THE WOMAN WHO MET HER MATCH

Fiona was born in a youth hostel in Yorkshire. She started working on teen magazine *Jackie* at age 17, then went on to join *Just Seventeen* and *More!* where she invented the infamous 'Position of the Fortnight'. Fiona now lives in Scotland with her husband Jimmy, their three children and a wayward rescue collie cross called Jack.

For more info, visit www.fionagibson.com. You can follow Fiona on Twitter @fionagibson.

By the same author:

The WOMAN WHO MET HER MATCH

FIONA GIBSON

avon

AVON

A division of HarperCollins*Publishers*
1 London Bridge Street,
London SE1 9GF
www.harpercollins.co.uk

A Paperback Original 2017

4

First published in Great Britain by
HarperCollins*Publishers* 2017

Copyright © Fiona Gibson 2017

Fiona Gibson asserts the moral right to
be identified as the author of this work

A catalogue record for this book is
available from the British Library

ISBN-13: 978-0-00815-702-9

Set in Sabon LT by Palimpsest Book Production Limited, Falkirk, Stirlingshire

Printed and bound by
CPI Group (UK) Ltd, Croydon, CR0 4YY

MIX
Paper from
responsible sources

FSC
www.fsc.org

FSC™ C007454

Acknowledgements

Huge thanks as ever to my amazing agent, Caroline Sheldon, and to Helen Huthwaite, Natasha Harding, Rachel Faulkner-Willcocks and all the wonderful Avon team. Cheers to Kedi Simpson, Yasmin Boland, Barbara Smith and Steve Fletcher for tips and reminiscences of budget travel to Paris back in the eighties. Thanks, lovely Nicki Wallis, for obligingly checking the French bits. Before this book was finished, I very naughtily snuck off for a few days to Ibiza with my girl pals. Jenno, Kath, Riggsy, Susan and Laura, thanks for making me laugh to the point of collapse and for filling me with sangria. We must do it again sometime (oh, we are?!). Huge thanks to Jimmy, Sam, Dexter and Erin for being all-round brilliant. Finally, a gratitude-filled shout-out to Misha McCullagh, who not only spent hours with me, filling me in on life as a department store beauty consultant, but also treated me to a restorative make-over. Naturally, I couldn't resist splurging on a few items from her counter. All in the name of research, of course.

For Maggie Dun
My first ever (and *best* ever) boss xxx

Prologue

The Summer of 1986

'It'll be good for you,' Mum announced. 'You'll improve your French; see a whole different side of life. You don't want to be stuck in boring old Yorkshire all summer, do you?'

She was applying her make-up at her dressing table mirror: two coats of spidery black mascara, frosted peach lips and a flash of apricot blusher across each cheek. She closed her small, tight mouth and swivelled round on the stool to face me. 'You might even meet a nice French boy. Oh, I hope so, Lorrie! Just think – your first boyfriend. *That's* what's meant to happen on a French exchange!' She turned back to her mirror, brushing on bronzer until her face took on a shimmery metallic hue.

At sixteen years old, I knew that people only said *it'll be good for you* when it was something you didn't want to do. And this was a prime example.

I didn't want a French boyfriend. I had never been out with anyone in Yorkshire – no one had even shown any interest in kissing me – and I doubted that my arrival in a foreign country would suddenly heighten my allure. I

1

didn't even want to go to France, *especially* not to a stranger's house. My French was pretty limited. I was fairly confident I could buy a cauliflower or report the presence of cockroaches in my hotel room but as for living in a French family's flat for an entire month? I was fully prepared for no one to understand a single word I said. Although I had tried to convince Mum that I'd learn just as much by studying my textbooks at home, she wouldn't listen. Once she had made up her mind, that was that; firm arrangements were made, my terrible passport picture taken in a photo booth with my hair scraped back so I looked like a potato, and travel tickets booked. Clearly, there was no point in arguing.

There were many other reasons why the thought of going to France scared me:

- I was to fly there, despite having never been on an aeroplane before. In fact, I had never been on *any* mode of transport where a talk on safety procedures was required.
- French girls were thin and sexy – and I was neither of those things.
- French people kissed on both cheeks just to say hello, i.e. much potential for humiliation. It was all about sex. *Everything* was. Even their nouns were either masculine or feminine.

In fact, I knew from occasional glimpses of French films that everyone was always snogging the face off each other. So what would *I* do while all that was going on? I would take photos of churches and force myself to buy things in shops. *Bonjour! Un chou-fleur s'il vous plaît, Madame. Merci, au revoir!* I would trot back to my penpal's flat with my cauliflower in a basket and sit and write postcards home.

In my own bedroom, which smelt of the tinned meat pie Mum had heated up earlier, I dropped a selection of cheap biros into my suitcase, wishing I was at least travelling with someone. However, despite Mum's insistence on using the term 'French exchange' – implying a load of British kids all singing excitedly on a coach – it was just me, being packed off to a stranger's place, alone.

It had all started when we were allocated penpals through school and I'd ended up with a terse-sounding Valérie Rousseau. Our correspondence so far had been rather basic ('What is your favourite sport?' 'Le ping pong,' I lied, not actually having one). Next thing I knew, Mum was on the phone to Valérie's mother, wafting her cigarette and putting on her Penelope Keith voice with the odd French word flung in: 'Merci, Mrs Rousseau. Lorrie is très excited to come and visit chez vous!' And that was that; the trip was arranged. 'Well, she sounded very nice,' Mum announced. 'Not that she speaks much English, but you'll be *fine*.'

I should also point out that my destination wasn't Paris. It wasn't even the Côte d'Azur, which I'd at least heard of. I was travelling alone to somewhere called The Massif Central, which sounded like an ugly office block with an enormous road system around it. For all we knew, Valérie's parents could have been alcoholics or child molesters – but this was the eighties and no one really worried back then.

I zipped up my suitcase and studied the instructions Mum had hammered out on her manual typewriter:

1. *Overnight coach to London Victoria Station.*
2. *Tube (Victoria Line, light blue, then Piccadilly Line,*

bit darker) to Heathrow Airport. Check which terminal on your ticket – I think there's a few?

3. *Get on plane. If you need anything, ask an air hostess. I'm sure they're very nice.*
4. *Arrive at Charles de Gaulle airport. Don't leave your small bag on the plane and remember to pick up your suitcase from luggage collection thing!*
5. *Train to Gare du Nord.*
6. *Go to jail. Go directly to jail! Do not pass go! Do not collect £200!*
7. *Not really, haha. Just change onto Metro (like tube but French) and proceed to Gare d'Austerlitz.*
8. *Train to Châteauroux. Valérie's Mum (Jeanne) will meet you there (you should have phoned her in Paris to say what train. Number is in your purse in case you lose these instructions. DO NOT FORGET TO PHONE!).*
9. *Have fun!*

I studied the sheet of A4 for the billionth time, prickling with annoyance at the Monopoly reference – as if this were the time for jokes! – and then went to find Mum. She was still in her bedroom, scooshing hairspray all over her coppery curls.

'Well, I'm all packed,' I announced.

She beamed at me. 'Good girl. Exciting, isn't it?'

I folded up her instructions into a neat little square. 'I'm a bit nervous actually.'

'What on earth is there to be nervous about?'

'Just . . . stuff.'

'What stuff?'

'Mum, I hardly speak any French!'

'You must do. You're studying it at school, aren't you?'

'Yes, but that's school French, not proper French like people speak in France . . .'

Mum tapped at her hair as if to ensure it was sufficiently crispy. 'Don't be so defeatist. You must've picked up a *bit* of vocabulary over the years. Now come on, Lorrie – we need to get going. Your coach leaves at ten and you don't want to miss it, do you?'

What would French teenagers make of me, Lorrie Foster, I wondered, with my jeans from the market and chubby little chipmunk face? I still hadn't believed that Mum would really send me off to a foreign country on my own. Now the moment was here, I wished I'd packed earlier – and more carefully – as she had been urging me to do, instead of being in denial and leaving it until the very last minute. But it was too late now to try and dress Frenchly. It was too late for anything because I was dragging my suitcase downstairs whilst trying to shake off the feeling that Mum simply wanted me out of the way for a month so she could have boyfriends over, or whatever it was she planned to get up to. My parents had divorced six years earlier. With her make-up and hair freshly done, she was clearly planning a night out after she'd shovelled me onto the overnight coach to London.

'I wish I'd had the opportunities you have,' she announced as she drove me, rather speedily, to the bus station. *What, the opportunity for a trip she didn't want to go on?* I sat in gloomy silence and stared out of the passenger window until she pulled up in the car park. Then, with a powdery cheek held briefly against mine, she bade me goodbye and warned me against the perils of drinking during the day. 'They love their wine, Lorrie, with *all* meals – even breakfast. Try to fit in with their ways but don't embarrass yourself, will you?' I promised

I wouldn't, and as I climbed onto the coach, I turned to give her another wave. She had already gone.

On the journey to London, I pressed myself against the coach's greasy window as the man beside me slurped noisily from a can of beer. Clutching Mum's typed sheet of paper, as if it were instructions for saving a life, I braved the short but turbulent flight. Whilst I had no need for the waxed paper sick bag I found in the seat-back pouch, I was still relieved to know it was there. As reminded by Mum, I dragged my case off the luggage carousel and made my way across Paris, becoming tearful only when I found myself unable to operate a French public telephone. With my ropey vocabulary and lots of miming, I managed to explain my predicament to an elderly lady who obligingly helped me to call Valérie's mum. From there I sped south, the train hurtling between endless rolling fields and towns with all kinds of exotic accents sprinkled like confetti over the letters, until finally I was greeted with two cheek kisses by Jeanne – who had a reassuring plump face – and Valérie, with her stern gaze and long black centre-parted hair, who looked as undelighted by my arrival as I was.

They lived in a sparsely furnished apartment above a bakery: Valérie, her kindly but permanently harassed mother (no dad was mentioned and I didn't like to ask), plus a mysterious older brother, Antoine, whom I had yet to meet. He was away camping with friends, I was told: *le camping*. Hey, I was picking up this French malarkey! In fact, I soon discovered I could cobble entire, rather wobbly sentences together – simply because, reasonably enough, no one spoke much English in a sleepy village in the middle of nowhere. Valérie certainly didn't – or at least, she didn't seem willing to make much effort. I gath-

6

ered that, as in my situation, her mum had been the one who had been keen for me to visit: 'I'm happy Valérie has English friend,' she explained falteringly, while her daughter glared at me over the rim of her mug of *chocolat chaud*.

By the end of week one, my French was severely put to the test with the arrival of my period. Having left it so late to pack, I had forgotten to bring sanitary towels. I'd spotted a box of Lil-Lets on Valérie's dressing table. However, as I feared tampons – and Valérie – I decided instead to approach her mother: '*Er, je suis beaucoup désolé, mais j'ai mon . . .*' No, no, period would surely be feminine. 'Ma, er . . .' Menstrual cycle? My *bicyclette menstruelle?* I stared as she slung three horse – horse! – steaks into a frying pan. 'Er, avez-vous une serviette, s'il vous plaît?' I blustered, sweating profusely now.

'Une serviette?' Jeanne frowned.

I nodded and smiled. 'Oui, s'il vous plaît.'

'Mais il y'a une sur ton lit . . .'

'Non, non, c'est, uh . . .' Try as I might, I couldn't scrabble together the vocabulary to explain that I didn't mean *that* kind of towel.

'Tu as besoin d'une autre?' Jeanne asked.

(Almost fainting with relief). 'Oui!'

She flipped the sizzling meat and took herself off to the airing cupboard, returning with a bath towel with an anchor embroidered on it: 'Voilà.'

I thanked her warmly and slipped out of the flat, managing to find what seemed to be the sole shop in the village that stocked *des serviettes hygiéniques*.

In a weird way, this incident boosted my confidence. Faced with having to fashion my own sanitary towels out of the virtually non-absorbent loo paper favoured by the Rousseau family – or the belligerent corgi who lived across the road – I had used my initiative and managed to avert disaster. Now, I felt determined to get to know the languid girls who hung around Valérie's apartment. Still too shy to join in properly, I remained on the fringes, trying to follow their conversations whilst affecting a bored – rather than panic-stricken – expression. When they were debating what exactly a British pop star might be singing about, I tentatively suggested that I might be able to help by writing out the lyrics. Valérie shrugged and said okay, if I wanted to – and so it began.

While Valérie still seemed to regard me as a particularly unpleasant smell, her friends seemed thrilled by this new service. Soon, I was filling my days by stressfully putting back the needle on Tears for Fears and Duran Duran singles while a clutch of honey-limbed girls fidgeted impatiently on the edge of Valérie's bed.

Culture Club. Paul Young. The Commodores. Phil Collins (a low point). I realised I could get away with a bit of guesswork – thus completing my lyric sheets faster – and no one would cotton on. In fact, by the end of my second week in France, whilst not exactly popular, I was verging on being accepted by the teenage population of the village.

Perhaps regarding me as a sort of project, Valérie's best friend Nicole had taken it upon herself to teach me how to apply make-up. Not a frosting of gaudiness, as favoured by my mother, but something altogether more subtle and incredibly flattering. So those gorgeous French girls did wear make-up after all. They just applied it properly, with a light hand. Under Nicole's stern eye, I learnt that a smudge of pinkish rouge and biscuit-coloured eye shadow, plus a little lip gloss, had a remarkably enhancing effect.

With her baby blue eyes and a fondness for a white

vest and no bra, Nicole was breathtakingly beautiful. I watched with rapt attention as she demonstrated how to curl lashes, and gushed thanks when she allowed me to use her make-up. I loved the smell, the packaging, the enticing shade names: *Bleu nuit. Bois de rose.* She gave me a couple of products she no longer used, and I topped up from the meagre selection at the village pharmacy. Life felt brighter. I took to 'putting on my face' and offering to run errands for Jeanne, feeling proud of being able to ask for things and trot back to the flat with everything on the list.

And then . . .

Antoine returned from *le camping*: a vision of messy blond hair, a smattering of stubble (manly!) and caramel limbs in battered old khaki shorts and a sun-bleached Depeche Mode T-shirt. Long, sweeping lashes grazed his chocolatey eyes. He smelt of grass and coconut. 'Hi,' he said with a smile, dumping a rucksack on the living room rug and kissing my cheeks (ooh!).

I'd been focusing hard on Duran Duran's 'A View to a Kill' but from that moment on, a fortnight into my trip, lyric services ground to a halt. Now, there were far more interesting things to keep me occupied. I'd never known a boy to show much interest in me before, but Antoine seemed to want to know everything about me. Or rather, he wanted to discuss the novels he'd read in English which, to my mind, marked him out as a genius (I had difficulty enough interpreting texts in my own language). His obvious eye-pleasing qualities aside, it was a relief to be able to communicate in my own language instead of forever worrying about using a wrong word.

Appalled by how much time I'd spent holed up in the gloomy apartment, Antoine appointed himself as my tour guide, and we soon became inseparable. Valérie seemed faintly relieved that I had been taken off her hands, and by now I could pick up enough from her conversations with her friends to know they were having a giggle about her brother and me. I didn't care. Those timely make-up lessons had boosted my fragile confidence, and the village, which had so far failed to make much of an impression on me, suddenly blossomed into the most beautiful place I'd ever seen. Antoine and I sat on the riverbank, chatting whilst dipping our bare toes into the cool water. We lay in a field, looking up at the turquoise sky whilst feasting on bread and cheese. I could hardly believe that such ordinary things could be so delicious.

The sun beamed down on us as Antoine took my hand on a walk through the forest. We were on our way to visit his friend Jacques, whose family kept goats and made cheese from their milk. As we picnicked in their untended garden, Antoine kissed me properly for the first time. It was like an electric current shooting through me. For days, we had just been friends hanging out, and now we were lying in each other's arms, snogging fervently in the long grass while his friend – thank you, Jacques! – wandered off to help his father with the goats. No one had kissed me that way, ever. It felt as if my hormones, which had been lying dormant like a pan of cold soup, had been turned up to a rapid boil.

When Antoine took me deeper in the woods, I was a little nervous; he was eighteen, he'd have kissed hundreds of girls not to mention having *done* it – of course he had, you could just tell. But I felt safe with him. We kept stopping to kiss some more, and he whispered that he couldn't believe I didn't have a boyfriend back home. I could have floated then, like dandelion fluff. I still couldn't believe that a boy like Antoine wanted to be with me in this way, when I suspected all of Valérie's friends fancied him.

We reached a lake, deserted and glittering with a wooded island in the middle, and stripped off to our underwear and swam. Me, Lorrie Foster from Yorkshire with a body the colour of rice pudding, swimming in my bra and knickers with a boy! 'You're so beautiful,' Antoine said afterwards, gallantly offering his T-shirt for me to dry myself. He praised my skin ('like cream'), my eyes ('dark, mysterious') and even my mouth ('so pretty, like a flower'). If he even noticed my chubby thighs or wobbly bottom, he didn't seem to view them as faults – and soon, neither did I. It was as if I was seeing myself differently, like the way you adjust the settings on a TV. Finally, I was seeing myself in full brightness.

My cheeks glowed and my badly highlighted hair seemed to acquire a new sheen that had never been apparent under drab Yorkshire skies. Every cell in my body seemed to shimmer from all the kissing we were doing. Because, of course, following that afternoon at the lake, we spent every possible moment in each other's arms, swiftly graduating onto the kind of 'petting' the sign at the swimming baths warned you not to do. Oh, we petted all right, but there was no pressure to 'go all the way' (as it was quaintly known back home), even when we were alone in the apartment, because the unspoken message seemed to say: this is *perfect*.

Every night, as I drifted off to sleep on the pull-out bed in Valérie's room, I could still feel Antoine's kisses hovering on my lips. I was madly in love, changed forever. The 'View to a Kill' lyrics remained untranscribed.

My last day in France loomed like a darkening cloud. We could hardly bear to talk about it. 'You'll come back,'

11

Antoine kept saying, as if to reassure himself as much as me. 'Or I could visit you. I need to find a job anyway – anything'll do. I'll save up and come to Yorkshire!' Try as I might, I couldn't picture him in our chintzy living room back home, being fussed over by Mum.

On the day I was leaving, we all squished into Jeanne's tiny car and drove to the railway station, where she and Valérie hung back awkwardly as Antoine and I hugged goodbye. *I love you,* he mouthed as the train pulled away. On the plane, I was crying so much the lady in the next seat gave me her embroidered hankie and said I could keep it.

Back home, I'd expected Mum to notice a difference in me immediately – to comment on my new, more sophisticated appearance and demeanour. I was certain she'd say something about the understated make-up I'd started to wear. However, she seemed more eager to tell me about Sue down the road who'd been coughing up bile, and how we'd have to cut back for the rest of the summer due to the exorbitant cost of my trip (I didn't notice any cutting back where Mum's make-up purchases were concerned). Only when I told her about Antoine did she sit up and take notice. 'He can come here for a holiday!' she enthused, and I wondered if it might actually be possible.

We wrote to each other, declaring our love, and then from a couple of letters a week, his airmailed missives dwindled to perhaps one a fortnight, then monthly, followed by a gaping void, during which I felt hollow and tried to tell myself the postmen must be on strike. However, the rest of our mail – the endless bills and Freeman's catalogues – seemed to be arriving without any problem. Maybe the French postmen were striking?

They weren't, of course. Antoine's life was simply

continuing without me; I had faded to him, like a newsagent's neglected window display. The occasional letter read more like an exercise in rudimentary English: *We played good at football on Saturday. Our apartment is painted outside. How is the weather in Yorkshire?*

Even at sixteen, I knew that asking about the weather suggested he was no longer obsessed with my creamy skin or mysterious eyes. Valérie had stopped writing too – my visit had been the death knoll to our 'friendship' – apart from to dash off a hasty note, informing me that Antoine was now 'madly in love' with Nicole, my make-up tutor. Tears rolled down my cheeks as I stared at her last flippant sentence ('I just thought you should know!'). Well, of course he'd end up with her; she was stunning. Yet I'd believed him when he'd said he loved me, and convinced myself that he was oblivious to the charms of his sister's friends. I could almost hear Valérie's cruel laughter as I screwed up her letter and threw it into my bin.

As autumn slid into a cold, wet winter, another letter arrived from France. 'Ooh, is it from that boy at long last?' Mum cooed, as I charged upstairs to my room to read it in private.

Dear Lorrie,
I hope you are well.
Valérie learns karate but broke shoulder.
Quite busy next few weeks.
Antoine

And that was the last I ever heard from the beautiful boy from the Massif Central.

Chapter One

30 Years Later

He's done that thing.

That thing of using a really old photo on his dating profile. How long ago was it taken? Ten years? Fifteen? This could be a fun guessing game. As if I wouldn't notice that his hair isn't in fact a lush chestnut brown as it appears in his picture but actually *silver*.

'Lorrie? Hi!'

'Ralph, hi!' *Force a smile. Don't look shocked. Don't stare at the hair.*

'Lovely to meet you.'

'You too . . .'

'Shall we go in then?' he asks brightly.

'Yes, of course!'

As the two of us stride into the Nutmeg Gallery, I try to reconcile the fact that the man I've had lodged in my head – with whom I've been corresponding via email all week – isn't the eerily youthful-looking Ralph I'd expected to meet. Dressed in a crisp white shirt, new-looking jeans and a blue cotton jacket, he is a perfectly presentable man of forty-eight. He has striking blue eyes, his teeth are notably good – shiny and white, probably flossed – and he's in pretty decent shape, suggesting that he does a bit of light jogging and goes easy on the booze. So why dig out a picture from something like 2002? When someone does that – and it contravenes the trade descriptions act really – it doesn't matter how attractive they are, because it's all you can think about.

And you feel sort of *duped*.

It was Ralph's suggestion to meet here, outside the gallery tucked away by a pretty stretch of the canal in Islington. Ideal, I thought. The art bit would feel pleasingly grown-up. I know I shouldn't still regard galleries in that way, being forty-six myself. I mean, I am mother to two teenagers, for goodness' sake. I shouldn't need to do certain things – like look at art – in order to feel like a bona fide adult. Then, after we'd sped through the gallery, we could get to the part I was really looking forward to: a chat in the cafe he'd mentioned, with tables overlooking the canal. 'Amazing home baking,' he'd said.

I'd had a good feeling about today, and not just due to the cake element. Ralph had been chatty and interesting in his emails: a solicitor – again, pleasingly grown-up – with hints of poshness and a warm, likeable face. After a couple of dud dates with other men I'd allowed myself a glimmer of hope. But now, well, he's just not what I expected.

'I didn't even know this place existed,' I tell him as we wander into the first gallery room.

'Oh, I've been here a few times. It's a charming little place.'

As we study the paintings – at least, I *pretend* to study them – a sense of awkwardness settles over us.

'So, how's it been so far?' I ask lightly. 'The whole, um,

online thing, I mean?' An older couple are perusing the artworks, and my voice sounds terribly amplified in here. Perhaps it wasn't such a great choice of venue after all.

'Oh, I've just started really,' Ralph says. 'In fact, you're the first person I've met.'

'Really? Well, I'm flattered.' Silly thing to say, I know. He probably just hasn't got around to meeting anyone else yet.

'What d'you think of these?' He indicates a row of small paintings, all in similar beigey hues. They are close-ups of various body parts – a forearm, a thigh, a rather septic-looking finger – each bearing a plaster.

'Not crazy about them,' I admit. 'It's all a bit medical, isn't it?'

Ralph chuckles. 'Yes, it is a bit. The permanent collection's much better – let's go take a look.'

We stroll through to an airier room filled with bright, splashy abstracts which are far more pleasing with their cheery colours. Ralph makes straight for a still life depicting a wobbly yolk-yellow circle on a sky blue background.

'That's quite striking, isn't it?' I remark.

He nods. 'Yes, it was always Belinda's favourite.'

'Belinda?' I give him a quizzical look.

'My wife,' he explains.

'Oh, right.' This floors me even more than the hair colour shock. From our email chats, I learnt that Ralph enjoys reading thrillers, cooking Asian food and jaunts to the south coast: reassuringly unremarkable stuff. One cat, no kids – 'Just didn't happen for me'. However, although a couple of relationships have been mentioned, no wife has popped up in our communications. I study the painting, wondering how I'm supposed to respond. *Really? Well, I can see she has excellent taste . . .* Or, *How about showing me more paintings Belinda loves?*

Now I can barely concentrate on the art at all as a terrible thought hits me. He said *wife*, not ex-wife. Surely, if they were separated or divorced, he'd refer to her as his ex. I mentally scroll back to the email where Ralph mentioned his situation, relationship-wise: 'I've been on my own for just over a year . . .' Not single, but on his own. Plus, the painting *was* Belinda's favourite; past tense. Which can only mean one thing: Belinda is dead.

I throw Ralph a quick glance as he finally tears himself away from the yellow circle painting and moves on. Is this why he suggested meeting at the Nutmeg Gallery – because Belinda loved it here? It makes sense, too – the vintage profile photo, I mean. He's still so deranged with grief, he couldn't get it together to find a more recent one – or perhaps she was in all of them, hugging him. God, how tragic. This is probably the first date he's been on since she died.

As we drift into the next room, I run through possible ways of broaching the subject sensitively: *So, erm, if you don't mind me asking, what happened with Belinda? Is Belinda still, er . . . 'around'?* Neither sounds quite right.

Ralph starts to stroll around, hands clasped behind his back as he gazes thoughtfully at the artworks. It's not paintings in here, but a collection of grubby old baskets with bits of frayed rope attached, dotted around on the parquet floor. On closer inspection, because I'm trying to appear suitably fascinated – and not like some heathen who only likes paintings of thatched cottages or kittens – each of the baskets has a small item inside. Nothing precious or beautiful, but the kind of stuff you might have crammed in the cupboard under the sink: rubber gloves, a bottle of Cif, a pair of rusty Brillo pads sitting snugly together as if they might start mating.

Although I know I should be open-minded, just as I'm trying to be open-minded about Ralph, I'm starting to think we should wrap up the art bit now and head to the cafe. That unmentionable thing – Belinda, his dead wife – hovers between us, but right now, with the elderly couple still lurking close by, isn't the right moment to bring it up.

'Interesting, isn't it?' Ralph remarks.

'Oh, er . . . yes, very.' *Be positive. It was his idea to come here and the poor man's bereaved.* 'What d'you think it's all about?' I ask.

My stomach growls as he gazes around. I was too intent on getting ready – black and white spotty dress, patent heels, full face of make-up and a ruddy blow-dry – to think about lunch and now it's gone 3 p.m.

'Well,' he says, 'I think it could be interpreted in lots of ways.' He pushes back his neatly cropped hair. 'I don't want to sound pretentious. You know how people can be about art . . .'

'Oh, yes,' I say, warming to Ralph a little now, but wary of *over*-warming to him out of pity. 'It's all cleaning stuff, isn't it, trapped in baskets? So I think it's about that terrible hemmed-in feeling you have when you've got the kitchen nice and shiny and then everyone storms in and messes it all up and you think, Christ, it's like Groundhog Day – bloody endless.' I smile, feeling pleased with myself.

'Oh, I don't think it's quite that.' He chuckles patronisingly.

I sense my cheeks reddening. 'No, well, I was joking. To be honest, this kind of art isn't really my—'

'I think,' Ralph interrupts, 'what we're seeing here is a

19

comment on the permanence of the enclosed objects, juxta-posed with the *impermanence* of the lobster pots—'

'Oh, is that what they are?' I glance at a galvanised bucket in the corner with a mop propped beside it. Are they part of the art as well, or did the cleaner just dump them there?

'Well, yes, what did you think they were?'

Rustic storage solutions? Quirky hats? As I'm not a fisherman I had no idea . . . 'Um, I knew they were *something* nautical,' I fib, not that it matters, as Ralph doesn't appear to have heard me.

'. . . And as you'd expect, they show distinct signs of weathering due to the erosive effects of the sea. And what the artist is alluding to here is . . .' I phase out, ceasing to listen for a few moments. '. . . Then again,' he chunters on, 'it could be more about the concept of cleanliness, of sterility in a world literally *milling* with germs and bacteria . . .' He stops and blinks at me. 'Do you think?'

'Yes, that could be it,' I remark, wandering towards the small white card on the wall, hoping that'll settle things once and for all. But all it says is:

I AM NOT A CRUSTACEAN by Thomas Trotter, 1991
Lobster pots and household objects

Which tells us nothing more, apart from the fact that the artist was born in the nineties, suggesting that he has never acquainted himself with a Brillo pad in any kind of useful way.

Now, close to the exit, Ralph is surveying a small pile of brownish tweed fabric lying on a wooden plinth. 'Another Thomas Trotter piece,' he observes. 'Hmmm . . . what's this one saying?'

I look at it dispassionately. It's saying: *What were you thinking, not even finding out if he's a widower or not? And now, because you pity the man, you're frittering away your precious Sunday afternoon with someone who insists on throwing around fancy words, which would be fine, maybe, in other circumstances. But who says 'juxtaposed' on a first date? Actually, I fancy going straight home and juxtaposing my arse with the sofa, thank you very much . . .*

In fact, if it wasn't for my kids, I wouldn't be here at all. They're the ones who forced me to join datemylove-lymum.com in the first place. 'Me and Cam were talking, Mum,' ventured Amy, my fifteen-year-old, fixing her wavy dark hair into a no-nonsense ponytail. 'We just thought you should . . . get out more. Do stuff. *Enjoy yourself.*'

Christ, they were worried about me. Didn't they think I was managing, holding down my full-time job in the beauty hall of a department store, whilst keeping things ticking along at home? I wasn't keen on the implication that I was anything less than a vision of contentment.

Cameron, who's seventeen, pitched in. 'We just thought you should, er, try one of those dating things . . .'

'Like Tinder?' I spluttered.

'No! God no. Tinder's for our age. There's others – ones for *older* people. It's what single women your age do. They have no way of meeting people any other way.'

'But I meet people all day,' I exclaimed. 'It's my job—'

'Yeah, we know about that,' he conceded. 'It's called traffic stopping . . .'

'But actually,' Amy cut in, smirking, 'it's taking innocent people hostage and forcing them to sit on your stool so you can plaster them in foundation.'

'Yes.' I nodded. 'I tie them up and gag them. I never told you that part.'

21

Cam tossed his choppily cut brown hair back from his handsome, angular face. 'Stop changing the subject. We're not talking about customers at a make-up counter. We mean, you know . . .' He winced slightly. 'Meeting a *man*.'

'Oh.'

'And we've already written your profile,' Amy added, her dark eyes glinting with amusement.

'What? All this plotting and scheming's been going on behind my back?'

'Yeah, it was fun,' she said, grinning. 'Stu helped us.' So my oldest friend – currently our lodger – was in on this too? The traitor!

Cam fetched his laptop to show me their 'work':

Our mum is a lovely outgoing and attractive person who would like to meet someone special. She is kind, sociable and loves a laugh with her friends. She is incredibly thoughtful and has brought us up all by herself for the past seven years. In all that time she has been single, not because there is anything wrong with her but because she has always put us first. But we are older now and both feel it's time for her to get out there, meet someone special and enjoy life to the full.

Mum is called Lorrie – short for Lorraine – and is forty-six (but looks younger). Why not meet her and find out how lovely she is?

Please get in touch,
Cam and Amy

Oh my God. It wasn't perfect, I decided as I blotted my sudden hot tears on a tea towel. It certainly wasn't what I would have written myself. But, like a child's lumpen rock cake lovingly transported home from school, you have to give it a try.

Slowly, the idea started to grow on me. Not in a 'finding a life partner' way – I'd had that in David, my children's father and lost him seven years ago – but the odd date now and again, just to liven things up. So I agreed to go with the profile my kids had so sweetly created, and see what happened. Perhaps I'd find a 'companion', like wealthy Victorian ladies used to have?

First of all I met the curiously named Beppie, a plummy 'lifestyle consultant' – whatever *that* meant – who charmingly remarked, 'If you're not looking for anything serious we might be able to have a bit of fun.' As if he might deign to sleep with me when there wasn't much on the telly. No thank you.

Marco, my date before Ralph, had perhaps three teeth in the whole of his head due to extensive oral decay, judging by the remaining examples (in his profile picture he'd had his mouth firmly closed). Was I being too fussy, hoping for something at least approaching a full set? Probably.

Yes, I get lonely, but for someone to hang out with there's always Stu, who's funny and kind and does possess teeth, and who I have known since we were school friends growing up in our beleaguered West Yorkshire town. We snogged just the once, under the stairs at a party in 1987 (my futile attempt to get Antoine Rousseau out of my head), and never mentioned it again. The unspoken message was that we knew each other too well as friends for anything else to happen, and the kiss had been a drunken accident. By our early twenties, when we drifted to London at around the same time, I'd almost forgotten it had ever happened.

23

I glance at Ralph now as he prowls around the gallery, reading all the little cards on the wall. Will this be a case of third time lucky with my online dates? I'm trying to remain positive.

He turns to me and indicates the bundle of brown fabric. 'Ooh, it's called "jacket for two". The idea is, we both get in it and wear it together.' He beams eagerly as I step back.

'But surely we're not supposed to touch it?'

Ralph shakes his head. 'No, it's an interactive piece. Look, it says over there on the wall, "Please wear me with a friend . . ."'

But we're not friends! 'Oh, no, I don't think so . . .'

He holds up the grubby-looking garment. 'Look, it's enormous.'

'It really is,' I agree.

'I think even *we* could fit into it!' What, me with my ample chest and sizeable backside? He's really not helping himself. 'Must have been specially made,' he adds.

'Yes. Wow.' I can smell coffee wafting through from the cafe. I'm starving now, to the point of light-headedness. Perhaps this, coupled with my pity for Ralph, is why I find myself standing there like some inert shop mannequin while he drapes half the jacket around me. It smells like an ancient sofa in a tawdry B&B as he feeds one of my arms into a sleeve whilst shimmying into the other half himself.

He buttons up the jacket with impressive speed. We are now both trapped in it, our bodies pressed awkwardly together. I can feel the thumping of Ralph's heart as he grins at me. 'We're a living sculpture!'

'Yes, lovely. Very good. What an amazing, er, concept.' What the hell am I saying? If Amy told me she'd been

24

cajoled into wearing a stinky jacket with a man, I'd be horrified. As a single parent, I hope I have raised her to have a darn sight more self-respect than I clearly possess. I'm sweating now, my special date pants clinging to my bottom (not that I was expecting to show them but, *you know*) as I fumble for the buttons.

'What's wrong?' Ralph exclaims as I struggle out of the jacket.

'Nothing. I'm just a bit hot, that's all. Think I might be having a flush. Look, Ralph, I'd really like a coffee now if you don't mind,' *i.e. enough of Thomas-bloody-Trotter and his so-called art!*

'Oh! Yes, of course . . .' He pulls his arm from the sleeve and dumps the jacket back on its plinth, trooping rather sulkily beside me as we make our way to the cafe.

As we order lattes, my gaze skims the array of baking on offer. 'A piece of carrot cake please,' I tell the girl behind the counter before turning to Ralph. 'Would you like something?'

'No, no, you go ahead, though,' he says.

We install ourselves at a table at the waterside. It's a picturesque stretch of canal, with a row of brightly painted narrowboats moored on the opposite bank. A mallard duck bobs along on the water, and a young couple stroll hand-in-hand along the towpath.

'Well, that was interesting,' I remark.

'Glad you thought so,' he says with a smile.

Silence descends, and I focus instead on sampling the carrot cake which, I have to say, is perhaps the best I have ever tasted.

'I've really enjoyed this afternoon,' Ralph adds.

'Oh, me too,' I say through a mouthful of delicately spiced sponge and creamy icing. I swallow it down, soothed now by the delicious cake and the slight breeze, and decide Ralph's not that bad really. This has become my marker of dating success: *he's not that bad really*. I glance at him as he observes the bobbing boats. 'I hope you don't mind . . .' I venture cautiously, poking at my cake with my fork. 'I mean, I sort of need to ask you this really, but, of course, I completely understand if you don't want to talk about it . . .'

He raises a brow. 'Yes?'

'Um, you know the painting with the big yellow sun? The one you said Belinda liked?'

'Oh, yes, it's called "Orb".' He sips his coffee.

I clear my throat. 'Look, I hope this isn't intrusive, but you said, "My wife". So I'm sort of assuming – well, you know, otherwise you'd have said *my ex* . . .' Hotness spreads up my cheeks. 'Is she . . . I mean . . . what happened to—'

'Oh, it was all very amicable. We married very young, silly mistake really. In fact, we're still married—'

'You're *married*?' I dump my fork on my plate.

'Well, yes, technically, I suppose . . .'

'Which means yes!'

'No – we're separated, split up over a year ago. Sorry, I really must stop saying my wife. I realise how confusing that sounds . . .'

'No, no, it's *fine*. So, where is she now?'

He shrugs. 'Moved north, to Halifax.'

'Oh, right!' I glance towards the canal, wondering whether or not to feel relieved. A narrowboat is chugging by, a man with a white beard at the helm, an elderly woman in jeans and a faded rugby top primping a tub of Michaelmas daisies on the deck. They both wave, and I wave back, then glance down at my cake which, although

26

I've made inroads, now seems huge and unwieldy. It's not that I'm trying to appear feminine and dainty. It's just, my appetite seems to have withered away. 'Er, would you like some of this, Ralph? I'm not sure I can manage it all.'

'Oh, no thanks, I stopped off for a sandwich before we met.' His mouth flickers into a smile as he adds, 'You tuck in, Lorrie. I can see you're a girl who *very* much enjoys her cake.'

I blink at him. Well, that's flipping charming, isn't it? Fatty, is what he means. Porky lady, cramming in the carbs and cheesy topping. 'I am actually,' I say with a terseness he doesn't seem to notice.

'Well, that's good,' he says with a smirk. 'A healthy appetite, that's what I like to see in a lady. Not your picking-at-a-lettuce-leaf type!'

'Okay, thank you, Ralph . . .'

He leans forward. 'Oh, I didn't mean—'

'No, it's fine, really.' That's it. I have to get out of here. I edge my plate aside and pull my phone from my bag, frowning as if something urgent might have happened at home. 'Sorry, but I'd better be going . . .' I slip my phone back into my bag and get up from my seat.

His face falls. 'So soon? That's a pity . . .'

'Yes, um, I've enjoyed the gallery, it's been a lovely afternoon but I really must dash . . .' Then I'm off, turning briefly to wave goodbye as I leave the cafe by its wooden gate, and striding towards the tube station, feeling leaden inside, and *not* due to the Nutmeg Gallery's home baking.

Chapter Two

Like a burglar, I creep into my house and dart upstairs before Stu and the kids can accost me. They know I'm back, of course. Stu has already called out 'hi', and I can sense them all waiting downstairs, keen to hear all about my date. That's what my personal life amounts to these days: cheap entertainment for my lodger and kids.

In the bathroom now, I start to cleanse my face. Primer, base, blush, tawny lips. Eye shadow – *three* shades – plus liner and mascara: what a fat waste of make-up. Lovely make-up at that; La Beauté is a premium brand. 'That just means expensive, Mum,' Amy observed. 'Why don't they just admit it?' She was right, and our gorgeous products are worth every penny – although of course, I would say that. I am La Beauté's counter manager in a beautiful, old-fashioned department store – a little like Goldings in Bradford, to which I would accompany Mum as a child, fascinated as she had her face done by one of the scarily made-up ladies who worked there. While there are La Beauté counters in stores all over the country, ours was the UK's first and remains the favourite among customers.

Somehow, despite being a global brand, the company still retains a cosy, family feel, and I can't imagine working for anyone else.

Plus, I *adore* cosmetics and the magical things they can do. Just as when Nicole taught me the ways of make-up in France, I still love the way it can change how a woman feels about herself: with confidence all buffed up, as if given a brisk shimmy with a chamois leather cloth. That's how I felt as I put on my face before setting out to meet Ralph. Now, though, I realise it was all wrong for a casual date at a gallery on a Sunday afternoon (and I'm supposed to be an expert on make-up!). I'm not a shined-up version of myself. I'm just a tired-looking middle-aged woman who's too fond of her cake.

Laughter drifts up from the kitchen, where Stu and the kids are bantering away. I sniff my cardigan sleeve. It pongs of that arse-smelling tweed jacket. I whip it off and change into a T-shirt and jeans, tie back my shoulder-length dark brown hair – hair that I not only blow-dried but *deep conditioned* for my date – and head downstairs to greet my public.

'So?' Stu grins at me.

I shrug and start to make coffee. 'Not good.'

'What happened?' Amy asks, still in her basketball kit from training this morning. 'Was he weird?'

Was Ralph weird, or is it me? I tell them about the un-dead wife, Ralph's arty pretensions ('juxtaposed!') and the fact that the photo he'd used was decades old. 'It's so much easier for men,' I grumble. 'They just come onto the site and write their own profiles, thinking they have the pick of all us desperate single mums . . .'

'No one thinks you're desperate,' Stu says with an unconvincing smirk.

'So what else happened?' Amy asks eagerly, folding her slender arms. I describe the lobster pots and the outsized jacket while they all stare, agog, as if enjoying a thrillingly diabolical Eurovision performance.

'What a twat,' Cam exclaims, chuckling.

'And he said,' I add, indignation bubbling up in me again, '"You're obviously a girl who *very* much enjoys her cake."'

'*Girl?*' my son sniggers, missing the cake significance entirely.

'Never mind the girl bit—' I start.

'Well, you do enjoy cake,' Stu teases, his greeny-blue eyes glinting. 'You're a cake appreciator. You wolfed that lemon sponge I made last weekend . . .'

'Oh, thanks—'

'C'mon, you're just a woman with a healthy appetite . . .'

'That's what Ralph said! Can we stop this? *Please?*'

Stu gives me a pained look as I slump onto a kitchen chair. 'Hey, what does it matter what some idiot said? Forget all about it and move on to the next . . .'

'There won't be a next,' I say firmly.

'Aw, Mum, don't be like that.' Cam gets up from his seat, towering above me at well over six feet, pale arms dangling from the sleeves of his unironed grey T-shirt. He bends to give me a little squeeze.

'No, I've decided, I'm coming off the site.'

'But you've hardly met anyone yet,' protests Amy.

'I have, love. I've met three and that's quite enough. I don't think I can go through with this anymore—'

'Oh, we'll miss the reports,' Stu says, pulling his trilling mobile from the back pocket of his scruffy jeans. Mercifully, this halts the interrogation. He snatches his ring-bound notepad from on top of the microwave and starts to

30

scribble with his phone gripped to his ear. 'Walnuts, cashews, agave nectar, medjool dates . . . yep, got all that . . .'

The kids amble off, and I load the washing machine as he falls into some light-hearted banter with the customer at the other end of the line.

Stu moved in with us last September, when his live-in relationship with Roz, an intimidating psychotherapist, finally fell apart. It was supposed to be a temporary measure, but he slotted in so easily that neither of us has seen any reason for him to move on – and of course the extra cash helps out. In fact, it was from a wine-fuelled chat around this very kitchen table that the idea for Parsley Force, Stu's emergency forgotten ingredient delivery service, was launched. We'd had a craving for posh crisps, and I'd joked that it would be terribly handy if we could just call someone up and bark, 'Salt and vinegar, please – 120 Pine Street!' down the phone. Stu had remarked that, surely, people were always needing things: snacks, booze, a missing ingredient from a recipe. What they needed was a hero to deliver it to their door. He'd been working as a motorcycle courier but really wanted to set up something of his own. This, he decided, would be perfect.

'But don't people read a recipe right through before they start, to make sure they have everything?' I asked. Apparently not, he declared with tipsy confidence. They just skim it and lurch right in and then . . . disaster! Dried mulberries are required! 'So why wouldn't they just run out to the shops? I mean, this is London, not the Shetlands. Shops are open all the time.' Too busy, lazy or drunk, he reckoned. 'Where will you buy the stuff?' I asked.

Stu rubbed at his darkly-bristled chin. 'Er, just in

supermarkets, obviously, or delis, specialist shops, whatever. Basically, I'll just be picking up all the annoying little things they've forgotten to buy.'

And so the business was born, with the aid of a hastily knocked-together Facebook page and some judicious advertising in local magazines. In partnership with his mate Bob, Stu took to zooming all over North London on his motorbike, giving me a fascinating insight into miniature dramas happening all over the city: 'We crave cheese and we're too drunk to drive!' And – frequently – 'Could you bring wine and cigarettes?'

'But who's Parsley Force *for*?' I wanted to know, a few weeks into their venture.

'People who call in help. The types who have cleaners, gardeners, all that.'

'Not me, then.'

'No, and you don't need any of that because you have me.'

He's right and, although I'd never imagined having a housemate at forty-six years old, I doubt if I could have found a better one. He leaves sauce bottles sitting on the table, lids off, but does loads of cooking and we never seem to run out of essentials anymore. He is incapable of grasping that bread doesn't need to be stored in the fridge, but he can deal with a bird that's flown in through the open kitchen window, catching it deftly in a tea towel before freeing it outside. He is not averse to running the hoover about, and on weekends, like an obedient Labrador, he goes out for the newspapers, which we lie about reading companionably.

He is handsome, certainly, in a mussed-up sort of way, and has been resolutely single since Roz called time on their relationship. Yet, when I suggested he tried online dating too, he gawped at me as if I had suggested colonic irrigation: 'Christ, no thanks. Too many crackpots out there.' Yet the meeting of crackpots is positively *encouraged* where I'm concerned.

He finishes the call now, shoving his phone into his pocket and beaming at me. 'Ingredients for vegan cheesecake. She hadn't realised her guests are vegan and she's now having to rethink dessert. I mean, that's not going to be a cheesecake, is it, by any stretch?'

And off he goes, just as my phone pings with a text: *Would very much like to meet again, Ralph.* What, to insult me some more about my fondness for baked goods?

Sorry, I reply, *it was lovely to meet you, but I'm afraid there wasn't any chemistry for me.* Yep, that old line. *Good luck with meeting someone,* I add before deleting him from my phone.

Chapter Three

The summer holidays used to be a source of low-level guilt for me – despite Pearl, our wonderful childminder, who soon became a close friend – but those days are gone. As Cam is working – albeit sporadically, helping to set up lighting for gigs – and Amy's sporting activities continue all summer long, nowadays I can trot off to work, leaving them to their own devices with a fairly clear conscience. Plus, Stu is around much of the time, not as a surrogate father or anything, but as a reasonably sensible adult about the place.

Although it amuses Cam and Amy to think of me dragging women by the hair to our counter in the beauty hall, it doesn't quite work that way. The approaching of customers is indeed called traffic stopping but no one is bullied or insulted. 'My God, you're really flushed! You need our new colour corrective powder!' I once heard a consultant from a rival brand saying to an aghast-looking customer. But that is not our way at all.

'Make a friendly approach,' I was instructed during training by Nuala, our fresh-faced area manager, when I joined the company ten years ago. 'No leaping out, scaring them, or accosting them with a mascara wand. You're there to sell products, of course. But no one will buy so much as a hand soap if they don't feel inclined, by which I mean happy and good about themselves. Your job is to help them feel that way.'

I soon discovered that traffic stopping isn't as terrifying as it sounds. After all, it's only make-up and skincare we're offering, not a rectal examination. Today, I spot a woman pushing a buggy containing a sleeping baby and holding the hand of a little boy, and figure that she might appreciate a little pampering. As we have a stock of colouring books in a drawer under the counter, I am never put off by the presence of small children.

'Excuse me,' I start, 'I wondered if you'd have a moment to try our new summer colours?'

The woman glances to the side as if I must be talking to someone else. 'Oh, er, I don't think—' she blusters.

'Wanna go,' mutters her son, who looks about four years old, tugging hard on her sleeve. 'Wanna go *now*.'

'Oh, Archie, we've only just got here,' she says wearily.

'Why are we here? It smells bad. I can't breathe!' He stares at her, his breathing now coming in audible gasps.

'For goodness' sake,' she groans as a terrible rasping noise emanates from his throat.

'What's happening?' I exclaim. 'Does he have asthma? I can fetch help—'

'No, he certainly doesn't have asthma,' the woman snaps.

'I can't breathe!' the boy gasps. 'It's horrible in here. Why does it stink of flowers? Aggghhhh . . . huuuurrrrr . . .'

Because it's the beauty hall of a department store . . .

'Stop this right now,' his mother barks, snatching at his

35

hand, at which Archie's breathing reverts instantly – miraculously – to normal. She turns to me. 'Sorry about that. What were you saying about summer colours?'

A moment of recognition passes between us as I remember myself, not with Cam – he was remarkably good-natured in department stores – but Amy, who couldn't bear the places, and would jab her poky fingers into the trays of make-up testers if I so much as glanced at a new product.

'They're lovely,' I say. 'Very fresh and easy to wear. Come over and I'll show you.'

Obediently, with her son merely muttering now, she manoeuvres the buggy to our counter where she obligingly hops onto a stool.

'Would you like a colouring book and some crayons?' I ask Archie. Although he merely scowls, I glance over to where my colleague, Helena, has just rung a customer's purchase through the till. 'Helena, could you give this little boy a colouring pack, please?'

'Sure, no problem.'

His mother shifts on the stool. 'I can't be too long, and I'm afraid I'm not planning to buy anything.'

'Oh, that's fine. We're just showing the new range, that's all.'

'I mean, I *really* can't afford anything. Is this stuff expensive?'

'It's a quality brand but really, it's *fine*. There's no obligation at all.'

On the floor beside her, Archie is leafing crossly through the colouring book.

'I'm Lorrie,' I add.

'Jane.' She smiles faintly.

'Nice to meet you, Jane.'

'It's all pictures of stupid ladies' faces,' Archie growls, tossing the colouring book aside. The drawings are lovely, the originals having been sketched by sisters Claudine and Mimi, the now-elderly founders of our company, who live in Grasse in southern France.

'Well, yes,' I say. 'The idea is, you can use the crayons to draw make-up on them . . .'

'There's no boys,' he complains.

'Yes, but you can make the ladies into whatever you like.'

He throws the pouch of crayons down. 'Don't wanna.'

Yes, you do. Give your poor mother a break, for goodness' sake, after your phoney asthma attack. 'You could make them ugly,' I suggest.

He brightens a little. 'Like with spots? And black teeth?'

'Yes, if you want to,' I reply as Jane exhales slowly, visibly relaxing as Archie starts to deface a picture with exuberance.

'Please don't put too much make-up on me,' she says.

'Don't worry, you look great as it is. Are you wearing any now?' A superfluous question, asked out of politeness: she is bare-faced, a little tired-looking but very pretty, her dark blonde curly hair pulled up into a haphazard top-knot and secured with a plain rubber band.

'Chance'd be a fine thing,' she says with a smile.

'Yes, I remember those days.'

Using a make-up sponge, I apply the thinnest layer of BB cream, and our newest eye shadow in 'tea biscuit' on her lids.

'Haven't worn make-up since Lila was born,' she adds, indicating her still-sleeping baby in the buggy.

I add a little eyeliner in a nutty brown, followed by mascara. 'Well, that's understandable. Other priorities take

37

over, don't they? But it's still nice to take a few minutes for yourself . . .'

'Or have a haircut,' she adds. 'D'you have children?'

'Yes, two – almost all grown up now. They're fifteen and seventeen . . .'

'Oh, tell me it all comes back,' she exclaims as I add a touch more liner. 'Your life, I mean. Feeling human again.'

'Yes, of course it does—'

'Before they reach their teens? Please tell me it happens sooner than that or I think I'll go stark raving mad!'

'Don't worry, it happens much sooner than that.'

Jane smiles, clearly enjoying herself now as Archie draws angry red spots and purple lesions all over an elegant illustration of a woman's face. 'Well, I hope I look as good as you do when these two are teenagers. But then, I bet you never let yourself go, even when yours were babies . . .'

'Oh, I did,' I say truthfully. In fact, I remember there were periods when the kids were well beyond babyhood and the very idea of putting on a face to greet the outside world was furthest from my mind. Of course, I don't tell Jane that, after I lost David, my hair didn't see a brush for days on end. It didn't occur to me to look in a mirror, and I only got dressed because friends urged me to.

David and I had been together for fifteen years – we'd never married, we simply hadn't felt the need – and I had forgotten how to be without him. After the accident, it was the children who literally kept me going. For them, I had to get out of bed every morning because ordinary life didn't stop. I was a lone parent now, ferrying them to and from Scouts and judo (Amy's short-lived obsession) and basketball (still her favourite thing in life). I turned up at school concerts – Amy sang in the choir, and Cam briefly flirted with the French horn – and parents' evenings alone, one of the kinder teachers always making the effort to come over and say, 'How *are* you, Lorrie? I know it's been a difficult time.'

Yes it was – because David was dead. I mean really dead, not a Belinda's-gone-to-Halifax scenario. It happened on one of those rare winter's nights when London is properly blanketed in snow, like in a children's story. We were happily cosied up for the evening in the house we still live in – 120 Pine Street, London E2, an ordinary little terrace made a little less ordinary by the original outdoor wooden shutters at the living room windows. With Cam and Amy in bed, David and I were looking out at the snowflakes falling slowly, illuminated by street lamps. 'Fancy some wine?' I asked, and David said yes, and because I was already in PJs he pulled on his thick padded jacket and a woollen beanie and headed out to the 7-eleven. Ever obliging, that's what he was like. Not a pushover – he knew his own mind, taught English in a challenging North London secondary school and took no nonsense from the kids there – but nicely old-fashioned in that he was willing to go out and buy wine, because I fancied a drink.

Because *I* wanted it, not him. Because I was worn out from a long week of working and being Mummy, and longed for a glass of something cool and chilled.

If I'd put on the kettle and had a mug of tea, it would never have happened.

If I hadn't been such a greedy wine-guzzling *lush*, it would never have happened.

If I hadn't had a bath after cajoling the kids into bed – and still been in jeans and a sweater rather than PJs – then maybe I'd have nipped out to the shop, and he'd still be with us now.

I try to push away such thoughts and pause to study Jane's face. She seems to have fallen into a sort of reverie. Choosing a neutral pinky-brown pencil, I outline her full lips, then apply a semi-sheer lipstick with a brush. Archie is now drawing thick round spectacles on the lady with the terrible skin condition in the colouring book.

The off-licence is only a five-minute walk away from our house, around the corner and down towards the Roman Road. And that's where it happened, just as David turned the corner, the car coming too fast on freshly fallen snow, skidding and slamming into him. And that was the end.

I brush on a little pinkish blusher, followed by translucent powder. 'All done,' I say, forcing myself to focus on my customer's now-radiant face.

'Oh . . . gosh . . .' Jane studies her reflection in the mirror. 'I look, well . . . human again!'

I smile as Archie gathers himself up from the floor. 'You look great,' I tell her. 'Really beautiful.'

She bites her lip and smiles. 'Thank you.'

'It was a pleasure.'

'I'm sorry, I feel as if I really should buy something but, you know, I can't justify—'

'Not at all,' I say, opening our drawer of hidden delights: a bevy of free samples. 'You can try this at home,' I add, dropping a mini lipstick into a crisp white paper bag, 'and this night cream's lovely. You know, you can actually *cheat* a good night's sleep . . .'

'Oh God, I need that,' she says, laughing.

I add a sachet of body lotion and a vial of fragrance.

'Thank you, are you sure?' They are tiny things, but she regards them like jewels. Her baby daughter whimpers in the buggy and Archie, still gripping a fistful of crayons, is tugging hard at her hand.

'Yes, of course. Take them home and enjoy them. I hope I'll see you again sometime.'

Her face breaks into a wide smile. 'You will, definitely. You've really made my day.'

'My pleasure . . .'

'*What* made your day?' Archie demands as Jane manoeuvres the buggy away from our counter.

'Oh, just having my make-up done . . .'

'Don't like it, Mummy.'

'Well, I do. I'd forgotten how lovely it feels to wear lipstick. And you know what, darling? That lady gave me a free one and I'm going to start using it every day.'

Chapter Four

Of course, it's not always like that, by which I mean not every customer walks away delighted. But usually, they feel a little better. It might simply be due to being tended by someone, or it could be the restorative power of make-up. I can honestly say that, once the storm had calmed, lipstick helped to pull me through the toughest period of my life.

After David died, I was allowed as much time off work as I needed. Stu and Pearl both turned up with home-cooked quiches and Tupperware cartons of curry and chilli to tide us over. My freezer was jam-packed with labelled plastic tubs, and Stu, a better-than-average baker, festooned us with more cakes than we could actually manage to eat. While my own mother didn't seem to know what to do with me, he and Pearl were there, almost constantly, sitting and listening as I went over and over that terrible night, and when there really wasn't anything left to say, they washed up and tidied and helped Cam and Amy with homework. To me, it seemed ridiculous that homework was still happening – that the *world* was still happening outside our house. Without children of her own – she and her husband had been unable to conceive – Pearl became far more than our childminder. She'd show up to take Cam and Amy to the zoo or the theatre, and became an auntie figure, woven into the fabric of my family. Whenever I suggested that she was doing too much for us, she insisted she'd rather be with us than stuck with Iain at home – 'the boring farter in the corner', as she termed him. At the mention of 'farting Iain', Cam and Amy convulsed with laughter. It seemed they were familiar with his gaseous emissions. As they had ricocheted through phases of being withdrawn and exploding with anger over tiny upsets, I was just terribly grateful that my children could still laugh.

My work colleagues visited too. Helena babysat, even though she'd only just started at our store, and area manager Nuala treated me to her cleaner for an entire day. I sat on the couch, feeling grateful but strangely redundant as Rosa cheerfully dusted and hoovered and our house emerged from its layer of grime and neglect.

At first, I didn't notice the La Beauté goodie bag Nuala had brought me. When I did, I just dumped it on a book-shelf. What was the point of taking care of myself or trying to look pretty? The very concept seemed ridiculous when David was no longer there. I wasn't even sure if I could ever return to work and enthuse over the plumping qualities of our latest serum. Perhaps I should retrain as a firefighter or a police officer, something that would make a real difference? But then, those jobs involved no small element of personal risk, and now Cam and Amy had only me to take care of them, I became terrified of some-thing equally dreadful happening to me, leaving them all alone. Even making a will, and citing Pearl as Cameron and Amy's guardian, did little to ease my fears.

One drizzly afternoon, Amy plucked the rope-handled La Beauté bag from the shelf and peered into it. Considering its contents useless, she tossed it aside on the sofa and a moisturiser, a night cream and a lipstick tumbled out. I only applied the lipstick because my lips were dry and sore. A couple of hours later, I happened to glimpse my reflection in the bathroom mirror. I looked better, I realised. More like the functioning human being I was pretending to be. I started wearing the lipstick daily and then I added a little base, some blush, a touch of eyeliner, as I had every day before the accident. I'd started to use the moisturiser and night cream too, soothed by the feeling of gently massaging them in. Taking a few minutes to apply my make-up each morning felt frivolous at first, considering what had happened. But it also meant I could face the day.

And slowly, I started to heal. Much to Mum's consternation, I returned to work: 'But what about the children?' she asked, suggesting that they would be better served if I stayed at home full-time. Yet how could I, when I needed to support us? They were at school, we had Pearl to look after them until I came home from work, and it was good for me to have some structure back in my life. I started to take pride again in being able to help customers to feel better about themselves, if only for the few minutes they spent perched on our stools. My world might have crumbled but small pleasures could be had in introducing a customer to our new, especially silken mascara. Now my job seemed to be less about meeting daily and monthly targets – although, for some reason my sales soared – and more a matter of sharing my love of beauty.

While life at home was hectic, stepping into our store brought an immediate sense of calm. Deliciously scented, and soothing even on the busiest days, it felt like the kind of place where nothing bad could ever happen. Now I understood why Mum had been so drawn to the lavish displays of frosted lipsticks and pearlised nail polishes in Goldings back in Bradford.

A few months after the accident, it all came out that Anneka Salworth, the thirty-two-year-old woman driving the car that killed David, had had an epileptic fit at the wheel. She had been told by her consultant not to drive, and was charged with causing death by dangerous driving. Her defence centred around the snowy road conditions, but she was found guilty and given a five-year prison sentence. I could have gone and seen it all played out in court, but took the kids camping to Cornwall instead.

It was late spring and still a little chilly, but building fires on the beach, and seeing Cam and Amy truly having fun for the first time since the accident, lifted my spirits more than any guilty verdict could. I even braved the freezing water with Amy. Swimming in the sea had been the thing she and David had loved to do together more than anything; he always adored ploughing through the waves. I am a rather feeble, splashy swimmer, and Cam always preferred to lie on a towel with a book. But we swam and cooked and laughed together, and during those few days my anger seemed to blow away on the sharp sea breeze. In fact, Anneka Salworth, with her droopy perm and doleful grey eyes – of course I'd Googled her and read the brief news reports – now seemed no more culpable than the snowy conditions that night, or me asking for a bottle of sauvignon.

I didn't want to blame anyone. I just wanted to at least *pretend* to be a normal functioning family, and for the three of us to find a way to be happy again.

Naturally, I still think about David every day but, somehow, during the past seven years, we have all managed to find a new way of living. Work has been a lifeline as I have risen up through the ranks to the position of counter manager. Today, business is brisk throughout the rest of my shift, and by the time I arrive home, Amy has headed off to her best friend Bella's while Cam, too, is on his way out.

'Got to go,' he says, giving me a speedy hug in the hallway. 'Last-minute call, emergency thing 'cause someone's sick. Gig on the Holloway Road . . .'

'Oh, that's great, love.' Hopefully, this line of work will continue throughout Cam's last school year. After that, he has vague notions to 'try and get into sound engineering', and I can't help thinking, what would his dad have made of that? But then, I can't think that way. Cam is a sociable, popular boy. He'll *get by*. 'Be careful,' I add as an afterthought, at which he stops at the front door and smirks.

'Be careful of what?'

'Oh, I don't know. Wires. Plugs. *Electricals*.'

He chuckles and pats my head as if I'm a fretful aunt. 'Don't worry. I'm not nine. I won't go sticking my finger into anything.' And with that, he's off, clambering into his mate Mo's revving, battered old van; Mo who, like Cam, is seventeen and barely shaves yet, so how can he possibly be in charge of a vehicle? It seems as scary a concept as the pair of them being let loose to perform a heart operation.

In the kitchen now, I wave through the window at Stu and Bob, his friend and business cohort, who are deep in conversation at the table in our tiny back garden. Prowling for something to eat, I discover prized treasure in the form of leftover spaghetti and fresh pesto – clearly Stu's work

– in a pan on the hob. Too hungry to bother with heating it up, I shovel it down straight from the pan before joining Stu and Bob in the garden.

'Hey, Lorrie,' Bob says, hands wrapped around a mug of tea. Parsley Force has certainly knocked back their beer consumption, as most of their call-outs happen in the evenings and late into the night.

'Hi, Bob. How's it going?'

'Really good,' he enthuses. 'Better than we could've hoped, amazingly.'

I glance at the A4 pad covered in scribbled notes on the wrought-iron table. 'Plans for world domination?'

He nods and grins. 'Well, expansion plans. Marketing, social media, that kind of thing. We've probably taken things as far as we can just relying on word of mouth . . .'

'He reckons we need to start promoting,' Stu offers. 'A newsletter, competitions, more activity on the Facebook page . . .'

Bob laughs, adjusting the black-rimmed spectacles that dominate his boyish face. 'Poor old granddad, afraid of social media. Thinks it's just some conspiracy to glean all our personal information . . .'

'Well, what else is it?' Stu retorts.

'It's useful,' I remark. 'What about keeping in touch with old friends? Everyone's scattered all over the place these days. How else would we all stay connected?'

'Er, via telephonic apparatus?' Stu smirks.

'Okay, but when are we supposed to phone each other?' I ask. 'We're all working all day and who has time for long conversations at night? Without social media, people would just fall off the radar . . .'

Stu shrugs. 'Friends who fall off the radar can't have been that important in the first place.'

'But I don't want to lose people,' I insist. 'And anyway, what about my dad? How else would we be able to keep in touch when he's 12,000 miles away in Australia? It's over a year since I've seen him for real but with Facebook I still get to see him in his silly yellow shorts, trying to light a barbecue, getting told off by Jill for squirting lighter fuel all over the prawns . . .'

Stu shrugs. 'Okay, there is *that* . . .'

'And it's how we'll spread the word,' Bob adds. 'Build up a wider customer base, get people talking, maybe even attract some press coverage . . .'

'Who'd want to interview *us*?' Stu asks.

'I don't know. Someone might find us inspiring . . .'

'You could be photographed looking all macho in your biker leathers,' I add with a grin. 'That could boost your customer base—'

'Or close us down,' Bob sniggers as I leave them to thrash out their plans in peace.

Alone in the living room, I find myself wishing the kids were around tonight. These days, I barely see them. Cam's often working or hanging out with Mo and the rest of his mates, and Amy loves being at Bella's. Who can blame her, with their semi-wild garden and the summerhouse Bella's dad built? Even at fifteen, the girls still love to 'camp' in it. Anyway, I shouldn't be reliant on my children for company.

I curl up on the sofa with my laptop and, being more of the Bob persuasion where social media is concerned, I log onto Facebook with the intention of catching up with Dad.

Ah, a friend request. I click it open and my heart seems to clunk.

Antoine Rousseau.

Antoine from the Massif Central? Antoine who saw me swimming in my C&A bra and pants? It *can't* be him. Occasionally, I've wondered what he's been up to over the years – and, okay, when I first joined Facebook I had a quick search for him. Okay, okay, I spent *hours* trawling for my teenage love – just out of curiosity, of course. There were so many men called Antoine Rousseau – none of them looking anything like the boy I remembered – that I gave up.

I stare at his name. As he doesn't have a proper profile picture, I'm still not convinced it's the Antoine who dumped me in favour of bra-less Nicole. The photo is of an orange sitting on a white plate. What's that all about?

I open his page but, as we're not Facebook friends, all I can see is a small selection of pictures: blowsy pink flowers in a garden, a glass of wine on a garden table. And, in bold black type, what looks like one of those motivational phrases, which I have an aversion to in any language and can't even bother trying to translate.

There *is* one picture of a person. As it's taken from a distance on what looks like an otherwise deserted beach, it's hard at first to tell whether it's him. I peer at it, and slowly he comes into focus.

A tall, slim man with light brown hair, squinting in the sunshine. A lopsided smile. Bit Boden, actually, in a loose, windblown checked shirt and stone-coloured chinos. My God, he does look like 'my' Antoine. In fact, I'm sure he is. What on earth possessed him to contact me now, thirty years since we last saw each other?

Bob's voice floats in from the garden. 'We need a proper website. People expect it. It's like a shop window . . .' His voice fades as I'm transported, as a shy and chubby teen- ager, back to 1986, and a lake deep in the woods where

49

the most beautiful boy I had ever set eyes on handed me his T-shirt to dry myself . . .

Antoine Rousseau, trampler of my tender sixteen-year-old heart.

Decline or accept?

Bastard.

I click *accept*.

Chapter Five

I sit there, poised for a message to say *hi, how are you? It's been a long time!* Pathetic, I know. Beneath my undeniably middle-aged exterior, I am clearly still that desperate schoolgirl yearning to glimpse a blue airmail envelope bearing a French stamp. *Lorrie Foster*, written in his spidery hand – oh, the thrill of it!

Irritated with myself – haven't I matured one iota during the intervening thirty years? – I call out goodnight to Stu and Bob, who have relocated to the kitchen table, and carry my laptop upstairs in the affectedly casual manner of someone planning to order some new saucepans from Amazon.

While I'm getting ready for bed, I keep checking Facebook, my gaze constantly flicking towards it as if I have lost all control of my eyeball-swivelling muscles. My fingers are tingling with the effort of not messaging him. *Hello Antoine,* I want to type, *this is a bit of a surprise!* Or rather, *Have you any idea how heartbroken I was, and how I took solace in all those 'forbidden' Viennettas Mum kept stashed in the chest freezer in the garage, plus stolen*

Dubonnet from her drinks cabinet? Of course, I don't really harbour any bitterness now. It was just a teenage thing, a holiday infatuation that fizzled out. After everything that happened subsequently – meeting David, having our children and then losing him – Antoine seems barely significant. But still . . . what does the shitbag heartbreaker *want?* Curiosity niggles at me like an itch, and I can't help wondering what he'd make of me now, aged forty-six, a generous size sixteen and currently wearing Primark pyjamas with penguins printed all over them.

Of course, now we're Facebook friends, I can access Antoine's entire photo archive and pore over his grown-up life. At least, the Facebook version which, as everyone knows, is carefully curated to demonstrate an unfailingly happy and enviable existence. However, as a test of will-power, I decide to postpone the pleasure. Instead, I prop up my pillows in bed and force myself into the calmer territory of eBay, where I try to concentrate on finding a suitable dress to wear to my mother's wedding in three weeks' time.

Mum's love life: now there's a template to avoid. She grumbled about Dad constantly, yet fell apart after turfing him out of the house when I was ten years old. There followed a series of ill-advised liaisons, all ending in heartbreak – but now, thankfully, she is deeply in love with a nice bit of posh called Hamish Sowerbutt, who's over a decade younger, terribly kind in his scatty way, and clearly adores her. The fact that I don't have my wedding outfit sorted is causing Mum no small amount of agitation. However, so far, I haven't found anything suitable. 'Remember it's a classy, formal affair,' she retorted recently. What is she expecting me to turn up in? Ermine?

Then I'm back on Facebook, unable to resist any longer,

and now examining numerous pictures of presumably corporate events Antoine has attended. The men are all dressed virtually identically in dark suits, the women in smart jackets and dresses in navy or grey. How disappointing. This is Antoine at work – all professional smiles and handshakes – and gives away nothing about his personal life. There isn't even anything to indicate the sort of company he works for, or what his job actually is.

In one picture, Antoine – again suited and, it must be said, dashingly handsome – is standing in front of an audience with a microphone, giving some sort of speech. I picture the honey-tanned boy with floppy, overgrown hair and golden skin, covering my neck in tiny feathery kisses. He now looks like the sort of man who has manicures. I stare and stare until each picture has imprinted itself onto my brain.

At around midnight, I hear Cam coming in. 'Okay, darling?' I call out.

'Yeah, good, thanks,' he replies from the landing. 'Managed not to fry myself on all those terrifying wires . . .'

'Glad to hear it,' I say with a smile. There's some pottering about, then music starts up in his room – low volume and pretty mellow, nothing to complain about really – and I detect a whiff of smoke, which Cam might have brought home with him, although of course, venues have been non-smoking for years. He's probably having a shifty roll-up out of his bedroom window. I know he does this – I've found the odd Rizla lying around, and those tiny cylindrical filter things. Although I don't love the fact that he smokes, he's assured me that it's only occasional. When you think of the kind of stuff he could be getting up to, is it really worth falling out over something like three roll-ups a week? Anyway, at his age – post-Antoine, having just started my first job – I was smoking proper ciggies, sneaking them out of Mum's packets.

Christ, I must have dozed off. I come to, groggily, with the main light still on and my laptop balanced perilously close to the edge of my bed. It's 3.47 a.m. 'Get a grip,' I mutter, placing it on my bedside table.

Just one more check . . . a message! Whoop!

Hi Lorrie, here's a recent pic from not so sunny Melbourne. Hope all's good with you and the kids, love Dad xxx

My father, grinning in a wetsuit, the wet black rubber with banana yellow flashing doing a sterling job of holding in his small paunch. His arm is thrust around Jill, his wife, who's bare-faced and grinning in a pink T-shirt, baggy shorts and a wide-brimmed straw hat.

Both looking great, I reply.

Hey, you're up late! Been out at a party?

Who comes home from parties at this hour on a Monday night? Oh God, plenty of people do. How old and sour I have become.

No, just having trouble sleeping for some reason. Night, Dad. Love you. L xxx

*

I manage to get through the whole morning at work without checking Facebook on my phone. But at lunchtime, on my way out to buy a sandwich, I crack and message him.

Hi Antoine, I type, my heart rattling only slightly, *what a surprise to receive a friend request from you. How are you?*

There. Pretty neutral, I'd say.

I glide through the afternoon, reminding myself that this is nothing – just an innocent little friend request – and the very fact that I'm all het up about someone I haven't seen since 1986 suggests that I really should get out more. Not on dates – *definitely* not dates – but out in the world generally. Take this summer, for instance. It's not just my shaky finances to blame for the fact that I have no holiday planned. It's the issue of who to go with. Naturally, Cameron doesn't want to come away with me anymore; he and Mo have a vague notion of going to a couple of festivals. Pearl, who works as a nanny to extremely well-heeled families these days, is due back soon from working in Dubai, but the last thing she'll want is to go away again. Other friends are happily ensconced with their families – *two*-parent families – and I can't imagine Stu would want to come away and abandon Parsley Force for a week. Anyway, we've never been on holiday together. I think he'd be a bit taken aback if I asked.

In contrast, Amy is off to Bella's family's holiday home on the Algarve. 'They're so looking forward to it,' Bella's mum, Cecily, tells me when she drops off Amy that evening. 'They've been talking about nothing else.'

'Thanks so much for inviting her again,' I tell Cecily as the girls disappear to the living room.

'Oh, she's such a pleasure to have around, and Bella

would be bored stupid, stuck with just her brothers for company.' She pauses and sips her tea at my kitchen table. 'How about you? Are you managing to get away?'

I shake my head. 'Maybe later in the year, I'm not sure yet.'

'I should have asked you to come too. There's room, you know, and you could get a last-minute flight, just fly to Faro and we'll pick you up—'

'Oh no, Amy would hate that . . .' I correct myself, 'I mean, she loves coming away with you. She had the best time last summer. It wouldn't be the same if I tagged along.'

'You wouldn't be *tagging*,' she insists, and it occurs to me that the real reason I have turned down previous offers to stay in Cecily and Gerry's Portuguese villa is because . . . well, I don't quite fit into their world. Although we have only got to know each other through our daughters' friendship, I admire Cecily immensely; she's a powerhouse of energy, taking charge of her four children without ever seeming to break into a sweat. However, en masse the Kentons are just a little too, well, perfect. No sugar is allowed in their house – ever. The only 'biscuits' permitted are seed-covered crispbreads by someone called 'Dr Kaarg'; Cecily is always asking Stu to pick some up for her when he visits a certain out-of-the-way supermarket which stocks the entire Dr Kaarg range. Plus, it's true that Amy enjoys the novelty of being away with the Kentons. Other people's families always seem a little shinier than your own.

To swerve us away from my lack of holiday plans, I fill Cecily in on my latest dating adventure – the living sculpture, the conceptual art – at which she honks with laughter, strawberry blonde curls tumbling into her eyes.

'Oh God, Lorrie. You *must* find a decent man who isn't completely weird. Let me find you one. There are lots at work, handsome guys in their forties, divorced, bit of baggage, but then who hasn't amassed some of that, at our age?'

'Oh no, please don't set me up. I'm not looking for any more dates . . .'

She helps herself to a slice of Stu's recent bake – a particularly moist and delicious gingerbread – and takes an enthusiastic bite. The sugar ban doesn't seem to extend beyond the boundaries of the Kentons' home. 'Well, what about meeting more men from that dating site?'

'Oh, no, I'm coming off that . . .'

'But you've hardly given it a chance!'

'I have, Cecily. Three dates is quite enough—'

'Three's *nothing* in that sort of world.'

I laugh. 'You don't know that sort of world. You have no idea what it's like to spend an evening with someone who drones on about how much he hates work – how the insurance business is *killing* him – and all you can do is stare at the three little brown pegs which you suspect might actually be teeth . . .'

'Ugh, really? It provides good stories, at least.'

But who wants to go on dates just for *stories*? I reflect as Cecily takes another bite of cake. She and Gerry have been together since, well, forever, and still adore each other. As well as Bella – who's an excellent pianist – they have Matthew, Oliver and George, all accomplished classical musicians with impeccable manners and hearty red cheeks. Their Victorian townhouse gleams with gilt-framed accolades.

'Oh, there *is* someone who's crawled out of the woodwork,' I add, lifting my laptop from the worktop. 'See what you think of this . . .' I open Antoine's Facebook page and click on the beach picture.

'Mmmm, he's a bit of a fox. Who is he?'

'First love,' I explain. 'Well, first obsession really, but it felt like true love at the time. Mum packed me off to France at sixteen to stay with my penpal. He was her older brother and he's just sent me a friend request . . .'

'So you had a thing with him?'

I nod. 'Just a holiday romance, I suppose, although there wasn't any "just" about it at the time . . .'

'Let's see more pictures,' she enthuses as I start to click through them. 'So many work events,' she adds. 'Conferences, meetings, that kind of thing . . .'

'It's all very corporate,' I agree, hearing the front door open and Stu striding in.

'Hey, Stu,' Cecily says with a smile.

'Hey, Cess.' He always calls her this. I'm not sure she likes it much, but she *does* like Stu, so she lets him get away with it. 'What's this?' he enquires, glancing over my shoulder. 'You're Facebook friends with an orange?'

'It's actually a person,' I explain. 'Remember Antoine, from that French trip? The one who stopped writing—'

'Not the shithead who broke your heart?' Stu asks.

'Yep, that's the one,' I say wryly.

He turns to Cecily. 'She was devastated. Cried for weeks. Of course, it was left to me to pick up the pieces . . .'

I sense my cheeks colouring as Cecily crooks a brow. 'And you accepted his friend request?' she remarks.

'Well, yes, but only because—'

'So, did he poke you?' Stu cuts in.

'Stu, she was only sixteen!' Cecily exclaims.

'No, I mean a Facebook poke.'

I laugh derisively. 'No one *pokes* anyone these days. No one's poked anyone since about 2007 . . .'

'No, I heard it was coming back,' he says, suddenly

58

quite the social media guru. 'People are poking each other all over the place. So, you didn't tell me he'd been in touch?'

Cecily and I exchange a quick look.

'It was only yesterday,' I remark.

'Oh, right. So, what does he want?' He cranes forward for a closer look, radiating disapproval.

'Just to be friends, I guess . . .'

'Friends?' he repeats.

'Yes, is there anything wrong with that?' I'm starting to feel rather crowded in now, and slightly regret turning this utterly *insignificant* incident into a public event. I decide not to mention that I have already messaged Antoine, and have yet to receive a reply.

'I s'pose not,' Stu says with a shrug, 'if you really *want* to be in contact again . . .'

'Well, I think he's gorgeous,' Cecily adds with a grin.

'He's all right,' I say lightly.

'Oh, come on! Look at those lovely dark eyes, Lorrie. The chiselled cheekbones. Very sexy in that polished professional sort of way . . .'

'Puh.' With a snort, Stu ambles away. He opens the fridge, peers inside and closes it again.

'Well, that's enough Antoine for me,' Cecily adds, jumping up. 'Better head back before I get overheated.' She turns towards the kitchen door. 'Bella darling? We really need to get going . . .'

And off they go, shortly followed by Stu, who's called out on another job – emergency unsalted butter required in Crouch End – so, with Amy enjoying one of her customary soaks in the bath, I hunker down at the kitchen table and scroll through yet more of Antoine's pictures.

More personal insights into his life is what I'm looking

for: a wife, a girlfriend, children. A couple of photos I missed earlier were taken at some kind of gathering in a garden, in which he's wearing a casual shirt and jeans, but there are no couply pictures, and there's nothing to indicate whether he's married or not. I examine picture after picture like some rabidly obsessed teenager, and when I check the clock on the cooker I realise over an hour has passed since Stu went out. That's how long I've spent gawping at someone I haven't seen since I was sixteen years old. What's wrong with me? I am forty-six, I have a tunic to iron for work tomorrow, there's a load of saggy old vegetables to dispose of in the fridge.

Allowing myself one final peek, I click on the picture that isn't of a person or thing, but a phrase – perhaps one of those mottoes for life. Nuala pins them up whenever we're all gathered together in a hotel for a La Beauté away-day: *Because every woman is beautiful.* Antoine's reads: *La vie est comme une bicyclette. Pour garder votre équilibre, vous devez continuer à avancer.*

Even I can understand the first bit. Google translates the rest: *To keep your balance, you must keep moving.* So this is the type of person he's turned out to be: a-life-is-a-bicycle sort of man. Right-ho. I go back to the corporate pictures, vaguely registering Stu arriving home and clattering about in the hallway.

A message pops up. Antoine!

Hey Lorrie, Thanks for accepting :) I'm very flattered that you remember me . . .

Remember? Is the man insane? Of course I remember!

60

Realise it was thirty years ago, he continues. *Where does all the time go?*

Oh, I don't know – it just keeps moving. On its bicycle probably.

So, he goes on, *what are you up to these days?*

I wait, but nothing more comes. So, how to respond? I rehearse the words in my head: *I am in charge of a highly successful make-up and skincare empire . . . Although I travel widely, what I love most is being with my two delightful teenagers in my beautiful house in a sought-after part of London . . .*

I glance down at Amy's dusty red and black basketball boots, dumped in front of the cubbyhole shelves that are meant for wine, but which are stuffed with random items such as gardening gloves, jam jars and obsolete chargers.

Stu saunters in, pulling off his crash helmet. 'Still in a sweat over your French fancy?'

'I'm not in a sweat,' I retort. 'Just a bit taken aback, that's all.'

He peers down at my face. 'Yes you are. You're all flushed and your pupils are dilated . . .'

I laugh awkwardly and try to angle my laptop so he can't see the message. Too late. His eyes light upon the screen.

'Ooh, he's messaged you. Are you going to reply?'

'I might . . .'

'What are you going to say?'

Jesus, it's like having another teenager about the place. *Any replies from datemylovelymum yet? Let me see!* 'Just . . . you know,' I murmur. 'Normal stuff . . .'

61

'Tell him what an amazingly handsome, adorable house-mate you have. Go on. Make him regret running off with that French girl, what was her name . . .'

'Nicole . . .'

'. . . And realise what a fuck-up he made of things. Make him *pine* for you, Lorrie . . .' He guffaws loudly.

For Christ's sake, is my entire private life to be held up for everyone else's cheap entertainment? I try to radiate calm – and mentally compose a suitable message – but it's impossible now with Stu hanging over me.

He extracts a Magnum ice cream from the freezer and rips off its wrapper. 'You know what you should put? You should say—'

'Stu, *please*!'

'Whoah, I'm only trying to help . . .'

'Yes, but you're sounding exactly like my mum. You know she used to tell me what to put in a thank you letter? "Don't just say thanks for the sweater, Lorrie. Say *what* you like about it – be specific about how you love the colour, the feel of it, how it goes with your jeans . . ."'

He licks the ice cream slowly. '*Please* don't say I'm like your mum.'

I stand up and go to touch his arm, but he steps away. 'Oh, of course you're not. I just meant—'

'I was only trying to help,' he cuts in like a petulant child.

I look at him, embarrassed now for acting like a lunatic over a casual friend request. 'Look, I know you were. But I really don't need anyone's help to message someone . . .'

'Yeah, I know.' He tries for a smile, but it falters. 'He uses a photo of an orange for a profile picture.'

I chuckle. 'Yes, he does. Seems like a bit of a jerk.'

Stu drops his Magnum, only half-finished, into the bin.

'You don't really mean that,' he adds, affecting a teasing tone as he saunters out of the kitchen. 'Anyway, if you're going to obsess over someone who broke your heart thirty years ago, then *I'm* not going to stand in your way.'

Chapter Six

It's a cool and breezy Wednesday morning and, after Stu's prickliness, I'm looking forward to throwing myself into a day at the store.

I didn't bother replying to Antoine's message last night. Instead, I went straight to bed, finally drifting off to the muffled chatter and laughter of Cam and Mo in Cam's room. No one had surfaced by the time I got up. I dressed quickly in my La Beauté tunic and the required smart black trousers, and applied my make-up – dark eyes, red lips, my professional face – on autopilot.

As I emerge from the tube station a text pings in from Cecily: *I have a theory about the lovely Antoine. He's newly divorced and thinking, hmm, who can I contact from my past? And you were top of his list!*

I smile, amused by her line of thinking. The thing is, when you're single, married friends are especially keen for you to 'get out there' and enjoy some dating adventures. Perhaps they miss that flurry of excitement, and want *you* to have some fun for them to enjoy, safely, from the side-lines.

I stop outside a closing-down Rymans and reply: *Top of the list? Very much doubt it. Will keep you posted!* And so to work, where I know precisely what my role is, and what's expected of me – unlike with the rest of my life.

*

'The lovely thing about this day cream,' I say, spreading a little across my customer's finely boned face, 'is that it's like wearing nothing, but all the time it's keeping the cells plumped up for at least seven hours, whilst helping to stop moisture evaporating from the surface . . .'

'You mean it doesn't sink in?' she asks.

'Well, yes, it does, but a very fine layer sits on top of the skin, acting as a protective barrier.'

'Do you actually *know* this?'

This takes me aback. I was surprised, actually, that this older woman agreed to come to the counter as I approached her. She'd glided in – tall, perfectly poised with erect posture – just after we opened this morning. I'd expected a brisk 'no thanks' and for her to saunter straight past.

'All our products have taken years to develop,' I explain, 'and when something new is launched we all try it over a few weeks. This is the cream I use every day.'

She smiles knowingly. 'Of course it is, but then, you have to say that.'

'I'd never recommend anything if I didn't feel confident that it works.'

She touches her cheek. 'It does feel rather nice, I have to say.'

I smile. 'Would you like to try some of our new make-up colours too?'

'Oh, is there any point at my age?'

I study her for a moment. What a face she has: almost sculpted, with an amazing complexion, her green eyes as striking as a cat's. In her mid-sixties perhaps, she is a vision of elegance in a simple blue cotton dress and a lace-knit black cardi. Her silvery bob, not a hair out of place, hangs neatly at her pointed chin.

'I think there's a point at any age,' I say, 'if it makes you feel good about yourself.'

She frowns briefly. 'Oh, go on then, why not? It's just, I've never been a make-up person, I've never actually worn lipstick . . .'

'No, well, I can do something very subtle for you.'

'And I do have something coming up – an important presentation which I'm actually quite nervous about. Silly, I know, at my age . . .'

'Not at all,' I assert.

She blinks at our array of eye shadows, looking quite baffled. 'Anyway, I'm thinking that make-up is somewhat necessary for such an occasion. It's just expected, isn't it, that one looks . . . polished these days? Could you give me some advice on that?'

'I'd be delighted to,' I say. 'I'm Lorrie, by the way . . .'

'Gilda.'

'Don't worry, Gilda, I won't do anything outlandish. Neutrals are best when you want to look professional. So, I'll start with our new primer . . .'

A small frown. 'I have *no* idea what primers do.'

'They just form a smooth base for make-up,' I explain, 'and contain tiny light-reflecting particles—'

'I don't want to look like a mirrorball!'

'Oh, you won't, because when I apply base over that . . .'

'So base goes over the . . . what's it called again?'

'Primer.'

Gilda chuckles. 'The base coat . . .'

'Well, sort of . . .'

'Like I'm a roughcast wall.'

I laugh, because she really is astoundingly beautiful and I don't think she's even aware of the fact.

She sits bolt upright as I apply a light cream base, and seems to be paying rapt attention as I talk her through the make-up. 'I'm using this neutral beige over your lids,' I explain, 'and some darker brown close to your lashes and along the socket line – this gives an impression of depth . . .'

'Not too much, please,' she murmurs.

'No, I promise it's not a lot. Just a smudge of liner and some brown mascara, it's much softer than black . . .' I add blusher and a subtle brownish-rose lipstick. Although it *is* a full face of make-up, the effect is subtly enhancing.

'So what do you think?'

Gilda swivels towards the mirror. 'Oh!' She regards herself for a moment.

Hell, she's horrified.

'Well, I have to say . . .' She peers more closely. 'Yes, I actually like it. Gosh, that's a surprise. It did feel like an awful lot of *stuff* you were putting on . . .'

I exhale with relief. Although I always care, it seemed especially important that Gilda – a lipstick first-timer – was happy with my handiwork. 'It probably did, if you're not used to it . . .'

She hops down off the stool. 'And I couldn't be doing with all that every day, good lord no . . .'

'No, of course not. But for a special occasion – for your presentation . . .'

'Yes, quite. You know, I think I might have a go myself.' She smiles. 'I'll take them, please.'

That's a bonus. I didn't expect a sale. 'Which products were you thinking of? Here's everything I've used today . . .'

I lay out the make-up on the counter, which she peruses carefully.

'Oh, I'll take the lot, darling. You're very talented, I can't quite believe how, well . . .' She pauses and checks her reflection again. '. . . How damn *good* I look!'

'You look wonderful. I'm so glad you're happy.'

I ring through her purchases and watch her stride away.

'God, she was gorgeous,' exclaims Helena, who's just returned from her break. 'I'd love to be like that when I'm her age. It gives me *hope*. And wasn't she pleased! Isn't that a great feeling?'

'It is,' I say truthfully, because that's what I love most about my job: seeing a woman light up with pleasure after I've applied her make-up. We get to know our customers a little, too, albeit for the short time they're perched on our stools. We hear about new relationships, break-ups, difficult mothers, career triumphs and disasters – the whole range of life's dramas. Making up someone's face is such an intimate thing. Often, a woman opens up, more than you'd ever imagine.

'You're definitely coming out tonight, aren't you?' Helena adds.

'Yes, of course. Looking forward to it . . .' It's Helena's birthday today – her thirty-sixth – reminding me that I'm by far the oldest team member here. As one customer put it, 'It's nice to get advice from someone who understands mature skin.' Ouch. She was right, though, and even our younger customers – barely twenty, some of them – seem to enjoy my rather motherly approach. I reassure myself of this on rare occasions when I panic about being put out to pasture.

At lunchtime, having picked up a sandwich, I install myself on a bench in the nearby tree-lined square and check my phone. Antoine has messaged again.

Hope you don't mind me getting in touch, Lorrie. I knew it was you right away. You have hardly changed at all.

Oh, please – flatterer. Yet I can't help smiling.

Where are you? Still in Yorkshire?

I take a fortifying bite of my sandwich and type:

Hi Antoine,
Lovely to hear from you. It was quite a surprise, I have to say. I'm in London – I've lived here pretty much all my adult life actually. East London, Bethnal Green. I live with my two teenagers and our lodger, Stu. Life's really good. How about you? Where are you living these days?

I'm poised, waiting for a reply; I can see he's online with his little green light on. There's a burst of laughter from a group of young women all stretched out on the grass. Despite the cool breeze, their skirts are hoiked up to maximise tanning potential.

Life is good thank you, he replies. *I live in Nice – very different from that sleepy place I grew up in, where nothing ever happened! Do you remember it? I have very happy memories of my time with you. :)*

Hmm. So he likes a smiley emoticon. Could it be interpreted as flirty, or would that be a wink? I'm not au fait with the language of commas and dots. Another message appears:

I have two teenagers too, Nicolas and Elodie.

Lovely names, I reply.

Thank you, of course I think so! And yours?

I have Cameron, who's seventeen – everyone apart from his grandma calls him Cam – and Amy, she's fifteen. She spends every spare moment at basketball training. Cam loves music and wants to be a sound engineer – or at least he thinks so. It's all rather vague at the moment.

They sound like great kids. Mine live with their mother in Paris so it's a long way. But we see each other when we can. They are fifteen and thirteen and growing up fast. It's hard to believe we were just teenagers ourselves when we met that summer! Do you remember?

Does he actually think I have no memory at all?

Yes, of course I remember, I reply, then add a smiley :)

Amy would be appalled. I've glimpsed her texts – they are littered with emoticons – but she reckons there's a cut-off age (twenty) for their usage.

Having finished my sandwich now, I'm starting to feel slightly ridiculous, sitting here on tenterhooks for another message. I can virtually hear Stu, carping into my ear: *'Your pupils are massive and you're all flushed! Jesus, Lorrie, look at the state of you . . .'*

Amazing wasn't it? Antoine types. **The best time!**

Wow – that's a bit . . . suggestive. Fragments of his long-ago correspondence – the spidery handwriting with its distinctly French-looking loops and curls – flutter into my mind as I get up and drop my sandwich wrapper into a nearby bin. *I'll never forget you,* he wrote in his letters back then. *I'll always love you, my beautiful Lorrie.*

I stop at the corner of the street. Five minutes left of my break. I type a message, feeling emboldened now.

Can I just ask what's made you get in touch with me now, after all this time?

Hell, why not? I want to know what he wants, and I've been far too reserved lately. Take the date with Ralph. What possessed me to just sit there, being pleasant, while he told me I was clearly very fond of my cake? Why didn't I say, 'Actually, that's incredibly rude of you and, while we're at it, I really couldn't give a toss about what Thomas Trotter is trying to "say" with his caged Brillo pads'?

I hover, staring at my phone like a fixated teenager. Perhaps Cecily was right, and Antoine is newly single and working his way through the list of all the women who've been in any way significant to him. Who would I have, if I was playing that game? Without David, there is literally no one. There have been others, of course – a few forgettables

71

before I met him, then more recently Pete Parkin from the electricals department at work, with whom I had a brief thing about three years ago, until he left to take up a deputy manager's position at Holland and Barrett. But he'd hardly feature on any list; in fact, I suspected we'd only got together because we were both lonely and ended up chatting at a work leaving do. We had absolutely nothing in common, and the sex, which happened just a handful of times – accompanied by the shrill squawks of his parrot in the living room – was a rather dismal affair.

I moved a few months ago, Antoine replies. *I'm still sorting through papers and photos, trying to throw things away. Do you find it hard to let go of things?*

Oh, yes. Our loft is stuffed with boxes and bags containing David's possessions. His books, paperwork, numerous shirts with frayed collars that he refused to throw away: they're all there, waiting for decisions to be made about their destiny.

Once, I got as far as packing up a dozen or so shirts for charity. I was halfway to the shop when I glimpsed a faded blue one poking out of the bag – the one David always took on holiday and threw on over a T-shirt when the beach turned cool. I pulled it out of the bag and briefly buried my face in it, certain I could smell his sun-warmed skin and not caring whether passers-by thought I was crazy. Then I hurried home and bundled the bag of shirts back into the loft.

That, Antoine types, *is when I found pictures of us!*

I stare at my phone. Pictures of us? I don't remember

many being taken, and the only one I have from that trip is of Valérie and me, sitting rather unhappily on the edge of her bed. I am smiling tensely and Valérie is pulling off one of her socks.

Really? I type. *I am amazed you have any from that long ago.*

Yes, he replies instantly, *it was lovely to see them. You know, I couldn't believe you had travelled alone, all the way from Yorkshire, with that piece of paper your mother typed. You were brave. Anything could have happened to you . . .*

Something did happen to me.

I thought you were clever, brave and beautiful . . .

My heart seems to slam against my ribs.

Look, here's one of the pictures . . .

My breath catches as a photo appears. It's a little fuzzy, and at first it's hard to believe it's really us. He's probably photographed the old print with his phone. But I remember it being taken now, by one of Valérie's friends on a blisteringly hot day. Antoine and I are standing on the old stone bridge in the village, squinting a little – or at least I am – at the camera. He is looking at me, and his slim brown arm is slung around my shoulders, pulling me close. I have dreadful hair – yellowy highlights clashing against my natural brunette, the style verging perilously close to mullet – but I look so happy. Both of us do. You can see it clearly, shining out of our faces, even from a thirty-year-old faded print.

Wow, I type.

It's lovely, he replies.

Apart from my highlights!

Highlights?

Those yellow stripes in my hair . . .

I swallow hard, poised to walk back into the store, wanting to remind him that his letters became rather blunt ('Valérie learns karate but broke shoulder!') before petering out altogether. I could tell him about my prowlings in the hallway at home, waiting for the postman, or the fact that I lied to Gail Cuthbertson, the mean girl at school, when she asked if I still had 'that French boyfriend'.

'Yes, if it's any of your business.'

'Let's see a photo of him then.'

'Don't have any.'

'Yeah, 'cause you made him up!'

Of course I don't hold grudges: not like my mother, who's still prone to muttering about my father's unwillingness to fix a dodgy plug – 'It's like he was waging a campaign to electrocute me, Lorrie. Like he wanted to shoot thousands of volts through my body!' And they broke up *thirty-six years ago.*

'Can't you just let it go, Mum?' I implored her the last time she dredged it up. 'It's a very long time ago and he's

74

safely on the other side of the world. No one's going to get electrocuted now.'

'Maybe Jill will,' she muttered, with a trace of gleefulness.

So, no – of course I'm not bitter about a teenage romance that fizzled out.

I thought you had lovely hair, Antoine replies now.

A busker starts playing a harmonica incredibly badly as another picture appears on my phone: the two of us again, this time lying on our backs in some grassy place – the goat farm perhaps – photographed from above. I guess his friend must have taken it. Of course, it was long before the days of selfies. My T-shirt is rumpled and slipping off one shoulder, and I am smiling broadly; that pouty photo face, the one all the girls do now, hadn't been invented then. Even if it had, I'd have been too filled with happiness to remember to pull it.

I stare at the picture, no longer registering the throngs of people all around because I'm just seeing me, a young girl madly in love for the very first time. My vision fuzzes as Antoine's message appears:

I have to tell you, Lorrie, it was the summer I came alive.

Chapter Seven

There's no time to reply and, anyway, I haven't the first idea how to respond. The summer he came alive? What does *that* mean? I hurry back into the store and find Nuala hovering at our counter.

'Ah, *here* you are, Lorrie.' She smiles tightly.

'Oh, sorry, were you looking for me?'

'No, it's okay, you're here now. Just wondering how things are going?'

Helena, who's helping a customer to select a blusher, throws me a quizzical look.

'Great,' I reply. 'We're all hitting targets, the day cream and serum are going especially well . . .' Nuala knows all this because our sales are carefully recorded and monitored. In her late thirties, authoritative but approachable and chatty with the team, she usually just drops by to ensure everything is tidy and just so. She might share some gossip from one of the other stores, and one of us will touch up her lipstick. Today, she doesn't seem interested in any of that.

'Just wanted to let you know,' she starts, pushing back

her sleek black hair, 'we're having a bit of a company meeting on Friday and it's really important everyone attends.'

'Oh, okay. What's it all about?'

'Just a little thing for all the counter teams in the south-east. There's a hotel booked for it. You'll receive an email but I wanted to see you personally . . .' She clears her throat and glances around anxiously. Although she's my boss, we have known each other for long enough to have developed a sort of friendship. However, today she is emitting definite don't-quiz-me vibes.

'Is it a training session?' I ask.

'Um, no, it's not training. Well, not exactly.'

'Come on, Nuala. Don't leave us all hanging like this.'

She smiles tersely and her neck flushes pink. 'Sorry, I can't say anything else. It's an early start, I'm afraid – 8 a.m. – and breakfast will be served. You'll be back here by noon.'

I glance at Helena, and then back at Nuala. 'You mean we'll *all* be there? But what about the counter?'

'Don't worry,' she says briskly. 'I'm bringing in a team to cover things here. It's only a few hours . . .'

'A team? What d'you mean?'

'Trainees. They'll manage,' she adds with uncharacter-istic sharpness.

'The counter will be manned by *trainees*?'

'It'll be fine, Lorrie. Trust me, please – oh, and you should all be in uniform for the meeting, that goes without saying . . .'

'Yes, of course,' I murmur, glancing down at my black La Beauté tunic with its white logo on the breast pocket. As if we'd turn up in T-shirts and jeans.

Nuala swipes her trilling phone from her shoulder bag

and purses her lips at it. 'Sorry, got to take this.' She steps away, hair half-covering her face, already murmuring into her phone.

I look at Andi, an eager school-leaver and our newest recruit. She pulls a 'what the hell?' face, but there's no chance to speculate, not with Nuala loitering nearby. Anyway, if something's afoot, we won't help matters by standing about gossiping.

I approach a customer, inviting her to try our new, ultra-light foundation, and fall into easy chit-chat as normal. 'You'll find it's as light as a BB cream, while smoothing out imperfections . . .'

'Oh, I'd like to try that . . .'

'Could you hop on the stool for me and we'll see which colour gives the best match?'

'Great,' the woman says. 'The thing is, foundation always looks orange on me . . .'

Antoine flickers into my mind as I dab at her face with a cosmetic sponge. Antoine, with his orange-for-a-face profile picture, who reckons he 'came alive' in the summer of '86.

'Oh, that *does* look good,' she exclaims, examining her reflection. 'I'll take it.'

'Great, would you like me to cleanse it off for you?'

'What, and look like my knackered old self?' She laughs, oblivious to Nuala who's still lurking close by, barking into her mobile now: 'Yes, they'll all be there. Of course I've said it's compulsory . . .'

My customer trots away with her purchase, and I busy myself with tidying up my counter area, while trying to ignore a niggle of unease about all of us attending this meeting. The company is strict about holiday leave; many of our customers are fiercely loyal and expect to see a familiar face at the counter. In fact, I can't remember a time when we have all been off at once.

Looking severely rattled now, Nuala finishes her call and turns to address us again. 'I meant to say, one or two counter staff might be asked to stand up and do a little talk at this, er, *thing*. It's nothing to panic about—'

'Really? What kind of talk?' I try to keep my voice level.

'Oh, you know, just a quick, spontaneous thing. The essence of what La Beauté is all about . . .'

I study her face. Her pale blue eyes look tired, and her lipstick has worn away.

'Any idea who'll have to do this?' Helena asks.

'Honestly, I have no idea. But I think we should all be prepared, okay?'

'So we should prepare, even though it's meant to be spontaneous?' I smile to show I'm *fine* with this, but Nuala's mouth remains set in a tight line.

'Really, it's nothing to worry about. All they want to see is a real passion for the brand . . .'

'Who's *they*?' I ask.

'Oh, just the head honchos, you know . . .'

I frown, confused by her vagueness; I know most of senior management by name. Her phone trills again, and she waves quickly, her glossy heels clacking as she marches away from our counter, past clusters of perplexed-looking assistants from the other counters, towards the revolving front door.

Andi widens her eyes at me. 'That sounds scary. I hate public speaking. I always feel like I might actually throw up.'

'It's no big deal,' I say, affecting a breeziness I don't feel, 'and it'll probably be good for us, whatever it is. Just a little team get-together to keep us all on our toes.'

The upstairs room in the pub that Helena reserved for her birthday gathering has been double-booked. So we've been bundled in with a crowd of incredibly loud twenty-somethings who seem surprisingly inebriated, considering it's only 7.30 p.m. Crammed around a too-small table, we all ooh and ahh as Helena opens her presents, enthusing over each one in turn. However, the larger group dominates, their choice of music pumping relentlessly from a speaker above my head.

'He says it was all moving too fast,' shouts a girl from the other party, inches from my ear. 'And now I hear he's moved in with that woman. You know the fat one who's, like, thirty?'

I glance around, and she casts me a look of disdain as if I have no business being here at all.

'Oh my God,' gasps her friend, flicking her tussled blonde hair. 'The one with skirt up her arse, cellulite on display?'

Helena's sister Sophie catches my eye across the table and grimaces.

'Yeah, don't know how he can stand seeing her naked.'

Our nondescript meals are brought by a glum waitress, and bear all the hallmarks of having hopped straight from freezer to microwave. I poke at my bland Thai curry, wondering when thirty was deemed ancient and whether I can get away with slipping off home pretty soon.

The two girls are still positioned right beside our table where they are continuing their annihilation of this unnamed woman. 'She must be at *least* a size fourteen,' the blonde one remarks.

'Yeah! God, it's disgusting. It always amazes me how some women allow themselves to get to that size.' I look down at my bowl, my appetite having waned, my curry watery and tepid. After our initial sterling efforts, our group seems to have given up on making ourselves heard above the din. Even Helena looks as if her spirits are sagging.

As our plates are cleared, I reflect that, at some point, Mum stopped mentioning my 'puppy fat', declaring instead, 'You're lucky, you can carry off your size because of your height.' Which made me feel like some vast ocean liner: strong, sturdy, reliable in high seas.

More people are crowding into the room now, jostling our table and shouting over our heads. The waitress seems to have forgotten that we've ordered another round of drinks, and I find myself yearning to be spirited home to Stu and the kids.

'Let's go somewhere else,' Helena says in frustration.

'Good idea,' remarks Sophie as the bill is plonked on our table, without the extra round of drinks. As we divvy it up, I make my excuses for a quick exit and hug Helena and Andi goodbye. That's one bonus of growing older; there's no shame to be had in ducking out early.

Liberated into the humid July night, I make my way towards the tube, finally getting a moment to consider Antoine's 'the summer I came alive' declaration. How am I supposed to respond to that, and why is he telling me now? Perhaps he was just hit by a wave of nostalgia, as I am occasionally. Only mine tend to feature David and the children, the four of us together, on a holiday or at Christmas, or just lazing around the house on a rainy Sunday afternoon. Sometimes, I miss him so much it causes an actual ache.

As light rain starts to fall, I step into Tesco Metro where I select packets of chilli and lime rice crackers to satisfy Cam's copious late-night snacking. Amy favours cheese – the pricier varieties, naturally – and it's as I approach the dairy section that my mobile rings.

'Hello?' I reach for a wedge of Brie.

'Hi, Lorrie. It's Ralph—'

'Oh! How are you?'

'Great. Look, I hope this isn't a bad time . . .'

'Um, I'm just shopping actually . . .' *And didn't I explain last Sunday that we wouldn't be meeting again?* I drop the cheese into my basket, confused as to why he's calling at all.

'Right,' he says.

'Ralph, you did get my text, didn't you? After our date, I mean?'

'Oh, yes,' he blusters. 'Yes. Sorry. I'm just calling because, uhh . . .' There's some anxious throat-clearing. 'I think I owe you an apology.'

'Really? What for?' The cake thing, he must mean.

Feeling generous, I select the smoked cheese Amy likes, the one with the terracotta-coloured skin.

'Oh . . . everything really,' he says with an awkward laugh. 'Mentioning Belinda, for one thing. I'm not sure what I was thinking. That's not what one does on a date, is it?'

'It's okay to talk about your ex,' I say lightly, 'and I did ask. Don't worry about it.' It's *slightly* less okay to infer that I'm a cake-scoffing heifer, not that I care about that now . . .

'. . . And going on about the art,' Ralph continues. 'Obviously, they weren't your cup of tea, those wound paintings, the Thomas Trotter installations . . .'

'Well, they were interesting.'

'No, I'm sorry. You must have found me a colossal bore . . .'

'No, not at *all*,' I say, firmly, making my way down the aisle.

'You're very kind, Lorrie. Anyway, what I wanted to say is, I was terribly nervous on our date. Does that sound pathetic?'

'No, of course not. It's nerve-racking, this online dating business, strangers thrown together like that. But look, Ralph, I'm in Tesco, I really must get on and—'

'The thing is,' he interrupts, 'I was pretty taken aback when I saw you.'

I stop and frown. 'What d'you mean?'

'Oh, please don't take this the wrong way, but you're really not like you appear in your photo . . .'

'Aren't I?' *Neither are you, Mr-dig-out-a-pic-from-the-90s!*

'No. I mean, your photo's lovely, of course – that's why I contacted you in the first place. But in real life you're much more, er . . .'

Oh, God, what now?

'. . . You're *beautiful*!' he exclaims.

I blink, wondering whether I've heard him correctly. 'Erm . . . that's very kind of you, Ralph . . .'

'No, I mean it. I think I was rather bowled over, and when I'm nervous I sort of . . . oh God, this is awful, I *am* sorry, but I wanted to impress you, I suppose.'

Something in me softens, and then I realise I'm doing it again. At the gallery it was poor, bereaved Ralph. Now it's poor, nervous Ralph. I must get a grip before I find myself agreeing to another date just because I feel sorry for him. 'Well, thanks for explaining,' I murmur.

'That's okay. Just thought, if I cleared the air, you might agree to meet me again, just for a coffee or something—'

'I'm sorry, but no,' I say firmly.

'Ah. Okay.'

'But there is something else,' I add. 'Something I'd like to say about our date, if that's okay.'

He coughs. 'Oh. Yes, of course.'

'It's about the cake thing.'

'The cake thing? I'm sorry, I don't—'

'Remember when we were in the cafe?' I cut in, emboldened now. 'You said something that came across as rather rude, actually.'

'Really?' He sounds aghast.

'Yes, you said, "You're obviously a girl who very much enjoys her cake."'

A small silence hangs between us. 'Oh. Was that impolite?'

'A little, yes.'

He sighs audibly. 'I'm so sorry. I meant it as a compliment actually. It's very attractive, you know, seeing a woman enjoying her food, tucking in with gusto . . .'

'Really?' I say, laughing now.

'Yes. Women these days – the ones I work with at least – it's all tiny trays of sushi for lunch, or maybe a dip and some crudités . . .'

'I'm not a crudité sort of woman.'

'No, I can *see* that.'

'Because I am a *larger* woman, you mean . . .'

'Well, yes, although I'd rather use the term *curvaceous* . . .'

Those few forkfuls of Thai green curry sit uneasily in my stomach. 'Pardon?'

'Or perhaps I should say *voluptuous*,' he adds, and

84

there's a catch to his voice now that makes me shudder.

'Perhaps you shouldn't,' I remark.

'I meant it as a compliment. You're very attractive. The way you carry yourself, your *body* . . .'

I frown, aware that his breathing has taken on a rasping quality. 'I'm not sure I'm comfortable with—'

'. . . When we interacted with the art,' he adds. 'I noticed it then, especially . . .'

'I beg your pardon?' I have stopped by the laundry detergents.

'When we – you know – tried on that jacket. It was rather . . .'

'Rather what?' I bark, flinging a bottle of fabric conditioner into my basket.

'It was, you know . . . quite *stirring*. I enjoyed interacting with you, Lorrie . . .'

It takes me a moment to process this. 'You mean in an art way? You were stirred by the art?'

'No, by being in such close . . . proximity to you. You see, when we were pressed up together I couldn't help but notice your marvellous figure . . .' *Oh my God.* 'I'm sorry,' he goes on, sounding a little breathless now. 'You see, since Belinda left, I haven't actually been physically close to anyone at all . . .' I am standing dead still. An elderly woman gripping a gigantic pack of loo roll gives me a quizzical look. '. . . And there we were, so close together, and it was rather . . .' His breath catches.

'Stirring?' I snatch a three-pack of yellow dishwasher sponges from the bottom shelf.

'Well, yes.' There's a sharp intake of breath, then another.

'Are you jogging, Ralph?'

'Jogging? No, no, I'm still at work—'

'But it's nearly nine o'clock!'

'Yes, I often work late,' he pants. 'Busy, you know. And I've been thinking about you. Been thinking how much I'd like to, uh, get to know you better—'

'You sound out of breath,' I cut in. 'Are you ill?'

'No, no—'

'Are you saying all this in front of your colleagues? Or are you the only one left in the office?'

'Oh, don't worry, I'm being discreet . . .'

I frown. 'Are you under your desk?'

'No, no . . .' His voice, I realise, has an echoey quality, as if he's in a small enclosed space. 'I'm in the gents' actually.'

'Oh!'

'Bit of privacy,' he adds as it dawns on me what he's actually doing.

'Are you in a cubicle?'

'Yes. Yes, I am.'

'And what are you doing exactly?' I ask sharply.

'I'm just thinking about our date, about me and you all buttoned up together in that jacket . . .'

Oh, dear lord. 'For God's sake, Ralph. Do you know how vile this sounds? How completely *creepy* it is to talk to a woman in this way?'

He makes a choking sound. 'I'm sorry, I just can't help—'

'I think you can help yourself actually,' I snap, 'unless you've stumbled into the office loo and your trousers and pants fell down and your hand has accidentally clamped itself around your penis.'

I end the call, plunge my mobile into my pocket and stride up to the nearest available till, dumping my basket with a clatter onto the counter. The girl at the till gives me a startled look, and the customer at the next till – a

86

huge bear of a man clutching a box of frozen toad in the hole – swings round to stare.

'Good on you, darling,' he says with a throaty laugh. 'You bloody give 'im what for.'

Chapter Eight

It's raining heavily by the time I leave the supermarket, causing people to duck into doorways or march quickly, heads bent against the weather. I hurry into the tube station, gripping my carrier bag tightly, the relaxing effect of those couple of glasses of wine having now worn off.

That's *definitely* the end of datemylovelymum and me. Any dating at all, actually. If it's adult male company I'm after, there's always Stu: amenable, funny, requiring no effort whatsoever in the personal grooming or acquisition of fancy lingerie departments. He has seen all my pants anyway: the full range from fancy black lace to saggy and greying. Mine and his are often laundered together, and sit companionably on the radiator drying side by side. They are even *touching*, sometimes. No one thinks anything of it. I have seen him trimming his nasal hair with his clipper, and he has watched with interest while I've applied some kind of acid solution to my recurring corn. We might as well be an old married couple – apart from the fact that we probably *like* each other more than most long-term partners do.

Who needs sex anyway? No one died from a lack of it, as far as I am aware. Neither Stu nor I have had any for a thousand years – well, ages anyway – and he, at least, seems pretty chilled out most of the time. A celibate life seems preferable now to running the risk of encountering any more men like Ralph. That's the thing with having big boobs, hips, bottom and all that: it tends to bring out the creeps. There seems to be an assumption that a larger woman is parading herself – 'flaunting her assets' in *Daily Mail* speak – and a certain type of man takes this as permission to make personal comments. 'I love a woman with curves,' growled Pete from electricals, kissing my stomach in his nicotine-hued flat, last time we were in bed together. 'God, you don't half give me an appetite, Lorrie. If we hurry up and get dressed we'll be able to use my two-for-one Groupon deal for that Indian buffet down the road.'

I'm still fizzling mad – not about Pete Parkin, but Ralph – by the time the tube reaches Bethnal Green station. I stumble out of the carriage, glowering at an elderly man who stares pointedly at my chest as he waits to get on. 'D'you really think,' I want to shout, 'that women don't notice when men are doing that?' I hope to God Amy learns to handle this kind of thing better than I ever have.

It's only when I'm halfway down my street, jacket damp from the rain, hair flat against my scalp, that I realise my bag of fancy cheese, fabric conditioner and chilli-spiked snacks is still trundling along on the Central Line towards Epping.

Damn it. Damn it all. I let myself into the house and call out a dull hello.

'Hi, Mum,' Cam replies from the living room. I find him lying prone on the sofa, TV blaring unnecessarily, seeing as he is reading a dog-eared novel. 'All right?' He delves into a family packet of crisps.

'Yes, just went to Helena's birthday do after work. You look tired, darling. Why don't you head up for an early night instead of lying here?'

'Aw, no, I'm all right.'

'D'you really need the TV on?'

'Yeah, I'm watching it.' His gaze returns to his book.

'Is Stu around?'

He shakes his head, grudgingly shifting up on the sofa to make room for me to sit beside him. 'Out on a delivery, I think.' That's disappointing. I need someone to offload to, about Nuala's surprise visit to the store today and, more urgently, Ralph fiddling with himself in his office loo, *ugh*. I need to turn it into something funny and I know Stu will be able to make me laugh about it.

'Hi, darling,' I say as Amy appears, fresh from her bath, her long dark hair wrapped up in a towel. 'What've you been up to today?'

'Shopping for my holiday.' She beams excitedly. 'Bella said Portugal's going to be even hotter than last year. Hang on, I'll show you what I bought.' She runs off and returns with a Topshop bag, extracting a couple of bikinis in her preferred sporty style: one plain navy, one jaunty red and white stripes.

'They're lovely. Bet you can't wait.'

'I can't,' she says, stuffing them back into the bag and snuggling on the sofa beside me. 'You okay, Mum?' She turns to look at me.

'I'm good,' I fib. 'Oh, there's just something coming up on Friday. It's on my mind a bit – a work conference thing. Only heard about it today.'

'What's that all about?'

'No idea but I might have to do a little speech.' I grimace. 'D'you mind if I try something out on you? It'll only take a few minutes . . .'

She recoils. 'Mum, you're *not* putting make-up on me!'

My daughter prefers the natural look; lip balm and a quick pluck of the brows and she's ready to go.

'No, no, not that. It's just, I'll feel better if I have some idea of what I'm going to say, in case they ask me. Can I just run through it with you?'

'Aw, can't we do it tomorrow? It's late, Mum . . .'

'It's only just gone ten, and Grandma's coming over for dinner tomorrow, remember?'

She eye-rolls at the prospect, which I choose to ignore.

Cam looks up from his book. 'How's the wedding planning going?'

I chuckle. 'On a par with a royal wedding, judging by the way she's acting . . .'

'When is it again?' Amy asks.

'Honey, I've told you this. It's just over two weeks away.'

'And where is it?' Cam wants to know.

'At Hamish's parents' place, that huge manor house of theirs. C'mon, you've seen the pictures . . .' They're just winding me up, sniggering at the thought of their grandma and her fancy-pants toy boy getting hitched. My kids are fully aware that her fiancé is sole heir to the Sowerbutts' ancestral home, nestling in extensive grounds in leafy Hertfordshire. From photos of Lovington Hall which Mum has proudly foisted on us, we've seen the lake, the stables, the panelled grand hall hung with eerie oil paintings of Hamish's ancestors in their hunting attire. Now partly open to the public, it's where he and Mum first met. She had taken a coach trip there with her friend Dolores to see an exhibition of historic textiles. Hamish had been pottering about in the tea room, and he and Mum had fallen in love over scones and a pot of Earl Grey.

If I was a little wary at first, it was only because Mum's liaisons tended to end in tears and trauma and a sharp incline in alcohol consumed. Although I could see why Hamish was transfixed by her – with her clingy outfits and full make-up, Mum is incredibly glamorous – I feared she was just after his cash ('and what attracted you to the millionaire Hamish Sowerbutt?'). However, they are clearly devoted to each other, and I've grown fond of Hamish: the way he twinkles as if enjoying an innocent, private joke, and the way Mum's complaints and criticisms simply bounce off him. Or *orf* him, as Hamish would say: *I do enjoy Great British Bake-orf. It's tremendous fun!* He is terribly, endearingly posh, and I don't think he has ever had to work for a living, which probably explains why he's been pretty useless on the wedding planning front; he simply doesn't have a clue how to get anything done. Amy once mentioned Argos in front of him and he had to ask what it was. Even his hair radiates poshness: a luxuriant sweep of gingery brown, like duvet wadding, and not even greying, just slightly faded as if left out in the sun. I like the way he talks fondly about his childhood nanny – still referred to as 'Nanny Bridget' – despite him being in his late fifties. My only concern is how naive and sheltered he seems; there's no ex-wife or children. I wonder if he's even had serious girlfriends and whether he realises quite what he's taking on in marrying Mum.

'Hamish's parents,' Cam says with a snigger. 'They must be, like, a hundred or something?'

'Not exactly,' I chuckle. 'Remember he's twelve years younger than Grandma.'

'Ugh,' Amy winces.

'There's nothing *ugh* about it, and it's not that big an age gap . . .'

'Yeah, you'd love it if I went out with a twenty-seven-year-old,' she teases.

'That's different. Anyway, she's happy, she loves him, that's what matters . . .' They're both chuckling again as I head upstairs to fetch my clutch of La Beauté products in order to practise a little talk. I know it'll thrill my children, listening to me burbling on about natural ingredients and skin-plumping properties.

In my bedroom now, I scoop together a selection of skincare and make-up and drop them into a towel to carry downstairs, like Dick Whittington with his sack. Back in the living room, I clear away the detritus of magazines and mugs from the coffee table and set out my wares.

Amy, whose long, silky lashes rarely encounter mascara, eyes them with disdain. 'Why do people pay huge amounts of money for this stuff?'

I mute the TV and click into sales mode. 'Okay, let me tell you about this – our new base. It's so light, it feels like you're wearing nothing. You can apply in the usual way, or if you twist the top, like this, it becomes a spray—'

'Like you'd spray a car?' Cam sniggers.

'Well, the same principle, I suppose – easy application, smooth coverage . . .'

'. . . Repels rust.' He munches on a crisp.

'How much is it?' Amy asks.

'Um, let's not get into that. I won't be talking about prices . . .'

'Go on, tell us how much that stuff is.' Cam leans forward with interest.

'It's £35.'

'£35,' Amy gasps, 'for something that's basically nothing!'

'Well, yes, it *feels* like nothing because that's what you want in a base. You just want it to smooth out imperfections . . .'

'What about this one?' She grabs a small white bottle from the table.

'That's our serum.'

'Why do people need that?' Cam asks, excavating an ear with a finger.

'Serum has a higher concentration of active ingredients than moisturisers do. It helps skin to look smoother, firmer, more glowing . . .'

'My skin *is* firm,' Amy remarks.

'Yes, honey, because you're fifteen . . .'

'But if I came to your stand you'd try to sell it to me anyway.'

'No, I wouldn't. I'd never sell a customer something she doesn't need—'

'Mum, you do! You do it all the time. That's what the beauty industry's about, to make women feel bad about themselves . . .'

It strikes me – and not for the first time – that if it were vegetables or fish or shoes I was selling, I wouldn't have to defend myself like this.

Amy adjusts her head towel as Cam escapes to his room. 'You'd never sell anything,' she goes on, 'if your customers didn't feel insecure. You want them to feel crap . . .'

'Of course I don't!'

'. . . So they spend a fortune, and then they go home and try it, and when it doesn't work like it was supposed to, they come back and buy something else . . .'

'Love, there *is* a positive side to it. You know, sometimes a woman might just need a confidence boost.' I think of

94

Gilda, perched elegantly on the stool. 'She might have something important coming up,' I continue, 'and, believe it or not, a bit of make-up can make all the difference to how she comes across. Look, can I just run through my talk without you firing questions?'

She pulls off her towel and tosses out her hair – hair which she regularly deep conditions with La Beauté's Nourishing Huile d'Amande Masque, I might add, in order to maintain peak lushness. 'Aw, I think I'll go up to bed. C'mon, it's only talking about make-up. You do it every day. How hard can it be?' Before I can protest, she's scooted out of the room too.

Alone now, I glance down at my products, realising it was silly to expect her to respond to my sales talk with enthusiasm. She has never fallen for the allure of beauty products, the way I did when French Nicole took me under her wing, and I learnt that make-up needn't be of the shimmery mask variety as favoured by Mum. Amy has never felt the need for lipstick. Her body is strong and agile, and while she has my dark eyes, she has also inherited her father's fine bone structure and full mouth – a natural beauty through and through. At her age, I felt podgy and plain. Make-up helped me, and I still stand by the fact that there is some value in what I do, even if Amy won't accept that. Okay, she'd probably respect me more if I was a social worker or ran a donkey sanctuary, but the truth is my job has kept a roof over our heads these past seven years.

Disgruntled, I carry my products upstairs and set them out on my bedside table, in the hope that they will somehow transmit inspiration into my brain during the night. I change into my PJs, replaying the evening's events: those girls' sarky comments about a supposedly gargantuan thirty-year-old woman ('at least a size fourteen!') in that dismal pub, topped off by Ralph perving over my 'voluptuousness'. Ugh. I flip open my laptop and click to my datemylovelymum.com profile, then go to settings where, without a moment's hesitation, I click on the red button.

Are you sure you want to suspend your account? the message reads.

God, yes, absolutely sure.

Click.

ACCOUNT SUSPENDED.

Good. I know their types now, joining the site thinking: aw, poor mums in their stained dressing gowns, desperate for a bit of attention. Tragic middle-aged women sitting at home reading *Take a Break* and nibbling custard creams; what they really want is a creepy phone call from a solicitor's office loo.

Maybe he thought I'm so sex-starved and desperate, I'd actually *enjoy* it. It's seeming less and less likely that I will ever enjoy a normal relationship with a man.

Curled up on my bed now, I log onto Facebook. Although I still haven't replied to Antoine's last message – his declaration about that summer making him 'come alive' – he has sent two more pictures without any accompanying comment. In the first, we are holding hands on a country lane and both looking back at the camera, smiling. How handsome he was, all tanned and rangy with a smile that flipped my heart. I thought I was chunky then, but in fact I can see now that I was a pleasant-looking girl: not eye-catchingly beautiful like Amy but pretty enough, and excited to be away from home.

The other picture is of me and him in his kitchen, cooking together as if playing at being grown-ups. I remember him showing me how to make soup with onions and beans and fresh herbs scattered in it. It seemed terribly exotic, and was delicious, I recall. At home, our herbs came from jars, our soup from a Heinz tin. Maybe Jeanne, Antoine's mother, took the photo. I can't imagine Valérie did.

My breath catches. A message has appeared.

It was so nice finding these old pictures!

I pause, wondering how to respond.

You're very quiet, Lorrie. Hope I haven't upset you by sending these?

I stare at the screen. What on earth does he want after all this time? In fact, why am I allowing myself to become all stirred up when I have this mysterious conference looming in two days' time? Oh, sod it. Sod Ralph and sod Antoine, suddenly rearing up in my life like this, bombarding me with photos from when I was fresh-faced and unlined and serum hadn't even been invented.

I glare at his profile picture – Mr-Quirky-Tangerine-Head – and tap out a reply:

No, I'm not upset now. But I have to remind you that you broke my heart.

Chapter Nine

Thursday, 6.13 a.m., still not properly light. I ease myself out of bed and check for messages.

Oh Lorrie, I'm so sorry. Did I really? It wasn't intentional. I was eighteen years old and an idiot. That summer meant a lot to me, you know. I thought you were a beautiful and fascinating girl. I loved getting your letters all about your interesting life in Yorkshire!

Oh, really? I remember it now: trying to amuse him with tales about how Mum behaved whenever a Man Came to the Door. It would go like this: quick peek through our ruffled lace curtains before answering it. If it was a woman – a neighbour or someone collecting for charity – she'd open it all normal with her feet stuffed into flattened-down slippers. But if it was a man, she'd rush about fixing her hair and smearing on lipstick in the convex hall mirror as if any visiting bloke might turn out to be a potential future husband.

Mum had called time on her marriage when I was ten. Although only in her mid-thirties, she seemed to hold the view that time was of the essence in finding a new man. Soon after the divorce – to her intense annoyance – Dad met a kind and courageous Australian lady called Jill, a single woman without kids and quite the adventurer. She was exploring Europe on her own, staying at cheap hostels and marching about in walking boots, corduroys and charity shop sweaters. The very opposite of Mum, I doubt if Jill owns even one item of make-up. She and Dad fell in love and relocated to her home city of Melbourne, where they eventually married. Mum has never forgiven him for finding happiness with someone else.

Thank God she has now – at seventy years old – found someone who loves her deeply, I reflect as I dress for work. I just wish she could relax and enjoy life instead of panicking about the wedding. After work, I have the pleasure of picking her up and bringing her here for dinner so she can delegate some tasks off her *colossal* list.

At work, my first customer happens to be an older bride-to-be. 'I'm so out of touch with make-up,' she explains as we peruse colours together.

'What sort of wedding are you having?' I ask.

'Oh, just two close friends as witnesses, my daughter and son-in-law, and my little granddaughter. I really couldn't face a lot of froth and nonsense. I mean, what's the point, really? We've both done it before. It's not about the show and ceremony. It's more about . . .' She pauses.

'. . . Just wanting to get married because you're in love?'

'Exactly.' She beams at me. 'So I'd just like to look like me, on a good day – on a *brilliant* day actually. You know those days when everything feels . . . just right?'

I laugh. 'I know exactly what you mean.'

In her early sixties, Maggie is a delight to make up and buys her entire wedding-day face, including our new foundation (£35 for something that's basically nothing! as Amy observed).

After work, I come home to find Stu and the kids crowded around Cam's phone, watching a YouTube video of baboons flinging themselves into a lake. I only have time for a quick cup of tea, before I'm on my way out again.

My mobile rings as I climb into my car. 'Hi, Mum, just setting off now.'

'Oh, good. You *are* still coming?'

'Yes, of course I am. Are you okay? You sound a bit—'

'It's nothing. Nothing to worry about. Well it *is*, but I don't want to discuss it on the phone . . .'

My chest tightens. She sounds horribly tense. 'Please just tell me what's happened, Mum. Aren't you feeling well?'

'No, I'm fine. Well, *sort-of* fine . . .'

It's a beautiful warm evening. I lower the driver's side window and exhale slowly. 'Hamish hasn't changed his mind, has he?'

'Of course not. It's not that . . .' She makes a small, whimpery sound. 'Please come over right now, Lorrie. I don't think I can cope with this on my own.' With that, she finishes our call.

Whatever it is – however shocking and dreadful – I wish she'd at least hinted at what's wrong rather than leaving me worried sick on the half-hour drive to Leyton, where she's lived for twenty years, lured down from Yorkshire by Brian Horley, a scaffolder whom she'd imagined would offer lifelong happiness but instead ran amok with her credit cards. And now, as I crawl through

100

traffic – my usual route is snared up with roadworks – my brain whirrs with terrible medical diagnoses.

By the time I pull up outside her small sixties block in a quiet residential road, I am feeling quite sick with dread.

I clatter up to her first-floor flat, where her door flies open.

'Well, thank goodness you're here.' As if am a tardy plumber and the whole place is flooded.

'What on earth's wrong?' I step into her living room. Immaculate as ever, and smelling keenly of furniture polish, it's a jarring vision of clashing patterned upholstery.

'Hamish's bloody parents' place, *that's* what's wrong. Look!' She grabs a paper wallet of photos from the cluttered sideboard and thrusts them at me. I take them out and flip through them; they are various interior and exterior shots showing Lovington Hall in all its glory.

'I've seen these before, Mum. What's the problem?'

I hand them back to her, and she jabs at one of the prints.

'It's not like this now. It's suffered storm damage, roof's in a terrible state, apparently. The grand hall's unusable . . .'

I frown. 'Aren't there other rooms you could use? The place is enormous.'

'I'm not having our reception in a kitchen or a billiard room . . .'

No, heaven forbid . . . 'Can't it be fixed in time? The roof, I mean?'

'No, because it's *historical*, a Grade One listed building. It can only be repaired with the right kind of slates . . .'

'Can't someone get hold of the right kind?'

She shakes her head. 'The original ones came from a particular quarry and it closed down fifty years ago. The roof tiles have to match, apparently.' She snatches her packet of cigarettes from the ornament-covered sideboard and lights one up.

'Oh, Mum . . . could you put the wedding back?'

'No, Lorrie. It's going to take months – maybe years – to import the right slates from God knows where. We could be waiting forever!'

I breathe slowly, trying to emanate calmness. 'Well, can't you have a marquee in the grounds instead?'

Her lips purse. 'Haimie's parents won't have that. It'd ruin the lawn, they said. Their gardener's very particular about it – it's taken years to get it looking that good . . .'

'But it's only a big tent . . .'

'Tell me about it,' she says, exhaling a gust of smoke.

I frown and step back. 'You can still have the actual ceremony in that lovely church, though, can't you?' I've seen photos of that too; Saxon, ridiculously picturesque, its vicar having only agreed to marry Hamish and my mother – a wanton divorcee – due to his family's standing in the area.

'Yes, but what about the reception?'

'Well, there must be other places nearby you could use. A hotel, a restaurant or a village hall . . .'

'A hotel instead of a Jacobean manor?' she exclaims. 'That's the whole theme, Lorrie – *Jacobean*. You know Dolores has made my dress? Tight bodice, red velvet, gold detailing – it couldn't be *more* Jacobean . . .'

'Um, could she *un*-Jacobean it, or at least tone it down a notch?'

Mum stares at me as if I've suggested she gets married in her bra and pants. 'What d'you mean?'

I shrug. 'Well, maybe hold back on the gold detailing?'

'You can't *un*-Jacobean it,' she splutters. 'The Jacobean-ness is the whole point . . .' A bubble of mirth starts to rise in my stomach. 'As if I don't have enough on my plate already,' she adds, tapping her cigarette into a large onyx ashtray.

'It has been a lot of work,' I concede.

'Tell me about it. Don't you ever have a wedding like this one, Lorrie.'

'No, well, I can't imagine I'll be having any weddings at all,' I say with a wry smile.

'Oh, please don't say that. Don't be so defeatist . . .' Funnily enough, I remember her saying exactly the same thing when she was packing me off to the Massif Central.

'I'm not defeatist – just realistic. Anyway, never mind that. It's *your* wedding we're concerned with now. I hate to see it stressing you out—'

'It doesn't help that Haimie's left it *all* to me . . .'

'Only because he didn't really want a huge do,' I remind her.

'He's perfectly happy with our plans!'

'Yes, of course he is, but he knows you're so much better at organising things than he is.'

At this, Mum seems appeased; I have learnt from experience that it's better simply to nod and agree and flatter her. However, I also know she's the one who's been driving the whole thing, and that Hamish is only going along with it to make her happy. 'I'd have settled for a nice quiet dinner,' he confided recently, 'but it's what Marion wants and it's her day.' *It's your day too*, I wanted to say, but thought better of it.

Perhaps I just don't get the huge, flouncy wedding thing with the towering cake and little gauzy bags of sugared almonds – dyed dark red and sprinkled with edible gold dust, to echo the Jacobean theme – never having been a bride myself. Naturally, Mum had been eager to know when

David and I were planning to 'do the decent thing, especially as there are children involved now'. We had to explain (through gritted teeth) that we were together and loved each other, and the kids were fine, thank you very much – we just had no need for the almighty palaver and expense. *I don't see why you're so anti-marriage,* she lamented. We weren't, we just didn't want it for us. *If you had a wedding planned, it'd be a great incentive to lose weight!* Thank you, Mum. *But what if he just ups and leaves you?* Well, he did leave – or rather, he was taken from us – and no signatures on the marriage register could have altered that.

'Let's go, Mum,' I prompt her now, as she stubs out her cigarette. 'Stu'll be waiting. He's cooking for us tonight . . .'

'Oh, Stu's going to be there! I wish you'd said.' Mum *adores* Stu. She always has, ever since he hung around in our kitchen as a teenager, politely deflecting her awkward quizzings: '*Any girlfriend on the go, Stuart? Bet there is. Ooh look, Lorrie, he's blushing! Read into that what you will . . .*'

All sparkly now, she pulls on a tan leather blouson-style jacket over her hip-hugging navy skirt and embellished blouse. 'Oh, I can't understand you and Stu, this *arrangement* you have,' she adds.

I blink at her. 'What d'you mean, "arrangement"? He moved in with us when he split up with his girlfriend and needed somewhere to live, and I was grateful to have a bit of rent coming in. Why does that seem so strange?'

'What I mean is, there you are, all alone with this wonderful person right under your nose, and you're not taking advantage . . .'

'You think I should take *advantage* of Stu?' I splutter with laughter.

'No, no exactly . . .'

'You mean, fondle his bottom while he's taking a carton of milk out of the fridge?'

Mum tuts and frowns. 'I'm being serious, Lorrie. It just baffles me. What a crying waste of a perfectly lovely man.'

In the hallway now, she checks her reflection in the mirror and rummages in her bag for her gold quilted make-up pouch. Out comes the lipstick and mirrored powder compact; a fresh coat of iridescent peach is hastily applied in preparation for some heavy-duty flirting with my housemate.

'I'm sure Stu doesn't feel he's going to waste,' I tease her. 'He's probably up to all sorts and I don't even know.'

'Oh, you *know* what I mean,' she says, shaking her head in exasperation as we make our way downstairs to my car.

Chapter Ten

Mum has never been the tactile type. She responds to hugs as if being frisked at the airport, which is why, I suspect, her grandchildren always insist on embracing her enthusiastically on arrival.

'Hello, Cameron,' Mum says, patting down her hair as she disentangles herself.

'Hi, Grandma. Great to see you . . .'

She endures Amy's hug with a rictus smile while looking around anxiously, probably for Stu.

'Looking forward to the wedding?' My daughter grins mischievously.

'Don't ask!' Mum exclaims.

'*We* are,' Cam adds, catching my eye, 'aren't we, Mum?'

'Yes, of course we are.' I catch him glancing at the clock on the hall wall. Although he's off out later to a party with Mo, I've asked him to hang around and at least have dinner with us. Not that my mother has ever been particularly interested in her grandchildren, or in young people at all, for that matter; 'One child is quite enough for me', she was always fond of saying when I was a kid, as if I was forever smashing windows and setting fire to things. She rarely involved herself in my life as I was growing up, aside from providing essentials (I always suspected she attended parents' evenings only for the opportunity to flirt with my rather dashing maths teacher). Of course she loves Cam and Amy in her own, rather distracted way, but if you were to ask her anything about their interests or young adult lives, she'd be stumped for an answer.

'Where's Stu?' She whips off her jacket and hands it to Amy to hang up for her.

'Hello, Marion, I'm here.' He strides out of the kitchen, hair a little dishevelled but still looking smart in a new white T-shirt, dark jeans and a stripy butcher's apron. The sparks that fly off her are almost visible as he kisses her cheek. No shying away *this* time.

'Hello, Stu,' she says, beaming at him. 'Busy in the kitchen, I see!'

'Er, yeah. It's just simple, I'm afraid . . .'

'I'm sure it'll be wonderful. You look great, Stu. Very handsome and trim. Must be all that zooming about you do!' Her tinkly laughter fills the kitchen as we follow him out through the back door to the garden.

'On my motorbike, Marion. Not sure that counts as exercise . . .'

'Yes, but out there in all weathers . . . you're terribly brave, I always think.'

Out there, in the wilds of Crouch End and Walthamstow.

He catches my eye and winks. 'I thought we'd eat out here, if that's okay for everyone. Seems a shame to waste such a lovely evening. Cam, Amy, can you help me bring things out, leave Mum and Grandma to have a chat?'

'Sure,' Cam says, clearly stifling sniggers as my mother

and I take our seats at the garden table. Dinner is brought out with remarkable efficiency: perfectly baked salmon with a chilli-spiked sauce, new potatoes flecked with chives, a multi-coloured salad, plus a beer for Cam and wine for Mum, as I'm driving her home and Stu is on Parsley Force duty later on tonight. There's a bottle of sparkling water, and another of orange juice, for the rest of us.

As everyone takes their places at the table, Mum fills them in on the Lovington Hall roof slate disaster. 'The trouble is, they're discontinued,' she laments, as if we're talking about a beloved shade of lipstick. God, I could murder a drink . . .

'The only thing to do is embrace it,' Stu remarks. 'Okay, your plans have been shaken up, but sometimes the best things are thrown together at the last minute—'

'But we've already sent out the invitations!' she exclaims as Stu fills her wine glass.

'That doesn't matter, Grandma,' Amy offers. 'You can find somewhere new and explain to everyone what's happened.'

Mum purses her lips. 'More work for me.'

'The thing is,' Stu adds, 'the huge, grand reception – that's not really what matters, is it?'

She turns to him, adoration beaming from her pale blue eyes. 'What d'you mean?'

'Well,' he pauses and gives me a quick look, 'it's really about you and Hamish, isn't it? You've booked the church and that's not going to change . . .'

'. . . And I can help you find another venue,' I add. 'I'll start tomorrow.' This is beginning to feel better. I beam silent thanks to Stu and the kids for being so calming and kind. Although Cam and Amy can't resist gently teasing their grandma, they're good kids really.

'. . . It might even turn out for the best,' Amy adds, filling her glass with orange juice.

Mum's mouth tightens. 'I'm not sure how.'

'Well,' Stu offers, 'a huge do like that might've been intimidating for some of your guests.'

'D'you really think so? Oh, I wouldn't want that.' She gazes at him across the table that he set, very prettily, with a small jar of flowers picked from our terracotta pots.

'Yeah,' Cam chips in. 'People might feel awkward in a huge mansion . . .'

'. . . A low-key party will be more intimate,' Stu adds.

'Hmm, perhaps you're right.' She smiles at him. 'This is delicious, Stu. I do wish Lorrie had learned to cook.'

Amy's mouth twitches as she catches my eye.

'It's just fish and salad,' he says nonchalantly.

'Just! You're so modest. Oh, I do wish you were coming to the wedding, Stu. You're virtually part of this family. You really should be there!'

He shrugs, feigning deep regret. 'I know, and I'm sorry, but you know I'm going to Venice . . .'

'Couldn't you go to Venice another time?' She tips back her wine.

'It's my sister's fortieth birthday party,' he reminds her. 'Sorry, Marion, but I don't think I'd be terribly popular with Dawn if I didn't turn up for that.'

Mum sighs heavily as if Dawn had arranged her date of birth to coincide with the wedding, purely out of spite. 'I just worry, you know,' she adds, 'about Lorrie having to come to the wedding alone.'

'She won't be alone,' Amy points out. 'She'll have us.'

'Yes, I know, but . . .'

'We'll look after her, Grandma,' Cam says, for which I

109

could hug him. 'And anyway, Mum's been dating, haven't you, Mum?'

The traitor! How dare he?

'Have you?' Mum asks, eyes wide.

'Just, um, this website thingie I joined,' I mutter.

'Oh, you're getting a man off the internet?'

'You make it sound like ordering a new suitcase,' I say with a strained laugh.

'Well, if it's come to that, I suppose it's better than nothing. You're not getting any younger, you know. Not far off fifty . . .'

'Thanks, Mum. I do realise that, I see myself deteriorating a little bit more every day . . .' I place my cutlery on my plate, appetite depleted. 'Anyway, I tried it, it was an utter disaster and I've now suspended my account.'

'Oh, Mum!' Cam's face falls.

'After all the work we did,' Amy exclaims, as if I'm a child who's just crayoned on a freshly painted wall.

'Yes, well, I gave it a go, didn't I?' I eye the wine bottle greedily and distract myself by getting up to clear the table.

'She gives up too easily,' Mum mutters as the kids and I carry the plates and dishes inside. '*That's* her problem.'

In the kitchen, I lean over the sink for a moment, watching Mum fawning over Stu – 'that meal was restaurant quality!' – and looking as if she'd dearly love to wriggle onto his lap and kiss him.

I carry out the cake Stu made – an impressive chocolate and orange sponge – which sends Mum into such raptures ('So moist!') she barely registers Cam and Amy making their excuses to leave. So keen are they to escape – Amy to her room, Cam to a party in Hackney – they even turn down the offer of a slice.

110

The air has cooled now. Mum lights up a cigarette. 'You know what I'm really annoyed about?' she remarks.

'No?' I ask, sitting down beside her.

'Hamish. I just feel so . . . let down.'

'But he couldn't help the storm,' Stu points out reasonably, 'and all the damage it's caused . . .'

'No, I realise that, but he *did* say I deserved a dream wedding after everything I've been through . . .' Oh no. She's reached the half-a-bottle maudlin stage, and her eyes glisten with tears. I catch Stu's eye across the table. 'Don't know why I'm even bothering with him,' she continues, waving her Silk Cut. 'I should just be on my own, pleasing myself. I mean, look at you, Lorrie. You don't have anyone and you're . . . *all right.*'

I stare at her wine. 'Yes, well, being single does have some things going for it.'

'Just don't think I have the energy left,' she burbles on, topping up her glass and slopping some onto the table where it drips down through the curly wrought-iron gaps. 'I've always had to do everything myself after your father left, and it was such a struggle sometimes . . .' *But you ended it!* I want to protest. *You said Dad was lazy, unmotivated. You told me, as a little girl, that your own mother had said you could have married better . . .* I remember the last picture Dad posted on Facebook, deeply tanned and encased in wetsuit, his arm clamped around Jill, who clearly thinks he's the greatest thing alive.

'Mum, you did fine,' I say, touching her hand with its outlandish engagement ring: a chunky diamond with rubies all around it.

She sniffs. 'Glad you think so. At least I was there, wasn't I, Lorrie, and not in *Australia*? Always there for you . . .'

111

'Yes, of course you were.'

Another swig of wine. 'Not like working mothers today . . .'

And what's *that* supposed to mean? 'Mum, plenty of mothers work. In fact, most do. It's normal. It's not 1957—'

She rounds on me, cheeks flushed, a cake crumb stuck to her bottom lip. 'Did you *have* to work, though? I mean, did it really make that much difference?' I stare at her, stuck for words. 'Shop girls can't be paid that much,' she adds.

I am vaguely aware of Stu's expression changing from feigned interest to one of concern. 'Well, I managed, Mum.'

'Oh, yes, and of course you have Stu here now. That must help.' She pats his thigh and he flinches.

I clear my throat. 'Of course it does, but I don't really see what your point is, Mum. Yes, ideally I'd probably have chosen to do something part-time when the kids were younger but I needed to earn—'

'Rather than being there for your children?' she cuts in.

And that's it. That's the point at which I bang down my glass of fizzy water on the table and leap up, knocking my chair which hits the table and causes my glass to tip over and roll off and smash onto the stone flags.

'Oh, Lorrie!' She gazes down as if it were precious antique glassware.

'Mum, you *know* why I work!'

'All I was saying was—'

'Who d'you think keeps us? Who pays every bill and takes care of two teenagers who'll hopefully go to college or university and will need supporting through that, and God knows how I'll manage—'

'Lorrie, it's okay!' Stu jumps up, feet crunching on

broken glass as he rests his hands on my shoulders.

I shake him off, aware of my eyes filling with tears. '*What* were you saying, Mum? Please tell me, I'm all ears—'

She stares at me, open-mouthed. 'All I meant was . . . children like being with their mothers most of all.'

Stu frowns. 'Marion, I don't think that's completely fair . . .'

'Never mind, Stu,' I cut in, turning to Mum. 'I've worked,' I add quietly, 'because I've needed to. Because I've been on my own . . .'

'Well, I was too!'

I stare at Mum's face, a mask of self-righteousness with her frosted blue shadow, lashings of bronzer and shimmery peach lips. Mum is glaring at me, mouth pinched. I'd like to think she's just worked up about the slate quarry and the silly Jacobean dress rather than having any real contempt for the way I've chosen to live my life. 'Mum,' I say, as calmly as I can manage, 'remember, you were the one who split up with Dad.'

She taps a pearly pink nail on the table. 'That's just splitting hairs. It was supposed to be a temporary thing, to knock some sense into him . . .' It certainly did that because he never came back . . . 'You have no idea what it was like, having no support. It was terrible for me!'

'But Dad did send us money,' I snap. 'Why are we having a contest over who's had it the hardest here?'

'Calm down, Lorrie,' Stu murmurs.

'No, I won't calm down! Why on earth should I?'

'. . . Barely gone five minutes and he met *that* woman,' Mum mutters. 'That Jill. That *naturist* . . .'

'She's a *naturalist*,' I correct her. 'It means she studies plants, wildlife, that kind of thing. In fact she specialises in botany. A naturist is someone who likes wandering about with their clothes off . . .'

'Splitting hairs again!'

My heart is hammering in my chest. 'You don't seem to realise how insensitive this is, considering what happened to David—'

'Well, I'm just saying—'

'Yes, but Dad didn't *die*, did he? I mean, he wasn't killed by a car?'

'He might as well have been,' she shouts after me as I storm towards the back door, colliding with Stu's prized pot of nasturtiums.

I barge into the house, wondering why I always rise to the bait where Mum's concerned – despite trying my damnedest not to – and whether I will ever stop missing David so much it hurts.

Chapter Eleven

I perch on the edge of my bed and glare at the array of La Beauté products crammed onto my bedside table. Products I should be thinking hard about in preparation for the meeting tomorrow, and writing enthusiastic notes about – 'a beauty boost from within!' – but which could now be tubs of goose fat for all I'm inspired by them.

I flop backwards and stare up at the ceiling, realising how petulant I'm being: me, the bona fide grown-up around here with the regular job, the extensive knowledge about cream vs powder blushers and willingness to be open-minded about conceptual art. I hope to God Amy had her headphones plugged in while Mum and I were arguing, as is her custom these days. I'm surprised they haven't had to be surgically removed.

Mum and Stu's voices drift up from the garden. Hers is alternately coquettish and whining, his a placatory murmur. I am hugely grateful to him, as someone needs to be on Booze Guard with her now. She's had quite enough. We've had all the familiar stages – maudlin, self-pitying, verbally aggressive – and who knows what might be next? Lunging at Stu and licking his ear? Pushing him onto the geranium trough and trying to straddle him? I stretch out on my bed and take a few deep, calming breaths, momentarily wondering what Cam and his mates are doing now and wishing, for just a moment, that I was his age – seventeen – but then, I'd still be recovering from being dumped by Antoine, possibly having just snogged Stu under the stairs and barely being able to look him in the eye for weeks afterwards.

That kiss was pretty heady-spinny if I remember rightly, but was never referred to again because we were mates who lent each other records, tapes, books. If friends happen to snog each other drunkenly at a party it's just brushed off afterwards as if it never happened. Occasionally I'd sense a frisson if we'd had a few drinks on a night out, but a few weeks later Stu started going out with Diana Cresswood, a grumpy girl with spiky hair who seemed to regard me with suspicion, and I had to pretend to be all interested when he played me the mixtapes she'd made him. From then on, there was no hint of anything other than us just being mates.

Mum's laughter drifts up – high-pitched and tipsy – and I shuffle to the foot of my bed so I can peer down to the garden. They are both still sitting at the table, deep in conversation; it looks like she's recovered from our little altercation.

Although it's nearly ten and dark out there, the outside light illuminates the garden very prettily. For years it wasn't a garden at all, but a yard where David would smoke the occasional ciggie, or we'd shove the odd broken chair or bookshelf. Following his death, I pretty much forgot it was there. Then last September, when Stu moved in, I began to see it for the tawdry dumping ground that it was. David had been gone for six years. It was time to move on and get our outside space together. 'It's a real suntrap,' observed Bob, who's not averse to a spot of gardening himself. Together, the three of us painted the bordering brick walls white, lifted a row of concrete slabs and dug out the earth to create a flower bed. We filled terracotta pots, with Bob advising on the varieties that would provide maximum colour all year round. I bought the ornate wrought-iron table from a junk shop, plus four charmingly mismatched cafe-style chairs.

'I don't understand why she acted like that!' Mum's voice cuts through the night air. 'Was it something I said?' Stu is explaining something – I can't catch it, his gravelly voice doesn't carry like hers – then he gathers up the glasses from the table and makes his way, followed by Mum, back into the house. He could receive a Parsley Force call at any minute; I really should go down and rescue him and, besides, I feel ridiculous now, sitting up here on my own like a flouncy teenager. Her insensitivity over David now seems less significant than her implication that I am living some kind of sad half-life without a partner. Or maybe it's not Mum at all. Am I just still feeling prickly about Ralph's call – the image of him panting in the loos proving hard to banish from my mind? Or perhaps I'm stressing about the work conference tomorrow? Nothing to worry about, Nuala insisted. Isn't that the kind of thing people say precisely when something awful's about to happen?

'Lorrie?' Stu calls up from the hallway. 'You okay?'

I emerge from my room and peer downstairs sheepishly. The two of them stare up at me. 'Er . . . hi. Yes, I'm fine.'

Mum purses her lips. 'Stu's kindly offered to take me home.'

'Oh. Are you sure, Stu? What if you get a work call? I'm happy to—'

'Honestly, it's not a problem,' he says quickly. 'Me and Bob want to go over a few things with the business anyway, so I'll stop off at his place afterwards. I'll be virtually passing your mum's.'

I have to say, I am hugely relieved to get out of being trapped in the car with her again tonight.

'He's taking me on his motorbike,' Mum adds with a note of pride.

'Will you be okay?' I make my way downstairs towards them.

'I said I'd take her in the car,' Stu starts, 'but she really wants—'

'I'll be *fine* on the bike. I do have a sense of adventure, you know.' She turns away stiffly as I go to hug her.

I clear my throat. Mum will never apologise, and I'm loath to end the evening on a sour note. 'Look, Mum,' I start, 'I'm sorry about storming off like that. I know it wasn't very mature of me. It's just, when you said—'

'No, it wasn't very nice, Lorrie, but let's just leave it at that, shall we?'

'I've just had quite a lot on recently,' I add.

She nods, choosing not to enquire what that might be, and turns instead towards Stu. 'D'you know, I've never been on a motorbike before. I'm a little nervous . . .'

'Don't worry,' I murmur. 'Just cling onto him *very* tightly.'

'Oh, I will!' she titters, virtually melting with pleasure as Stu fixes the strap of his spare helmet beneath her chin. 'Don't go too fast now, Stu,' she adds. 'That's a powerful machine you've got there, and I'm precious cargo . . .' Funnily enough, her angst over Lovington Hall's Grade

118

One listed status seems to have faded, such is the soothing effect of my housemate's presence.

'Bye, Mum.' I go to kiss her chardonnay-flushed cheek, which she offers grudgingly.

'Amy,' I call upstairs, 'Grandma's leaving now . . .'

She appears, dutifully, and plants a kiss somewhere near my mother's ear.

'Bye, Grandma. Nice to see you.'

'Bye, love,' Mum says vaguely as Stu pulls on his biker jacket. 'Ooh, look at you,' she cries, 'all macho in your leathers!' And out they stride, with Mum virtually *shimmering* and Amy scuttling back upstairs, leaving a trail of mortification behind her.

I stand in the doorway, watching as my mother clambers onto the back of Stu's bike, jamming her arms around his waist and her thighs tightly against his hips. Rather belatedly, I remember the alcohol issue. 'Stu, is it okay for Mum to ride pillion? I mean, she's been drinking . . .'

'She'll be fine,' he asserts.

'It's not as if I'm *driving* the thing,' she trills as I wave them off, as if they are my children heading off on a fantastic adventure. Mum lets out a whoop of delight, clearly fancying herself as Marianne Faithfull in *Girl on a Motorcycle* as they speed away.

Back inside, to blot the vision still lingering in my mind, I load the dishwasher and prowl around the house, gathering up the small items Cam and Stu – but mostly Amy – leave scattered in their wake: shoes, jotters, hairbands, T-shirts, the odd sock, tiny packets of chewing gum with one or two pieces left in, a crumpled piece of paper with GINNY BENSON *quince jelly, half doz quail eggs, white truffle oil, pule cheese* scribbled on it in Stu's jagged script. It strikes me that I have never eaten any of these things.

119

I don't even know what 'pule cheese' is. I guess the types whose shopping lists read 'teabags, bleach' just go out and buy the stuff themselves.

It's Ginny Benson I'm thinking about as I carry an armful of Amy's bits and pieces upstairs to her room. Ginny Benson with her quails' eggs, who, I'm certain, isn't reminded by her mother that she isn't getting any younger, or that she's probably messed up her children irreparably by going out to work.

I step into Amy's room. 'All right, Mum?' She smiles tentatively. She is lounging on her bed, long legs stretched out, in the black vest top and tracksuit bottoms she favours for sleeping.

'I'm fine, love. I'm off to bed, though. This big work meeting's happening tomorrow so I really need a decent night's sleep.'

She gathers herself up and crosses her legs. 'Worried about it?'

'No, no. It'll be fine . . .'

'What was Grandma annoyed about earlier?'

'Oh, nothing really. Nothing important.'

She reaches out for my hand and I sit beside her on the bed. While the trophies at Cecily's house are lovingly shined up and displayed with space around them, giving them the reverence they deserve, Amy's basketball cups are jammed onto a shelf in between books, jars of pens and soft toys with missing eyes. She refuses to have them displayed in the living room where everyone would see them. To her, it's the *doing it* that's important, and being part of her team – not the gleaming trophy with her name etched on as Most Improved Player. 'It didn't sound like nothing,' she offers now. 'I heard shouting, Mum. You and Grandma . . . what was she going on about?'

'Oh just that I shouldn't have been a working mother, that's all.'

She splutters. 'Why not?'

'Because . . .' I shrug. 'Because it meant I couldn't be here for you all the time.'

Amy peers at me in confusion. 'Well, we went to Pearl's and we loved it there. She did so much stuff with us – games, baking, painting. It was great.'

'She did more with you than I did,' I say wryly.

'That's *not* what I mean. You did stuff too but you had your job and the house to look after as well. You were busy, Mum. It was *fine* . . .'

I twist a corner of duvet cover between my fingers: a simple light blue stripe, the kind of design she always chooses. 'Was it really so great, having a childminder?'

''Course it was. Mums go to work,' she adds firmly. 'It's not the eighteen hundreds.'

I smile. 'I know, darling. She just has a way of getting to me, that's all.'

'I'm so glad you're not like Grandma, Mum.'

'Thanks, darling. She's not so bad. Just a bit wound up about the wedding, I guess . . .'

She smirks. 'No, she's always been like that.'

I hug her goodnight, and try to thank her but can't quite convey why it means so much to hear her talking that way. How often does a child acknowledge that a parent hasn't made an almighty hash of raising them? Almost never. Perhaps things have been okay, just the three of us, after all.

In my own bedroom, I gather up all my La Beauté products from my bedside table and stuff them into a drawer. No need to have them looming at me as I go to sleep. Nuala was right, I know our ranges inside out;

nothing's going to faze me tomorrow. Instead, I change into PJs and sit up in bed with my laptop and log onto Facebook.

Antoine again. He is online too.

Sorry to bombard you with messages, Lorrie. I get the feeling you don't want to be in touch. That's okay. I understand. You must still be angry with me.

I think of Mum, angry at Dad for having the nerve to meet someone else and moving to a little beach-side apartment in Melbourne – *over thirty years ago.*

I'm not angry, I write. *Just been busy, that's all.*

Aware of Stu's motorbike pulling up outside, I realise how abrupt my message sounds, how pissed off and grudge-holding. Stu clomps into the hallway and shuts the front door.

I enjoyed seeing those pics, I add, *although I was a little disturbed by my 80s hair . . .*

Antoine is typing, Facebook tells me. At the sound of Stu coming upstairs, I slip out of bed and poke my head around my bedroom door.

'You're back quick. You didn't go to Bob's, then?'

'Nah.' He gives me an inscrutable look.

'Everything okay with Mum?'

He smirks. 'Huh. S'pose so. Just never ask me to do *that* again . . .'

I peer at him. His hair is still flattened from his motor-

122

bike helmet, his bristles erring towards pre-beard. 'She didn't try and *kiss* you, did she?'

'Um, well, not quite.'

My stomach clenches. 'Not quite? Jesus, Stu, I was joking! What d'you mean?'

He wanders into the bathroom, partly to tease me, I suspect, to keep me guessing. I scamper in after him and watch as he splashes water onto his face and dabs at it with a towel. 'She seemed a bit wobbly, said she felt all disorientated from being on the bike . . .'

'Couldn't have been anything to do with the wine,' I remark.

'No, 'course not.' He chuckles. 'So I helped her upstairs, made sure she could get her key in the door. She started going on about how her Jacobean dress won't look right, now the wedding plans are up in the air. I tried to persuade her it'll be fine, she'll look great . . .'

'Stu . . .' I stop and wince. 'Please don't tell me she launched herself at you . . .'

'Christ, no.' He laughs. 'But she did insist on tottering off and trying the dress on, said she needed my opinion. "All right," I said. I mean, she's your mum, isn't she? What else was I supposed to do?' I shrug wordlessly. 'So she disappeared off to her room and reappeared in this, this . . . gown.' His mobile trills. He swipes it from his back pocket, frowns at the screen before I can see who it is – not that it's any business of mine – and declines the call.

'And then what?' I ask.

He rubs at the space between his eyebrows as if trying to erase the memory. 'Well, she paraded around her living room in it, and I told her it was lovely but that I really needed to go. She said, "Wait, help me get this thing off . . ."'

'Not that old line,' I say, appalled.

'Yeah. She said the zip was stiff, being Jacobean . . .'

'But it's just a normal, modern zip!'

'Hmm. Well, I just gave it a little tug . . .'

I cover my face with my hands and peer at him through my fingers. 'You didn't *undress* her, did you?'

He looks at me, eyes wide. 'What else could I do? I couldn't leave her trapped in it . . .'

'Yes, you could! She could have slept in it and somehow struggled out of it in the morning, maybe asked Mr Tomlinson from upstairs to come down and help . . .' We both splutter at the thought.

'Well, she wasn't having any of that. She was quite agitated, you know, and kept saying, "Get it *off* me" and asking why was I being so uptight when there are certain people – *naturalists* – who wander about with no clothes on all day . . .' We are now both laughing convulsively. 'So, what else could I do? I yanked on the zip and the dress fell to the floor and I rushed off to the bathroom and found her dressing gown hanging on the door, thank God . . .' He is doubled up with laughter. 'And I bundled her into it.'

'Oh, my God, Stu. I'm so sorry—'

'It's not your fault your mother's a sex pest.'

I wipe tears from my cheeks. 'She adores you, you know. Thinks it's a terrible waste, you living here . . .'

'Huh?'

'You know, me and you not being a couple. God.' I dab at my cheeks with my pyjama sleeve. 'Maybe it was all an elaborate plot, falling out with me tonight so you'd be the one taking her home . . .'

He pushes a tumble of dark, wavy hair out of his eyes. 'I tend to have that effect on the older demographic.'

I study him for a moment. 'Really? You mean *other* older women have propositioned you?'

'Don't be ridiculous,' he mutters, cheeks colouring.

Now, of course, I am fascinated. 'Stu, what else has happened? Is it one of your Parsley Force customers? Has someone tried to jump on you when you've dropped off their fresh figs?'

'What are you *on* about?'

I can feel the heat from here, radiating from his cheeks.

'They have! They've said, "Hang on a minute" and pretended to rush off to find their purse, and come back wearing a see-through negligee with nothing underneath, and then turned the dimmer switch down . . .'

'You've watched too much rubbish porn.'

'I've never watched *any* porn!' I exclaim truthfully.

Stu chuckles. 'And no one has dimmer switches anymore.'

'Actually, Mum does.'

'God, does she?' He shudders.

'*And* a negligee with peonies all over it; I've seen it drying on that wire stand in her bath . . .' We are on the landing now, giggling like the teenagers we once were, over Jacobean dresses and the fact that Mum thinks he's hot. 'I'd better go to bed,' I say finally. 'Early start for this conference tomorrow.' We say goodnight and, as I climb back into bed, I find myself wondering what Stu meant by the older demographic, seeing as he ducked out of further questioning. There's been no evidence – and certainly no information shared – about any encounters with women since scary Roz chucked him out. 'He's always *between* things, that's his problem,' she moaned when she appeared on my doorstep to drop off the last of his stuff. 'Between jobs and projects,' she clarified. 'Never fully *in* them. I might consider having him back if and when he finally grows up.' Without wishing to be disloyal to Stu, I just murmured that I understood, and decided not to remind her that he was in fact working as a motorcycle courier, albeit sporadically. 'Thanks for taking him in,' she added, as if he were a stray dog she'd found sniffing around the bins. Yet he's not between things now. He's busy and motivated, and Parsley Force seems to be flourishing. I'm so proud that he turned a crazy, wine-fuelled idea into something real.

Cam arrives home then, calling out a cheery goodnight from the landing.

'Have a good time, love?' I ask through my closed bedroom door.

'Yeah, great.'

With no further info forthcoming, I lift my laptop onto my bed and log onto Facebook. I know I planned an early night but one last quick peek won't hurt.

Antoine has messaged me.

I love the pictures too, and your 80s hair was great! Look, this might be a bit forward but I'm in London on business this week, arriving Sunday afternoon as I have a breakfast meeting first thing on Monday . . .

Antoine in *London?*

. . . I know it's short notice, he continues, *but would you like to meet for a drink?*

A drink. Sounds so casual, as if we are just old friends. But we're not, are we? Friends keep in touch. They don't stop writing out of the blue. They make an effort, and spend time together, and we haven't seen each other in thirty years.

I blink at the screen, mulling over possible ways to

126

reply. I'm scared, that's the problem. Scared because the last time he saw me – just a girl, quite a pretty girl, I realise now – I had skin like a peach and, despite feeling terribly plain, an actual *waist*. Now I'm a middle-aged woman who's terribly fond of her cake . . .

Just a quick, friendly drink, though, for old times' sake. Where's the harm in that? And he's older too. He's a middle-aged man in a suit who just so happens to be coming to London on business. He just wants to catch up. He's not going to judge me and, anyway, what do I care if he does? After three-teeth-Marco and pervy Ralph, isn't a fun night out with a delicious Frenchman precisely what I need?

Trying to project calm – rather than rabid enthusiasm – I type out my reply:

Sounds great. How about Sunday evening, about eightish? Would that work for you?

Cam stomps to the bathroom, and the loo flushes repeatedly; I assume he's done his party trick of using almost an entire loo roll, thus blocking its workings. I'll have to sort it out with a straightened-out wire coat hanger tomorrow. Bet Ginny Benson's never troubled by such thoughts as she waits for her truffle oil delivery.

There's some muttering and more flushing, then Antoine's reply appears:

Perfect. I'm staying at the Neal Street Hotel in Covent Garden – I'll wait for you in reception. How wonderful to see you after all these years! xx

Chapter Twelve

So worried am I about sleeping in – despite my alarm clock being set, backed up by the alarm on my phone – that I jerk awake next morning at 5.47 a.m. with no chance of drifting back to sleep. Still, plenty of time to re-read my little exchange with Antoine last night, just to satisfy myself that it did really happen – that he's coming to London.

Having unblocked the loo with my patented coat hanger method, I shower and consume an entire cafetière of coffee as I get ready. I pull on my uniform tunic, and select my smartest black trousers; they are a little tight at the waist, I discover, but okay if I remember to hold in my stomach. I choose low heels, polished to a high sheen, plus the simple silver earrings that Pearl brought back for me last year after a nannying stint in Switzerland. She doesn't work as a childminder anymore. Nannying for wealthy families overseas is far more lucrative and, as she put it, she 'needed adventures' after it transpired that her husband Iain had been having an affair with an intern at the publishing house where he worked. This was three years ago, when Iain was forty-seven. Daisy was eighteen. 'Operation Yewtree,' Pearl spat out, whenever we discussed his new liaison. Iain tried to patch things up after Daisy had, in Pearl's words, 'realised that spending her Saturday nights in with a boring middle-aged man isn't that much fun'. But by then, Pearl had binned his possessions, redecorated their home to her personal taste and begun to enjoy living in a flat 'that isn't filled with his black moods and farts'. She has, she has asserted, no desire to meet anyone new, and there are no children to badger her into joining a dating site.

Sensing that the earrings will bring me luck today, I turn my attentions to my hair, first blow-drying it, then obliterating any suggestion of fullness by scraping it back and securing it in a tight bun. The effect is either sleek professional or hostile doctor's receptionist, I can't quite decide which.

Make-up wise, we're talking full face: it's expected for work, although now I choose more muted shades than usual. *Neutral colours are best when you want to look polished and professional.* I find myself replaying the advice I gave to elegant Gilda in the store. It feels oddly like talking to myself.

By the time I'm ready to leave – at 7 a.m. – no one else has emerged from their rooms. I check Facebook, and discover that Antoine has messaged me his mobile number, which I store in my phone immediately before sending him mine. Then I log off and leave the house quietly, with an unsettling feeling deep in my stomach as if I am going to court.

*

The Davenport is a bland modern hotel at the Euston end of Tottenham Court Road, a step up from a Travelodge or a Premier Inn. There's nothing terribly alluring about it. Across the street, teetering along in terribly uncomfortable-looking heels, Andi, our newest team member, shouts my name and waves. She waits for a gap in traffic before darting towards me.

'Oh, I'm so glad to see you,' she exclaims. 'I wish they'd told us what this was all about. I could hardly sleep last night.'

'Me neither,' I say truthfully. 'It'll be fine, though, once things get started. These conferences are usually quite fun.'

She casts me a doubtful look. 'I'm just no good at speaking in front of people. Will they ask me, d'you think?'

I squeeze her arm as we make our way into the hotel foyer. 'I've no idea, but try not to worry. You're warm and friendly and that's all that matters. That's what the management wants to see.'

Andi musters a weak smile. 'God, I hope so—'

'And they're just *people*,' I remind her. 'Most of them do the same job you do. There'll be a few bigwigs, but I've met most of those from various seminars and they're *fine*. They're just like us . . .'

We both turn as a tall and rangy blonde woman in a black linen suit and nude heels strides towards us. She is clutching a thick wodge of documents, and a pair of huge sunglasses are perched on top of her head. 'You're here for the La Beauté conference?'

'Yes, that's right,' I reply.

She jabs a cherry-red nail in the direction of one of the corridors leading off the foyer. 'Down that way, last door on your right. Please pick up a name badge on your way in.'

Hmm, no niceties there, then.

I assume a purposeful stride as Andi and I head off together and collect our badges from the dozens arranged in neat rows on a table.

Fixing them on, we step into the already bustling conference room. Rows of plastic chairs have been set out before a small raised stage with a lectern positioned dead centre. Behind it, the elegant swirl of the La Beauté logo beams from an enormous screen. Our entire skincare range has been laid out on a cloth-covered table to the right, and another table displays our make-up collection. It all looks impeccably organised, and I try to ignore the niggle of unease about being given only two days' notice for this. And what about our counter back at the store? I'll be checking the morning's sales the minute we get back.

Although croissants, pastries and a selection of fruit have been laid out for us, no one seems to be eating anything. Normally I'd be right in there, ogling the glistening pains aux raisins and squidgy blueberry muffins. I have never quite managed to shake off my childish joy at being faced with a hotel breakfast buffet but now I can't stomach a thing. D'you hear that, Ralph, office-toilet-perv? There's about a mile of baked goods on offer and I am merely pouring myself a coffee from a stainless steel pot.

Clutching my cup and saucer nervously as if I've never handled such items before, I glance around the room. Andi is still lurking anxiously at my side, like a little girl on her first outing to playgroup. I smile – serenely, I hope, my cup jiggling only slightly – in recognition, at some of the women who are hovering around. As we're 'a much-loved niche company', as Nuala puts it – i.e. small fry to the industry's major players – most of the London sales staff know each other even if we work at different stores.

I catch Nuala's eye, and she waves distractedly, then turns away to continue chatting with a modelly-looking guy in tortoiseshell specs and an expensive-looking pale grey suit. He has one of those angular jaws that looks chiselled from rock. 'It's a bold, brave move but it's definitely the way forward,' he booms, and I catch Nuala nodding, wide-eyed. 'Knock the competition into a cocked hat,' he adds, with a horsey laugh.

'Lorrie!' I turn to see Helena, pink-faced and clearly harassed, peeling off her black jacket whilst hurrying towards me. 'Delay on my train. Thank God it hasn't started yet . . .'

'No, you're fine, don't worry. Just take a few moments to calm down. Are you okay?'

She exhales with relief as she looks around. 'Yeah, I guess so. Who's that guy Nuala's talking to?'

'No idea.'

'Jesus. This looks like a pretty big deal, doesn't it?'

I agree that it does, and watch with interest as Nuala and Mr Chiselled are joined by a bird-like woman in a knee-length red dress which clings to her tiny waist. Another two men in suits stride over and they all start bantering loudly. The woman in red throws back her head, her black bob swinging as if she's in an advert, and laughs shrilly: 'Oh Gerard, you crack me up!' It's as if there's a private party going on that the rest of us haven't been invited to. 'Yep,' she adds, 'I'm ready. As ready as I'll ever be, haha!' With that, she tears herself away from the group and strides onto the stage, where she claps her hands sharply. 'Could everyone please take their seats for the presentation?'

Everyone swings round to face her. If that was me up there, I'd be worrying about looking sweaty or my pants

132

working their way up my bottom. Clearly, though, she does this kind of thing all the time. She widens her eyes expectantly, and there's a great deal of scurrying and scraping as forty-odd people settle into their chairs. Andi, Helena and I bag three seats together as a reverential hush descends on the room.

'Hello everyone,' the woman starts, 'and welcome to our La Beauté conference. I'm Sonia Richardson and I'm the new CEO of La Beauté UK.'

'New CEO?' I mouth, aghast, at Helena. 'What's going on?' We've never had one before. Claudine, Mimi and their own management team ran things from the offices in Grasse.

She pulls a baffled face as I turn back to face the stage. So that's what this is about: someone new put in place, perhaps due to Claudine and Mimi wishing to step back from the running of the business. Well, that's understandable; our founder sisters are well into their seventies. I take a deep breath, trying to convince myself that everything's going to be okay.

Sonia Richardson's smile lifts and widens. Her perfect teeth shine out at us, like a freshly painted gate. 'It's so good to see you all together,' she continues, 'for what promises to be an inspiring morning for all of us. And now, to kick things off, I have a *very* important announcement to make . . .'

Chapter Thirteen

Everyone sits bolt upright, faces turned to the new boss. Sonia smooths down the front of her red dress, then glances over her shoulder as the words **A NEW WAY FORWARD** flash up on the screen. 'Right,' she says briskly, 'this is the focus of today's conference – the reason you've all been invited here. I know you haven't had much notice but it's been important to keep these developments under wraps.' Small pause for effect. 'I'm here to tell you that La Beauté is under new ownership.'

I gawp at her, wondering for a moment whether I've misheard. There are several audible gasps, and a collective murmur ripples across the room.

'Who owns us now?' Andi hisses, but all I can do is pull a *no-idea* face in return.

'As you're all aware,' Sonia continues – we all quieten down immediately, like scolded children – 'we have always been a niche brand that's attracted an incredibly loyal following.' She pauses. 'So how do you think our customers would describe us right now? Please speak up. I'd like to hear your opinions.'

The room is hushed. Mr Chiselled, who is hovering near the stage like Sonia's minder, clears his throat. I should say something – of course I know how they'd describe us – to break the silence that's stretching uncomfortably.

At the end of our row, an eager-looking girl with a blonde crop shoots up her hand. 'Er, we have a personal approach.'

Sonia purses her lips. 'Yes, very good,' she remarks in a voice that says, *That's not very good, is it?* 'But then, I doubt whether there's a successful brand who wouldn't claim to have that. Of course it's personal. We are selling beauty, not tile grouting. Could you expand a little, please?'

I glance back at the girl who's now shrunk into her beige stackable chair, twisting her hands together on her lap. 'Um, well . . . I just think, er, that's why our customers are so loyal, you know? They like coming to us, they enjoy the experience . . .'

'Well, that's a good start, isn't it?' Sonia's tone is cruelly mocking.

'. . . Because we don't just thrust the latest product at them. We take the time to chat, to get to know them a little, ask about their jobs, their lives, their families . . .' My heart goes out to the girl as she struggles on.

'Yes, excellent.' Sonia's eyes are already scanning the room. 'Anyone else like to contribute?'

No more hands are raised. Now there's a surprise.

She waits, one hand resting on the lectern, the other plonked on her bony hip. 'Yes?' Her gaze lands on someone in the row behind me. I glance round to see Zara, the counter manager from the Knightsbridge store.

'Well, it's all about trust,' she begins.

'Yes, of course they trust us when we're recommending products for their face.'

I shift uncomfortably and adjust the waistband of my trousers. Sonia is pacing the stage, face set hard, in the manner of a stern GP. What does she know about our business, and our relationship with customers? Bet she didn't start on the shop floor.

'I mean, we are not hard sell and never have been,' Zara adds. 'It's just not our way.'

'But we are in the beauty business,' Sonia says, now addressing the room, 'and I'm here to tell you that's how things are going to change. We are putting the word *business* first.' She jabs a remote control, and up it flashes on the screen in fat black type: **THE BUSINESS BEAUTY.** What? Someone's made a mistake. The words are in the wrong order. It's like saying, 'I fancy a sandwich cheese.'

'Yes, loyalty and trust were – *are* – important,' Sonia goes on, 'but La Beauté is no longer a family-owned company. As of yesterday, the brand was taken over by Geddes and Cox which, as I'm sure all of you know, is one of the biggest companies in Britain and probably the most diverse, product-wise.' I glance at Andi, who pulls an alarmed face. '. . . And what Geddes and Cox are extremely keen on – in fact, what is required of us now – is to boost sales to a level where we are out-performing the big guns. We are talking major expansion and a whole new, highly-driven approach.' Sonia pauses again, allowing this information to sink in.

Big guns? We are talking about a touchy-feely company, started by two sisters over forty years ago, who concocted all-natural lotions and face creams using wild flowers from their own garden.

'Bloody hell,' Helena whispers.

'. . . which might seem like a huge undertaking,' Sonia goes on in strident tones, 'and, well . . . yes, it is!' She

136

beams around at us as if rallying us for battle and flicks her remote control.

AGGRESSIVE GROWTH appears on the screen.

Christ, it sounds like cancer.

Then:

What does this mean?

NPC = zero sale. zero commission. zero growth

NO! to the NPC.

Sonia glances at Mr Chiselled who nods approvingly. 'Now, who is familiar with the NPC?' Silence. A waitress stops tidying up the ravaged croissant display and glances towards the stage. 'Really?' Sonia prompts us. 'Hasn't *anyone* heard of this term?'

A sea of blank looks. Sonia juts out her chin and smiles curtly. 'The Non-Purchasing Customer, of course. She's a waste of time and resources and something we must learn to manage if we are to achieve our goals.'

What? I refuse to think of someone like Jane – the knackered mum who was grateful to be looked after while her little boy defaced our colouring book – as a waste of anything. She'll come back and buy something one day – but even if she doesn't, so what? What difference does it make really?

Sonia turns to the screen, flicking her remote control again with a dramatic flourish, as if it will now cause the dreary conference room walls to slide apart to reveal a swimming pool.

A new message appears: **Maximising profits through minimising stool time.**

What? So they're planning to limit how often we go to the loo? This is crazy. I won't be treated like a naughty child . . .

'. . . The focus will move firmly towards rapid gains in

137

market share,' Sonia drones on. 'We'll be implementing measures to assess competitors' promotional drives and retaliate with our own aggressive strategies . . .'

My stomach feels leaden. This is definitely no longer our delightful company, with Claudine and Mimi at the helm, who sent me a handwritten condolence letter after David died: *Please take as much time as you require with assurance that you will be paid in full. We are sending you much love from Grasse.* They even followed it up with a spa voucher – never used, but a kind gesture – six months later, plus an open invitation to visit them with my children any time I needed a break. That's what's so special about working here. Despite being a global brand it's always had that family feel.

'What's the company approach to stool time right now?' asks Sonia with an arched brow, scanning the room for a raised hand.

'Erm, I'm sorry,' murmurs someone at the back, 'but I don't think we know what it is. I mean, I've never heard it before—'

'Really? Well, that is a surprise!' Sonia emits a small, mirthless laugh. 'It means the time a customer takes up when she's sitting on one of our stools, basically eating up our resources and profits. So, what's the maximum allocation at present?'

'We, uh, don't have one,' the girl replies.

'Well,' Sonia announces, 'that will certainly have to change . . .' And now the screen fills with a shouty directive:

STOOL TIME FOR MAXIMUM SALES POTENTIAL: 3 minutes 27 seconds.

The world has gone mad. My armpits are sweaty and, as the room has grown warmer, my feet seem to have expanded in the glossy black shoes which normally fit me perfectly.

'This,' Sonia announces, 'isn't just a figure plucked from the air. In the run-up to the acquisition, we conducted an enormous amount of research to demonstrate how long we need to assign valuable stool time to a customer in order to maximise the possibility of a sale.'

Three minutes, twenty-seven seconds? Will we be issued with stop watches? And what are we supposed to do if a customer lingers a little longer? Push her off the stool, or attack her with a sharpened lip pencil?

'So you see,' Sonia concludes, 'we are seriously changing the way we operate and I think – I *hope* – you'll all embrace our new approach and give your all to what promises to be an exciting future for every one of us.' She stops and looks round, as if anticipating whoops and cheers. The room remains deathly silent. 'And now,' she adds, 'we'll break for coffee – just fifteen minutes – after which one of our top salespeople will give a talk on how we plan to move seamlessly into this, our new, thrilling phase.' Her gaze hits the centre of my forehead like a laser. 'Lorrie Foster, I've heard excellent things about your performance and management skills. Straight up here after the break, okay?'

'Sorry?' A sharp stab of pain shoots up from my left toe.

She smiles pertly and strides off the stage, at the precise moment that a cluster of young waitresses glide in with trolleys bearing more pots of coffee and tea.

I glance round and see Zara striding towards me.

'So you knew all about this?' she barks. A clear message beams from her almond-shaped brown eyes: *traitor.*

'No, of course I didn't! I had absolutely no idea.'

'But you've prepared a talk about how we're all going to move forward?' She widens her eyes expectantly. Some of her team have gathered around us. They loom over me as if they might kick me in the shins, or at the very least burn my furry pencil case with a cigarette lighter.

'Honestly, I didn't know any more than you did. This has been totally sprung on me—'

'Nuala popped in a couple of days ago and said some of us might be asked to talk,' chips in Helena, ever the ally. 'It just sounded like a casual thing. No one knew about the acquisition.'

Zara's coterie glare at me, clearly still disbelieving, as if I must have known all along about Geddes and Cox and their stool-time rule. Hotness surges up my chest as we all make our way to the refreshments table.

'Well, I suppose it's an honour to be asked to *address* us all,' snaps Cleo, who works at the Notting Hill store. She flares a nostril at me and snatches a biscuit from a tray.

'Yes, I suppose so,' I murmur. I pour a coffee I don't want, and clutch the too-small cup with the clumsy saucer as hostility radiates all around me.

'Who made that up?' someone mutters. 'That non-paying NPC thing?'

'I think you'll find it's a standardly used term,' booms Mr Chiselled, who seems to have sidled over without anyone noticing.

'But used where?' Zara counters.

'In the beauty industry of course.'

'So what other beauty brands do Geddes and Cox have?' someone else pipes up.

'Um, none at the moment,' he says without a trace of humility, 'but with this acquisition we're serious about grabbing a major market share.'

Sensing my lifeblood ebbing away, I step back from the hubbub and lean against a wall which bears a smattering of drawing pin holes and Blu-tack smears. All these awful, unfriendly phrases: minimising stool time . . . aggressive growth . . . and, the corker, *The Business Beauty*. It's only my job, I remind myself, trying to keep things in perspective by thinking of non-work matters: like Antoine, on Sunday night! What about that? I have a date. No, no not a date. A casual drink with a friend from the past. Christ. The very thought of it, coupled with the gallon of coffee I must have consumed today – on an otherwise empty stomach – does nothing to quell my anxiety.

I dump my cup and saucer on the table. Spotting Nuala looking stranded by the skincare display, I make my way over to her.

'Hi, Lorrie,' she says dully. 'This is all very, um, interesting, isn't it?'

'Yes, you could say that. So how long have you known?'

'Only since Tuesday and I couldn't say anything. I wish I could but, honestly, I'd have lost my job . . .'

I nod, feeling sorry for her now. She's not a stool-time type either. 'Did you put my name forward to do a speech?'

She pushes her shiny dark hair behind her ears. 'Yes, but only because you're the best.'

'Glad you think so,' I murmur, 'but what should I say? I had no idea any of this was happening—'

'Just relax, be yourself . . .' She pats my arm as if I am seven and about to perform a wobbly solo on a recorder at the school concert, and beetles away.

Hell, coffee break must be almost over. I sneak out into the corridor, away from the sly glances from Zara and the others, in an attempt to collect my thoughts. As well as my feet puffing up, the waistband of my trousers is now pinching into me like cheese wire. Must be nerves, filling me up with wind. Pre-public-speaking bloat, is that a thing? A girl with a mousy ponytail lumbers past me, dragging a vacuum cleaner. I tug at my waistband and try to rearrange my expression to show that I am calm, just taking a moment.

The door to the conference room opens. The blonde woman who greeted us at the start of the day steps out into the corridor. 'Ah, Lorrie, here you are! We're all ready for you now.'

Chapter Fourteen

Keep calm, I tell myself as I walk towards the stage. *They're only people. People who pick their noses and do all the normal stuff – even Mr Chiselled sits on the loo with his trousers down.* I glance at him, trying to imagine the scenario, and he flashes a joyless smile.

Beside him sits Sonia, back rod-straight, hands placed loosely on her lap. Clearly, *her* outfit doesn't threaten to slice her through the middle when she sits down. She's just a young thing, I reflect as I step up onto the stage. Early thirties, at a guess, possibly even younger. She might come across as intimidating but I bet she'd have a full-on meltdown if her boiler broke.

The blonde woman hurries towards me and clips a tiny microphone onto the front of my tunic. I cough to test it. The noise ricochets like a thunder clap across the room. One of the besuited men flinches and throws Sonia a concerned look.

I take a deep breath, picturing Amy's face now, my clever and confident daughter who was her team's top scorer last season and regards the beauty business – the *business beauty* – as a load of old tosh, or rather, *tosh a load of*. She's probably right.

My caffeinated heart hammers away as I gaze at the sea of faces before me. 'Erm, hello,' I start. 'I'm Lorrie Foster and I'm a counter manager for La Beauté . . .' *Breathe, don't forget to breathe.* My throat is sandpaper dry and it feels as if a small radiator has been strapped to my chest. 'Well, it's very interesting, seeing the new direction the company is going to take,' I continue, aware of the wobble in my voice. 'And of course, selling products is important because without that, none of us would be here.' My gaze sweeps the rows of blank faces. Zara and her team, all lined up at the back, are gazing dispassionately as if tolerating a dreary talk by someone trying to flog timeshare apartments.

My mouth has completely dried up now – my tongue feels desiccated – as I try to figure out what to say that'll be relevant to Sonia's speech. Are they expecting me to enthuse about limited stool time and how we might deal with those dastardly customers who just want to browse? My brain has emptied itself of coherent thoughts. 'So,' I mutter, 'I think maybe we need to address the issue of the NCP.'

There's a small flurry of laughter. 'That's the car park company,' Sonia trills. '*NCP car parks*. I think you mean *NPC*?'

'Oh, yes. Yes, of course.' My heartbeat accelerates and I catch Helena's eye. She smiles encouragingly. Andi raises her brows, willing me to go on, to get this over with so we can hurry back to work and somehow struggle through the afternoon in our lovely fragrant store. 'The NPC,' I repeat carefully. 'Well, this is very new to us, isn't it? Thinking of our customers in this way?' I scan the room

144

again and register the odd tentative nod. 'Because to me,' I add, my voice a little stronger now, 'it seems to go against everything La Beauté stands for.'

As soon as I've said it, my nervousness seems to ebb away. I *know* what to say now, and how to say it. For the past decade I have been immersed in this company and used its products every single day. I can *do* this.

I glance sideways at Sonia and her besuited coterie, then turn back to the front. 'Because every woman we meet is an individual with her own hopes and concerns. The fact is, she has willingly come to our counter, and we should respect her for that, whether or not she decides to make a purchase.' I stop, take a deep breath and plough on: 'She's likely to be a busy person who has given us her time when there's probably a hundred other things she could be doing. Shouldn't we value that? Should we really regard her as a problem or a drain on our resources?'

The atmosphere is changing in the room. My colleagues are relaxing, shoulders shifting, and I pick up the odd murmur of agreement. 'Anyway,' I continue, 'a woman who enjoys the counter experience might decide to treat herself that day, or she may take away nothing more than a good feeling, a sense of happiness, and if that happens, then we have done our job very well.'

I clear my throat and continue. 'For instance, recently I had a new mum with her little boy and baby at the counter. Her name was Jane. She just needed – I don't know – to be taken care of for twenty minutes or so. To be treated and enjoy a little respite from all the responsibility, you know?' I catch Nuala's eye. She is smiling broadly, then glances around as if fearful of being told off. 'And then,' I go on, feeling as fired up now as when I told Ralph to stop his toilet perving, 'there was an older

145

lady, an absolute beauty, in her sixties, who said she'd never worn make-up in her life – can you believe that? Not even a lick of mascara!' Laughter fills the room. 'But even so,' I continue, 'she enjoyed the experience because it was new to her.' I pause, picturing Gilda as she studied her reflection in the mirror: *I like it. Gosh, that's a surprise. Thank you very much!* 'I mean,' I add, 'can you imagine trying your first lipstick at that age and discovering you love the effect? What a pleasant surprise that must be!' There are more murmurs of approval.

I look back at Sonia. Her mouth is set firm like a trap, the sinewy bits of her neck jutting out, reminding me of poultry.

Aware of tiny knots forming in my stomach, I turn back to the audience and spot Zara, who seemed to have me down as some kind of Geddes and Cox turncoat, and who is now nodding and mouthing, *Go on!*

'Lorrie?' Sonia is waving at me. 'I think you've said enough, thank you . . .'

I turn to block her from my vision. 'So,' I continue, picturing Cameron and Amy now, feeling proud of their mother even though I peddle face creams for a living, 'I believe our approach is just right and I know that Claudine and Mimi, our founders, would agree when I say that any woman, no matter how much money she has to spend, is welcome to stop by again and again, and it doesn't matter if she takes up a whole *hour* of stool time . . .' I lace the phrase with distaste – 'because looking after her is what our job is all about.'

I stop, and smile. My trousers seem to have loosened and I can breathe normally again. Even the pinchy sensation in my toe has abated. As I remove the microphone from my tunic, the applause starts, tentatively at first, then building until the room fills with a gale of clapping, and even the odd cheer. I laugh, filled with relief, and stride past Sonia who gives me an alarmed look as if I have just vomited down the front of her red dress.

I hand my microphone back to the blonde woman and bob back down onto my seat. 'Oh my God,' Andi breathes. 'You were amazing!'

'Well, we'll see . . .'

'Totally brilliant,' Helena says, grabbing my arm. 'Thank God someone around here still talks sense!'

The sharp clack of heels causes the hubbub to die down. Sonia has reclaimed the stage. 'Okay, thank you, Lorrie. That was very . . . illuminating. Now I'll hand over to Dennis Clatterbrock who's spearheaded the acquisition. He'll take us through a brief overview of La Beauté's new parent company.'

So that's Mr Chiselled's name: Dennis Clatterbrock. I'd have had him down as a Dylan or a Ben.

I don't take in much of his speech, apart from the fact that Geddes and Cox's main focuses are their screen wash, stock cube and tomato fertiliser brands. How very *relevant* to all of us sitting here, eager to return to our counters and get on with the business of selling eye shadow. 'Tomo-Grow,' he's boasting now, as a photo of plasticky-looking tomatoes appears on the screen, 'outperforms the nearest competitor by thirty-seven per cent. We're talking sixty-two per cent growth year on year . . .' Is he talking product sales or huge, bulging tomatoes? 'That's three units sold every minute. It's idiot-proof. Takes the gardening out of gardening . . .' Luckily, Stu pretty much takes care of our plant maintenance. I just 'help'. We even have a couple of tomato plants of our own – they have actually borne fruit, amazingly – although Stu prefers to use a natural organic feed.

I watch Dennis Clatterbrock, tall and imposing with an actorly voice, his fleshy hands resting on the lectern as pie charts and graphs flash up onto the screen. His supposedly 'brief overview' seems to be rumbling on for a week. I feel like the teenage me, fidgeting impatiently as Mrs Rippon, my English teacher, rambled on about the symbolism and metaphors in *Macbeth* until nothing seemed to make sense anymore. Perhaps there's something wrong with me. At the very least, I seem to have a faulty attention span, and Cam has already surpassed me in the general knowledge stakes. I can't even tell what's proper art and what's just been left lying about by the cleaner – that mop and bucket at the Nutmeg Gallery – or even identify a lobster pot.

My stomach growls as, finally, Dennis Clatterbrock turns his attentions to our beloved French brand. '. . . Ascertain whether a customer has expressed a *specific* product need prior to allocating stool time . . . We are not in the business of giving away products for free . . . Samples are to be used as add-ons, as a thank you to those spending over £100 . . .'

For God's sake! We usually dish out freebies like sweets. They cost the company pennies. What's with the meanness all of a sudden?

'. . . So thank you, everyone, for coming this morning,' he concludes. 'I hope you're as excited as I am to be part of the Geddes and Cox family. Take a look at our website, familiarise yourselves with our product portfolio and be reassured that today is the day we go from strength to strength.'

And that's it. There's a short, stunned silence, then we all rise from our seats and shuffle past the messed-up array of pastries and fruit towards the exit, funnelling through it in muttering groups, and step out into the bright summer's day.

'Blimey,' Helena mutters.

'You did really well there,' says Nuala, scuttling towards us. I catch her glancing around, as if scared of being caught fraternising with the lowly counter staff.

'Thanks,' I reply, 'although it's probably not what they wanted to hear . . .'

'Well, we'll see, won't we?' she trills, leaping away in order to hail a cab. She doesn't offer to share one with us. Too mortified, probably. Instead, Helena, Andi and I take one together and barely say a word the whole journey back to work. It's as if we're too stunned to even speculate as to what might happen next.

Back at the store, the three of us take over from the rather frazzled-looking relief team. Clicking into counter lady mode, I advise on eye creams, loose powders and our top-of-the-range hydrating gel. I traffic stop as if nothing untoward has happened today, and do complete make-ups for a couple of young women who are giddy on prosecco, having enjoyed a boozy lunch.

Rather childishly, I am terribly generous with free samples, delighting the women with tiny pots of cream and serum even though they have only purchased one item each. 'Wow, are you sure? Thank you!'

'Yes, of course. Take them home and enjoy them . . .'

Come and get it! I feel like crying, wishing I could send a hail of complimentary mascaras flying across the floor for customers to scramble over. Because what my job really boils down to is making people happy; it's simply what I do.

Or at least, it's what I *did*.

Chapter Fifteen

Back home, I find Cam and Mo in the garden, passing Mo's new guitar back and forth as if it were a baby they've just brought home from hospital.

'Be careful,' Mo warns my son. 'Don't be so rough. You nearly clunked it on the table . . .'

Both in rumpled band T-shirts and baggy shorts, they're installed on our spindly wrought-iron chairs, the table littered with the remains of a pizza and an ashtray, I happen to note. Hmm. I've delivered the smoking-is-bad sermon before and I'm not planning to lecture him now.

'All right, Mum?' Cam says, somewhat belatedly, picking at a pizza crust.

Maybe I am. I'm still feeling quite proud of how I handled myself up on that stage this morning. 'Good, thanks,' I say, not expecting him to remember that I've been to a conference.

'There's broken glass all over,' he adds, glancing down at the ground. Of course – the breakage during the tense dinner with Mum. I'd completely forgotten to sweep it up.

'Oh yes, just a little accident when Grandma was here.' Dutifully, I fetch the dustpan and brush and sweep it up, then leave the boys to their musical endeavours.

As Amy is over at Bella's and Stu, presumably, is out on deliveries, I throw together a quick bowl of pasta, lifting it from the doldrums with the remains of Stu's home-made pesto from a kilner jar in the fridge. Mmm, it's so *basilly*. He really is terribly handy to have around the house.

Sufficiently fortified, I fetch my laptop, install myself at the kitchen table and study Geddes and Cox's website. While I have nothing against stock cubes or even tomato fertiliser, I can't imagine how a brand like La Beauté will fit in alongside them. I find profiles of key team members – Sonia Richardson and Dennis Clatterbrock beam, fakely, from a gallery of similarly executive types – and sense a stab of yearning for what already feels like the 'old' ways. Presumably there'll be no more kind and encouraging messages from Claudine and Mimi, or those occasional afternoon teas in a fancy hotel that they'd invite key counter staff to whenever they came to London. What will happen to our founders now? Will they still be connected to the company in some way? I can't help feeling that they've sold out, but what would I have done, in their shoes? Perhaps they'd simply had enough. Yet I wish, perhaps naively, that we'd had some warning. 'We're a family,' Claudine told me when I emailed to say thank you for the spa voucher. 'We try to take good care of the people who work with us.' Next time they were in London, the sisters made a point of taking me for lunch – alone – to check I was managing okay. What would *they* make of terms like stool time and NPC?

Cam and Mo wander in, bickering good-naturedly as

they amble up to Cam's room. I switch on the radio and position it at the kitchen window, then pull on Stu's grubby old gardening gloves. With Pulp's 'Common People' drifting from the kitchen window – Stu and I have reached the 6 Music lifestage – I experience a sense of calm as I pluck straggly weeds from the plant pots and between the paving stones. Although I'm enjoying this simple task, I still regard the tomato plants, with all the care they require – the pinching and pruning and spraying with a special kind of tea – as exotic reptilian pets and so decide they're best left alone.

Stu arrives home and gives me a keen thumbs up through the kitchen window. 'Good work,' he mouths.

I laugh, feeling oddly proud of my efforts, and sweep up the weeds before giving everything a good dousing with the watering can. Working *inside* the house is never as gladdening as this. I've tried to garner some kind of satisfaction from domestic work but still haven't managed to find any. The part of parenting I loved was the playing, the reading stories, the taking off for a weekend with a tent and sleeping bags stashed in the boot – all the fun and adventures. As I mentioned to Ralph – clearly, he was riveted – when you clean a room you're actually just counting the seconds until someone stomps in and trashes it again.

Stu appears at the back door and holds out my phone, which he has a tendency to answer, like an efficient secretary. 'Pearl's home,' he announces.

'Oh, great!' I smile and take it from him, relieved that she's back. I am always eager to see her during her brief spells between jobs abroad. 'Hey, welcome home. I've missed you!'

'Missed you too,' she says. 'Just got back this morning . . .'

'Can't wait to hear all about it. Shall we meet up? When are you free?' Her month in Dubai seems to have stretched indefinitely.

'Well, I'm out walking Toby in London Fields right now. God, he was pleased to see me. Poor Mum and Dad, though. They're brilliant dog-sitters but they always seem quite bereft when I take him home . . .'

I laugh. 'How about I come out and meet you? I can head out straight away—'

'Great,' she says.

Fifteen minutes later we're hugging at the edge of the park as if it's been years since we've seen each other.

'So,' she says as we fall into step, 'the family has this top-floor apartment, 360-degree views, pool with little underwater lights and a fountain, all that . . .' She pauses as Toby, her wiry rescue terrier, stops to greet a passing Alsatian.

'Sounds amazing.'

'Oh, it was. And the only people in it pretty much all of the time were the cleaner, the other nanny and me.'

'The *other* nanny?' I turn to Pearl in surprise. Tiny and trim in skinny jeans and a baggy black sweater, she wears her ash-blonde hair cropped short and her face devoid of make-up apart from customary red lips. At forty-nine, she could easily pass for a decade younger.

'Yep, the Connaught-Joneses have two, at least when they're in Dubai—'

'And what do they do? For jobs, I mean?'

'Both lawyers by day, with incredibly active social lives by night. Barely saw them for the whole month. They hardly saw their daughter either.'

'And there were two nannies for one little girl? What was the point of that?'

153

Pearl laughs. 'To ensure that Lois's every need was catered for in case, you know, one of us had to nip to the loo or prepare her lunch or something. So, most of the time, we were both hovering around her, fussing really, and the other nanny, Cleo, was getting quite competitive about it: "Hey, Lois, come over here for a story while Pearl tidies up . . ."'

'Only they had the cleaner for that . . .'

Pearl nods. 'Exactly. I suggested to Cleo that we set up a shift pattern but that didn't work. So we were scrambling over each other, foisting attention on her . . .'

'Lucky girl . . .'

'Not really. She just wanted her parents, hurled herself at them whenever one of them happened to come home.' She pauses, and Mum's accusatory tone flits into my mind: *All I meant was, children like being with their mothers most of all.* 'God, it's so good to be back and be normal,' Pearl adds, squeezing my arm. 'Don't suppose you fancy a drink?'

'Oh yes, I could murder one.'

As we make our way across the park to the pub, I fill her in on recent developments at work.

'I'm sure you'll be fine,' she asserts. 'They need people like you who know the company inside out.'

'They were all so young, though – the new management, I mean. Young and ballsy and thrusting . . .'

'Who needs *thrusting* in the beauty business?'

'Well, they think we do! They seem to think we're this gentle outfit who just trundle along, being kind to people, never pushing a sale . . .' I pause. 'Which we are, I suppose.'

'Yes, but a lot of your customers are our age, aren't they? They want someone who understands them . . .'

'I hope you're right,' I murmur.

154

Although the pub is bustling on this warm summer's evening, a young couple happen to vacate one of the outside tables as we approach, and we claim it quickly.

'White wine?' Pearl asks.

'Yes please,' I say, as she hands me Toby's lead. He strains to watch her as she disappears into the pub, panting excitedly as she reappears with our drinks. 'Looks like he's really missed you,' I remark.

'God, yes. He's been following me around the flat all day, nuzzling against me, trying to lick my face . . .' She laughs and ruffles the top of his head.

'Maybe I should get a dog. Must be lovely to have someone so delighted to see you every time you come home.'

'Yes, but you have Stu for that.' We laugh, and she gives me that look; Pearl seems to think that, one day, Stu and I will glance at each other over a plate of toast on a Sunday morning and realise we are desperately in love. 'How's that mad business of his going?'

I sip my wine. 'Pretty well, amazingly, and mostly through word of mouth.'

'All those harassed North London cooks . . .' She clasps a hand to her chest. '"Oh, my God, I'm fresh out of chervil!"'

'And he'll literally zoom off at any hour of the day or night . . .'

'Where does he get the stuff?'

'Any supermarket en route, or a specialist shop if he needs to. He's become an expert on pretty much every North London food store and their opening hours.'

She beams. 'So simple, so clever. Aw, darling Stu. Your first love.'

I laugh and push back my hair. 'We were only ever

mates, you know that. That French guy, Antoine, was my first love . . . remember I told you about him?' Pearl nods. 'Well, he's been in touch on Facebook. He's coming to London on Sunday, we're meeting up . . .'

'Wow! How long since you've seen each other?'

'Oh, only thirty years—'

'So, what's he like now? Assuming you've forensically examined all his photos?' She raises a brow.

''Course I have,' I admit with a grin.

And so the evening goes on, with us sniggering over my teenage Antoine obsession, the way I prowled about waiting for the postman, and once stopped him in the street and asked, 'D'you have anything for number seventy-two?' Sorry, he said, he wasn't allowed to hand out mail in the street. We chuckle over Pearl's first love – a boy at her judo club, which caused her to continue with the sport, even though she detested being thrown around and sat upon, until an ankle sprain forced her to quit. By our second drinks we are convulsing with laughter over Ralph's bile-making panting in his office loo, and she is dismayed that I've suspended my datemylovelymum.com account.

'Aw, what about all the work your kids put in, researching the sites, choosing the best one—'

'Oh, come on! They just chose the one with the funniest name.'

'Well, writing your profile, then—'

'It was just a bit of fun to them,' I remind her. 'Not an exam essay. I mean, their futures won't be affected just because their couple of paragraphs didn't result in me meeting someone I actually want to see a second time.'

Pearl tuts and delves into a packet of crisps. 'I think you should have a few more goes.'

I smile. 'You're making it sound like a coconut shy.'

'Well, the more balls you throw, the better your chance of knocking one off . . .'

'Sage advice,' I tease her as we finish our drinks and set off for one final circuit of the park.

A tall, red-headed man waves in the distance, and Pearl waves back. His syrup-coloured spaniel pulls on its lead.

'You know him?' I ask.

'Yes – well, sort of. It's a dog thing. His spaniel's called Rosie. When you have a dog, you get to know all the other dog people but you rarely find out the humans' names.'

'Toby looks pleased to see them,' I remark as he pulls forward, yapping excitedly.

'Oh, yeah, he *loves* Rosie. They usually have a play about, bit of bum-sniffing, the usual date stuff . . .' No sooner has she uttered the words when the man unclips Rosie's lead, just as Pearl frees Toby. They bound towards each other in a whirl of wagging tails.

'Hey, haven't seen you in a while.' The man smiles as he comes over, and what a smile he has: wide and warm and unguarded. He is wearing a faded sweatshirt over dark jeans and his red hair catches the evening sun. The park, I realise now, is milling with dog people stopping to chat, exchanging pleasantries while their charges play in the fading evening light.

'Been away in Dubai for a month,' Pearl explains.

'Oh, a nannying job, right?'

'That's it,' she says.

'Rosie's missed Toby. Look at the pair of them now.' Like proud parents they turn and watch as the two dogs scamper together, Rosie's ears flapping, Toby's tail a blur of delight.

'It's so lovely to see,' I remark, cheered by the sight of them playing.

'Best thing about having one,' the man remarks. 'I wasn't sure, you know, about fitting in the walks on top of work and everything else, and of course, my daughter promised she'd take care of all of that . . .' He laughs.

'And does she?' I ask.

'Not a chance. She loves her, of course she does, but her idea of walking Rosie is to take her to the street corner and back, and now she's off travelling . . .' He shrugs good-naturedly. 'So it's just the two of us. Luckily, I can take her to work with me . . .' He calls Rosie, and she charges towards him, obligingly allowing him to clip on her lead. 'I have an off-licence,' he adds. 'You might've seen it, just across from the tube? It's called Tipples . . .'

'Yes, I know it,' I say.

'I'm changing the name,' he adds quickly, 'and sprucing the place up. Planning wine tastings, gin evenings, that kind of thing . . .'

'Count us in for those,' Pearl says with a smile. It's a little more challenging for her to attract Toby's attention, so enraptured is he with his friend. Finally, she manages to secure his lead, and the three of us fall into step.

'So where's your daughter travelling?' I ask.

'Thailand, Cambodia, Vietnam . . .' The man smiles again, and I register the pale blue of his eyes. 'Terrifying for me,' he adds, laughing.

'God, yes, I can imagine. I'd be tempted to put a tracker device on mine.'

'So you have teenagers?'

'Yes, both still at home. My daughter's fifteen, my son's seventeen, so not long till I'm an empty nester . . .'

He nods, and we stop as the dogs investigate an alluring

158

clump of long grass. 'Well, it feels like I'm there already.' He indicates Rosie. 'Luckily, I have her . . .'

'They're the best company,' Pearl adds. 'Affectionate, undemanding . . .' She turns to me. 'You should get one, Lorrie.'

The man chuckles. 'So you're Lorrie and . . .' He rakes back his hair. 'Funny, isn't it, how we know each other's dogs' names—'

'And not each other's,' Pearl agrees. 'I was just saying that to Lorrie. I could probably tell you the names of pretty much every regular dog in this park, but none of the owners. I'm Pearl—'

'And I'm Eric . . .'

'So you live around here?' I ask.

'Yep, just five minutes away. And you?'

'Pine Street. Been there for what seems like forever – well, since the kids were tiny, anyway.'

'So it's just you, your teenagers . . .'

'And our lodger, Stu . . .' I break off as my phone rings in my bag. It stops as I pull it out.

'Everything okay?' Pearl asks, catching my concerned expression.

I sigh and check the time on my phone; somehow the evening has flown by and it's gone 10 p.m. 'Three missed calls. Mum's been trying to get hold of me. I'd better call her . . .' I turn and hug Pearl. 'I'm so glad you're back, and nice meeting you, Eric . . .'

'You too,' he says, flashing another disarming smile. 'Maybe we'll run into each other sometime?'

'Hope so,' I say, tension gathering deep in my gut as I say goodbye and call Mum. Perhaps she wants to apologise for inferring that she had it so much harder, what with throwing her husband out of the house instead of him dying in the road . . .

159

'Lorrie, at last! I've been calling all evening, tried your landline, Stu said you were out with Pearl . . .'

'Yes, we just had a quick drink. Didn't hear my phone. Is everything okay?'

'Um, I *suppose* so . . . but I have to say, I'm rather upset.'

I inhale deeply. 'What about?'

'Well, the wedding of course!'

'Oh,' I frown. 'Has something else happened?'

'You *know* what's happened. It's all changed now, hasn't it? The venue, the theme – everything—' Her words morph into a sob. I suspect more booze has been consumed.

'Oh, Mum. Does there really need to be a theme?'

'Well, Haimie doesn't seem to think so . . .'

'Maybe he's right? And look, I said I'd help you find another venue. There must be somewhere within easy reach of the church—'

'There's just no time!'

'Yes, there is. I can make some calls tomorrow—'

'Oh, is this your Saturday off?'

'No,' I say with exaggerated patience, 'but I do get breaks, Mum . . .'

She sniffs loudly. *Thank you, Lorrie, for offering to spend your lunchbreak ringing round every darn village hall in the vicinity . . .* 'I'll need a different dress,' she adds.

'Mum, the dress is fine. *Stu* said it's lovely . . .'

'Oh. Did he?' I sense a flurry of pleasure, and then: 'But it's Jacobean! How ridiculous will that look in some tawdry little hotel?'

'Mum, you'll look beautiful . . .' I turn into our street, eager to end this conversation before I step into the house.

'Can you come shopping with me tomorrow?' she barks.

Oh, dear God . . . 'I've told you, I'm working . . .'

'Ah, yes, of course . . .' Yep, that's me – *always* working,

160

leaving my almost-adult children to forage for food in supermarkets' bins . . . 'Sunday, then? Or are you working then too?'

I pause a couple of doors away from my own, weighing up the prospect of enjoying my day off, and taking my time to get ready for my date – sorry, *drink* – with Antoine, against being trapped in a Phase Eight changing room with my mother.

'No, Mum, I'm free on Sunday.'

'We could go shopping then. What about your own outfit for the wedding? Have you bought anything yet?'

'No, but there's plenty of time . . .'

'Let's go shopping together then, on Sunday. Come on – it'll be fun. Can you *please* do this for me?'

I sigh as I let myself into my house. 'Okay, Mum, if it'll make you feel better. Sunday, I'm all yours.'

Chapter Sixteen

The following lunchtime – a gloriously sunny Saturday, with a sky such a brilliant blue it looks painted by a child – I am hunched in the so-called staff 'canteen' making numerous calls to hotels, restaurants and village halls out in the wilds of Hertfordshire.

Hardly anyone uses the canteen; understandably, as it isn't one anymore. Whereas a few years ago it was a popular subsidised staff restaurant, cost-cutting measures have reduced facilities to a kettle, an industrial-sized tin of Nescafé, another of powdered milk and a temperamental vending machine stocked with the kind of confectionery you rarely see these days (Caramac, Fry's Turkish Delight). There is also a small fridge, which seems to be used solely by Craig from homewares, who brings in a tuna sandwich in a grey Tupperware box every day. On the plus side, it's eerily quiet, and therefore ideal for my wedding venue search.

Of course, everywhere is booked. I must be insane to think anyone can casually call up a venue at such short notice. *August next year, you mean? What . . . this year?*

Haha, no, I don't think so, but good luck with that! At one place I ring – an ostentatious modern hotel that looks as if its sole purpose is weddings – the woman I speak to clonks down the phone as soon as I mention the date. 'Shotgun wedding, is it?' barks a cocky-sounding young man at a golf club function suite, even though the term hasn't been in common usage since, well, *Jacobean* times.

With my lunchbreak ebbing away, I start to wonder how I've ended up taking this on, which leads me, rather irrationally, to feel cross that my parents didn't at least produce one more child, so at least there'd be someone to share this with.

Any luck yet?

That's Mum texting.

I'll have to Google more places tonight, I reply. Immediately my phone rings, and it's the radiant bride-to-be again.

'I'm just not sure about you getting any old place off the internet.' She says 'off the internet', as if we were talking about discreetly packaged Viagra.

'It's how you research things these days, Mum.' *In fact, it's how it's been for about the past fifteen years . . .*

Craig strolls in and smiles benignly before extracting his plastic tub from the fridge and parking himself in the seat opposite me.

'Yes, but it just seems very, I don't know, *risky*,' Mum whines.

'Well, it's the only way I can help,' I explain, trying to erase the tetchiness that's creeping into my voice. 'It's just not feasible for me to drive all over Hertfordshire, checking places out personally.'

'Oh!'

A terse silence hangs between us.

Craig has peeled the lid off his tub, emitting a powerful fishy smell, and nibbles at his sandwich like a rodent.

'Mum, it'll be okay. We'll find somewhere. But, look, I really should get back to work.'

'All right, love,' she says, sounding choked now, and causing a little needle of guilt to stab at my stomach. We say goodbye, and as Craig uses a licked finger to gather up the crumbs left in his tub, I decide to make one last call. I have tried the number several times already and left increasingly pleading messages on an answerphone. Now, a person answers: an elderly-sounding gentleman named Walter Fadgett, keeper of Little Cambersham village hall, just five miles from the church where Mum and Hamish are to be married. His establishment is indeed available on the day my mother is to be betrothed. '£8.50 an hour, love,' he explains.

'That's fine,' I enthuse.

'Used to be £7.50, but we're building up funds to replace the cistern in the ladies' . . .'

'No, no, £8.50 is perfect . . .'

'It's a bit cracked, you see, but still functional . . .'

'I'm sure it's *great*.'

Sandwich finished, Craig is now hunched over a word search magazine.

'And you will tidy up afterwards?'

Of course I will. I'll clean the floor with my tongue if it means I can book the place . . . 'That's no problem at all. Um, is there any chance Mum and I could come over tomorrow afternoon and take a look?'

'No problem, love. The ladies from the Evergreen Club are having a birthday bash but they won't mind you dropping by. They love a bit of a singalong, that lot. Perhaps your mum might like to join in?'

'I'm sure she will,' I say, my mouth twitching as we finish the call.

Craig looks up and smiles as I head for the door. 'Very efficiently done. Took my daughter six months to find a venue for her wedding.'

I laugh, as if my last-minute approach was entirely intentional. 'Yes, it's amazing, isn't it, how complicated weddings can become?'

'Tell me about it,' he chuckles.

As I make my way along the beige-painted corridor I bring up a picture of Little Cambersham village hall on my phone. An unremarkable pebble-dashed building, it has a moss-smattered roof and a rather saggy wooden lean-to attached to one side. It's not a grand family seat but, Christ, at this stage it will have to do.

Unwilling to embroil myself in another conversation, I fire off a text to Mum. *Just found the perfect wedding venue close to the church. We can check it out on Sunday after shopping. Can you ask Hamish to meet us at Little Cambersham village hall at 3? It's only fair that he sees it too. PLEASE do this, Mum.*

Back at the counter, bolstered by my success as a wedding planner, I throw myself into cheery work mode. Saturdays are generally our busiest days, and as the afternoon progresses we serve numerous regular customers who are stocking up on favourites. However, free samples are handed out sparingly, and when traffic stopping we offer to demonstrate a single product rather than giving full make-overs (far too time-consuming under the new regime). As I'm ringing through a purchase, I spot the approaching spectre of our new chief.

In a tightly belted black dress and towering heels, Sonia Richardson strides towards us. As yet, there have been no repercussions after my little speech yesterday, but the sight of her isn't a welcome one.

I fix on a bright smile. 'Hi, Sonia. This is a surprise. How *are* you?'

She flicks back her dark bob and smiles grimly. 'Hi, Lorrie. Hi, girls. I'm fine, thank you. Just here to get a feeling for what happens on the floor, so please carry on.' She bares her startlingly white teeth, then leans against the counter and folds her slim brown arms.

Although a woman is perusing our lipstick testers, I am unsure whether to approach her or to engage Sonia in chit-chat, to find how things are going in the tomato fertiliser market these days.

'Please don't mind me,' she reiterates, in the manner of a stern boarding school headmistress conducting a dormitory inspection. And so, feeling horribly scrutinised, I ask the customer if she needs any help.

Perhaps in her early fifties, she has the air of someone who finds acres of make-up in gleaming packaging quite intimidating. 'I think I do, actually. I've been wearing the same old natural pinky-brown lipstick for about twenty years and it's washing me out.' She adjusts her silver-rimmed spectacles and smiles apologetically.

'Natural's fine,' I assure her. 'It's easy to apply and suits everyone, and you don't have to even think about it. But I agree, sometimes it's fun to try something a little bolder . . .'

She nods and studies our selection of reds. 'I like the look of these but I've never worn red in my life. I mean, they're all so similar, but different . . . how on earth does one choose?'

166

I glance towards Sonia. Her immaculately-outlined lips are pursed, and her gaze drills into my forehead.

'Well, the thing is,' I continue, 'red can be intimidating but there actually is the right shade of red for everyone.'

'Really?'

'Yes, d'you have a few minutes so I can show you a couple of options?'

The woman nods and climbs onto the stool. Although this is the part of my job I love most, I sense my confidence seeping floorwards as I select two options to try. I have *never* felt nervous when interacting with customers; at least, not since those first few days when I was let loose in the store, and even then the counter manager, Nicky, was so encouraging I soon relaxed into my own way of doing things. However, now I am aware of Sonia watching intently, as if she were a store detective convinced I'm about to slip a pot of night cream into my pocket.

I cleanse off the customer's lipstick and brush on a red – 'Wow, that *is* nice!' she enthuses – then remove it before applying another, all the while conscious of stool time ticking away, like a cab driver's meter, under Sonia's unwavering gaze. 'What d'you think?' I ask brightly.

The woman studies her reflection. 'I do like this one. But maybe the first . . .?'

'Mmm, yes, that was slightly warmer. Both look great on you.'

She picks up each lipstick and studies it in turn. 'Or this one? I'm not sure I can apply it like you did. Won't it smudge, the first time I have a sip of coffee?'

'Well, these are our all-day lip shades – they stay put through drinking, kissing, everything really – but it's best to outline first. Our true red pencil works with both of these shades, it's a brilliant all-rounder, and we also do a

167

lip base which keeps the colour in place even longer . . .'
I am frantically up-selling now, and a twinge of despera-
tion has crept into my voice that's never there normally.
The words BUSINESS BEAUTY pulse into my brain, and
I picture Dennis Clatterbrock with his pie charts and
graphs, his market-leading screen washes and stock cubes.

My customer sighs and tries both of the lipsticks again
on the back of her hand. 'I'm really not sure . . .'

'Take your time,' I say, picturing a huge clock ticking.
She shakes her head. 'I'm sorry, I have to dash off. I
don't suppose you have any samples, do you? Just so I
can get used to wearing red for a day or so . . .'

'Yes, of course,' I say without thinking, as we do in fact
have chic cardboard folders containing four tiny vials of
colour, with a mini brush.

I make my way over to the freebies cupboard. Like a
hostile Alsatian, Sonia appears to be guarding it. 'Excuse
me,' I start, 'could I just get something from the cupboard
please?'

'Oh!' She feigns surprise. 'Yes, of course.' She shuffles
to one side, allowing me just enough room to crouch
down and open it. I rummage about, aware of her glaring
at me as if I might be accessing crack cocaine. Grabbing
a sample of lip colours, I straighten up and hand it to my
customer.

'Thanks so much,' she says, then strides away, the letters
NPC flashing neon-bright above her – but what was I
supposed to have done? Lied, and said we had no samples
to give out, and cuffed her on the head for wasting approx-
imately twelve minutes of stool time?

With Sonia watching – she makes no attempt to engage
with customers or make pleasantries with us, her under-
lings – the day crawls along agonisingly slowly. Only when

I spot Gilda, my elegant older customer, do my spirits rise.

'Gilda!' I exclaim, over exuberantly. 'Lovely to see you again.'

She looks a little startled – she probably doesn't remember me – then taps her female companion on the arm. After briefly conferring, they turn towards me. 'Hello,' Gilda says warmly. 'I was hoping to see you again. I was telling my friend – this is Kathryn – that I've been using the bits I bought from you, and it's been quite fun!'

'I'm so glad to hear that,' I say. 'Have you done your presentation yet? You mentioned—'

'Oh, yes, I'm amazed you remembered. Yes, it went well. I did feel quite, well, professional, you know. Sort of different, all made up . . .'

Kathryn smiles proudly. 'Gilda's being modest. She's chair of the board of a children's charity and just nailed a hugely lucrative partnership . . .'

'. . . In fully made-up armour,' Gilda says, laughing.

As we fall into a chat about her work-related travelling – 'She's off to Guatemala in September,' Kathryn adds – Sonia's hostile presence seems to fade, and I start to feel more positive. Instead of being the kind of person who can't stand up to her own mother, perhaps I'll blossom into being *this* sort of older lady: assured and confident, full of adventure and fun.

'Well, it's been lovely seeing you again,' Gilda says warmly.

'You too. Do drop by any time. Our new autumn colours are due in any day . . .'

'I might just do that,' she says, smiling, as she and Kathryn make their way towards the lifts.

Sonia steps towards me. 'Well, not much happening around here today, is there?'

'Oh, it's been really busy actually.' I sense myself starting to sweat.

'You were chatting for quite a while there, though, when you could have been traffic stopping . . .'

'I did, I stopped Gilda and Kathryn—'

'. . . Grabbing friends doesn't count.'

I catch Andi giving me an incredulous look.

'They're not friends,' I murmur. 'I've only met Gilda once before, and she bought lots of products then—'

'But not this time,' Sonia observes curtly.

'Er, no.'

'So it was *wasted* time.'

I open my mouth to speak, to justify and defend myself, but can't think of how to do it. 'Can I just ask,' I manage, aware of Helena's anxious glances as my cheeks start to glow, 'what we're supposed to do in that sort of situation?'

Sonia looks momentarily put out. 'Well, I don't know. That's *your* job, isn't it? It just shouldn't happen, at least not as frequently as I've observed in the short time I've been standing here . . .'

'So, what should I do? *Punish* them somehow?' My heart seems to be banging audibly. I know I'm being difficult and now I can't stop. 'It's hard, though,' I go on, 'because they haven't actually done anything wrong, have they? I mean, it's not as if they've *stolen* anything – unless you count stool time . . .'

My chest tightens as we stare at each other. Sonia swallows, her mouth pursed, her fingers balled into tight little fists. She glances round at Helena, who's pretending to tidy the counter. I look at my new boss, realising how badly I'm handling this 'new direction', the direction of pie charts and market share and hard sell . . .

Sonia's nostrils flare as she smooths back her hair. 'Can we grab a quick coffee in the canteen please, Lorrie?' she asks in an eerily pleasant voice. 'I'm sure your team can manage things here.'

Chapter Seventeen

Craig has left his Tupperware carton open, emitting its fishy whiff, on the communal table.

'So,' Sonia starts, fixing me with a cool gaze from the opposite seat, 'I think it might be helpful to clear up a few things between us.'

'Yes. I'm sorry. I just meant—'

'I've never been spoken to in that manner at work,' she adds crisply.

I nod. 'I know and I'm sorry.'

'No, you *don't* know, Lorrie. It might be the way you've always conducted yourself but—'

'It's not!' I cut in. 'I was just . . . a bit het up, I suppose, with all the changes that are happening. I mean, it's come as quite a shock, the whole take-over thing . . .'

'These *take-over-things* have to be kept strictly confidential until they're finalised . . .'

'Yes, I realise that, and of course I always try to make a sale. I know it's important. It's just, I find that customers are put off if I come on too strong . . .' I tail off and glance at the cluster of chipped mugs sitting by the sink.

There's been no further mention of hot drinks. Clearly, neither of us is desperate for instant coffee spooned from the industrial-sized tin of indeterminate age.

'The thing is,' she says, adopting a patronising tone now, as if addressing a child, 'at Geddes and Cox we need salespeople who *embrace* change.'

'Oh, I do! I really do. I *love* change.' A desperate edge has crept into my voice.

'Are you sure? Because that's not the impression I got just now.'

'No, well, I'm fine with it, truly. Everything's *fine*.'

'Hmmm.' Sonia examines a perfectly oval fingernail and looks back at me. 'Because . . . well, it's difficult to say this, but in my experience a resistance to change is often . . . an age issue.'

I blink at her. 'How d'you mean?'

'Well . . . the younger ones, Helena and Ally . . .' *Andi. Her name's Andi, for goodness' sake.* '. . . I get the impression they're more open to our new way of doing things than you are . . .' *No, they're just too scared to speak out!* 'Busying away, they were, while you were standing there gossiping about the music school that woman's planning to set up in Rio de Janeiro or wherever it was . . .'

'Guatemala,' I murmur. My nose is tingling, threatening to start running and, ridiculously, I can feel tears welling up behind my eyes. An hour ago I was all chuffed with myself for finally getting hold of Walter Fadgett and securing his £8.50-an-hour village hall. Now I'm being ticked off by a woman who's never sold a lipstick in her entire life. 'I like to show an interest in our customers' lives,' I offer feebly.

'Yes, well, that's all very nice, but back to the *age issue* . . .' She pauses, and a feeling of dread judders up my body. Perhaps she is considering 'retiring' me, like a grey-hound that's past its useful racing life? Am I to be packed off to a home for knackered old beauty salespeople? Sonia leans forward. 'In my experience, Lorrie, the older staff are the ones who want to keep things rattling along in the same old way, year in, year out . . .'

Oh, God. She views me as the team dinosaur. She's going to have me put down.

'. . . And I have to say, your refusal to embrace new ideas really worries me.'

I look down and twiddle the delicate antique ring that Mum gave me for my fortieth birthday. I assumed she had long disposed of the jewellery Dad had given her – offloading it to those suspect types who turn up at the door, saying, WE WILL BUY ALL YOUR GOLD (yes, for about £2.50), and I was surprised and delighted to be given this piece.

'I *am* happy to embrace new ideas,' I murmur. 'The conference was only yesterday and I stood up and spoke in front of everyone. I hope you saw then how committed I am, and how passionate about the brand . . .' *And how, as single parent to two teenagers, I damn well need to cling onto this job.*

'Are you, though?' Sonia asks.

'Yes, of course! Have you looked at my figures? There's hardly a week when I haven't met target and most of the time I'm well over. In fact, last year I was one of the top salespeople in the whole of the South East. Perhaps, if you could spend more time at the counter—'

'I don't have time to nursemaid anyone,' she snaps.

'You don't need to do that,' I manage to squeak out, blinking rapidly to hold back the tears.

Sonia sighs. 'Okay, but I want to make it absolutely

174

clear that we need key team members to stay on message. Can we rely on you to do that?'

'Yes,' I say weakly, feeling as if I've been slapped.

'Well, that's what I needed to hear, Lorrie.' She stands up and dusts down the seat of her dress, as if the hessian chair might have contaminated it. 'Let's get back to the floor, then. We all have work to do.'

There's no further discussion as we travel down to the ground floor. At the counter, she bids us a rather terse goodbye before zooming away.

Helena scuttles over. 'What the hell was that all about?'

'Oh, she just wanted a little chat about me staying on message . . .' I shake my head as if it was nothing.

'Christ, she didn't give you a hard time, did she?'

'Not really,' I say, unable to face going into it now. 'Just, you know, stuff about company policy . . .'

'You look pretty shaken up,' Helena says gently.

I inhale and fix on a big smile as a potential customer wanders towards our counter.

'I'm fine,' I say, turning to the woman as she tries a concealer on her wrist. 'Hi, can I help at all?'

'Oh yes, if you wouldn't mind. I'm not sure if I should buy a concealer or just a more concealing base . . .'

I start to explain our range with its wondrous skin-enhancing properties. As she hops obligingly onto the stool, I make a silent vow to stay on message – of course I will. I'll have one of Dennis Clatterbrock's sodding pie charts tattooed onto my forehead if that's what it takes.

*

I don't plan to go over the whole sorry episode that evening at home. It won't help matters and, anyway, there's nothing

I can do. Sonia already has me down as a pusher of free lip colour samples, and who knows where that might lead? Next thing, I'll be lurking in alleyways and slipping passers-by full-sized pots of Ultra-Deluxe Creme de la Nuit. In fact, as I travel home on the tube, I'm wondering whether a new career might be in order, but how does a forty-six-year-old woman go about changing direction? Oh, I know glossy magazines are full of enterprising types who threw in their humdrum administrative jobs and started making chutney, and now they're supplying Waitrose and being festooned with chutney rosettes . . . but does that actually happen to people like me?

Stu has always been a radial direction-changer. 'Forever *between* things,' as his ex put it, but that wasn't quite true. And now, when I think about it, his various employments – mechanic, manager of a motorbike shop that was swallowed up by a bigger company (hmm, familiar), followed by a hair-raising stint as a motorcycle courier and now the driving force behind the dispatching of emergency goji berries (or was that last season, and it's all about dried cherries now?) . . . well, I can see there's been some logical progression. But what am I good at, apart from peddling serum?

My seemingly faltering career is the last thing I want to discuss as I step into our house. I call out a cheery hello from the hallway, and poke my head around the living room door where Amy and Stu are chatting companionably about her forthcoming holiday with Bella's family.

'We haven't eaten yet,' Stu remarks. 'Thought we'd wait for you.'

'Oh, that's great, thanks. I'll just get changed . . .'

I head up to my room, grateful to pull off my tunic, trousers and shoes – it feels like shrugging off Sonia's disappproval – and slip on my comfiest PJs, ignoring the niggling thought that dressing for bed at 7.35 p.m. is a terribly old-person thing to do. So what? I'm not under scrutiny now. I cleanse off my make-up, splashing on cold water again and again until my skin feels as shiny-clean as a baby's.

Installed at the kitchen table, I sense the day's tensions ebbing away as Stu regales me with tales of a woman in Kilburn who had some kind of breakdown because he hadn't managed to source a particular kind of cheese. 'Ass cheese,' he says flatly.

'What?' Amy snorts, having been lured through by the aroma of spicy chicken sizzling in the pan.

'Well, Balkan donkey actually,' Stu corrects himself. 'The thing is, I can usually get hold of the stuff, but my trusty deli has discontinued the line.'

I chuckle and try, unsuccessfully, to focus on the delicious plateful Stu has put in front of me. However, the spectre of Sonia Richardson sneaks back into my mind and I can barely finish it.

'Everything okay?' Stu asks as I set down my cutlery.

I nod. 'Just a bit of an off day, that's all. I did manage to book a new venue for Mum's wedding, though—'

'Oh, that's great!' he exclaims.

'But then our new boss came to the store, and well, she seems to think I'm too gnarly and ancient to get to grips with the New Way, and basically I have the wrong attitude.'

'You don't look *old*,' Amy insists.

'Thank you, sweetheart,' I mutter.

'Seriously – I mean it. You look younger than Cecily . . .' She shovels in her dinner with her customary gusto.

'Amy, that's just not true.'

'Yes, you do. You could pass for, um . . .' She falters. 'Forty!'

I smile unsteadily. 'It's not really about that anyway. It's more . . .' I shrug. 'It's the *inside* of me that's old. I'm set in my ways, apparently, afraid of change . . .'

'No, you're not,' Stu insists. 'D'you know, without you I'd never have had the nerve to set up the business? Apart from Bob, you're the only person who didn't think I was a raving nutjob . . .'

'Actually,' I say with a smile, 'I *do* think you're a raving nutjob.'

He grins as Amy gets up from the table and delves into the cookie jar before wandering away, munching a cookie. 'Oh, c'mon,' he adds. 'I hate seeing you like this. Tell you what, why don't we do something tomorrow to cheer you up? We could get out of London, head for the coast, I'll take us somewhere on my bike . . .'

I shake my head. 'No, I can't. I have the pleasure of taking Mum wedding dress shopping tomorrow . . .'

'But she has a dress. I had the pleasure of seeing her modelling it.'

'I really am so sorry about that,' I say, shuddering.

'Not your fault . . .'

'. . . And anyway, she's decided it's not suitable so we're going to find another one, and then we're checking out the village hall I've booked, to see if it passes muster . . .'

'Right. So, you'll need a drink after all that, won't you? How about we do something tomorrow night? Bob can cover deliveries—'

I pause and look at him. 'I'm out tomorrow night too.'

'Ah, right. Meeting Pearl?'

'No . . . Antoine.'

I catch him giving me an inscrutable look. 'Antoine? You mean orange-for-a-face Antoine?'

'Yes,' I say with an awkward laugh.

Stu frowns. 'What's he doing in London?'

'He's here on business . . . '

'On a *Sunday*?'

'Yes, because he has a breakfast meeting on Monday and needs to make an early start.'

Stu looks nonplussed at this, and wanders over to the sink to fill the kettle, turning on the mixer tap with such force it spurts all over the front of his T-shirt. 'Shit!'

I try to suppress a smile. 'You *know* not to turn it on too hard.'

He mutters something under his breath, tugs off his T-shirt and drapes it over the back of a chair. Clad just in jeans now, I'm surprised to see how tanned he is; he must've been topping it up in the garden between deliveries.

'You're not . . . being *funny* about this, are you?' I venture.

'No, of course not. It's great to see you getting out and about.'

I chuckle. 'You're making it sound as if I'm ninety-seven.'

His face creases into a smile. 'Yeah, well, keep your wits about you, won't you? Don't let him feel you up inside a smelly old tweed jacket . . .'

'I promise you, there'll be none of that.'

He nods, seemingly reassured. 'So where are you meeting him?'

'At his hotel.'

'His *hotel*?' Stu splutters.

I open the washing machine door and crouch down to stuff in Amy's dirty laundry from the plastic basket. I really must train her to attend to such duties herself. 'Yes, in the *bar*,' I say, bewildered by his parental attitude. He

179

didn't make this kind of fuss when I was setting off to meet Beppie who just fancied a quick shag, or three-teeth-Marco.

'Great, well, just don't let the fucker break your heart again, that's all.'

I straighten up, unable to determine whether or not he's joking. 'It's just a drink because he happens to be in London, Stu. It's nothing.'

'Yeah,' he mumbles, 'I just don't want to see you being messed around, that's all.'

My heart seems to soften, and I step towards him and hug him tightly. 'You're so lovely and caring, you know that? But I was sixteen then, and I'm forty-six now. No one's going to mess me around.'

Chapter Eighteen

Despite a late night with Mo and the gang, Cam seems oddly keen to accompany me and his grandma on our day out. Not only to Little Cambersham village hall but firstly – and even more surprisingly – to the enormous out-of-town shopping mall that Mum favours.

'Just fancy a day out,' he says, climbing into the passenger seat of my car.

'Are you sure, love? I mean, we're choosing Mum's dress first and I know how much you hate shopping . . .'

'Aw, that won't take too long, will it?' His face pales. 'Stu didn't mention—'

I laugh. 'Ah, so he suggested you should come, did he?'

Cam shakes his hair out of his eyes. 'He just thought, y'know, that I could be a sort of . . .'

'A buffer,' I suggest.

He nods and grins. 'Yeah. Or a referee, I guess.'

I pull away from the parking space and smile, grateful to my son, and to Stu, despite him being so prickly last night.

We pick up Mum, with Cam obligingly moving into

the back seat, from which he gazes serenely at the sprawl of retail parks and car showrooms as we edge our way through the suburbs towards the mall. Mum *loves* a mall, or a 'shopping arcade', as she still calls them, viewing them as a vast, multi-stored version of Goldings back in Bradford: everything under one roof, no need to negotiate the outside at all.

On arrival, as predicted, she wants to make a beeline for Phase Eight while Cam ambles off to Starbucks. Eschewing the idea of a traditional wedding dress – thank heavens – Mum has decided to opt for the 'classy frock' option. However, Phase Eight fails to yield delights . . . as do Hobbs, Jaeger, LK Bennett, Monsoon and a whole host of other stores which I'd never heard of but seemed perfectly promising to me. I suggest John Lewis, with its many concessions – 'I'm getting *married*, I need to see the full ranges!' – and, with inspiration rapidly swilling away, Marks and Spencer. Mum snorts derisively. 'Maybe if I was just after a pair of pants.'

Onwards we tramp, with Mum shunning the offerings at Laura Ashley, Jigsaw and Coast. To my alarm, she glances briefly into the window of Agent Provocateur but I manage to whisk her away. In Jacques Vert, she deigns to try on a pistachio shift in layered damask, but it's deemed 'too mother-of-the-bride' and thrust back at the salesgirl after being tried on, with bronzer smudged around the neckline.

In a shop frequented mainly by teenagers – 'No harm in looking,' Mum trills – she admires a revealing 'little number', as she terms it, which might possibly have been tacked together from hankies. Although I hate to say it – and it's appalling to even *think* this way – it probably wasn't designed with a seventy-year-old woman in mind.

'I know it's quite young,' she concedes, giving the flimsy fabric a lustful stroke.

'It is a *bit*, Mum . . .'

She laughs. 'You never dressed young, even when you *were* young!'

I gawp at her, remembering that right now I could be on the back of Stu's bike, zooming down to the south coast. 'What does that mean exactly?'

Mum chuckles as we leave the store. 'Only joking, love. But, you know, I do think I have the figure to pull off something quite risqué, don't you? Turn a few heads? Ha – that'd set the cat among the pigeons with Hamish's buttoned-up family . . .' I nod mutely. 'I'm lucky,' she adds as we march along the brightly lit concourse, 'with my fast metabolism. You take more after your father . . .'

Well, thank you kindly. While we're at it, shall we criticise me some more on my day off? We stroll past a garish stationery store, its window filled with aggressive-looking greetings cards covered in expletives. HAPPY BIRTHDAY YOU GRUMPY OLD BASTARD . . . WE'LL MISS YOU, FUCKFACE. Who buys these things? Still, I am tempted to pop in to buy Mum a notebook in which she can list my many faults:

Had the audacity to work when her children were little.

Failed to marry her children's father – thus denying fascinator opportunities – and now, of course, it's too late.

Not a very good cook.

Always dressed like a geriatric, even when sixteen.

Fat.

Onwards we plod while I picture my darling amenable son immersed in one of his mangled novels, sipping his cappuccino, still being of the age where he enjoys spooning the chocolatey powder off the top.

'Are you going to the gym these days?' Mum enquires as she swerves, without warning, into an otherwise deserted branch of Karen Millen.

'Not at the moment, no. Not for about six years, actually.'

At first, I assume we've landed here by mistake. I have never quite 'got' Karen Millen, my impression being that everything is super-tight with alarming cut-away sections, requiring shoulders and back on display and throwing up all manner of bra conundrums. But perhaps that's because – as Mum pointed out – I have never 'dressed young'.

'Have you ever thought of going back?' she enquires, the hangers clanking as she peruses the rails.

'Er, not really, Mum. I can't imagine how I'd find the time, to be honest, and it's so expensive.' To distract her, I select a surprisingly simple dress in pale grey silk.

'Too old,' she remarks.

'Oh, it's not an age thing. I mean, I don't feel too *old* for the gym. I just don't enjoy being trapped in a sweaty room with all that terrible equipment—'

'No, I mean that dowdy dress,' she says briskly, scowling at it as I return it to the rail. 'I'm going to be a *bride,* Lorrie. Every bride should feel youthful on her big day!'

The sales assistant, a fresh-faced redhead who looks only marginally older than Amy, glides over with a bright smile. 'Hi, can I help you?'

'Oh, we're here for my mum, actually. She's looking for something for her wedding . . .'

If the girl is taken aback, she is adept at hiding the fact. 'How lovely. Shall I leave you to browse for a while?'

'Yes, thank you,' Mum says grandly, as if the store has been closed to the riffraff in her honour, and now busying herself by scrunching delicate garments in her fist.

184

'What are you doing?' I hiss.

'Checking if they crease,' she replies. 'That's the sign of quality fabric. It doesn't crease when you scrunch it.'

Now the assistant is frowning at Mum, but is clearly too scared to ask her to stop the scrunching.

'How about this?' Mum holds up a white body-con mini dress.

I shake my head. 'It looks like a giant support bandage. You know, like runners wear for a bad knee.'

She eyes me coolly. 'I think it's *lovely*.'

'Well, it is, and it's obviously great quality, you've been crushing it up in your fist for about ten minutes and yet it's completely uncreased.' I inhale slowly, trying to quell the ball of agitation that's building inside me. Is it normal, to become so riled after just ninety minutes spent with one's mother? Pearl doesn't feel that way – she goes out of her way to spend time with her parents – and nor does Stu, whose widowed mum still lives in Yorkshire and dotes on him. 'Don't you think it's a bit on the . . . tiny side, though?' I venture.

'You just said it was giant!'

I catch the eye of the salesgirl. 'Giant for a support bandage. Tiny for a dress.'

'You're so uptight,' Mum huffs. 'I don't know where you get it from, this perpetual worrying about what other people think. I mean, look at Cameron, take a leaf out of his book—'

'What does Cam have to do with this?'

'Such a lovely boy. So calm, nothing seems to ruffle him . . .' In a fit of rebellion, she marches to the back of the store with the white dress.

Well, of course it doesn't, I muse, irritably flicking through a rail of teeny-tiny quilted skirts. He is seventeen years old. He does pretty well at school, earns enough money to fund his active social life, and will never be roped into the organisation of his mother's wedding.

'Shall I pick out some other dresses,' I call after Mum, 'in case that one's not quite right?' *For instance, in case it makes you look like an Egyptian mummy?*

'If you like,' she sing-songs back as she disappears into the changing room.

With jaw clenched I continue to browse the rails, half-heartedly looking for a dress for myself and wondering if everything needs to be body-con these days. I mean, I thought that was over years ago. But it seems to have reared up again, like a troublesome pimple, requiring a person to eat virtually nothing at all.

Mum's gym-related enquiries churn around my brain as I gather together a selection of alternative dresses for her to try on. I joined the gym a year or so after David had died. Although it was more than I could afford, I'd read that exercise 'released endorphins' and figured that grappling with the terrible fixed weights might make me feel marginally less insane. I only went once. Even grief failed to make me thin. However little I ate, my body clung onto its pillowy reserves, as if they were a duvet – or a quilted skirt – that someone might try to snatch away at any minute.

'Lorrie? *Lorrie!* Come here!'

Shit. Mum's strangulating herself with the support bandage. I hurtle towards the changing room – look, Mum, I'm exercising! – and find her having emerged from her cubicle, encased in the white sheath.

'So, what do you think?'

'Er, I think . . .' I bite my lip.

Mum twists and turns, angling her hips and tilting her

bottom hither and thither as if to prove she can at least *move* whilst wearing it. It's not that she doesn't have the body for it. Her figure is enviably trim, the result of a lifelong dedication to Ryvita and cottage cheese – with the addition of pineapple whenever caution was thrown to the wind – plus the appetite-quashing effects of Spring Vegetable Cup-a-Soup ('Only fifty calories a serving, Lorrie. Shame you don't like it!'). However, it's such a young style – and so organ-squeezingly tight – that I can't help wincing. Mum is a striking-looking woman. She'd just look so much lovelier in something more elegant.

'Well?' she prompts me.

'I think there's a bit of a bra issue,' I say, diplomatically.

She glances down at her breasts which, I have to say, are impressively perky for *any* age. 'Yes, you're right. It's spoiling the line. I'll take it off.' Back in she goes, grunting behind the closed cubicle door and reappears, still wearing the bandage dress but with nipples visible. 'Better?'

'Erm . . .' I grip the alternative dresses and grimace. 'It's a bit . . .' *Nipply?* No, that won't do. 'I'm just not sure about the white, Mum.'

'Well, I am a bride,' she exclaims, and something inside me shifts uneasily. I picture my son, probably starting to wonder where we are by now, and experience a powerful urge to be with him.

'Yes, I know, but I think you could choose something . . . much prettier, don't you?'

'Oh.' Her face softens.

'And less . . . *stark*? Here, look – I picked out a few for you . . .' I hand her the dresses and, grudgingly, she disappears back into the cubicle.

For what feels like weeks, I peruse the shop with its lime sandals and cream leather handbags adorned with

187

buckles and gilt chains. In a few hours' time I'll be meeting Antoine, and I haven't given a thought as to what I might wear for that. I thought I'd have ages to plan my outfit but the day is rapidly slipping away, and we still have to drive out to Hertfordshire to check on the hall.

'Well?' Mum has reappeared, now wearing a fitted cobalt blue dress with delicate gold embroidery detailing around the neckline. It's incredibly pretty and sweet.

My heart shifts a little. 'You look lovely, Mum,' I say truthfully.

She bites her lip. 'Oh, I'm not sure . . .'

No, really – you do. And your grandson is probably on his third coffee by now, and I have a date tonight with a man I haven't seen since 'A View to a Kill' topped the charts . . . 'Honestly, I don't think you'll find anything better.'

She sighs, turns sideways and frowns. 'It's not very . . . weddingy, is it?'

'That doesn't matter. The colour is wonderful on you.'

She smiles coquettishly and steps out into the main shop – 'I need to see it in better lighting' – where the assistant enthuses that the dress could have been designed with her in mind.

'Oh, go on then,' she says, beaming. 'I'll take it.'

A clutch of deeply tanned twenty-somethings wander in, all long, highlighted hair and muscular calves. They probably don't even notice us but, if they do, I like to think they would agree that Mum looks sensational. Minutes later, she is linking her arm with mine, shimmering with pleasure, as we leave the store.

In the next shop, she shuffles and sighs impatiently as I try on a fitted dusky pink dress with a cream lace collar – just one single garment, requiring five minutes' waiting

188

time – which happens to fit perfectly and does wonderfully flattering things to my waistline. My phone bleeps as I'm getting dressed, and I snatch it from my bag, expecting Cam to be enquiring as to our whereabouts. *Just landed at Heathrow,* Antoine has texted. *Very much looking forward to seeing you tonight.*

Mum smiles quizzically as I emerge from the changing room. 'Oh, you didn't let me see. How was it?'

'Lovely. I'm going to buy it.'

'You do look pleased with yourself,' she teases. 'See, it's not so bad coming out shopping with me, is it, darling? We should do it more often.'

Chapter Nineteen

We find Cam immersed in a novel at a cafe table littered with muffin crumbs, and make our way to the car park.

'Got my dress, Cameron,' Mum announces.

'Great,' he says, mustering enthusiasm.

'Do *you* have your outfit picked out?'

He smiles as we arrive at our car. 'Er, no, but I'll find something, Grandma.'

'It'll be much easier,' I add, 'now there's no theme.'

'Yes, well,' she says, only slightly grudgingly, 'I suppose it might turn out for the best now that Hamish's parents won't be involved. You know they've hardly *welcomed* me . . .'

'Oh, Mum, I'm sure they'll come round eventually.'

She wrinkles her nose as she buckles herself into the passenger seat. 'They think I'm not of their class.'

I glance at her. 'Well, does it matter what they think? Hamish loves you. Anyone can see that.'

'Yeah, it's Hamish you're marrying,' Cam offers gamely, 'not his mum and dad.' This seems to appease her and as we pull out of the car park, I send silent thanks to Cam for being here today.

I have yet to meet Hamish's mum and dad – does he even call them that, or is it Mummy and Daddy in those circles? – and I'm intrigued to do so. Clearly, they are of the landed gentry type, and whenever I picture their home it's cluttered with muddy wellies, bouncy spaniels and fishing rods. My own in-laws – naturally I regarded them that way, despite David and I not being married – were a no-nonsense but kindly couple from London's East End, Lionel a tailor and Patricia a doctor's receptionist. They adored Cam and Amy, their only grandchildren, but passed away – Lionel first, followed by Patricia a mere three months later – the year following David's death. The previously buoyant couple seemed to be suddenly beset with a raft of chronic health concerns; it was as if they couldn't bear to carry on living after losing their only child. So, with Dad in Australia and Mum being too distracted to fully engage with my kids, grandparental attention has been fairly thin on the ground. Perhaps that's why Cameron is so incredibly kind to his grandma – at least, for a seventeen-year-old.

Aided by Google maps on his phone, he guides us through the leafy lanes of Hertfordshire. We pass through villages of red-brick terraces and Tudoresque cottages. Whilst I've never had the urge to leave London, I can see the appeal of softly rolling hills punctuated by the occasional church spire. We pass the gated entrance to Hamish's family seat, its north turret just visible through the woodland. Although Mum has visited Lovington Hall several times in the year she's known Hamish, she doesn't drive and therefore has no concept of where anything is, and seems quite surprised when I point it out.

'I assume Hamish is meeting us at the village hall,' I remark.

'Well, I told him to be there at three,' Mum says, 'like you said. But there's no need, you know. He'll just say it's *fine . . .*'

How dare he be so easily pleased! 'Yes, because all he really cares about is you and him getting married. Can't you see that's all that matters?'

She glances at me and frowns. 'Well, yes, I suppose you're right.'

I touch her hand. 'Can't you just relax, then, and appreciate that?'

She rubs at her eyes. 'Of course I can,' she murmurs, causing my heart to squeeze a little. It's no wonder she finds it difficult being so adored; she's simply not used to it. After Dad, none of Mum's subsequent men were terribly nice to her. Following credit-card-thieving Brian, she hooked up with John, a borderline alcoholic with a roving eye, then Larry who had the audacity to suggest she might have a boob job 'for me'. For him! As if it were as simple a procedure as trotting out to buy some fancy knickers. Then along came Hamish, who's been so unswervingly sweet and devoted in his old-fashioned way, suggesting that Mum move into his own modest cottage a few miles north of Lovington Hall only after they're married. I hope to God she doesn't screw things up.

'Nearly here,' Cam announces. 'Next on the left, Mum . . .'

The narrow lane, which looks as if it doesn't actually lead anywhere, takes us right to the front of Little Cambersham village hall.

Mum gazes out, seemingly not registering Hamish's gleaming racing green Daimler parked on the weed-punctured gravel, or indeed her husband-to-be standing beside it, hands clasped behind his back. She unclips her

192

seatbelt. 'This can't be it, surely? This shabby little place? Your phone must be wrong, Cameron.'

'Phones are *never* wrong,' he chuckles as we all climb out of the car and greet Hamish, who is dressed in his customarily formal attire of pale blue shirt, a tie with some kind of emblem on it, and beige slacks.

'Hello, darling,' he says, kissing Mum's cheek.

'Hello, sweetheart.' She musters a weak smile.

'This is exciting, isn't it?' he enthuses. 'Well done, Lorrie, for sorting it out!'

'Oh, it was *nothing* . . .'

Mum pulls a face as if trying to dislodge a morsel of food embedded in her back teeth. 'Is this *it*?'

'Yes, Marion – look.' Hamish slips a kindly arm around her shoulders and indicates the peeling wooden sign which hangs between two rotting windows.

'I think we're going to have to go back to the drawing board,' Mum mutters. 'Are you sure there's no chance of reopening that quarry, Haimie?'

'Not in time for the wedding, no, darling.' He smiles reassuringly and catches my eye.

The four of us step into the hall, where Walter Fadgett greets us amidst what appears to be quite a lively gathering. His face is almost entirely covered in abundant white beard, reminiscent of Captain Birdseye, and he grasps my hands warmly. 'Hello, hello, welcome to our humble abode!'

'Thank you,' I say, sensing Mum bristling beside me. 'Sorry we're a bit late. Hope we're not getting in the way . . .'

'Not at all,' he says jovially. 'It's just the Evergreen Club having a birthday gathering . . .'

'The Evergreen Club?' Mum exclaims, as if it were code

193

for the Spanking Society. She narrows her eyes at the dozen or so rather boisterous elderly ladies who are all seated around a long trestle table strewn with the remains of sandwiches and cake. The room is filled with shrieks of laughter, and someone has just popped a cork on a bottle of champagne.

'Yes, the place is well used,' he explains. 'It's a real hub of the community. So, this, as you can see, is our main social area . . .' He waves an arm grandly, and Mum's lips seem to wither as she surveys the plainly decorated room. The walls are beige, the lighting of the fluorescent strip variety, and a large cork pinboard is covered in splodgy paintings created, a stuck-on note reveals, by the children of the Sunday School. Another note, taped to the door of a wall cupboard, warns, MUGS FOR MUMS AND TODDLERS GROUP ONLY.

'Well, I think it's very jolly, Marion,' Hamish declares.

'It's great, Mum,' I offer, willing her to agree. 'Plenty of room for everyone . . .'

'Let me show you around,' Walter says, guiding us around the facilities – the tiny Formica kitchen, the bathroom with a single washbasin and cracked cistern, 'but still in good working order,' he adds proudly.

'The loos aren't up to much,' Mum hisses as we make our way back into the main hall.

'Mum, they're fine. No one's going to notice. It's not as if they'll expect Molton Brown toiletries . . .'

She turns to whisper something in Hamish's rather hairy ear, and he frowns and squeezes her hand.

'They're having a perfectly lovely time,' he murmurs, 'and they're not going to be here at our wedding, are they?'

The Evergreen ladies clink glasses. 'Like to join us?'

calls out a woman with an immaculate helmet of lilac hair.

'Thanks, but we're just looking around,' I reply pleasantly.

'This lovely couple are having their wedding reception here,' Walter announces with a note of pride.

'How wonderful!' the woman exclaims. 'Sure you can't manage a glass of champagne?'

'No, really—' I start.

'Ooh, are you the husband-to-be?' a lady in a loudly-patterned dress exclaims. 'Look, Jessie – a toy boy. Maybe there's hope for us yet!' There's a ripple of laughter as Mum scuttles towards the door.

'Well,' she mutters, stepping outside, 'it might be fine for the Evergreen Club . . .'

'Grandma, listen.' Cam takes her arm. 'It might look a bit . . . *y'know*. But I can sort the lighting. I do it all the time for gigs . . .'

'This isn't one of your *gigs*, Cameron . . .'

'No, but I can borrow all the gear, make it more, uh, weddingy . . .'

'You can do whatever you like,' Walter says, having followed us out, 'as long as it's all cleared away afterwards, of course.'

'We have to clear up after our own wedding?' Mum turns to Hamish in alarm.

'Me and the kids will take care of that,' I say quickly.

'You'll do nothing of the sort,' Hamish announces with uncustomary force. 'We have a wonderful cleaner at Lovington Hall. She'll see to everything. I think you've done marvellously, Lorrie, finding this place so quickly. Now we just have to let everyone know about the new venue.' Before Mum can protest anymore, Hamish is

195

murmuring that they really should go now, so I hand Mum her Karen Millen bag from my car. Mum is staying at Hamish's cottage for a few days in a rather nondescript village a short drive away. The plan is that they'll live there when they're married. Although I worry about how Mum will handle living in the country, I can't quite see Hamish in Mum's 1960s East London maisonette.

Mum tilts her head and throws me a pitying look, then turns to Hamish. 'Oh, I do wish Lorrie had someone to bring with her. My own daughter, coming to our wedding alone . . .'

Not this again . . .

'I'm sure she'll be fine,' Hamish says kindly. 'Lorrie's a very capable girl . . .' *Girl*, God love him.

'Are you sure Stu can't make it?' she asks, frowning.

'Mum, he'll be away in Venice at his sister's fortieth, you know that. Just relax, okay? All that matters is that you and Hamish have a wonderful day.'

*

The atmosphere is lighter as Cam and I drive home. First the dress, and now the hall; everything seems to be coming together. And now I have a date to get ready for. My stomach swills with nerves and anticipation as we crawl back through the suburbs.

Antoine Rousseau is in London. And I'm meeting him in – Christ – two hours' time. I let us into the empty house – Amy has been out holiday shopping again with Bella and Cecily, and I assume Stu is on deliveries.

'I might stay over at Mo's tonight,' Cam remarks.

'Okay, love. I'm out tonight too. Remember that French guy I met when I was sixteen?'

196

He nods, clearly not remembering; understandably, things I got up to as a teenager hold little interest for my kids.

'I'm meeting him for a drink in Covent Garden,' I add, at which he chuckles.

'Don't get offended if he says you like cake,' is his parting shot as he hurries out of the door.

I snigger and head upstairs where I undress quickly, flinging my clothes onto my bed and glimpsing my 'generous', unexercised body in the dressing table mirror. Should I force myself back to the gym at some point? In the normal scheme of things, I don't dwell on how my body might be 'improved', preferring to focus instead on the superficial (hurrah for make-up!). However, in the aftermath of spending time with Mum, I tend to view myself through her eyes, as someone who really should acquaint herself with a stairmaster – if such instruments of torture still exist – which reminds me that I am in fact ravenous, having not eaten since breakfast.

I text Antoine: *Should I eat first or shall we have dinner?*

Let's have dinner, he replies. *I'll reserve a table at the hotel if that's okay. Do you have any dietary restrictions?*

I smile at his query and tap out a reply: *No, I eat everything.* A knot of anxiety tightens in my chest. Now I sound like a heifer.

Under the hot blast of the shower, I rake at my legs and underarms with a razor in the manner of scraping ice off a windscreen – not that he'll see, but that's not the point. I dry off and, still wrapped in a towel, I stare at the dresses hanging in my wardrobe. There aren't many, but still, after expressing an opinion on dress after dress with Mum, I am incapable of making a decision. All I know is that the pink one I bought today is, whilst lovely, far too posh for a casual drink.

As I try on a selection, I discover that a couple are, depressingly, too tight around the middle. The black-and-white spotty frock I wore on my Ralph date – which does fit – evokes unsettling memories, and my simple red shift looks far too 'ta-daaahhh, I'm *so* excited to be seeing you!' So, jeans it is, with a stripy top; hell, I hope he doesn't think I'm trying to look French. Since when did it become the law that all middle-aged women must dress like Breton fishermen?

I curl my lashes and apply my make-up, aiming for a natural look to show that tonight *isn't* a big deal at all: just a touch of primer, base, concealer, three shades of eyeshadow, eyeliner, brow pencil, blusher and ample mascara, plus La Beauté's famous all-day lipstick which, I realise now, is actually quite a lot of make-up, and I really do look *terribly-excited-to-see-you-Antoine*, entirely by accident. Still, no time to tone it down now, and at least I've managed to hold back from dabbing on some glittery highlighter on my brow bones. I gather up my make-up and stuff it into its pouch, cramming it into my shoulder bag as I scamper downstairs.

The front door opens and Stu walks in. 'Hey, you look good! Where are you off to?'

'I'm meeting Antoine, remember?'

His brows shoot up. 'Oh, God, yeah! It's the big night. I'd forgotten.' He pulls off his helmet and tries, unsuccessfully, to un-flatten his hair with his hand.

I frown. 'Not too much, is it? The make-up, I mean?'

'Not at all. You look amazing. Really lovely. So, um . . . how did it go with your mum?'

'Really well,' I say, tugging on my jacket. 'We found her a dress and bullied her into giving her seal of approval on the village hall . . .'

'Get you, pulling it all together . . .'

I laugh stiffly. There's a sort of forced jollity between us, and now I'm aware of Stu giving me a curious look. 'What's up?' I ask.

'Nothing. So, um, I hope you have a good night . . .'

'Thanks.' I peer at him, trying to read his guarded expression. 'I'm quite nervous actually.'

'What is there to be nervous about?'

I throw him a baffled look. 'What he'll *think*, obviously . . .'

He shrugs. 'What d'you think he'll think? "Wow, Lorrie Foster's grown up into a beautiful woman!"'

I reach for his hand and squeeze it. 'Thanks. You're making me feel so much better.'

He shrugs. 'Anyway, he knows what you're like now, doesn't he? Don't tell me he hasn't pored over your Facebook photos . . .'

'Well, yes, I suppose he might have.'

'He *will* have,' Stu says firmly.

I smile at the thought of Antoine scrolling through my pictures, the way I have with his. 'Oh, I know I'm being silly. It's just a drink, no big deal at all. And at least I don't have those awful yellow highlights anymore . . .'

'You looked cute with those yellow highlights,' Stu calls after me as I step out into the night.

*

And that's what I tell myself as I stride, already running late, towards the tube station: that our teenage thing was no big deal, and that Antoine Rousseau was merely a brief amusement sent to rescue me from spending my entire trip scribbling down the words to pop songs. He saved

199

me from bottom-of-the-barrel lyric transcribing, that's all.

On the tube, I pull my compact mirror from my make-up bag and check my face. I brush my hair and powder my nose like an elderly lady might, and touch up my red lipstick. As long as it doesn't involve spraying clouds of perfume, or sawing at toenails or plucking hairs from the chin, I have no problem with engaging in beautification on public transport. In fact, I think there's something quite elegant about seeing a woman fixing her face in a cafe or on a train. Tonight, though, the make-up isn't working. I am emitting an aura of abject terror; if my face were an exhibit in a gallery, it would be called something like 'urban decay'.

I snap my compact shut and plunge it back into my bag, conscious of hotness radiating from my face throughout the carriage. I'd assumed it was a gradual thing, this age-related dwindling of oestrogen, but it seems to rear up in waves and right now I am in the throes of a full-on perimenopausal sweat. I snatch a crumpled copy of *Metro* from the next seat and flick through it. An entire page is filled with photos of 'beach-ready' bikini-clad celebrities. I discard the paper and try to soothe myself with non-Antoine-related thoughts, such as: my successful day out with Mum and Cam, and how lovely it'll be to see Mum and Hamish get married – as long as she goes easy on the booze and lets me just get on with doing her make-up instead of hectoring me ('is a *bit* more bronzer too much to ask?'). Then, as I try to dredge up more soothing thoughts, I somehow spin backwards in time to a hot July day in '86, the day Valérie had been snide about me using 'her' shampoo and called me 'ma grosse' with a smirk as if we were genuine friends and this was her pet name for me: 'Fatty.'

That's what I was like at sixteen: forever worrying about how others viewed me. My own daughter breezes through a life filled with friends and sporting successes. She thinks of her body in terms of strength and speed – of what it can *do* – rather than a perpetual source of humiliation. I wouldn't be feeling like this if I was the kind of woman who strides into Karen Millen and thinks, 'Ooh, gorgeous, sexy clothes!' rather than, 'Bra issues.'

The evening is warm and muggy as I emerge from Covent Garden tube station, the pavements thronging with people all heading out for the evening. I speed-walk down Long Acre, turn left into a narrow street and spot the hotel. It's a discreet boutique affair in stark contrast to the bland, faceless place where Dennis Clatterbrock ranted on about his tomato fertilisers. The hotel's name gleams in gold above the doorway. I stop outside and peer in, realising I am still boiling hot. I pull off my jacket but the prospect of carrying it elegantly – tossed nonchalantly over my shoulder, or bundled under one arm like a tantrumming toddler? – seems far too tricky a prospect so I shrug it back on.

A group of guests emerge from the hotel, all chatting and looking happy about the night ahead. I step into the wood-panelled foyer. The polished floors are strewn with faded rugs, and antique tapestries hang on the walls; everything is ageing perfectly. I glimpse my reflection in a tarnished gilt-framed mirror and see myself as a rather tired-looking woman of forty-six, whose last date resulted in listening to a man masturbating while I bought fabric conditioner in a supermarket. It's just not how I'd imagined my adult life would pan out.

I pause, trying to steady myself as I eye the entrance to the bar. And there he is, sitting waiting for me in a stripy armchair in the far corner. Antoine Rousseau, so handsome with his dark eyes and chiselled features, my breath catches in my throat. He's just as I remember him; older, of course, but all the lovelier for it. He hasn't spotted me yet. It's just a drink, I tell myself. He just happened to be coming to London on business and, in an idle moment, thought, 'Why not?' He had a quick search on Facebook and there I was.

He turns and sees me and stands up: not the boy of eighteen just back from *le camping,* but a man – a tall and utterly gorgeous man, more striking than his gangly teenage self, with a smile that sends me spinning back to that summer.

The summer *I* came alive too.

He strides towards me. 'Lorrie! It's good to see you!' He hugs me and kisses my cheeks.

'Hello, Antoine,' I say over my clattering heart. I smile awkwardly and try to smooth down my hair.

He steps back and surveys my face as if he can't believe I'm standing there. 'Lorrie Foster, after all these years. And don't you look beautiful? You really haven't changed at all.'

Chapter Twenty

I laugh because I don't know what else to do. 'Thank you,' I manage, 'but I'm sure that's not true. Still, at least no mullet these days!'

'Mullet?'

'Oh, erm, that hairstyle, you know – long at the back, bit spiky on top like a pineapple.' He blinks at me. 'George Michael, Duran Duran, Kajagoogoo . . .' Hell what am I *on* about?

'Kajagoogoo?' Antoine looks baffled.

'Eighties band. I probably wrote out the lyrics to some of their songs . . .'

He breaks into a smile at the recollection. 'I remember that. All that writing! Poor girl, I thought. I'll have to take her away from all of this.' He touches my arm and a spark shoots through me. 'Shall we sit down?'

'Yes, of course . . .' Ohh, that accent, I reflect as we make our way to the two velvety armchairs at the small table in the corner of the bar. The lighting is flatteringly dim, the room filled with the hubbub of chatter and laughter and unobtrusive jazz. An aproned waiter strides over.

'A white wine, please,' I say.

'Sancerre?' he suggests.

'Oh, yes. That would be lovely.'

'A glass of Merlot for me,' Antoine says, then turns to me. 'So, it's been quite a while, hasn't it?'

'Yes, it has. I couldn't believe it when you popped up on Facebook . . .'

'Well, I came across those old pictures of us and decided to take a look. You weren't hard to find. There were a few Lorrie Fosters, and I knew you might be married and no longer a Foster at all . . . *have* you been married?'

I shake my head, momentarily floored by his directness. 'No, I haven't. How about you?'

'I was, but that's over now. So, you didn't mind me sending you a friend request?'

'Not at all. It was lovely to hear from you.'

His gaze meets mine and my insides seem to somersault. 'I wasn't sure if you'd want to be in touch,' he adds. 'I thought, will she be *horrified* to hear from me out of the blue like this?'

I sip my wine, willing him to go on. I want to sit here all night listening to Antoine talking so Frenchly; if I could get away with it I'd record him secretly on my phone.

'Of course I wasn't horrified. It was a wonderful surprise . . .'

'And I knew this trip was coming up,' he continues, 'and I thought, maybe she's ended up in London, like she said she wanted to? It was just a hunch.'

'Well, I did and here you are!' I seem to be having trouble saying anything sensible.

'Yes, just for one night, unfortunately . . .'

I assess his face: the dark, compelling eyes, the cheekbones and chin clearly defined. His light brown hair is neatly cut with a hint of grey at the temples. He is wearing a crisp blue and white striped shirt and black trousers – he's made an effort, or perhaps this is the way he dresses all the time? – and smells gorgeous, of something spicy with a hint of orange. He looks, I realise, as if he is on a proper date, and I wish now that I'd gone for the spotty dress from Nutmeg Gallery day, or even the red one. What made me choose jeans and a Breton top, as if I was nipping out for milk?

'. . . Flying back to Nice at nine tomorrow night,' Antoine continues. 'Wish it was longer. I do love London, I'm usually here a couple of times a year' – all these visits to my home city and I didn't know! – 'and I've often thought, I wonder, well . . .' He breaks off and I sense the hormonal hotness surging up again.

'So, what does your company do?' I ask.

'Recruitment. Headhunting. We're based in Paris but set up a new division in Nice. We're looking at designing new appraisal procedures to roll out across the company.'

'Sounds interesting.' His English is flawless, laced with that gorgeous French accent. I am finding it difficult to concentrate on what he's saying.

'Oh, it's not really so interesting.' He laughs self-deprecatingly. 'But it's all about getting the best out of people, identifying their strengths, focusing on performance and the pursuit of excellence within the commercial landscape.' He runs a hand over his hair. 'Do stop me if I'm boring you.'

'No, no, not at *all* . . .' Normally, this kind of talk wouldn't have me gripped in rapt attention. But right now Antoine could be describing the chemical make-up of owl droppings and I'd still sit here happily and soak it all in.

He smiles, seeming flustered for a moment. 'Um, what was I saying?'

'Commercial landscapes,' I prompt him, noticing now how terribly attractive his eyelashes are.

'Oh, that's enough about me. So, tell me about your work. It's make-up, isn't it? That's what you do?'

'Yes, that's right . . .'

'And do you enjoy it? I imagine you're very good at it.'

'Well, I hope so. It's selling, basically, although it feels more, uh . . .'

'. . . Creative?'

'Yes, I suppose it does. It's a lovely company I work for. French, actually, set up by two sisters from Grasse.'

'That's fairly close to Nice . . .'

'Really? There was talk at one time of key team members going over for a weekend, a sort of celebration of beauty. The founders, Claudine and Mimi, like to stay in touch with the staff. I guess they see themselves as sort of maternal types . . .' I tail off and sip my wine; it's in a different league to the usual cheap stuff I quaff at home. Never mind learning to appreciate 'difficult' art. Buying less, more expensive wine would surely make me properly grown-up. 'But big changes are happening,' I add. 'We've just been taken over by Geddes and Cox, have you heard of them?'

'Yes, of course—'

'Well, I have to admit it's been a bit of a shock. Looks like there'll be no trips to Grasse now.'

'That's a real pity. So, what about your family? Your children's father?'

Ah, that one. I should have figured out how I'd handle this, and now it feels wrong to talk about David, to spring it upon Antoine out of thin air. 'He's not around,' I say quickly. 'It's just me and the kids, and we have a lodger – Stu, he's an old friend from up north. Helps to pay the bills, you know. So, um, you mentioned that your kids live in Paris . . .'

'Yes, that's right – they're with Nicole, their mother—'

'You mean Valérie's friend Nicole?' I exclaim. *White-vest-no-bra Nicole, who taught me the ways of make-up?*

He smiles. 'Yes, she was my wife. You remember her?'

'I do, yes. Very tall, slim, long blonde hair . . .' *Baby blue eyes, prominent nipples on permanent display . . .*

'. . . and completely crazy,' he adds, 'although it took me a long time to figure that out . . .' Nicole, who he dumped me for so heartlessly! Not that I care about that now. He was just a boy, and what eighteen-year-old would remain faithfully in love with a girl who'd gone back to England when he had a real live girlfriend-in-waiting right there?

Antoine checks his watch; a simple white face with a matt black leather strap. I can't think of any other man I know who wears one. 'We should go through for dinner,' he says as, right on cue, our waiter glides over and tells us that our table is ready. He deftly places our drinks onto his tray, and we follow him through to the dining room.

'Will this be okay for you?' he asks.

'Yes, great,' Antoine replies as we take our seats at a table next to a window.

'Look at those lovely flats out there,' I remark, glancing out at the courtyard as we are handed menus. 'Imagine living there, tucked away in Covent Garden.'

'It's a great part of the city,' he says.

'It is, but I don't come here very often. I suppose I tend to think, Covent Garden, street theatre, jugglers and all that.'

207

He smiles. 'So, which part of London d'you live in?'

'Bethnal Green in the East End. We moved there when I was expecting Cam, our first child. It's always felt buzzy and friendly, and there's quite a community feel. It's become gentrified of course, like pretty much everywhere.'

'And before that, where were you?'

'In Hackney. Well, Hackney Downs, actually – more like Clapton. A tiny two-bedroomed flat, three floors up, not so great for a baby and bit of a crazy area back then – I mean, there was a park, but you were likely to get attacked by some nut with his snarling devil dog so we thought, okay, enough of "lively" areas with the dodgy cab firm with its terrible cars – you know the type, you glance down and spot a great hole on the floor of the passenger seat, you can see the actual *road* . . .'

I break off and laugh, taken aback by the way Antoine is looking at me as I chatter incessantly now. It's as if he *knows*. Amidst the babble about taxis and devil dogs he *knows* something happened to me after we moved. 'So we bought a little terraced house,' I continue. 'You could do that back then. It wasn't half a million for a shoebox like it is now.' Agh, now I've lurched into house prices! I never talk about stuff like this. What's got into me tonight? One large glass of wine, that's what – on a stomach that hasn't seen food since breakfast, and after a day spent schlepping around every high street chain known to womankind.

'Oh, we should decide what to eat,' Antoine says as the waiter reappears.

I quickly scan the menu, delighted to see that, despite the panelled elegance of the room, many of the dishes would come under the banner of nursery food. 'Would it be terribly immature of me to go for the macaroni cheese?'

'Not at all,' the waiter says. 'It's our speciality. It's been on the menu for ten years.' I think of joking *not the same batch, hopefully,* but think better of it.

'And I'll have the seabass,' Antoine says, quickly perusing the wine list which we haven't glanced at either. 'Did you enjoy the Sancerre?'

'It was lovely, yes.'

'We'll have a bottle of that then, please.' He catches my expression as the waiter leaves. 'This is my treat tonight.'

'Oh, no, I couldn't possibly—'

'Please, Lorrie, I want to.'

I smile. 'That's very kind of you. So, tell me about your life,' I prompt him, 'in Nice.'

'Well, I have to say it's terribly work-focused. I live alone, in a top-floor apartment – it's lovely, I listen to music, read a lot, run along the beach sometimes, try to look after myself, you know . . .'

I relax again as he enthuses about running – 'it's almost meditative' – and by the time our food arrives, beautifully presented on fine white china, we are talking over each other as people do when it feels as if there's so much to tell, so much to catch up on. It strikes me that *this* is the kind of date I'd hoped for when I'd allowed myself to be frog-marched into the murky territories of datemylove-lymum.com.

The waiter appears and removes the empty wine bottle from its silvery container.

'Another?' Antoine suggests, terribly un-Frenchly, I'd have thought: I'd always assumed it was only us Brits who guzzled in copious quantities.

'I'd love to, but don't you have a meeting first thing?'

'Oh, that'll be *fine*,' he says breezily, and so another

bottle arrives and now I'm hearing how beautiful Nice is, how diverse and exciting.

'You should visit me sometime,' Antoine suggests.

'That would be fun,' I say lightly.

'No, I mean it. I'd love you to.'

'Well, maybe one day,' I say, dismissing it as a tipsy suggestion as our table is cleared and we are handed the dessert menus. I choose a chocolate tart which somehow manages to be cloud-like *and* sinfully rich.

'That was delicious,' I say finally, as Antoine pays the bill. 'You must let me treat you sometime.'

'Okay,' he says, grinning, 'you can – when you visit me in Nice.' Then, without further discussion – Antoine merely suggests 'You can show me around London' – we leave the restaurant and step out into the warm night.

As we wander towards Soho, I tell Antoine how different it was when I arrived here, aged twenty and thrilled to be a part of it all. Living in a rowdy houseshare with a bunch of girls, I loved the sleazy bars and cheap Italians where we'd fuel ourselves on spaghetti carbonara in preparation for nights on the town. I was temping at the time, and somehow managed to eke out my meagre earnings so I could go out nearly every night. My friends and I hung out in shady drinking clubs, deep down in the bowels of townhouses or up dingy staircases, requiring a rap on the door and a few moments' nervy hesitation as the owner – usually a fierce middle-aged woman with make-up trowelled on – would decide whether or not to let us in. I'd met David in one of those scuzzy little places. We'd found ourselves squashed together on a decrepit sofa at 3 a.m., and stayed there happily sipping terrible wine until we were finally tipped out into the bleary morning light.

'I'd always wanted to live here,' I tell Antoine as we

meander the streets, 'right from when I was a little girl.'

He smiles. 'You wanted to escape from Yorkshire, I remember you saying. You wanted to live someplace where you could be yourself, be anyone you wanted to be.'

'Really? You remember me saying that?'

He laughs lightly. 'I remember lots of things.'

We stop and, for no particular reason, find ourselves looking into the window of a bakery. It's just a chain, as most places are around here these days.

'So do I,' I say, smiling.

We are looking at each other now, and perhaps it's all that wine but I am mesmerised by his face. The boy I kissed on that bridge, and at the goat farm and down by the lake, is here in Soho! How could that possibly be? 'What time is it?' I ask.

He checks his grown-up-man's watch. 'Ten past one.'

I'm amazed at where the time has gone. 'Really? That late? I really should be getting home . . .'

'Me too. I suppose I should be sensible. Shall we get you a taxi?'

'Yes, I think so.' I glance down the street for a yellow light, and that's when Antoine takes my hand. My heart seems to somersault as a cab drives by.

'You really are very beautiful,' he says.

I look at this man, the first person to kiss me properly in a way that sent fireworks exploding in my head, and then somehow we are kissing now, spinning back to 1986 and I'm sixteen again, with my mullet and terrible high-lights, and all the people and traffic of London fade away.

We pull apart and smile. 'Oh,' is all I can say.

Without my noticing, Antoine's arms have wrapped around my waist. 'Well, *that* was as magical as I remembered it.'

211

'It was,' I murmur.

'It's been so good to see each other again.'

'Yes, it really has.' Over his shoulder, another yellow light catches my eye. 'I should get this cab,' I add reluctantly.

He turns and flags it down. 'Can I see you again? Before I leave, I mean?'

'I'd love to, but aren't you working tomorrow?'

'Yes, but we can't leave it another thirty years. That would be insane—'

'No,' I say, laughing, 'I'd be – Christ – seventy-six . . .' The cab pulls to a halt beside us.

'My meetings finish at two and I don't need to leave for the airport until six . . . I don't suppose you're free?'

'Yes, I'm off tomorrow . . .' I step towards the cab's open passenger window.

'Let's text to arrange it.'

'Great,' I say, turning to the driver. 'Pine Street, E2 please.' The driver gives me an amused look and nods.

I look back at Antoine. 'It's been a wonderful night. Thank you for dinner.'

'No – thank *you*, Lorrie. I've had such a great time. So d'you think you can forgive me for stopping writing to you all those years ago?'

I chuckle. 'I think so, just about.'

He shakes his head. 'I was such an idiot.'

'No, you weren't. You were just a boy and it's *fine* – of course it is.' I climb into the cab and ease into the back seat.

'Pine Street,' the driver reiterates.

'Yes please.' I glance back to see Antoine standing there. He is smiling and raising his hand to wave and looks, I realise, a little shell-shocked, as if something has happened. Well, it has.

The driver pulls away, and perhaps it's just the wine and the kisses but London looks amazing tonight, a swirl of lights all around. I close my eyes momentarily, trying to steady my pounding heart.

'Hey, love,' the cabbie says. My eyes ping open, and I catch him observing me in his rear-view mirror. 'Looks like *somebody* had a good night.'

I laugh, assuming he's noticed I'm a little tipsy – and on a Sunday night too. But when I pull out my compact mirror to check my face, it seems that La Beauté's famous all-day lipstick isn't quite as kiss-proof as we claim.

Chapter Twenty-One

It's almost 2 a.m. by the time I'm home and the house is silent. Like a late-homecoming teenager with booze on her breath, I creep in, closing the front door quietly behind me and hanging my jacket on the hook in the hall.

I pad upstairs to the bathroom and wipe away my make-up, and when I examine my freshly cleansed face in the mirror I see that just-kissed look, a gleam in my eyes and a mouth that just won't stop twitching into a delighted smile. I think about Antoine's dark eyes, his lips, that brush of his tongue, and my body starts tingling again. I clean my teeth briskly, trying to normalise myself in case Stu or one of the kids should get up for a pee and discover me looking all freshly snogged.

Tucked up in bed, I'm convinced I won't sleep – my heart still seems to be rattling away at an alarming rate – but what feels like moments later, I am coming to, with daylight beaming in through the gauzy white curtain and Antoine's kisses still lingering on my lips. I pull on my dressing gown over my pyjamas. At just before nine, Stu is the only one up, also still in PJs – his loose-fitting checked bottoms and a plain grey T-shirt – and making toast. 'Hi,' I say, which morphs into a throat-clearing cough.

'Hey, *here* you are.' He leans against the worktop and smiles. 'Didn't hear you come home last night, dirty stop-out. Thought Frenchie-boy had snuck you into his hotel!'

I laugh stiffly. ''Course he didn't. As if I'd do that on a first date.'

It's a joke, but seems to miss its mark. 'So it *was* a date, then?'

'Oh, you know, just a drink. And dinner . . .'

'Pretty late for dinner . . .' He snatches the toast as it pops up.

'Well, er, we had a walk around Soho . . .' *And the most delicious kiss, the kind that almost stops you breathing . . .*

'Sounds great.' I watch Stu as he manhandles the lid off a jar of crunchy peanut butter, wondering why he's behaving like this. There was none of this prickly quizzing after any of my previous dates. 'Did you mention the fact that he totally broke your heart?' he asks, slathering peanut butter onto his toast.

'No, of course I didn't!' I exclaim.

He takes a big bite and munches it thoughtfully. 'So, will you keep in touch, d'you think?'

My back teeth clamp together, and I busy myself by making coffee which Stu usually does, only he seems to have forgotten this morning. 'Actually, we're meeting up again today.'

He wipes his mouth on his hand. 'I thought he was here on business?'

'He is, yes, but his meetings finish at two.'

'Two o'clock? It was hardly worth him coming over!'

I watch, stuck for words, as he studies the remains of

215

his toast and, apparently having gone off the idea of eating it, drops it into the bin. 'It was just meetings,' I say rather feebly.

'Yeah, whatever,' he says, leaving me staring, bewildered, as he strides out of the kitchen.

While he showers or potters about upstairs – I'm really not concerned with what he's doing when he's clearly in a godawful mood – I sip my coffee at the table and flick through the weekend papers. Amy emerges just after ten in search of breakfast, followed by her brother shortly afterwards. They bustle around the kitchen, making toast and filling bowls with Rice Krispies; there always seems to be a huge amount of activity and receptacles used whenever teenagers fix themselves something to eat. Kitchen trashed, they drift off to watch TV in the living room. There's been no quizzing about last night's date, probably because they realise there'll be no undead wife/stinky jacket hilarity. Or maybe they've forgotten I was out at all.

I check my phone for texts – nothing – then Facebook, my heart performing a sort of flip on seeing Antoine's message.

Great to see you last night! Would you like a picnic in Hyde Park today?

Sounds perfect, I reply. *We could meet at Hyde Park Corner tube station. Shall we say 2 o'clock? Would that work for you?*

Yes, looking forward to it! I'll bring us something to eat. So happy we can meet up again :)

216

I spend the rest of the morning in a scruffy tracksuit, rattling through household chores with uncharacteristic speed and enthusiasm. Stu reappears and grabs his crash helmet, leaving with an overly cheery goodbye; still a little stung by his attitude this morning, I focus on showering and dress in preparation for meeting Antoine.

'I'm going out for a few hours,' I tell the kids as I'm about to leave; jeans and a T-shirt today, park-appropriate with minimal make-up. It would seem strange to turn up all dolled up for a picnic when I wore jeans to an elegant restaurant in a boutique hotel.

'Are you back on that website?' Cam swivels from the sofa with interest.

'No, love . . .'

'You're not seeing Jacket Man again, are you?' Amy asks.

'No, it's not Jacket Man. It's Antoine, the French guy . . .'

'Him *again*?' Cam exclaims, raising a brow to suggest that it's something significant.

I laugh lightly. 'We're just going for a walk in Hyde Park before he catches his flight. That's all.'

And this time, I set out without even the faintest fluttering of nerves. The day is breezy and bright, the sky a wash of pale blue, and my heart feels as light as a cloud. Oh, that kiss last night! I keep grinning stupidly, and have a ridiculous urge to do a little jump on my way to the tube station. Antoine Rousseau, after all these years! I step onto the train, banning myself from even considering the fact that he is flying home to Nice tonight.

He's waiting when I arrive, this time more casually dressed in a black T-shirt and jeans, at the top of the steps at Hyde Park Corner station. 'Hello, you,' he says warmly, pulling me in for a hug.

'Hi, Antoine.' His arms are around my waist as he holds me. We pull apart, and he bends to pick up a brown canvas bag with greeny-blue handles, emblazoned with the initials F&M.

'What's in there?' I ask.

'Our picnic, of course!'

I peer at it. 'Where did you buy it?'

'Fortnum and Mason.'

'Really?' I exclaim. 'You bought our picnic there?'

'Yes?' he says in an enquiring tone, and I laugh. 'What's funny?' he asks, smiling.

'The way you said it. Sort of, "Don't you buy all your picnics from Fortnum and Mason?"'

He chuckles, but I can tell he's still a little confused as we make our way into the park with the sun beating down on us. There are joggers and elderly couples, and a group of Japanese tourists are trying to work out which path to take. Rugs and blankets are strewn on the grass. Picnics in all guises are being picked over all around us: a toddler's birthday complete with balloons, a group of women all wearing white shirts and black skirts, perhaps just released from their shift somewhere. There are numerous dogs, ranging from small, scruffy mutts to regal King Charles Spaniels, the whole scene laid out before us as if to show how lovely and diverse London can be on a bright summer's day.

'How did your meeting go?' I ask as we settle on a shady spot beneath the sprawling branches of an oak.

'Oh, really well,' he says with the kind of confidence that suggests it's nothing really, nipping over from Nice to London for half a day's work. 'So, are you hungry?'

'I am, yes.' I watch, transfixed, as Antoine pulls out a white paper cloth. He tears off its clear cellophane wrapping

218

and spreads it out on the grass, then begins to set out our food.

When he suggested we had a picnic, I'd pictured a couple of sandwiches, but here is a plate of gravlax and a tiny pot of dill sauce, and salads of roast peppers, charred aubergines, asparagus and exotic cured hams. There are strawberries and cheeses, seed-covered crackers and, most pleasingly, a bottle of rosé.

'This is amazing!' I exclaim. 'It's really all for us?'

'Well, I can't take it home,' he says with a grin, then apologises for the plastic glasses, plates and cutlery as if I'd be likely to say, *Well, that's just not good enough*.

If last night was our reintroduction, today seems so natural, as if the thirty-year gap never happened. We eat, and we drink, and it feels as if my heart has stopped as Antoine gently kisses my lips. 'You're a beautiful woman, Lorrie,' he says.

I smile, not knowing how to respond. No one says things like that to me. Well, Stu does occasionally, but not like that. 'You look great,' he might tell me in a morale-boosting way, to reassure me when I'm scampering out on a date. But this is different. Antoine holds my hand, and I kiss his neck gently, sensing him shiver slightly at the touch of my lips. We kiss again, then he leans back, surveying me, his dark eyes meeting mine.

'So, what happened?' His voice is gently enquiring, his fingers still wrapped around mine.

'About what?' I'm genuinely confused.

'About your children's father. I sensed last night, that there was something . . . I hope it's okay to ask?' My stomach seems to clench. 'Of course, if you'd rather not talk about it . . .'

I pick at tufts of grass, rubbing them between my fingers.

'No, it's fine, really. I do want to tell you.' And out they tumble: all those terrible details about head injuries, life-support machines and death, for the first time in years because, naturally, everyone I'm close to knows precisely what happened. I didn't tell Ralph or Beppie or three-teeth-Marco. Pete Parkin from electricals had heard that my partner had died in an accident, but other people's tragedies are unnerving and the unspoken rule was that we wouldn't discuss it. Our most common topic of conversation was his parrot, if I recall.

'. . . and everything calmed down,' I explain now, 'but of course, it didn't really, at least, not *inside* me. It was still there. The accident, I mean.'

He nods. 'It's the sort of thing you never recover from. You can't expect to.'

I sip my wine – it's lukewarm now – and consider this for a moment. 'Well, you do start living again, and of course, there was Cameron and Amy to think about, so I couldn't just fall apart—'

'You were allowed to, though. It was to be expected.' He wraps an arm around me, and I lean into him as my eyes mist.

'I'm sorry, I'm going on about this too much.' What am I thinking, blurting all of this out?

'Of course you're not . . .' He kisses the top of my head. It feels both loving and protective.

'It's not very cheering,' I murmur.

'No, but we don't need to be cheering, do we? Can't we just be ourselves?'

I turn and look at him. 'You're right, and I can't tell you how refreshing that is.' I reach for a strawberry and bite into it. 'I've been on a few dates recently. Nothing that led to anything. In fact, they were disastrous really.'

I run through a brief résumé of men I've met during the past few weeks, and soon the mood lifts and we are laughing, both giddy on wine all over again.

'These men must be crazy,' Antoine exclaims.

'Well, it was an experience, I suppose. Something to amuse the kids . . .'

'Can I say something?'

'Yes, of course.'

'I really think – well, I don't quite know how to say this, but I think you're an amazing person.'

'Why d'you say that?'

'Well, everything you've done. Since David died, I mean. Keeping everything together, building your career . . .'

'Career,' I repeat with a disparaging chuckle.

'. . . and raising your children alone. I know how tough that is. Well, I *don't*, obviously, because Nicolas and Elodie live with their mother hundreds of miles away in Paris, but it's a hard job. It's always changing. They seem to love you madly and then they can't bear to be with you. It's as if they suddenly become allergic to their own parents!'

'It's exactly like that,' I agree.

'And you never quite know what to do for the best.'

I smile and snuggle closer to his chest. We must look like a couple, I decide. Just an ordinary couple having a picnic on a gorgeous summer's day. 'Tell me about it. But, you know,' I add, 'in some ways I've been terribly lucky . . .'

'Really? Why?'

'In the way that my friends stepped in – Pearl especially. She was our childminder and she sort of filled the gap, you know. She was there for us. Still is. And then there's Stu—'

'Ah yes, your lodger.'

I nod. 'He was brilliant. Did all the guy things. Flat-pack building, fixing appliances, stuff I *could* have done but—'

'You appreciated the support.'

I nod. 'So we were sort of . . . mothered.'

'What about your own mother?' Antoine pauses. 'I'm sorry, I don't know if she's—'

'Oh, she's alive, yes. Very much so. In fact she's getting married the week after next – her second time. It's on a par with the royal wedding actually . . .' And I tell him about 'Haimie', the aristo in-laws, the slate quarry and abandoned Jacobean theme. I explain that, although she tried to help after David died, our collective grief seemed to unnerve her and she gave the impression – not that I blamed her – that she was always counting the minutes until she could go home. In turn, I learn about Antoine's own wedding, to Nicole, when she was just twenty and he was twenty-two, which came about 'only because her family couldn't handle the idea of us living together and not being married. They are deeply religious and I'm not. I was never good enough for them,' he adds with a shrug. Now I recall Nicole's home being a gated affair behind imposing, blond stone walls, while Antoine had grown up in a cramped flat with a cracked shower cubicle – no bath – above a baker's. 'We broke up after a few years, but got back together and had the children,' he adds, then: 'Remember last night,' he says, 'when I mentioned you coming to visit me?'

I nod. 'That was just the wine talking, Antoine.'

'No, it wasn't – honestly. I'd love you to come for a weekend. It's a fascinating city, I'm sure you'd enjoy it so much . . .'

I don't quite get this. Is he inviting me over for a sight-seeing trip, or something else? I sense a sudden snag of uncertainty. The head-spinny kisses, the Fortnum and Mason picnic, the invitation to France; this all seems too good to be true. 'Let's just see,' I say.

Antoine frowns. 'You think it's too much?'

'No,' I say quickly, 'but I have the kids to think about—'

'Yes, but they're almost all grown up!'

'And I get so few weekends off. Only one in four . . .'

He pushes back his hair and squints into the sun. 'But surely, if you want to take a holiday—'

'Let's just enjoy the rest of today,' I say quickly, touching his hand.

He nods and smiles as we start to pack up the remains of the picnic. We walk along the edge of the lake, where he takes my hand; we buy coffees and find a vacant bench, where we sit so close together I can feel the warmth from him.

'Lorrie . . .' Antoine hesitates. 'I wish I hadn't stopped writing to you.'

'Oh, it really doesn't matter. That was all so long ago.'

'Yes, but I used to love your letters. All the funny things about your mother!'

I smile and lean into him. 'My mother who's currently freaking out that I don't have a date for her wedding.'

He frowns, clearly not comprehending. 'Didn't you say it's in two weeks' time?'

'No, I mean a man to take with me. *That* sort of date. You know – I'm upsetting the numbers, the symmetry . . .'

'I'm sure men will be queuing up to accompany you!'

'No, they're not – and that's fine. I'm forty-six years old, I can handle going to a wedding on my own.'

He squeezes my hand. 'Of course you can.' Then he catches himself and checks his watch. 'Oh, I'm so sorry,

I really must go. I have a taxi picking me up at the hotel at six—'

'Yes, of course.' We both jump up from the bench and stride towards the tube station. We hit rush hour and stand, our bodies pressed together, laughing as the train jolts us as if we are an ordinary couple travelling home from work together. Except when we get out at Covent Garden, it feels anything but ordinary because, outside his hotel, he takes me in his arms and holds me tightly.

And right there, in a bustling side street with people passing us as they make their way into and out of the hotel, we are kissing as if we will never see each other again.

As we kiss, the years fall away until I am no longer a middle-aged woman – a pusher of blushers, supposedly 'resistant to change' – but a girl again, dispatched on a terrifying French exchange which turned out to be neither an exchange, nor terrifying, but the most wonderful thing that had ever happened to me.

'Goodbye then,' he murmurs.

'Goodbye, Antoine.' I turn quickly and hurry back to the tube station and my real, Fortnum-and-Mason-picnic-free life, feeling deep in my heart that this can't be the end, and I simply *must* see this man again.

Chapter Twenty-Two

I find Stu in the kitchen, phone clasped to his ear in mid-conversation as he scribbles in his notebook. 'Parma ham, fregola, pine kernels – ready-toasted if poss, yeah, got that . . . Truffle oil, that organic raw cider vinegar in the tall thin bottle, yeah, I remember . . .' His dark brows shoot up as he smiles in greeting. '. . . Two bottles of burgundy – okay, yep, the one with the big house on the label, yeah, you can't go wrong with the big house, can you? Haha . . .' He scribbles some more. 'Within the hour, okay? Yeah, buzzer's broken, I remember. You'll hear the bike, or I'll text you when I get there . . .' He finishes his call and turns to me. 'Fun afternoon?'

'Yes, lovely, thanks.' Considering his recent iffiness about my dates, I am reluctant to elaborate further.

He picks up his helmet from a kitchen chair, clearing his throat as he clips the strap under his chin. 'Look, I'm sorry if I've been a bit weird about this grand reunion thing of yours.'

I roll my eyes. 'It's not a grand reunion.'

'Yeah, well, you know what I mean. This *thing*, whatever it is.'

He slips his notebook into the pocket of his leather jacket and pulls it on over his grey T-shirt.

'You have, actually. I mean, you've been pretty touchy. I know you don't want to see me being messed around, but—'

'Yeah, like you were last time? I do remember, you know, you crying at school, getting teased by that awful girl with the plaits – what was her name again?'

'Gail Cuthbertson – but I was sixteen years old, Stu. I'm all grown up and sensible now.' I grin, trying to make light of it.

'Yeah, 'course you are, and so is he. I know it's all different now.' He shrugs. 'It's just . . . you seemed to be jumping in, that's all. Being a bit obsessed.'

'I'm not obsessed! How can you say that?'

'And I don't want to see it all going tits up for you.'

'Well, there's no need to worry your pretty little head,' I tease, tapping his bike helmet with my nails. 'I'm just having a bit of fun, that's all.'

'So, are you going to see him again?'

'Oh, I don't know. I mean, we live in different countries, we have very different lives . . . he has invited me to stay with him, though.'

'What, in France?' he exclaims.

'Well, yes. That's where he lives. I won't, of course. I mean, I can't just scoot off to Nice at the drop of a hat . . .'

He is already making for the door. 'Why not?'

'Stu, I'm just not going, okay? It would be ridiculous. I've seen him twice in thirty years and I hardly know him.' *Congratulations, Lorrie, for almost managing to convince yourself you made the right decision not jumping at the chance. Turning down the offer of a weekend in Nice with the most fanciable man you've laid eyes on in, well, since*

David, twenty years ago . . . well done for being a boring old stick-in-the-mud!

'Wouldn't it be weird,' Stu adds, 'if you ended up with him after all this time?'

I laugh involuntarily. 'I think that's *highly* unlikely.'

'Stranger things have happened,' he says with an exaggerated shrug, and then he's gone, clattering along the hall and shutting the front door firmly behind him.

I stare after him, trying to figure out whether he's trying to warn me off Antoine or thrust us together, because his attitude is extremely confusing. Sure, he doesn't want me to be hurt. Yet he never showed any concern when I was trotting off to meet those strangers from datemylovelymum.com. Even when I was seeing Pete with the parrot – when Stu was still living with scary Roz – he didn't seem too concerned about how things would turn out.

The warm summer's day has tipped into a humid evening, and the air feels heavy with impending rain. With Cam and Amy occupied with several friends upstairs, I heat up a vast quantity of pizza – feeling slightly shamed, considering the Fortnum and Mason delights I devoured by the Serpentine – and retreat to the living room while they all surge into the kitchen and dive upon it.

My phone bleeps: a text from Antoine, reading simply, *Lovely to spend time with you Lorrie x.*

I smile and tap out a reply – *Lovely to see you too xxxxx* – deciding that five kisses is perhaps a little excessive and deleting two, then three, then putting one back. I finally leave it at a demure two, and fire it off. And now, because the kids and their friends are back upstairs in their rooms, I am free to log onto Facebook and stare at pictures of Antoine. How *dare* Stu insinuate that I am obsessed?

227

I ogle Corporate Antoine in an array of beige conference rooms, and Casual Antoine on the beach. I pore over his various comments about all manner of trivia, and then rake through his entire picture library again. Ten o'clock comes and goes – two hours I've spent hunched over my laptop – then eleven, at which point Cam and Amy's friends start to drift off home.

'Bye, Lorrie. Thanks for the pizza.' Mo's head appears around the living room door.

'Oh, you're welcome, Mo. Everything okay? Going away this summer?'

His handsome face angles towards my screen, and he smirks. *She's on Facebook,* his amused look says. *How quaint.* 'Uh, me and Cam might do something. A festival, maybe, if we can still get tickets . . .'

'Yes, he mentioned that.'

'Yeah. Depends on money and stuff.' More teenagers clatter downstairs. Mo grins and raises a hand, and is gone.

Midnight arrives, and with it the startling realisation that Stu hasn't returned – is that five hours he's been gone now, on one delivery? I seem to have lost track of time. I set my laptop on the sofa and check the street from the living room window, hoping to hear the approaching growl of his motorbike. Rain is falling steadily. I open the front door and peer out. The only people in sight are a young couple hurrying into a house on the corner.

I get ready for bed, no longer drawn to Antoine's Facebook profile but aware of a niggling sense of unease somewhere in my ribcage. Ever since David's death, I've found it hard to relax if the people I care about fail to show up when I expect them to. I'm being silly, of course. It's not unheard of for Stu to receive more calls when he's out, in which case he'll simply work through them until all deliveries have been made. Or perhaps he decided to head over to Bob's instead, to discuss further expansion plans for the business? He might even have decided to stay over; I know Bob has a spare room in the converted pub he's just moved into. But surely Stu would have let me know? Although we don't monitor each other's movements, there's an understanding that we sort of check in, because we don't want to cause each other any worry. I have never set out on a date without telling Stu precisely where I'm going, and who I'm meeting.

I call his mobile, which goes straight to voicemail. I check the weather again – insistent heavy rain – and, remembering that I have Bob's number, I tap out a text, rewording it several times so as not to sound too alarmed: *Hey Bob, Stu went out on a delivery a few hours ago and hasn't come back yet, don't suppose he's with you? Am sure it's nothing. Thanks, Lorrie.*

I send and re-read it. I sound like his anxious mother.

Sorry, comes the reply, *haven't heard from him either, just tried to call but he's not answering. Everything okay you think?*

Yes, he's probably had a few more calls. He'll no doubt be back soon. Thanks anyway.

Is that what's actually happened, though? I climb into bed, with calculations whirring in my head – was it about sevenish when he set out? Even with two or three more deliveries, this is still taking way too long. Stu is on intimate terms with every North London supermarket, deli and specialist store, and can snatch the required items with remarkable efficiency.

I lie still, staring at the ceiling whilst trying to calm my breathing. The delicious effects of the rosé wine with Antoine have long worn off. I close my eyes and commence the favoured activity of the middle-aged woman: night-time worrying.

Before David died, I would be unconscious within minutes of climbing into bed, shattered from a long day at the counter and coming home and trying to compensate for not being able to greet my kids with an array of home-baked goodies on their return from school; ridiculous parental guilt, as Cam and Amy had numerous after-school activities, or they'd have had a perfectly lovely time at Pearl's. The four of us would catch up on each other's days, and David might even have suggested a board game; he had a seemingly endless supply of enthusiasm for doing stuff with the kids. Then suddenly there were just three of us, and I noticed it would take me longer to drift off to sleep as I succumbed to a loop-tape of fretting: about Amy, always excelling at sports, but what about English, maths and science? Might things have turned out differently if her dad had still been there to enthuse her? I worried about Cam, too, who frequently lost crucial textbooks and seemed 'rather dreamy', according to his class teacher.

Of course, I've involved myself in their homework, I remind myself, eyes wide open now at nearly 1 a.m. I've done my best. As they moved up to secondary school I bought study guides and tried to familiarise myself with photosynthesis and the Battle of Trafalgar. But have I done enough? What about tonight's dinner – a load of cheap pizza chucked in the oven, probably seething with additives and saturated fat?

I sit bolt upright in bed, grab my mobile from my

bedside table and try Stu's number again. I don't care whether he thinks I'm being neurotic.

Hi, you've reached Stu from Parsley Force, please leave a message, I'll get back to you soon as I can . . . bye!

'It's me,' I croak. 'Just wondering where you are, is everything okay? I'm sure it is. It's just . . . ha, I know I'm being silly. It's just the rain, you know. It's a terrible night. I worry about you skidding and coming off the bike or something . . . yes, I know I'm being mad. Just humour me. Call me please, would you? I don't mind what time.'

And I wait, primed for the trill of my phone but hearing only insistent pattering against my window as the rain comes down.

Chapter Twenty-Three

Stu still isn't home when I wake up with a jolt at 6.23 a.m. I know this because I am already up and tapping gently on his bedroom door. 'Stu?' I call out softly. 'Are you there?' No reply. I hover on the landing, wondering whether or not to push the door open. He wouldn't mind if I went into his room, but I decided when he moved in that it would be solely his domain, his private quarters away from me, Cam and Amy and our assorted personal gubbins. I certainly wouldn't march straight in without warning if I thought he was there. What if he was splayed, naked, on his bed? What if he had company and I hadn't realised? Christ – perish the thought.

I peer around the door and see the double bed neatly made, his glossy books on motorbikes and outdoor adventuring, plus a couple of Jack Kerouacs and Truman Capotes, stacked tidily on the shelf. Rather sweetly, there are also a few of the Jennings novels he loved as a boy, their spines peeling from much handling. He keeps his room in pretty good order, with a stack of clothes folded on a chair, a small selection of man toiletries – including

La Beauté's newest male fragrance, a present from me, its box still sealed in cellophane – on the chest of drawers. Two pairs of rather scruffy black shoes, plus burgundy Converse, are lined up beneath the window. On another shelf sit various photos in cheap clip-frames: of Stu and a bunch of his mates from the motorcycle shop where they worked, all grinning goofily at the camera on a day out at the coast. There are his parents, Bernard and Barbara, also at the seaside somewhere, sitting side by side with ice creams on a bench.

My stomach twists at the sight of a blurry shot of me and David, with Stu sandwiched between us, gangly arms flung tipsily around our shoulders. David looks incredibly young – but then, he always did have one of those eager boyish faces: 'Looks so much younger than you,' as Mum was fond of saying, adding quickly, 'but only when you stand side by side.' Hmmm. She was right, though. In this photo we were at the wedding of friends with whom I've long lost touch. I remember a yellow marquee somewhere in Wiltshire and Stu asking me to dance, and then him stumbling off and being rather too enthusiastic with the free champagne, slipping on a drinks spillage and cracking his head on a chair leg. He had to be bundled into a cab and escorted by David back to the ropey B&B where the three of us were staying. David had always regarded Stu as a bit of a loose cannon, and this didn't help his case, especially when he failed to surface for the full English breakfast next morning. Although the two of them got along fine, David always regarded Stu as *my* mate, and they never socialised together if I wasn't there.

The front door opens. I spring out of his room, heart thumping, as if I've been rifling through his pants drawer. 'Is that you, Stu?'

'Yeah,' comes the gruff reply.

Relief surges over me. He's alive at least, and in the kitchen now; I can hear the tap gushing. Still in pyjamas, I bolt downstairs to find him glugging from a tumbler of water.

'*Here* you are,' I exclaim.

'Hi.' He smiles awkwardly.

I blink at him, knowing I shouldn't be annoyed or demand an explanation as to where he's been all night. He's a grown man, not an errant fifteen-year-old, and it's no business of mine what he gets up to, but . . . 'I called you three times last night,' I start.

He pulls off his leather jacket and dumps it over a chair. 'Did you? Oh, God, I didn't mean to worry you. Time just ran away—'

'Time ran away?' I repeat, conscious of my burning cheeks. 'But you've been gone all night! Where on earth were you delivering to – Kuala Lumpur?'

'No, er, Kilburn actually.' He studies the floor.

'Kilburn? But—' I stop abruptly as it dawns on me: the possibility that the handsome, dark-eyed Parsley Force man doesn't just deliver fancy foods. He's stayed the night with someone. Of course, there's no reason why he shouldn't, and he certainly doesn't need to ask my permission; he can do whatever he likes. It's just that this hasn't happened since he's lived here – and even before scary Roz, Stu was never a casual shagger – and I'm not quite sure what to make of it.

I clear my throat and take in his dishevelled appearance. His dark, wavy hair is flattened in some places and sticking up in others, his T-shirt badly creased. 'Sorry,' I murmur. 'I know it was silly. I was just panicking and I couldn't sleep. I even texted Bob, so now he'll be all worried too.

It was such awful weather, I thought you'd had an accident or . . .' I tail off and glare at him.

'Sorry. My phone, er . . . well, this is a bit embarrassing, but it sort of broke.'

'It broke? How?' Oh God, now I am interrogating him like a vexed teacher. *And how did this jotter get into such a disgusting state?*

'It kind of slipped out of my jeans pocket.' He turns to open the fridge and takes out the milk, and that's when I spot it.

The mark on his neck.

'Stu?' I stare as he spoons coffee into the cafetière. 'What's that bruise?'

'Huh?' He clicks on the kettle and stands there with his back to me – staring at it, as everyone knows you have to watch a kettle while it boils.

I step towards him, both shocked and fascinated at the sight of a love bite on a properly adult man. 'Let me see!' I demand, peering closely.

He jumps back. 'Let you see what?'

'That mark. Oh, my God, it *is*. You've been bitten. Someone was at your neck last night!'

He clamps a hand over it. 'Just leave it, would you? Can we *not* make a big thing out of this?'

'C'mon, let me have a proper look. Oh, I'm feeling all nostalgic, Stu. It's like a relic from a bygone era – I don't think I've seen once since 1989. I thought they'd died out, like snow-washed denim and Betamax videos . . .'

He's blushing furiously. 'Okay, very funny . . .'

'So,' I splutter, 'where were you last night when you were breaking your phone and getting bitten?'

'Nowhere!'

'You were *somewhere*, Stu.'

235

Even his ears have turned a furious pink. 'Just . . . someone's place, that's all.'

'A vampire's place? Like, one of those creepy Hammer Horror kind of houses where you're likely to get an artery savaged?' Even he manages to snigger at that. 'You should put something on it,' I add, 'like toothpaste, I'm sure that was the thing when people used to suck necks, or is that just a myth?'

'No idea,' he huffs.

'Shall I see if I can dig out a polo neck? Or a cravat?' Although I should be getting ready for work, I can't bear to tear myself away. 'Come on – tell me. Who is she?'

He coughs and grabs the nearest utensil to hand – a vegetable paring knife – to stir the cafetière. 'Her name's Ginny Benson, okay?'

'Oh, the one who likes that weird cheese!'

Stu squints at me. 'What are you on about now?'

'I found one of your lists lying around and her name was on it. It just stuck in my mind. So, she's the one who called last night?'

'Yeah.'

'The fregola, raw cider vinegar one?'

He nods. 'That's her.'

'Oh, Stu. You shagged one of your customers, talk about providing a full service . . .'

He winces. 'Thanks for putting it so delicately.'

'Fregola,' I chuckle. 'What is that anyway? Another kind of cheese, or a sexual practice?' I am now laughing uncontrollably. 'Don't tell me you gave her fregola on a first date? Isn't that rushing things a bit? I thought it was the kind of thing you had to work up to . . .' He, too, is sniggering, albeit in a pained, trying-not-to sort of way. '*Was* it your first time with her? Or are all your deliveries

236

actually secret visits to Ginny's place with the broken doorbell and, in fact, Parsley Force is just a cover-up for a rampant sex thing you've got going on?'

'Oh, for God's sake,' he blusters.

'What is it anyway? I need to know, Stu. Please tell me.'

'What's what?'

'Fregola. I'm worried now. I'm forty-six years old and I've never had it; I virtually feel like a *virgin* . . .'

He touches his neck distractedly, as if hoping to erase the mark with his fingers. 'It's pasta. Just very small pasta.'

'Aw, like mini macaroni? That's not so thrilling.'

'More like . . . little beads really. In fact, it behaves more like couscous when you cook it . . .'

'Well, that's good to know.' I beam at him. 'So, did you waive the delivery charge?'

He splutters. 'Christ, Lorrie, it's like living with the bloody Gestapo . . .'

I'm still laughing hysterically as I make my way upstairs, both thrilled and appalled by the damage inflicted on my friend's neck. What kind of grown woman has a desire to mark a lover in that way? Maybe she's bitten him in other places too. The mind boggles. I've never had a love bite myself, although I remember a period at school when they were as de rigueur as mullets, and Wendy Settrey and I were so desperate to be part of it all that we bruised each other's necks with our fingers. 'Twisters,' they were called, and mine was apparently as convincing as 'that French boyfriend you went on and on about'.

In the bathroom now, I pull off my PJs, stuff my hair into a polka-dot shower cap and wash quickly. In record time, I dress for work and apply my make-up; I can have the full face in place in under four minutes.

Back downstairs I find Stu, sipping his coffee at the kitchen table.

I slip on my jacket. 'So, Ginny Benson? You know her pretty well, then, I take it?'

He shrugs. 'She's just a customer. I've been over a few times – just to deliver,' he stresses.

'But this time . . .' I prompt him.

He frowns at the chipped rim of his mug. 'Well, yeah, she was getting stuff ready for a dinner – a *supper party*, she calls it – and she was all tearful when she came to the door; said the guy who was supposed to be coming just called to say he couldn't make it.'

I feign a concerned face. 'All those pine nuts – wasted. So, uh, you consoled her, I assume?' Another shrug. 'God, Stu, it sounds like a bad porn movie.'

He smiles faintly, reddening again. 'Well, we got talking, you know. She invited me in and I had a cup of tea with her. Heard the whole story, about what a useless arse he is and how stupid she felt, trying to impress him with elaborate food like some kind of Stepford wife . . .'

'So you felt sorry for her. Don't tell me it was a pity shag?'

'I'm not going into it, okay?' He shakes his head as if not quite sure what kind of shag it was.

I smile and rub his shoulder. 'D'you feel sullied?'

He frowns and looks up at me. 'Kind of. Is it really that bad?'

I study the small bruise. It's not the kind of accessory you'd expect to find on a forty-seven-year-old man. Not even Cam has had one, to my knowledge. 'Well, it's *visible* but it's not . . . you know. Not horrendously livid . . .'

'Cheers for that.'

'It's more of a casual marking of territory, like a dog peeing against a fence.'

238

'Okay, you've made your point.'

I pause, feeling quite sorry for him now, and imagining having to face *my* customers with my neck all ravaged. Christ – I'd have to feign an injury and slap a plaster on it. 'Did you realise she was doing it? I'd have said, "Stop! What d'you think you're—"'

'Lorrie, just leave it!' We blink at each other. 'Sorry,' he mutters. 'It's just a bit embarrassing, that's all.'

I exhale and study it again. 'D'you want me to put something on it?'

'Toothpaste?' He frowns.

'No, something better than that. But I need to be quick, okay? I'm running late now . . .'

I retrieve my make-up bag and, moments later, we are agreeing that La Beauté's Concealer Deluxe in mid beige is a perfect match for Stu's skin tone.

'Aw, Lorrie. You're a genius. Thanks.' He examines his now flawless neck in my compact mirror.

'Any time,' I say lightly. 'Spots, blemishes, neck bites – you know where I am.' With that, I step out into the bright, clear morning, still stunned over Stu and Posh Cheese Ginny, and wondering why the thought of his little adventure is making me feel rather odd.

Chapter Twenty-Four

As it turns out, that's the only make-up I apply today as a new directive has come from head office that 'full makeovers are to be offered on a strictly appointments-only basis'.

'We can still do them,' Andi says, rebelliously. 'No one will ever know.'

'But what if someone from management drops by?' Helena asks, frowning, and I understand her concern; since the takeover it's felt as if we are under surveillance.

'Let's just concentrate on shifting products,' I say, alarmed at how the phrase has popped into my lexicon. 'We need to go all out to sell today. Traffic stop as if our lives depend on it. Push the travel kit, the cream blushers, the men's range . . .'

'You know it's virtually impossible to get men to the counter,' Helena points out.

'Well, we'll just need to try.' I exhale loudly. It hardly seems possible that yesterday I was lying in Hyde Park, my head fizzing with fireworks as I kissed a beautiful Frenchman and strolled along the edge of the Serpentine, holding his hand.

'Let's get on with it then,' Andi says, loyally, immediately trotting across the floor and swooping on a sharply dressed older man with neat greying hair. He shakes his head tersely and marches on.

However, we manage to *shift product* all right. *Interested in the mascara, you say? Well, how about our creamy base for eyes – to make eye shadow glide on beautifully – and perhaps a pot of sparkly highlighter which, admittedly, isn't essential, but lights up the face for a night out? Or, you need a blusher? Well, how about a foundation to show off said blusher to maximum effect?* A flurry of sales flies through the till.

I grab a quick sandwich for lunch, eaten on a bench in the leafy square around the corner, and consider texting Antoine . . . but to say what exactly? That I'm thinking about him? Then I'll be waiting for a reply, wanting to constantly phone-check when I need to be working flat out to show our new bosses that we are definitely 'on message', and hard-selling is our priority now.

Back at the counter, I rev myself up for the afternoon shift, my spirits lifting when Gilda appears, all smiles, at the counter. 'I'm looking for something for my friend,' she explains. 'The one I brought in with me—'

'Oh, yes, Kathryn . . .'

'Gosh, you have a good memory. Well, her birthday's coming up. What d'you think she might need?'

It's a difficult question, because one woman might feel that all she 'needs' is a little translucent powder, whilst another will consider the entire kit pretty much essential in order to sustain life. 'Her colouring's similar to yours,' I remark.

'You remember that too. You *are* good at your job . . .'

I smile, and show her a selection of products for eyes

and lips and then, ignoring a twinge of guilt, I suggest that a blusher would be useful, plus a powder and, hell, why not throw in a BB cream too?

Gilda surveys the make-up I've set out on the counter and pulls a startled face. 'Oh, that's a bit too much, I'm afraid . . .' Her gaze scans the products. I've done this all wrong; she is overwhelmed by the choice.

'The blusher?' I suggest.

She exhales heavily. 'Would that seem odd, do you think? As a present, I mean – a little pot of pink stuff, all on its own?'

'Well, you could add a lipstick,' I suggest, aware of her enthusiasm waning as she glances around the store, perhaps surveying the floor for a less pushy salesperson, before adding, 'Tell you what, I'll mull it over and come back later.'

'Great,' I say with a bright smile. But of course she doesn't, and after a bustling morning there's a distinct lack of activity around our counter as the afternoon crawls on. A couple of teenage girls fiddle about with our testers, covering their wrists with lipstick and enquiring about prices, but baulk when Helena tells them.

Stu floats into my mind, and I wonder how his concealer is holding up.

My mobile rings in the pocket of my tunic. So boggled was I by Stu's love bite this morning, I forgot to put it on silent as is required for work; I glance around quickly and, with no customers nearby, decide to answer it. 'Hello?'

'Lorrie? Hi, it's Sonia Richardson here. Got your number from files. Hope now's a good time . . . d'you have a minute?'

My gaze skims our *Marie Celeste*-like counter. 'Yes, of course . . .'

'Just a follow-up really, to our little chat the other day. Thought it might be useful for us to get together again,' she continues in an overly perky tone, the kind a doctor's receptionist uses to deliver terrible news. *Your test results are back. There's just one small issue we're concerned about . . .*

'Okay, no problem . . .'

'Great. Just so we're all clear on everything. So, perhaps you could pop into head office?'

'Of course.'

'I was thinking tomorrow morning, shall we say ten o'clock?'

'Tomorrow?' I exclaim. 'But I don't even know where—'

'262 Liverpool Street,' she chirps. 'Come up to the fourteenth-floor reception and I'll meet you there.'

My mouth seems to have completely dried out. 'Sonia, could I just ask what this is about? I mean, it seems quite unusual and at such short notice . . .'

'Oh, not at all. We're a major operation, Lorrie, not the cosy little set-up you've been used to, run by two little old ladies in the South of France.' She laughs humourlessly. 'We do things properly here – appraisals, staff development . . .'

'I'm having an *appraisal*?'

'Oh, nothing as formal as that . . . so, see you in the morning?'

'Yes, of course,' I say, trying to normalise my voice. 'I'll be there at ten.'

We finish the call, and I glance at Helena, who's giving me an alarmed look. 'You okay?'

I smooth down my tunic and wipe the perfectly gleaming counter with a tissue. 'I'm not sure. That was Sonia. She wants me to go to head office tomorrow for, well, a sort of *follow-up*, she said . . .'

243

'Oh.' Helena pulls a face, then quickly corrects it. 'It's probably just something about company policy – stuff you need to know as counter manager . . .'

'Yes, maybe,' I say, realising with no small wave of relief that my shift is over.

I leave the store, determined not to spend the whole evening fretting about what might lie ahead. What I need is a drink and, as I travel home on the tube, I'm willing Stu to be around and in the mood for a stroll to the pub. However, when I get home there's no sign of him; perhaps he's out on deliveries, or sloshing truffle oil all over Ginny's naked stomach – who knows anymore? With Cam out at Mo's, only Amy is home, cross-legged on her bedroom floor, packing for her week's holiday with Bella's family. 'Hi, darling, how's it all going?'

She frowns at the open suitcase. 'I keep taking stuff out and putting it back in again.'

I survey the numerous rolled-up T-shirts in rainbow hues. 'That's a *lot* of T-shirts . . .'

'There's about fifteen.'

'Fifteen, for a week?'

'Yeah, you know what Bella's like. She'll be taking twice as many as this . . .'

I smile and plant a kiss on the top of her head. 'I'll miss you, darling. You will text me, won't you?'

She screws up her face. 'Might not have time.'

'Oh, surely you can manage—'

'I'm joking,' she exclaims. ''Course I'll text you . . .' She looks up and narrows her eyes. 'You look a bit upset. It's not about me going away, is it?'

The front door opens, and Cam and Mo's giddy laughter ricochets around the hallway. 'Hi,' I call down, but they either fail to hear me or can't be bothered to answer. I look back at Amy. 'No, it's not about you going away, love. I'm happy for you, especially as we haven't been away this summer. I just, well, you know my company's been taken over?' She nods. 'Well, my new boss wants me to go straight to head office tomorrow morning for some kind of appraisal.'

'They're probably just going to offer you another job,' she says breezily. 'Maybe even a promotion? Wouldn't that be great?'

I frown. 'It sounds awful but it hadn't occurred to me that it might be something positive.'

'Why wouldn't it be? What are you scared of?'

'I'm not scared, love, it's just been quite stressful—'

'C'mon, Mum. You've been there ages – years and years and *years*. You're always getting best sales person-of-the-whatever, aren't you?'

I shrug. 'Well, a few times, yes . . .'

'You won that magnifying mirror, the one that shows up all the horrible pores?'

'Yes,' I laugh bashfully, 'I did.'

'And these new bosses have come along and realised they don't know anything about creams and serums – and you do, your head's *full* of that stuff, you think of nothing else . . .'

'Thanks,' I say, laughing.

'So they want you to move out of the store and into a more, uh, management thing . . .'

'I hadn't thought of that,' I murmur, wondering now if my head really *is* full of serum, slopping around all the brain cells. It would explain a lot: my inability to stand up to my mother, my apparent reluctance to embrace change.

Amy grins. 'You might even get to develop new products!'

'Well, *that* would be great . . .'

She drops a bundle of underwear into her suitcase. 'So they're going to offer you a better job, and loads more money and then me and you, and Cam if he wants to – we can all go away on holiday together next summer, or maybe even sooner, maybe Christmas . . .'

'I guess we could . . .'

'I mean, in a year or so I'll probably start going on holiday on my own,' she adds, giving me a significant look.

I raise a brow. 'If I say you can.'

'Mum, I'll be sixteen! *You* went away then. You went to France with a list of instructions on how to get there done on Grandma's old typewriter . . .'

I smile and brush a strand of dark hair from her eyes. 'Yes, I know I did, darling, and I realise you're growing up and will want to do things with your friends. I understand that and I'm not planning to stop you . . .'

Amy squeezes my hand. 'So you'd better make the most of me while I'm here.'

I smile and re-roll some of her T-shirts so they fit neatly into her suitcase. Just being in my lovely, sunny daughter's company convinces me that everything's going to be okay or, at the very least, that I can handle whatever Sonia throws at me. 'I plan to, darling,' I say, 'and yes, maybe we can all go away together. Let's see, shall we? Let's see what tomorrow's meeting brings.'

Chapter Twenty-Five

Geddes and Cox's headquarters are situated on the top four floors of an enormous blue-tinted glass block close to Liverpool Street station. Although my appointment is at ten, I have somehow wound up outside the building forty-five minutes early so I nip into Pret for a coffee – already my third cup of the day – plus a croissant, and perch on a high stool by the window, telling myself it'll be all right because I know my job inside out, all the while scattering croissant crumbs all over myself.

I finish my coffee, dust myself down and text Stu, seeing as our paths didn't cross last night; I heard him coming in long after I'd gone to bed. *Scary meeting with new big gun at head office this morning,* I type. *Wish me luck!*

I pause, waiting for a reply, and when one doesn't come I make my way back through the brisk-walking morning crowds. As I take big, assured strides, I am conscious of acting the part of the breezy businesswoman, perhaps one of those women in the photos with Antoine at corporate events. We're always being told that French women don't get fat, and that their children don't throw food or misbehave in any way whatsoever, suggesting that these immaculate beings are somehow better equipped than we are in dealing with life's tricky issues. Perhaps I could pretend to be French? Would that be in keeping with the brand?

My phone bleeps with a text: it's Stu. *Hey missed you this morning. Didn't hear you leave. Good luck!!*

Thanks, I reply. *Crapping myself.*

Aw don't do that, he teases. *Unprofessional.*

I slip my phone back into my bag and, almost at the main entrance now, glance upwards nervously. Although I know I'm being ridiculous, I can't shake off the fear that Sonia is spying from on high, sniggering with binoculars jammed at her eyes. Although I am wearing my La Beauté tunic, black trousers and smartest jacket, I still feel rather dishevelled. It's a cool, breezy day, and my hair keeps escaping its neat ponytail. I'd like to whip out my compact mirror and check my lipstick's okay, but what if Sonia *is* studying me from up there on the fourteenth floor?

Instead, I step straight in through the revolving doors and make for the lifts at the far end of the marble-floored foyer.

'Excuse me!' barks a mustachioed man from the front desk.

I swing around. 'I have an appointment with Sonia Richardson at Geddes and Cox . . .'

'You need to sign in.'

'Oh . . .' Three beautifully groomed women stride by as I scuttle over to sign the sheet on the man's clipboard. He hands me a laminated visitor's badge, which I pin onto the lapel of my jacket, despite wanting to say, 'I work for this company, I'm part of this. I am a counter manager for La Beauté, don't you know!' Ridiculously, I want to text Stu again: something short and to the point, like: HELP! Or, SEND GIN!!! But what could he say? 'Chin up'? or 'You're bloody great, stop worrying'?

I wait for the lift, focusing hard on Amy's theory that it's probably good news, and my breathing lightens as it arrives.

The three women all stride in with me, bringing a heady merging of their perfumes. 'Fourteenth,' barks the one with an Amazonian build and tautly muscled legs, the kind of woman you could imagine nailing the 200-metre butterfly race. I jab the button like a lift operator. 'So,' she turns to her colleagues, 'I hope she knows what she's taken on because there's no way we're going to hit forecast.'

Her petite colleague, auburn hair pulled into a tight chignon, nods gravely. 'I don't know what they were thinking, taking on that tired old brand . . .'

'*Tired?* It's positively knackered!'

'Still, if anyone can turn things around—'

'*You-know-who* can . . .'

'Yes, and Dennis—'

'It's hysterical,' Amazonian chips in, 'him having anything to do with make-up. I mean, what does *he* know?'

'You know why they've bought it, of course,' says the shortest of the three, clutching her leather briefcase to her chest.

'For the name,' says the auburn one.

'Yep,' agrees Amazonian. 'Keep the name but totally rebrand it. Drag it kicking and screaming into the twenty-first century . . .'

The lift doors open and the women march out. Feeling quite sick now, I step out into a grey-carpeted corridor. The women have trotted into the glass-walled office ahead, where there is another reception area. This is it: the control centre of Geddes and Cox. Claudine and Mimi flash into my mind; that sweet letter they sent after David died, the bouquet of flowers delivered to my home, the spa voucher I never got around to using. I take a deep, audible inhalation and walk in.

'Can I help you?' A short-haired girl in a stiff-looking blue shirt looks up from the desk.

'Hello, I'm here to see Sonia Richardson.'

She casts me a doubtful look. 'And you are?'

'Lorrie Foster . . .'

'Ah, here you are!' Sonia has appeared around a partition and smiles tightly as if I am late, which I am not; it's bang on ten o'clock.

'Hi, Sonia.' I force an eager smile.

'Thanks for coming over. Come this way.'

I scuttle behind her as she marches through the vast open-plan office, in which highly professional types are already making calls and tap-tapping at keyboards. The mood is serious, productive; I've always wondered what goes on in these sky-scraper office blocks, and this is it. My mouth feels dry and tastes sourly of coffee. From the windowed side of the building, London shimmers, proud and enticing, beneath a cloudless sky.

We swerve into a corridor which smells of new carpet, where Sonia opens a door into a windowless office. Two men immediately leap up to greet me.

'Lorrie, hi! Thanks for coming.' Dennis Clatterbrock beams and shakes my hand firmly.

'Oh! Hello.'

'Nigel Wareing . . .' The other man – a portly chap whose white shirt strains across his stomach – grasps my hand with his rather clammy one. 'I'm from HR. Just thought I'd sit in on this if it's all right with you.'

'Yes, of course it is . . .' *Why the heck is he here, and what do they expect me to say?* '*No, it's not all right, please remove this man immediately*'? He flashes large, protruding front teeth and sits down again.

'Coffee? tea?' A young blonde girl has poked her head around the door.

'Not for me, thanks,' Sonia replies, and both men shake their heads as Nigel-from-HR pours everyone a glass of water from the jug on the table.

Sonia looks at me. 'Would *you* like coffee, Lorrie?'

'Oh, no thanks, I've had about three cups already, I'm completely caffeined up . . .' Great – give the impression that I'm a jangle of nerves before we've even started.

'Need a bit of a kick-start in the morning?' she asks, smirking.

'Don't we all?' I mutter, silently chastising myself as I take a seat. *For Christ's sake, calm down. You're here for a meeting, not to have your fingernails torn off.*

Realising I'm sweating profusely, I take off my jacket and drape it over the back of my chair.

'So,' Sonia starts, fixing me with a level gaze across the table, 'as you know, there are going to be some big changes with La Beauté as a brand. We wanted to invite you here to talk about that, about your performance and goals in the immediate future . . .'

I nod, trying to radiate calm. Sonia shifts in her seat.

'We do think it's important,' Dennis offers, picking up her thread, 'to establish gateway markers for goal-oriented development.'

'Yes, of course.' I realise I'm digging my nails into my palms.

Sonia sweeps back her dark bob. 'The thing is, Lorrie –

and this is why Dennis and Nigel are here too – to make sure everything is handled fairly and properly . . .' She glances at the men – Dennis beside her, Nigel next to me – and goes on: 'We're taking the brand younger, aren't we, guys?'

'Much, *much* younger,' Nigel says with a nod.

'How much younger?' I ask. *I mean, are we talking mascara for toddlers here? Night cream for babies in utero?*

'Teens, twenties,' Sonia says airily, 'and because of that – and please bear in mind that this is absolutely nothing to do with your performance . . .' My performance? What the actual hell? 'We need to consider our image, what we're saying to girls who come into our stores with money to spend – no dependants, no responsibilities, just lots of lovely cash to blow on themselves . . .'

'Can I just say something?' I interject.

All three of them stare at me. 'Yes, of course,' Nigel mutters.

'Well . . . of course younger customers are important because hopefully, if we treat them well, they'll stick with us throughout life. But, you know, it's the older – I mean, our properly *grown-up* customers who are more inclined to treat themselves. They value quality and care about their skin – what's going on underneath, I mean. It's not just a quick fix they're after—'

'Yes, but these *older* women . . .' Dennis shudders visibly, as if having trouble grasping the concept. I'd guess he's late twenties, early thirties tops. Probably spends his weekends plugged into his Xbox. 'What I mean is, they get to an age when – oh, I don't know how to put this delicately . . .' He emits a high-pitched giggle that's at odds with his executive image.

'. . . Where there isn't any point?' Nigel suggests.

252

'Well, yeah!' Dennis exclaims. 'I mean, once they're in their sixties, seventies, whatever . . .' I stare at him, hardly able to believe what I'm hearing. Mum shimmers into my mind, looking lovely in that cobalt blue dress we chose for her wedding day. '. . . they're going to stop spending anything on themselves because . . .' He pauses.

'Because what?' I manage to blurt out.

'Well, being realistic, women need to accept there's a point when *nothing's* going to work for them anymore,' he concludes, fixing me with a cool stare.

The room falls silent. I thought we were about to discuss gateway markers – whatever *they* are – and now we seem to be building up to the annihilation of all women over thirty-five. Sonia clears her throat. I am conscious of an insistent thudding against my skull.

'But these women do spend money on themselves,' I mutter.

'Yes, on coach trips and knitting patterns,' Dennis remarks with a gravelly laugh.

How bloody dare he! He guffaws at his own joke, and Sonia smiles tightly.

'I think what Dennis is trying to say,' she adds, 'is that we need our key counter staff to reflect our new, more youthful demographic and because of that . . .' Her smile seems to set. 'Well, we have a proposal for you.'

I shift uneasily and try to ignore the nausea that's rising in me.

'You're obviously very passionate,' Dennis offers, rubbing at an eyebrow.

'Yes, I am,' I reply, willing myself to hold it together. 'I love my job. I've been doing it for ten years and I can't imagine ever wanting to do anything else, to be honest.'

A hint of pity flickers across Sonia's cool grey eyes.

'Yes, well, ten years is a long time and we don't like to see anyone becoming stagnant . . .'

'But I don't feel stagnant!' I sit bolt upright in my chair so as to appear as alert and un-stagnant as possible.

'No, but the thing is, we feel – we *all* think, don't we, guys? – that you might be better suited to one of our other, less youth-oriented brands.'

I blink at her, not sure that I've heard her correctly. 'But I'm a beauty counter manager,' I manage to croak out. 'It's what I *do*, it's what my contract says—'

'Yes, but that's the thing about Geddes and Cox,' Dennis chips in. 'It's our ethos to be broad-thinking and fluid, so we encourage key team members to move across brand . . .'

'Encourage or force?' I snap my mouth shut.

Sonia leans forward, her face set in a frown. 'We never *force* anyone, do we, guys? That's why we're here today – to offer you choices – and I *promise* we won't make you do anything you're not a hundred per cent happy about.'

My breathing seems to have shallowed to that of a small rodent. I sip some water, dribbling a little down my chin, which I try to blot surreptitiously on the cuff of my carefully pressed tunic.

'So,' she continues, forcing a smile at Nigel, 'perhaps you'd like to run through the options, *Nige*?'

'Yes,' he says eagerly, delving into a brown leather bag on the floor beside him and extracting a clear plastic folder containing several sheets of A4 paper. He flips quickly to the second page, angling it so I can't read it. 'Firstly, we have the option of a very generous settlement which, given the current climate, I'm sure you'll agree is fair and proper . . .'

'You're paying me off?' I exclaim, my fist knocking

against my water glass so its contents swill perilously.

'Oh, we wouldn't use that term. In fact, the other option – and I do hope you'll consider this as we all feel your passion, your energy, could be a real asset to one of our other brands . . .'

'Which brand d'you have in mind?' I glare at the three of them, no longer caring about appearing keen and un-stagnant.

'Crumble Cubes,' Nigel replies, in a put-out tone as if I have insulted one of his children.

'Crumble Cubes? You mean those stock cubes that come in little yellow packets?'

Dennis beams at me. 'They're the ones. Do you use them?'

'No! I mean . . .' I pause, conscious of sweat sprouting from my upper lip. 'I don't cook much. I'm not really interested in—'

'Oh, you'd need to be familiar with the market,' Dennis says, assuming a headmasterly tone. 'But we are excellent at training, keeping our key staff up to date with the latest developments . . .' Why do they keep referring to me as one of their 'key staff' when they clearly want to give me the boot? '. . . Cookery courses,' he goes on, as if this might lure me, 'and visits to the cutting-edge production plant where Crumble Cubes are manufactured . . .' He thinks I want to watch a *stock-cube-making machine*?

'And where is that?' I snap.

He looks down at the table. 'Warrington.'

A hush falls on the room. The thudding has amplified in my head and has been joined by a needling pain in my chest; I can't have a heart attack now, not in front of Sonia and Dennis and 'Nige' – the *guys* – when Cam and Amy still need me.

I clear my throat and take several deep, calming breaths.

'So, what sort of role would I have, within Crumble Cubes?'

'PR and marketing,' Sonia says brightly. 'Just as an assistant at first, of course – Lindsay Newlands heads up the department, I think you could learn a lot from her.'

I nod, horrified by the wetness that's welling up behind my eyes. 'Could I, er . . . have some time to think about this?' My voice seems to have shrunk to a tiny peep.

'Yes, of course,' Dennis says, reaching an arm towards me; for one awful moment I think he might pat my hand.

'Thank you.' I get up from my seat and pull on my jacket. Dennis checks his watch ostentatiously and gets up too, while Nigel makes a big show of shuffling his sheaf of papers together.

'Don't go to the store today,' Sonia adds, her voice syrupy now as she tips her face towards me. 'In fact, take a week off, Lorrie. Think things over. The main thing' – she beams simperingly across the table – 'is that you make the right decision for *you*.'

Chapter Twenty-Six

I leave Geddes and Cox clutching the clear plastic folder of documents in which, apparently, Sonia and 'the guys' have detailed the choices on offer to me. And what choices they are: redundancy, or being shunted off to the world of Crumble Cubes. I stop by a vacant shopfront and flip through the papers, my eyes landing upon the amount they are offering me to quietly go away. It's a lot. It would certainly keep me and the kids going for a few months, but after then, what next? Of course, I could apply for jobs with another beauty company; despite Sonia's disparaging view of me, I have a wealth of experience and an excellent track record. But do I really want to start all over again, with a brand I don't feel any affinity with?

A young homeless man looks up at me from the shop doorway. To my shame, I hadn't even noticed he was there. 'All right, love?' he asks wearily.

'Yes, thanks.' I look down at him; an unravelling blanket partially covers his dirty jeans, and his face is so thin, his cheekbones are almost protruding. He looks, I realise with a start, around Cam's age. I rummage in my purse and hand him a two-pound coin.

'Thanks, darling. You have a good day.'

I smile, say goodbye and walk briskly to the tube, ashamed at worrying so much about my future in blusher sales while young people are sleeping rough, yet unable to stop replaying the meeting over and over in my head. So much for promotion. So much for staying where I have been perfectly happy for the past ten years. They want to get rid of me. They are only offering the Crumble Cubes option so they can say they have given me a 'choice'. But I am not a PR person, and I will not take a job that involves promoting those nasty little salty cubes. I would rather clean toilets, thank you very much.

I step into the tube carriage and take a seat, catching the eye of the middle-aged man in an Iron Maiden T-shirt sitting opposite. He frowns and gives me a concerned look. I realise tears are dripping down my face. I wipe them away with my hands and spend the rest of the journey sitting with a fist bunched at my cheek, as if that will somehow stop any more from spilling out.

At my station now, I trudge up the steps, seized by an urge to flop on the sofa and eat cake. Maybe Stu has been baking again, if he's had the time? Hmmm, unlikely; clearly, he has other distractions now. Will he just pop round to Ginny's place for more biting, or will they go on proper dates – i.e. the pub, dinner, cinema? It's totally up to him, of course, what he does.

I turn the corner into our street and check it, instinctively, for any sight of his motorbike. It's nowhere to be seen. I unlock our front door and pace from room to room; on this bright, sunny Wednesday, no one is home. A flurry of texts reveals that Amy, Bella, Cam and Mo are all in the West End, having managed to secure two-for-one tickets to the opening of a new movie. I need to talk to another human being – Stu, preferably, although he's probably *delivering fregola* – or, even better, someone who knows about employment law . . . like Antoine. He works in HR, but in France, obviously. What if it's all different there? Plus, I don't feel entirely comfortable, segueing swiftly from fervent kissing to the rather dispiriting matter of my being shunted off to some culinary graveyard featuring the lower end of the savoury flavourings market. I mean, it's not the kind of thing you brag about on Facebook. *Hey, friends, guess what my new job is! Thinking up new and interesting things to do with chicken stock. Anyone have any suggestions of where we might like to STICK those handy little cubes?* And then – I know I must be really losing it now – I picture Dennis Clatterbrock lying face down and whimpering on a bed at the doctor's surgery, the ones they cover with a paper roll to avoid staining, and the kindly doc saying, 'Try to relax, Mr Clatterbrock. It'll be far more painful if you're all tensed up.'

Mildly cheered by the vision of his agonised writhings, I undress and stand beneath the shower's blast for longer than I can ever remember. Afterwards, as I pull on old jeans and an unlovely, faded pink sweatshirt, I'm reminded that I have, in effect, been awarded a free week off, during which I could . . . well, *what* could I do, and who could I do it with? Amy's going to Portugal tomorrow, Cam's usually busy doing his own thing, and as for Stu . . . well, Kilburn is calling, obviously. I try to push away another wave of despondency and make myself a dismal cheese sandwich, reminding myself that I shouldn't be dependent on Stu and the kids for company anyway.

I could join a gym! I reflect, nibbling at my lunch at the open back door. How about that, Mum? Maybe, if I worked out for twelve hours a day – and ate nothing – I'd be lovely and trim in time for her wedding. I might even meet a muscle-bound man while I'm thrashing away on a stationary bike. Someone to accompany me to the nuptials, to save Mum from the shame of having her daughter turn up 'alone'. Or what about gardening? Don't they call this 'gardening leave' after all? Nigel whatever-his-name-was should have presented me with a ceremonial shovel along with that plastic folder. Handy for digging my own grave, considering I'm past my sell-by date, and far too old to care about looking presentable. *Women need to accept there's a point when nothing's going to work for them anymore.* Well, thank you, beauty expert Dennis Clatterbrock! Why don't we dish out prettily packaged cyanide pills so our older customers can finish things off once and for all?

I stare out at the pots of geraniums, the bushy tomato plant – would being offered a job with Tomo-Gro be more or less insulting than Crumble Cubes? I can't decide – and the explosion of orange nasturtiums in the trough. For once, their vivid colours fail to cheer me. And it dawns on me, as I bat away a persistent wasp, that Sonia and her 'team' have effectively given me my whole *life* off, and I haven't the first idea what to do with it.

'I'll come over right now,' says Pearl when I call her.

'Can we meet in the park instead? I know I've only just got home but I'm feeling kind of claustrophobic already.' Which, I realise as I set out to meet her, doesn't bode well for the future.

She is waiting for me at the street corner. When Toby sees me, he starts wagging his tail, which is gratifying; *two* friendly faces, after the morning from hell.

Pearl hugs me tightly. 'God, Lorrie. This is outrageous. They can't just fire you or shunt you off into another job. What would those French ladies say about this?'

I shake my head. 'I assume Claudine and Mimi aren't in the picture anymore.'

'Okay, but there are rules about this kind of thing – procedures companies have to follow. And if they really don't want you they have to give *reasons* . . .'

We start to follow the path that loops the edge of the park, passing groups of chattering mums with toddlers and an elderly man fanning his face with a newspaper and chatting to himself on a bench. 'Well, the reason is that the brand's going younger and I'm too old.'

'Too old? That's insane!'

'They don't seem to think so. Okay, I might be forty-six in normal years, but this is the beauty industry we're talking about . . .' I bend to ruffle Toby's head. His soft fur is momentarily soothing. 'How long are dog years again?'

She shrugs. 'Seven, I think . . .'

Spotting another dog some metres away, Toby scampers towards it for as far as his extendable lead will allow. 'I'd say make-up years are roughly the same, so that would make me, uh . . . three hundred and twenty-two.'

Pearl splutters – 'God help me then, being fifty next year' – and raises a hand in greeting as we spot the auburn-haired man in the far distance. Eric, I remember his name is, with Rosie the spaniel. Eric, whose off-licence is called Tipples and whose daughter has gone travelling. See, Sonia Richardson, my brain hasn't completely seized up! I am still functioning, still capable of contributing to *the business beauty*.

Wearing faded jeans and a washed-out checked shirt,

Eric towers above a gaggle of teenage boys as he passes them on his way towards us.

'Hey, this is a nice surprise.' His face breaks into a heartening smile.

'Hi, Eric,' Pearl says as the dogs bound towards each other. We all fall into step as we continue our way along the path.

'Day off today?' Eric asks, turning to me.

'Oh, um, I had a meeting this morning but wasn't needed after that.'

'A surprise afternoon off? How lovely. Always a bonus, isn't it?'

I grit my teeth. 'Yes, I guess so.'

'I've given myself the afternoon off too, left my able assistant in charge for a few hours.' He pauses. 'So, what d'you do, Lorrie?'

He remembers my name. I glance sideways at him, taking in the amiable face – kindness shines out of his light blue eyes – and the slightly gangly walk, the bounding energy he exudes. Don't they say that owners begin to look a little like their dogs? He has a spaniel-like quality, I decide.

'I work in the beauty hall of a department store.' I pause. 'Or rather, I thought I did. We've just been taken over by a huge company and I was hauled into head office this morning and offered . . .' I pause. 'Well, I'm sort of being pushed out, but you don't want to hear about that.'

'Yes, I do,' he insists. 'That shouldn't happen to anyone in this day and age. So, what's the story?'

I hesitate, because I'm not in the habit of blurting out personal stuff to strangers – but something about Eric's openness makes it feel okay. So out it all comes, with both he and Pearl agreeing that I mustn't make a deci-

262

sion – mustn't do *anything* until I've sought legal advice.

'I can't afford a lawyer,' I remark, studying the mottled tarmac of the path as we walk.

'Well, there's Legal Aid,' Eric offers. 'Everyone's entitled to representation if it goes to a tribunal.'

My stomach shifts uneasily. 'How can someone like me take Geddes and Cox to a tribunal? They're enormous!'

'So?' Eric frowns. 'They still can't ride roughshod over their employees. You hear about people winning unfair dismissal cases all the time. Don't be afraid of taking them on. What are their reasons anyway?' He snorts derisively. 'I bet they're calling it "restructuring".'

'No, they're calling it, "You are too old."'

'For God's sake, that's ridiculous!'

'That's what I said,' Pearl says vehemently, turning to me. 'What about the Connaught-Joneses? Maybe they could help?'

'Who are the Connaught-Joneses?'

'Don and Romilly, the couple I worked for in Dubai. They're both lawyers. They live about ten minutes' walk away, actually – amazing apartment in a gated development, gym in the basement, a lift to take their car into *another* basement below that . . .'

'I'm in the wrong business,' Eric laughs.

'Yeah, Don's a criminal defence lawyer but I'm pretty sure Romilly's area is employment, contracts, that kind of thing . . . I can check, if you like?'

An elderly woman with a terrier greets Pearl and Eric before moving on.

'But they're seriously rich, aren't they? I mean, they have two nannies—'

'Plus their London nanny who won't travel abroad, she's terrified of flying . . .'

'Okay, *three* nannies. They didn't get that way by working for people like me.'

'I don't mean hiring them officially,' Pearl says firmly. 'I mean having an informal chat, that's all. I can text Romilly, see if she'd be willing to give you a bit of advice. We're meant to be meeting up anyway, they're talking about taking me over to Australia in November . . .'

'That would be great,' I murmur, trying to quell the growing sense of dread in the pit of my stomach. All this lawyer-talk, the idea that I should go into battle with Geddes and Cox; it feels terrifying, and I wonder if I should be grateful for the chance – at my hoary old age – to embark on a new career in the stock cube world.

We part company with Eric as we reach the swings.

'Well, good luck,' he says warmly. 'Hopefully I'll run into you sometime – or do pop into the shop. You know where I am. I'd like to hear how it's all going . . .'

I smile. 'Okay – and thanks for the advice. I could probably do with some of those speciality gins actually.'

He laughs and gives Rosie's lead a gentle tug, and off they wander, his spaniel glancing back constantly, clearly not terribly delighted to be going home.

'Nice guy,' I remark, seeing him glance back, just briefly, before turning the corner and disappearing from sight.

'Oh, yeah, Eric's lovely.' Pearl flashes a mischievous smile. 'There's something about him, isn't there?'

'Yes, there is, definitely.' We both smirk as we fall back into step.

'And not just the fact that he owns an off-licence.'

'No, it's a plus, though,' I chuckle. 'You should ask him for a drink sometime. He seems friendly, interested—'

'Interested in *you*, you mean,' she teases, flashing a grin.

'Oh, come on,' I exclaim. 'What makes you think that?'

'The way he latched on when you talking about work – all attentive, giving advice . . .'

'He was just being helpful,' I say, laughing now, 'and anyway, it's you who's friendly with him.'

She shakes her head. 'He's not remotely interested in that way, and neither am I . . .'

'Really?' I study her face. 'You wouldn't just like something – you know . . . casual?'

'No thanks. Not even casual at the moment because casual gets complicated and you know what? I've had enough of complicated for a little while.' She grins, pushing back her short blonde hair. 'It's funny, but before Iain took up with Daisy – Christ, why am I talking like a Victorian lady? – I'd occasionally think, wouldn't it be nice to be single? Like, when he'd forget to take the bins out and I'd have to chase the bin lorry down the street in the morning – in my pyjamas, always the most embarrassing ones – and I'd think, why the heck am I with this person? I mean, what am I getting from this?'

'Oh yes, I remember the bin lorry dash.' In fact, Pearl seemed to run their home single-handedly whilst child-minding full-time, before she moved into lucrative, top-notch nannying with its frequent trips overseas. How lucky I felt, having a man like David, who was fully involved with family life. Until I'd got to know Pearl, it hadn't occurred to me that there were still men around who had managed to glide into middle age without ever having acquainted themselves with a mop or a bottle of Fairy Liquid. Iain, so often inert in his armchair, crossword to hand, seemed like a throwback from the 1950s.

'And now,' Pearl continues, 'I realise I was right all along. About being single, I mean. It actually suits me. I like not having to pretend to enjoy the box sets someone's obsessed with – just because they want company when they're watching TV – and I *love* never being mad about the bins.' She beams at me. 'Anyway, what about you? You haven't told me what happened with Antoine! Come on, I *need* to know . . .'

We stop as Toby strains towards a scattering of pale, fat chips. 'Tell you what,' I say, 'I really should get back and knock some dinner together. Don't suppose you fancy coming over and I can tell you all about it?'

By the time we're back at my house, Pearl is up to speed with the Soho kisses, the Serpentine kisses, the kiss outside Antoine's boutique hotel before he flew back to Nice . . . many, many kisses, all recounted, I realise now, in the fervent, frankly *obsessive* tones of an infatuated teenager. Have things really not moved on since 1986?

'It's like a film, isn't it?' Pearl enthuses, leaning against the sink. 'First loves reunited. God, Lorrie, how exciting. It's meant to be!'

I laugh. 'One of those films where it all, inevitably, goes horribly wrong and there's actually a wife at home . . .'

She pulls a face. 'Oh, come on, you don't really think that, do you?'

'Of course not. And yes, there was something . . . magical about it, I suppose. Sort of . . . *fireworksy*, you know?' I start to lift components for the dinner from the fridge – half a roast chicken, potato salad, some greenery, a bowl of guacamole, all knocked together by Stu – whilst filling Pearl in on the other aspects of my time spent with Antoine: the ambling and chatting and picnicking, the meanders around Soho simply to stretch out our time together.

'He wants me to visit him in Nice,' I add as the front door opens.

'Really? Well, you absolutely must go. You *have* to see

him again . . .' She turns and greets Stu as he clatters in. 'Hey, I hear Parsley Force is taking the world by storm, one clump of chervil at a time!'

He laughs bashfully and pulls off his jacket, leaving an uncharacteristic fine grey wool scarf looped around his neck. 'It's doing pretty well, I suppose. We can't believe it sometimes – how reluctant people are to go to the shops . . .' He turns to me. 'So, what were you two just saying? Who should you definitely see again?'

'Um . . . Antoine,' I say brightly.

I wait for a reaction – a comment on how obsessed I am, or at least an eye roll – but it doesn't come. Instead, he merely says, 'Oh, right!' in an oddly jovial manner, and bends to fuss over Toby who's sniffing around our kitchen. 'How are you, little man? Fancy a bit of chicken?' He tears a sliver of meat off the bird and requests Toby to sit – which he does, obligingly – and pulls off the scarf, perhaps forgetting why it's there in the first place.

With a laser-like instinct Pearl spots the offending mark immediately. 'What's that bruise, Stu?'

'Nothing,' he says, quickly turning away.

She snorts with laughter. 'Bit long in the tooth for neck decorations, aren't you?' She sniggers some more while Stu protests *okay, yeah, it's pretty hilarious, can we now please let it lie?* 'I'll never be able to let this lie,' she announces, greeting Amy as she wanders in with her swimming kit bag slung over her shoulder, followed swiftly by Cam. Thankfully, the kids have either failed to notice the love bite, or are so horrified that they cannot bear to speak of it.

As we all sit down to dinner, out it all comes about my terrible meeting this morning, and the fact that Sonia clearly wants me out. Naturally, everyone is aghast.

'You can't let them get away with this,' Stu asserts, echoing Eric's opinion earlier.

'What about the French ladies?' Amy asks, dark eyes wide with concern. 'Can't they stick up for you?'

I shake my head. 'I doubt if they're even involved anymore. Anyway, I don't want you worrying, okay?' I muster a smile. 'There must be something else I can do, if it comes to that . . .'

''Course there is,' Cam says, patting my arm very sweetly before I switch the conversation to the more cheering topic of Parsley Force.

As Stu regales Pearl with tales of the more bizarre items he's been called upon to deliver, it strikes me that this is my family now, the one I've made for myself, and I really couldn't ask for anything more.

Amazingly, Pearl is not only familiar with, but has actually *tasted* pule cheese. 'The Connaught-Joneses had it delivered when they were in Dubai. It's one of the most expensive cheeses in the world, made from Balkan donkeys—'

'It's made from donkeys?' Amy exclaims.

'Well, their milk, obviously, and there are only about a hundred of the right kind of donkey, and that's why it's so expensive.'

Cam and Amy look amazed.

'I like the stuff with the orange skin,' Amy announces and we all agree that, really, food poncery has shot off the scale, and what could be better, really, than a simple roast chicken like this?

'Especially when I do it,' Stu remarks.

I nod, setting my cutlery down on my empty plate. 'I have to admit, you are the best roaster of chickens I've ever known.'

'And that,' Stu says with a teasing grin, 'is the most touching thing anyone's ever said to me.'

It's almost 11 p.m. when we see Pearl out, yet she shrugs off the suggestion that Stu should walk her home. 'What, when I have this little man to protect me from harm?' she laughs. Toby, no more threatening than a hot-water-bottle cover, looks up with adoration in his eyes.

'Well, if you're sure . . .' At the sound of his phone trilling from the kitchen, Stu races to retrieve it, leaving us alone on the doorstep.

'So,' Pearl prompts me, 'what d'you think about going to Nice?'

I smile, turning the possibility over in my head. I am on gardening leave. Amy is going to Portugal tomorrow, and Cam is perfectly capable of looking after himself. There is not one reason why I shouldn't go . . . unless Antoine has had a change of heart? Now, *that* would be humiliating . . . 'I'll see,' I murmur. 'Stu will probably think I've completely lost my mind.'

Pearl frowns as she loops Toby's lead around her wrist. 'It's not about Stu, though, is it?'

'No, of course it's not.'

'Do what's right for you. That's what's important . . .'

I laugh, inhaling a lungful of cool night air. 'Sonia Richardson said something like that this morning.'

'Yes, but the difference is, I *mean* it.' We hug, and I watch her making her way along our well-kept terraced street with its shuttered windows, pausing as Toby sniffs at a doorway.

Turning back into the hallway, I climb our stairs and curl up on my bed with my mobile and compose a text. *Hi Antoine, I know this is very short notice but I have an unexpected week off work and could come to visit you*

269

*this coming weekend. Would that be okay, if I can book
a flight for Friday?*

I roll over onto my back, gaze fixed upon the ceiling
rose, vaguely aware of Stu heading out into the night. The
kids are still pottering around; they are often up later than
me these days. I have friends with older children, and
when I realised this happened – that their offspring no
longer trotted obligingly to bed at 8 p.m. – the concept
seemed terrifying. What if these crazy young people
decided to make chips, or poked knives into the toaster?
Of course, none of that happened because they were
virtually grown-up, as mine are now. In reality, there's just
amiable chatting downstairs, then music played at a
respectfully low level in Cam's room.

My phone pings. *That's wonderful news! I have some
time to take off. Please let me know when you're arriving
and I'll be there to meet you at the airport. So looking
forward to seeing you again, A x.*

I smile and pull on my pyjamas, bringing my laptop
into bed with me – not to ogle his Facebook photos this
time but to book a flight to Nice. Then, despite Nigel
Wareing's folder of documents currently sitting on my
bedside table, I drift away happily, knowing that the day
after tomorrow I will be back in the arms of the frankly
– and *Frenchly* – delectable Antoine Rousseau.

It feels, as Pearl put it, as if it was meant to be.

Chapter Twenty-Seven

Amy is leaving for Portugal. On this hot and heady Thursday afternoon she leaps out of our car and hugs Bella. Ours looks like a dented boot sale toy compared to the Kentons' enormous vehicle. Their vast silver beast occupies two parking spaces and is currently being loaded with suitcases by Gerry, Bella's rugby-loving father.

'Call us any time, Lorrie,' Cecily insists, chivvying her kids to do up their seatbelts while dispatching orders to Gerry to go back inside to fetch the iPad and remember to turn on the burglar alarm.

'Thanks so much for taking her,' I say. 'She's been counting the days.'

I look at her family and sense a snag of – what exactly? Envy? Probably, yes. It's not the car, the immaculate three-storey townhouse, or even the Kentons' holiday villa on the Algarve that I covet. It's being part of the excitement as they all jostle and joke, revving up for an adventure, finally silenced by a strident Cecily as she smooths back her dishevelled hair and shouts, 'Right, you lot! Shut up for a minute or we'll forget something vital.' She beams at me. 'Sure you don't want to squeeze in?'

'Thanks,' I laugh, 'but I'm going away myself tomorrow – to Nice.'

'Nice? Oh – that's where Gerry and I had our first weekend away. God, *that* feels like a lifetime ago. What a beautiful city – lucky you.' She hugs me, and I manage to gather up Amy and hold her tightly before she slips away and hops into the car.

Although the kids know I'm going away – and that I'm visiting Antoine – it's of little concern; now there are no hilarious stories about derelict teeth or stinky tweed jackets, they seem to have lost interest in my dating endeavours. I have yet to tell Stu, and am aware that I'm actively putting it off, but never mind that now because Amy is waving, and Cecily and Bella too, and in a blur of yelled goodbyes, they're off. A lump forms in my throat as I watch them disappear around the corner. They're only going for a week, but it still feels like a wrench to see my daughter heading off so happily. With a sharp pang, I realise it's those family holidays with David that I'm missing right now.

I drive home, wondering whether parental unease about separation ever leaves a person. As I park close to my house, I take a moment to reflect that, if Cam decides to apply for a sound engineering course out of London, he might be leaving soon for good – and Amy will follow and then, well, it'll be just Stu and me.

'Hi,' I call out as I let myself into the hallway.

'Hi,' Stu replies from the kitchen. I find him standing by the sink, looking rather awkward, clutching a mug of coffee. 'Amy get off okay?'

'Yep, without a backwards glance,' I say, smiling. 'So, er . . .'

272

'So, um . . .' We both stop, and I frown at him.

'Everything okay?' I ask lightly.

'Yeah, yeah,' he says quickly. 'I, um, noticed your boarding card – you left it on the coffee table . . .'

'Oh.' I sense my cheeks burning. 'Yes, I was going to tell you. Just haven't had the chance—' I go to fill the kettle, splashing the front of my top with the cold tap.

'You don't need my permission, Lorrie.'

I turn and meet his gaze. His eyes are guarded, his mouth a flat line as he plonks his mug on the table. 'No, I know that. But of course I was going to mention it . . .'

'So, tomorrow, eh?'

'That's right . . .' My scalp prickles with unease.

'Well, I think it's great!' He forces a smile and thrusts his hands into his jeans pockets. Leaning against the cooker now, he has the demeanour of an awkward teenager being forced to make conversation with his friend's mother.

'D'you really mean that?' I venture.

'Yeah. I mean, why shouldn't you go? After all that crap you've had at work lately . . .' He tails off. 'Anyway, I have something to tell you too, and I'm sorry – I know it's shitty timing . . .'

I frown. 'What is it?'

He exhales loudly. 'Look – the last thing I want to do is leave you in the lurch, so I'll pay rent until you find someone. I know you'll say no but I insist, okay? It's the least I can do—'

'Stu,' I cut in, 'what are you talking about?'

He meets my gaze, and now my insides seem to knot tightly together as I realise what he's trying to tell me. 'It's just . . . with Bob's new place. It's a hell of a mortgage he's taken on. He just mentioned it in passing, and we

273

thought it'd be, I don't know, maybe handier if I moved into his spare room?' He looks down at the floor.

I stare at him. 'Handier? Handier for *what*?'

'Well, you know – for business stuff. Getting the website set up, the blog, all that stuff he's always going on about and giving me a hard time for not doing . . .' It's an excuse, and we both know it. They have managed perfectly well so far. They have phones, for goodness' sake, and Bob only lives a couple of miles away. Communication is possible. 'It's been great living here,' Stu continues, cheeks flushing now, 'and this is a fantastic house – so handy for everything, five minutes' walk to the tube . . .'

I blink at him, wondering why my oldest friend is talking like an estate agent. 'I don't want just anyone living here,' I say sharply. 'I asked you, because we're friends . . .' *At least, I thought we were,* I reflect bitterly. *What the hell's got into you lately? Has that neck bite affected your brain?*

'I know that, but you can vet them carefully. There are those websites, those let-a-spare-room places. Maybe a student would want it? Actually, I'm sure a mate of Bob's is looking, some bloke from Leeds, coming down for a six-month contract in the City . . .'

'So why doesn't he move in with Bob?'

'Oh, I don't think Bob knows him *that* well . . .'

I turn away and de-hair the matted brush that Amy left on the table. 'I thought you were happy here,' I murmur.

'I am! And we'll still see each other, of course we will. I'll still pop round and roast you the odd chicken. If you behave yourself I might even knock you up one of those lemon drizzle cakes you're so fond of.' He tries for a smile but doesn't quite make it.

'That would be nice,' I say bleakly.

As he busies himself by unloading the dishwasher, I run through all the things I might have done to upset or annoy him: not cooked enough, not appreciated his culinary efforts enough, laughed at his love bite, made too many fregola jokes, booked a flight to Nice . . .

'Stu,' I start, 'is there really no other reason? If there is, I'd rather know.'

'No, of course there isn't.' He throws me a distracted look, as if to say, what on earth would it be?

'Is it . . . something to do with Ginny Benson?'

'No! Jesus . . .'

'Are you annoyed that I gave you a hard time for staying out all night?'

His face softens and he steps towards me. 'You didn't. You were just worried. It was kind of sweet, how concerned you were . . .'

'I mean, you're forty-seven. You can do whatever you like.'

'Yeah, don't look it though, do I?' he jokes.

I try to muster a smile. 'You don't, actually. Must be all that skincare I give you that you never use.' He chuckles, which I interpret as permission to gently quiz him further. 'So, um, have you seen her again since that night?'

'Er . . . yeah. We went for lunch yesterday and then to a gallery.'

I arch a brow. 'Not cleaning products in lobster pots, I hope?'

'Nah, just some Victorian watercolours that have to be kept locked away in the dark, they're that delicate and prone to fading. They're only allowed out on public display for one week a year.'

'What were they like?'

Stu's smile triggers a fresh wave of sadness in me.

275

'Faded.' Then his phone rings, and he scribbles down an order; I can almost see the trail of relief he leaves behind as he rushes off.

Well, it was only meant to be a temporary thing, I reflect as I choose tops and skirts and dresses and place them in the suitcase on my bed. It was just a stopgap after his split with Scary Roz, and he's been here nearly a year now, and perhaps that's enough. Maybe, despite his seemingly easy, jocular relationship with Cam and Amy, he's actually had enough of living with teenagers, of smelly basketball boots left lying around and my kids' mates forever clomping in and out. Or perhaps it's me.

He's right – I could easily find a new lodger. Whether or not I actually need one depends, I suppose, on whether I go for the Crumble Cubes option or the pay-off. Oh, I'll miss his moist lemon drizzle cake and him looking after the garden, tending our tomato plant. I'll miss finding a kilner jar of fresh pesto in the fridge, and us lazing around reading the Sunday papers together, but I can manage without all of those things.

It's Stu himself that I'll really miss. Lovely, sometimes belligerent Stu, who insists on storing bread in the fridge and happens to be my very best friend in the world.

*

'Lorrie?' The voice is abrupt, the number unknown. I close my suitcase and perch on the edge of my bed.

'Yes?'

'Hi, it's Romilly Connaught-Jones. I'm a friend of Pearl's. She asked me to call you, said it's pretty urgent . . .'

'Oh! Yes, it is. Thank you for ringing me. I have a slight

issue at work and she said . . . at least she thinks you might be able to give me a bit of advice—'

'Well, I'm off work today,' she cuts in. 'Lois is running a temperature and you know how it is, you hate to leave them but, in fact, our nanny is perfectly capable of taking care of things for half an hour while we have a chat. D'you want to pop round? Pearl says you're local?'

'That would be fantastic. When would be convenient?'

'Now, actually. I can't promise anything but hopefully I can set you off in the right direction.'

'I'd so appreciate that.'

She rattles off the address, and I rummage for a scrap of paper and pen from my dressing table drawer. I rake a brush through my hair, slick on a coat of morale-boosting lipstick and grab the wad of documents Nigel Wareing so kindly prepared for me. Clutching my phone so as to find my way, I set out with the faintest kernel of hope that Romilly Connaught-Jones might be able to help me figure out what on earth I should do with my life.

Chapter Twenty-Eight

Craven Court is a converted leather factory with a collection of former outhouses dotted around the grounds. As I'm buzzed in through the main entrance I take a moment to assess my surroundings. I have walked along this street to pick up the kids from various friends' houses, but had never realised the development was here. Bordered by high brick walls, the landscaped grounds – there are lawns, well-tended flower beds and a decked seating area – seem to have a rarefied atmosphere all of their own. I look up at the block and glimpse tasteful curtains, designer lampshades, a section of expensive-looking sofa. I press Romilly's bell as directed, and the door pushes open.

'Come in, come in,' she says distractedly, beckoning me into her third-floor apartment. 'Excuse the mess. You know what it's like when your child's ill. Everything falls apart.'

From a room at the far end of the oak-floored corridor, a woman and child are chatting in hushed voices.

'I'm sorry to hear she's not well,' I say.

'Oh, she'll be fine. I needed a day off, to be honest.

278

Work's been crazy. Come through, I'll make us some coffee. Do sit down. Tell me all about it.'

I'd expected Romilly to be rather fierce and immaculately turned out, but in fact she is make-up-less, with growing-out highlights, and wearing a baggy grey sweater and jeans that swamp her tiny frame. Her feet are bare, toenails unpainted, and there are dark shadows beneath her pale green eyes. I perch on a stool at the island unit and glance around the kitchen as she fiddles with a fancy coffee machine. As she selects mugs from a cupboard, I start to tell her about the ten years I've worked for La Beauté, how much I love my job, and the recent changes that are sending shockwaves through the company.

'I love La Beauté,' she exclaims. 'So simple and unpretentious and it just works beautifully.' She laughs. 'But then, you know all that.'

'Yes, I do,' I say as she places a cup of coffee, plus milk in an elegant white jug, beside me. 'Thank you.' I take a sip. 'It really is good of you to see me.'

'So, what's happened exactly?' She opens a packet of biscuits. They are ordinary rich tea. There's no fancy food lying around the place, no evidence of Serbian donkey cheese.

'Well, basically I was called into head office with one day's warning and presented with this.' I pass the wad of documents over to her.

While she reads, I glance around the kitchen. It has that showroom feel, all granite worktops and sleek, glossy white units, and the room is *huge* – perhaps three times the size of mine. I'd expected it to be pretty grand. However, what I hadn't imagined was the clutter and detritus of family life: splodgy paintings stuck to the enormous silver fridge, and a pinboard entirely covered

279

with a mishmash of photos, scribbled lists, tickets for concerts and, amazingly, a takeaway menu from the popular, and incredibly cheap, Indian restaurant by Bethnal Green tube station.

She looks up at me. 'So, there have been no verbal or written warnings?'

'No,' I pause. 'Well, there was a casual chat in our store's canteen about me staying on message, whatever that meant. Something about older staff tending to be resistant to change . . .'

'But nothing formally noted?'

I shake my head.

'And your performance, your sales . . . there's nothing they've highlighted as a problem?'

'My sales are fine,' I say firmly. 'I consistently meet target and my area manager put me forward as one of the top salespeople in the South East, which I, er . . .' I tail off, figuring that she doesn't need to know that I was presented with a magnifying mirror.

'Yes, very good,' Romilly says briskly. 'So the only issue raised was your age, am I understanding this correctly?'

'That's right – because they want to take the brand younger.'

A furrow appears between her brows. 'Which, apart from being completely unacceptable, seems to go against everything the company stands for.'

I frown at her. 'What d'you mean?'

She hops off her stool, fetches a wafer-thin laptop from the worktop and sets it in front of us, clicking on Geddes and Cox from her search history. 'I looked at their website just before you arrived. See, it says here: "At Geddes and Cox we take pride in offering a stimulating and nurturing environment in which every employee is valued and respected, regardless of gender, race, religion, disability, sexual orientation or age."' She stops and looks at me. 'Or *age,* Lorrie. Anyway, no company can fire someone because of that. It's just not on. They can't even sweep in and announce you're being made redundant – not without proper consultation.'

I sip my rapidly cooling coffee, taking in what she's said. Girlish laughter floats along the corridor. 'So, what should I do now?'

Romilly snaps off a fragment of biscuit and pops it into her mouth. 'Call a meeting, sit down and tell them you've sought legal advice and that you intend to take them to a tribunal. It's out-and-out discrimination and you have a clear-cut case of constructive dismissal.'

I inhale and smooth back my hair. 'But I don't think . . . I mean, I can't afford—'

'Companies can't do this, you know.'

'So, should I lie, then? I mean, I know we've spoken but I haven't hired you, have I? I haven't *officially* sought advice . . .'

'Of course you have,' she says. 'You've seen me. That's enough. They own a make-up brand now – how can they possibly risk being accused of age discrimination? Just the mention of a tribunal will be enough to shut them up. I think you'll find that these so-called choices miraculously disappear, and you can happily continue in the job you love,' she adds, smiling.

'Really? Wow. Thank you.'

She shrugs, as if it was nothing. 'Best of luck, Lorrie. I hate to see this sort of workplace bullying. Please let me know if you have any more problems after you've spoken to them.'

Thanking her again – profusely – I make my way

downstairs. So I can say 'my lawyer' now, I reflect as I leave Craven Court – at least, sort of.

The day is warm and bright and, despite Stu's shock announcement, my spirits have lifted. Amy will be up in the air by now. Cam has gigs on Friday and Saturday night, so he'll be occupied too. As for Stu and me . . . well, we'll still be friends, won't we, just as we always have been? Maybe he'll introduce me to Ginny, if it looks as if it's going somewhere.

Hungry now – I skipped breakfast – I take a detour and pass Tipples which, in fact, is no longer called Tipples but Spirited, which I have to agree is a much better name. The sign has been redone, hand-painted as is the favoured style among the chi-chi shops around here. I peer in and spot Eric at the counter with a cluster of customers around him. A couple are bantering jovially as he wraps a bottle in tissue paper, and he catches my eye and waves. There's an expectant look on his face as I wave back, but he looks far too busy to be interrupted now, so I walk on.

As my stomach growls hollowly, I stride on past the row of cheerful independent shops until I reach a small cafe. It's one of those jolly, homespun places with wipeable gingham tablecloths and a blackboard outside: *No Wi-Fi here! Come in and talk to each other! Pretend it's 1993!* I step in and order an Americano and a croissant at the counter – 'actually, I'll have a piece of chocolate cake too, please.' I carry my tray towards the only vacant table and flinch. It's Ralph, the toilet wanker. He is sitting opposite a round-cheeked woman with long, rather messy light brown hair, who looks at least a decade younger than he is. Wearing what looks like a man's checked shirt, she is chatting away, but he is clearly not listening. He is poking at his teeth with a toothpick and scanning the room.

His eyes meet mine and widen in shock. The message flashes across his face, as if in neon: 'I'm pretending I've never met you! Please do likewise!' His female companion registers the connection. As she blinks at him, Ralph quickly erases his panicky look and rearranges his face into a smile. 'Lorrie, hi!' His cheeks are blazing, his timing all askew. 'How nice to see you.'

'Hi, Ralph.' Look at me, with my croissant *and* a cake!

He turns back to the woman. 'This is, er, Lorrie, we met at a work thing . . .' He flashes me a pleading look. 'This is Belinda,' he adds. 'My wife.'

'Hello, Belinda,' I say levelly. 'Nice to meet you.' Definitely not dead, or in Halifax for that matter.

'Nice place, this,' she says pleasantly.

'Yes, I think it's just opened.'

'No Wi-Fi's a lovely touch,' she adds, 'although it's dragging Ralph out of his comfort zone . . .' She chuckles. 'Always plugged into something, he is. Squirrelled away with his gadgets!'

Hmmm, bet he is, the perv. 'Well, I'll leave you in peace,' I say, making my way past their table.

'We're just leaving actually.' Ralph scrambles up, followed by a slower-moving Belinda who, I see now, is around seven months pregnant at a guess, her hand running protectively across her belly.

I settle at the vacant table and watch them leave, with Ralph holding the door open for her, being gentlemanly. *Hey, Belinda!* I want to yell after her. *Are you aware that your husband prowls for women on datemylovelymum. com and phones them while masturbating in his office loo?*

Of course, I don't do that. I just pick at my croissant, reminding myself that Ralph is just one lone, creepy man

– but unable to shake off the feeling that the entire male species is something of a disappointment right now.

*

Although I tell Stu about my cafe encounter when I get home – it's a relief to have something both funny and awful to gossip about – we don't discuss when he might move out, and nor do we talk about my trip to Nice tomorrow. It's as if I have an angry-looking spot on my face that he's decided it best not to mention. At around 9 p.m. he heads out without much in the way of a goodbye, vaguely mentioning something about 'helping Ginny with a few jobs around the house'. It's so tempting to joke, 'Is that a euphemism?' but I think better of it.

I spend the rest of the evening checking and rechecking the contents of my suitcase. There have been no more messages from Antoine, and I sleep fitfully, my stomach a flurry of nerves about my forthcoming trip. I listen out for the sound of Stu's bike. However, when I emerge from my room next morning, he hasn't come home. Whether he feels awkward around me, or is simply madly in lust with Ginny Benson – it's impossible to know.

It's Cam who sees me off at 10 a.m., gamely carrying my suitcase downstairs and hugging me as I step out to climb into the waiting cab for City airport. I'll have to wait until after my trip to get in touch with Sonia. There simply isn't time now, and I'm hoping I'll be so buoyed up after two days with Antoine that I'll handle it all with seamless confidence. Hmmm, we'll see.

'Have a great time, Mum,' Cam says. 'You really need a break after all this work stuff.'

I smile, taking in his handsome face that's losing its

childish roundness, the cheekbones more prominent now. 'Sure you'll be okay, love?'

''Course I will. Wasn't I fine when you went away with Pearl that time?'

'That was one night, love, to Brighton. This is two, and I'll be out of the country—'

'Mum, I'm *seventeen*. Just go!'

I laugh and thank the driver as he loads my small wheelie case into the boot, glancing back to see Cam one more time; my tall, handsome, rather skinny son who could do with a tad more exposure to sunshine, and is perfectly capable of looking after himself. He'll have Stu for company anyway. As he didn't mention a moving out date last night, perhaps he'll change his mind about living with Bob? Maybe it was a spur of the moment thing, and he hadn't thought things through properly.

As the driver pulls away, I think of sending Stu a jokey text, just to lighten the atmosphere between us, but I can't quite think what to say. Instead, I call Mum to tell her about my jaunt to meet my teenage love, expecting at least a smidge of enthusiasm. 'But the wedding's next Friday!' she exclaims. 'Just a week away—'

'Yes, and I'll be back home on Sunday evening. I'm only going for two nights.'

'I'd just like you around,' she says huffily. No, *Have a great time, Lorrie*. No, *How exciting! I'm thrilled for you*.

'Well, I'll be around next week,' I say, 'and what about Hamish? Can't he help with any last-minute jobs?'

'Chance'd be a fine thing,' she mutters. 'His parents are insisting he stays with them at the moment to try and sort out this slate business. I think they're importing them from Bavaria – can you imagine? They're so demanding—'

'Not for much longer,' I cut in, smiling. 'From next

Friday he's all yours. So, are you looking forward to living in his cottage, Mum?'

'I suppose so,' she says with a sigh.

'And you'll rent your place out – is that the plan?'

'Oh, we'll deal with the details later. I can't be doing with all that now.'

We finish the call and Mum fades away, and now it's Antoine I'm thinking about; we'll have two whole days together, and two *nights*. My heart flips as I glance out of the cab window at an aeroplane, its trail a streak of fuzzy white against a searing blue sky.

Chapter Twenty-Nine

I can't read during the flight. I can't even focus on short, non-challenging articles about make-up or food in the in-flight magazine. I keep studying the little plane, nudging along its route on the overhead screen, calculating how long until I'm there and wondering how it'll be, seeing Antoine on home turf and, more significantly, what about tonight – i.e., actual night-time? Three years it's been since I've slept with anyone. Three years since Pete Parkin in that soup-smelling flat with the parrot squawking away in its cage. Perhaps it'll just be a platonic thing between us – although, after the way we were together, I somehow doubt it.

Do I want to do it? Oh God, yes. If those kisses were anything to go by, it'll be fantastic, as long as I can remember what to do. My legs and underarms are shaved, bikini line too; I am primped and primed and frankly scared witless. What will he make of my spongey stomach, my less-than-toned thighs and my bottom which, luckily, I can't study too closely? He's never seen me naked – not even back in '86. There was a bit of passionate teenage fumbling and that was it. It'll be okay, though, won't it? Like riding a bicycle. I repeat the mantra silently – *to keep your balance, you must keep moving* – and vow not to drink too much.

The stewardess trundles along the aisle with the trolley, and I order a startlingly strong coffee – and then another – helping me to achieve maximum jitteriness as we begin to descend, the Côte d'Azur laid out before me. I stare out of the window, awestruck. A glittering sea, the coastline a majestic swoop: it's almost too dazzling to be real. Before I know it, we're landing with a colossal screech and I'm out of my seat, hauling my case from the overhead locker and speed-walking – at one point I break into an actual trot – through passport control and customs – *rien à déclarer!* – and there he is, looking adorable in a soft blue shirt and jeans. His smile is as wide as the ocean as he cries, 'Lorrie!' and throws his arms around me. 'Here you are! I can hardly believe it!'

'Neither can I,' I say, laughing. He pulls me close and kisses my lips, then leans back and looks at me. 'What an amazing view from the sky,' I babble, dizzy from the kiss. 'Of course, you've seen it dozens of times . . .'

'It is incredible,' he says with another smile, taking my case from me as we make our way out of the airport building to the car park. 'Right, here we are. Not too far to my place.' He has a new-looking black Peugeot, shiny and undented; a businessman's car. I catch him appraising me as he lifts my suitcase onto the back seat.

'You look wonderful.'

I glance down at my red dress. 'Thank you.'

'So chic. Red suits you.' *And I am wearing my very best knickers and bra – black lace, a birthday gift from Helena – underneath.* Yep, those date pants again – last worn on my date with Ralph but, thankfully, that hasn't tainted them . . .

Antoine drives smoothly, negotiating the traffic at a confident speed as he tells me what he has planned for us. 'We can drop off your luggage at my apartment. I don't know if you might like to rest, or have a nap, before we go out . . .'

Is that code for 'let's get down to it right away'? I glance at his handsome profile, the mouth set in a slight smile, and inhale the smell of freshly valeted upholstery.

'. . . I'd like to show you the old town, the promenade of course, *la Baie des Anges* . . . it's very busy, touristy, but you can get a feel for the city . . .'

'Sounds great,' I say, trying to take it all in.

'. . . And perhaps a gallery, maybe two? D'you like art, Lorrie?'

'I *love* art.' *In fact,* I decide with a wry smile, *it wouldn't be a date without someone's paintings to peruse . . .*

He flashes a grin. 'For lunch, there's a favourite place I have – it's Turkish. You enjoy Turkish food?'

'It's my favourite!' I have never had proper Turkish food, but right now, as we turn off the motorway and make our way into the city, I feel ready for anything Antoine wishes to present to me. My real life back in London – Crumble Cubes, Mum's wedding, Stu moving out – is simply floating away.

Antoine's place is situated at the top of a steep, narrow hill, the street shaded by trees, the walls in front of the sun-bleached apartment blocks shrouded in dazzling pink flowers. 'Well, here we are,' he announces as he pulls into what seems like an unfeasibly small parking space. It's a modern block, its front grounds as well-tended as those of Craven Court, the entrance area floored in sparkling black and white chequered tiles.

He carries my suitcase as we trot upstairs and lets us into his apartment on the top floor. 'I hope you'll be comfortable here,' he says.

Comfortable, as if I might find it lacking in some way! 'I'm sure I will be. It's lovely.' I scan the wide, spacious hallway, then the living room where he sets down my case. It's impeccably tidy, everything just so, furnished with a tasteful grey sofa, a couple of inviting-looking soft leather armchairs and a coffee table bearing a small pile of news magazines. The huge window overlooks the sprawl of the city, and the shimmering ocean beyond.

'How long have you lived here?' I ask.

'Just three months. The company found it for me. I'll make us some coffee – would you like some?'

More coffee to send my heart rate off the scale? 'Yes please . . .' I smile, realising I have said yes to everything he's suggested so far. How pleasing this feels, having someone else make the plans, the decisions, and all I have to do is relax and let the adventure unfold.

While Antoine potters about in the kitchen, I study the well-ordered bookshelves, the decorative items dotted around – a speckled glass vase, an expensive-looking scented candle in a jar, an amber-coloured glass bowl.

He brings out our coffee and sets it on the low table.

'I'd love a place like this,' I tell him. 'It's so bright and airy. My house – well, it's Victorian, bit scruffy and in need of attention, kids' stuff scattered about everywhere . . .' My gaze lights upon a framed photo of a teenage boy and girl, swimming in turquoise water. They are dark-haired and tanned with bright white smiles. I go over to study it. 'Are these your children?'

'Yes, Nicolas and Elodie. He's fifteen, she's thirteen. That was taken last year on our holiday in Corsica.'

290

I smile. 'They look so happy.'

'Oh, it was an amazing trip. We hired a car, drove up the mountain roads – so narrow, a drop of hundreds of metres – terrifying!' He pulls a faux-terrified face. 'And we found a mountain pool, so clear and fresh – not like the sea. If you've never swum in a mountain pool . . .' I inhale and glance back out of the window. I want to get to know this city, I decide. *I want to get to know you, Antoine Rousseau; I want to know everything about you and then who knows what'll happen? Maybe one day we'll be swimming in a mountain pool too, just like that time at the lake in the forest* . . . 'Anyway,' he murmurs, stepping towards me now and pulling me in for a kiss, 'we have lots of fun things to do' – which I *think* could be suggestive, my entire body tingling at the thought – but, no, we settle down with our coffee, while Antoine fills me in on the art the city has to offer. 'There's Chagall . . . do you like Chagall?'

'I love Chagall,' I exclaim, wondering if I am picturing the right style of painting, or am I mixing him up with someone else?

'. . . There's the Musée Matisse, the Gallerie Renoir . . . there are a lot of cultural places. We are very lucky here.'

Yes, you are, I muse, and I am too.

'I don't want to tire you after your journey,' he adds.

'Oh no, it all sounds lovely.'

Antoine smiles. 'I like that about you, Lorrie, your keenness, your energy . . .' See, Sonia Richardson, he doesn't think I'm clapped out and stagnant! 'So, if you're ready . . . or would you like to shower and change . . .'

'No – I'll just quickly freshen up, if that's okay?'

'Of course it's okay. Do what you like here, make it your home. I'll just put your suitcase away.'

I pick up my shoulder bag and follow him to a huge, airy bedroom; again, there's a stunning view over the city, a sliver of azure sea in the distance. The bed is neatly made with grey linen, and enormous; my stomach flutters as I glance at it.

'The bathroom is this way,' Antoine announces, leading me back along the corridor towards it. The shower, which is fixed over the bath, is one of those rose kinds that make you feel as if you're being rained on. There is a bidet – *naturellement,* this being France – and for a moment I'm transported back to a holiday with David and the kids, and Cam's amusement on seeing such a thing. He was around seven at the time. 'Look,' he exclaimed, 'a little bath for your bum!'

I turn to Antoine. 'Thank you. I won't be a minute.' Alone now, I examine my face, cheered to note that the tension around my eyes from my meeting at Geddes and Cox's headquarters seems to have melted away. I splash water onto my face, clean my teeth, smear on a little tinted moisturiser and apply a coat of lipstick. That's enough, I decide.

And then we're ready, my red dress perhaps a tad too dressy for a day exploring the city, but what the hell? I feel bold and confident and entirely comfortable in the sensible ballet flats I chose for travelling.

'It's just a fifteen-minute walk to Chagall,' Antoine says. 'Is that okay?'

'Yes, that's fine. I love to walk,' I say truthfully.

He beams at me and kisses my lips. 'You look beautiful, Lorrie. Just as you did in London. Just as you did at sixteen.' I laugh, taken aback by the compliment. 'Come on then, let me show you my city.'

He takes my hand as we make our way towards the

front door – I glance into two more bedrooms, the kids' rooms presumably – and he's still clutching it as we head downstairs. As we step out into the Mediterranean sunshine my heart soars with excitement at the thought of the weekend ahead. While I'd never have opted for gardening leave, I am determined to enjoy every moment of my stay.

I find that I do love Chagall. His colours glow as if lit from behind, like stained glass; swirling paintings depicting flying people clutching each other's hands, and gorgeous mythical animals. 'Which is your favourite?' I ask as we drift from room to room.

'Oh, I can't choose just one,' he says. 'They are all beautiful. It's impossible.'

We pause in front of a canvas depicting a naked couple embracing, surrounded by an angel and jewel-coloured birds. 'I *love* this one.'

'It's very romantic,' he says. I smile, delighted that he thinks so too, and that there's no, 'Oh, what Chagall was alluding to here was . . .' I don't need to speculate why he chose to paint goats or serpents or a bride riding a winged horse. Thomas Trotter should come here and learn a thing or two, and forget the Brillo pads in a cage. These are simply the most dazzling paintings I have ever seen.

From the gallery, we amble slowly through tree-shaded streets towards the old town, where I take numerous pictures on my phone of shuttered houses and painted window boxes bursting with flowers, just ordinary things which seem so thrillingly French. I photograph a rusting iron gate, a house number painted on a ceramic tile, a bicycle propped against a terracotta wall, with a wicker basket on the front – an actual *basket*, for popping your baguettes in!

Antoine gives me a bemused look. 'So, you've never visited the South of France before?'

'No, I've only been to France twice. Once – well, you remember that time . . .'

He smiles and his fingers wrap around my hand. 'I do. It was wonderful.'

'And the other time was about ten years ago, with David and the kids. We stayed in a sweet little hotel in Brittany. The kids were thrilled by the supermarket, everything being so different. Amy grabbed a huge plastic bottle of Orangina from a shelf and dropped it, it exploded all over the floor—'

'Oh, how awful . . .' He looks shocked, which wasn't the reaction I'd expected – but then, French children don't run amok in supermarkets. 'Here,' Antoine says, stopping to indicate a narrow street with washing strung between balconies. 'There's a little restaurant down here that I had in mind.'

It's delightfully noisy and bustling, all the tables seemingly occupied. A group of harassed-looking German tourists are hovering at the entrance, seemingly debating whether it's worth the wait.

'Antoine!' A waiter beetles over and greets him warmly, and we are whisked around the corner, past tables laden with plates overflowing with exotic salads and skewered meats, to a tiny room at the back. Although I'm too thrilled and coffee-fuelled to have worked up a proper appetite, everything smells incredible: earthy and spicy and demanding to be tried.

'What would you like?' Antoine asks when we have installed ourselves in our seats. I frown at the unfamiliar menu, not knowing where to start. 'We can just have a selection?' he suggests.

'That sounds great.'

The friendly waiter reappears; Antoine addresses him by name – Jean-Philippe, I love those joined-up French names – and proceeds to rattle off an array of dishes we'd like. I try to focus hard, deciding I'll need to dust off my long-neglected French if Antoine and I are to become a *thing*, not that I showed a particular talent for language, even back at school. Still, I'm doing okay here, and congratulate myself on being able to pick out several words from the conversation as the men banter away – until I realise they're all 'kebab', bringing to mind those meaty hunks on a revolving spit, which always seemed so alluring after a night out in Soho.

However at Grill Istanbul, they are nothing like that. We pick over succulent morsels of skewered lamb, pomegranate-jewelled couscous, a zingy tomato salad scattered with mint and raisins and, ooh, pine kernels too. There are slivers of marinated aubergine, crunchy potatoes in a garlicky sauce, and a bottle of crisp white wine . . .

'Yes, the children love to stay with me,' Antoine is saying – we are sticking to fairly safe territory, conversation-wise – 'and it's a nice change for them. They love the sea, the sun. They usually do their studies in the morning and then we spend some time on the beach.'

'They study when they're staying with you?'

'Yes, of course.' He smiles and spears an aubergine.

'Well, I'm impressed. So, um, how often do you see them?'

'A couple of times, since I moved here . . .' Twice, in three months? I'd be pining for my kids, but think better of suggesting that it must be hard for him. '. . .Elodie wants to go to music college,' he continues, 'and Nicolas, well . . .' He breaks off and laughs. 'It's all football with him, he's crazy about it, even in the summer—'

295

'Amy loves basketball,' I cut in, but he doesn't appear to hear me.

'He's away at summer school now – a sports college. It's hard, five hours' training a day – plus studies, of course – but then . . .' He shrugs. 'What else would he do?'

I nod. 'It's good that he's so . . . dedicated.'

'They both work hard. Elodie plays her violin two hours a day.' He beams at me. *Two hours a day?* Blimey – how does the poor girl find time to do anything else? 'I'm a terribly proud father, I'm afraid.'

'Well, I think that's wonderful.'

Our plates are cleared and, despite my protests, Antoine insists on paying again, just as he did in London. Having eschewed dessert – in my excitement over the wonderful food, I have managed to eat way too much – we step out into the sunshine, ready to take in the other delights he has planned for me.

We drift around the Matisse gallery, which I also love – the colours, the intricate cut-outs! I am reminded of Cam and Amy covering the kitchen table, and most of the floor, in snippets of paper and glue. I once went to work with a red paper heart stuck to the back of my La Beauté tunic and Helena had to peel it off.

Having had our fill of art now, we stroll along the promenade where I gasp at the spectacle of it all: the ornate hotels with golden domes, and all the elegant people strolling – no, *promenading*.

A woman in a slouchy black dress hurries towards us. 'I found this,' she cries, holding a sparkling ring inches from my face.

'Oh, er . . . it's lovely.'

'It's yours?' she asks.

'No, it's not mine . . .'

'You have it!'

I study her face briefly, the dark brown eyes, the heavily lined forehead and elfin chin. 'No thank you. Perhaps you should hand it to the police?'

'No time,' she says distractedly. 'Please take it, I can't have it, it's not my religion to have rings—' She tries to press it into my hand. 'Please, just a little money to feed my family . . .'

'Oh, er, yes, of course . . .' I slip a hand into my bag and feel for my purse.

'Lorrie, let's go,' Antoine says sharply, and I throw the woman an apologetic look before scurrying alongside him.

'That was sweet of her,' I say, glancing backwards.

'It wasn't sweet. It was, what's the word . . .' He frowns. 'A hoax. A scam – that's it. Happens all the time here. They probably have a whole sack of worthless trinkets under the bed . . .'

I look at him and laugh, mildly embarrassed by my naivety. 'Well, it's quite . . . resourceful, I guess.'

Antoine slips an arm around my shoulders. 'If I hadn't been here you'd have given her money, wouldn't you?'

'Only a few euros, what does it matter?'

He gives me a bemused look, adding, 'Well, I think it matters. It's deceit, isn't it? She singled you out because you looked gullible—'

'Yes, okay,' I cut in, eager to change the subject now. But maybe he's right, and if I wasn't all happy and giddy, my head full of those dazzling Chagalls and Matisses . . . well, perhaps I'd be less inclined to admire the woman's resourcefulness. After all, we behave differently away from home. For instance, we drink in the late afternoon, as Antoine and I are now, having stopped at a charmingly ramshackle bar with wobbly metal tables outside. He has a beer, I have wine, and I sense a glow of pleasure spreading through me as he touches my hand. It's almost 5 p.m., and I feel – in the best way possible – as if my feet have barely touched the ground since I arrived.

'I've had a wonderful day,' he says, 'have you?'

'It's been lovely, Antoine. Thanks so much for showing me around.'

'Oh, my pleasure. Shall we eat soon?'

I pause, picturing the array of dishes entirely covering our table at Grill Istanbul. 'I'm not sure if I can just yet.'

'More art?'

'I'm not sure I can manage that either . . .'

He laughs and leans into me, nuzzling my ear, sending a shower of sparks shooting through me. 'I'm joking. We're too late now anyway. Shall we have another drink here or just head back to my place? I can fix us something to eat at my apartment.' He catches the waiter's attention with a nod.

'That sounds like a brilliant idea,' I say, thinking, *Yes please, let's forget the drink and jump into your bed right now.*

He lets us into the flat and pours us wine, putting on some gentle classical piano music in the background. We sip from our glasses and stand at the window, watching the sky darken. He sets out bread, and a variety of cheese, ham and fruit on the coffee table. But we don't eat anything because the moment we sit down we are kissing, fireworks shooting in my head as he strokes my hair. Then he takes my hand and leads me through to his bedroom where he draws the floaty white curtains, then unzips my dress, so slowly I'm pretty sure I stop breathing until it drops in a soft heap onto the floor.

He unclips my bra, still kissing me – impressively

dexterous, Antoine – and swiftly pulls off his own shirt, jeans and underwear (snug stripy pants, very fetching). We fall onto the bed where the poshest knickers I have ever owned are disposed of too, flung onto the floor like a piece of litter. I am *not* thinking, hell, what does he think of my stomach and thighs? Is he finding them terribly wobbly and not like the taut French fillies he's probably used to? At least, not *much* – and soon not at all – because he obviously likes them very much as he's kissing me all over, sending my body into some kind of ecstatic state.

It's *wonderful*, when it actually happens. So wonderful, I think I go wild, a bit shouty even as my brain spins off to some other place. Oh my *God*, it's amazing. I can't remember sex ever being like this. It must have been – with David, certainly – but all I can think right now is: so this is what it can be like. I had forgotten how it feels to be lost in the moment and desired.

Afterwards, we lie still, holding each other. I can feel the thump of his heart. He smiles languidly and kisses my lips. 'Are you okay?' he asks gently.

I realise tears have sprung into my eyes because it's the first time I've done it since David died – *properly* done it, I mean. Pete Parkin didn't count. I wipe my eyes, hoping he hasn't noticed. 'Yes. Yes, I'm more than okay . . .' I whisper it, but what I really want to do is cry out, 'I can still do it! D'you realise what this means to me?'

It means, I want to tell this gorgeous man, who's now turned away and is snoring softly, that my body is still capable of experiencing the most exquisite pleasure. It means I can still *feel*.

Chapter Thirty

We doze on and off, or at least I do. Antoine is properly asleep, lying on his back, his chest rising and falling with his breath. I'd like to curl up close to him but don't want to wake him. The glow of the city's lights creeps through the curtains, and he looks quite beautiful. I find myself studying him, as if to convince myself that I really am in his bedroom, having *done* it, and not just in a terribly workmanlike way, like those aerobics classes I forced myself to attend, briefly – going through the motions whilst thinking: *Surely we must be nearly finished now?*

I smile, hugging the feeling to myself because tonight – well, it was different. I close my eyes to replay the highlights – i.e. all of it – then open them in order to gaze at Antoine again: the mussed-up light brown hair, the fine cheekbones, the full lips. The closed eyelids, which I want very much to kiss, but fear might startle him. So I just turn on my side and watch this sleeping man, to whom I wrote fervently – 'I feel like my heart's going to burst!!' – in my teenage handwriting, when I still did little circles for the dots on i's.

An eye opens sleepily, and a bemused smile flickers across his lips. 'You're looking at me,' he murmurs.

'Well, you look lovely, lying there.'

He blinks at me. 'I'm being *observed*.'

I sit up and draw my knees up to my chin, glimpsing the clock on the wicker bedside table: 1.37 a.m. 'Am I freaking you out?'

'No, not at all,' he says gruffly. 'Let's get some sleep, though. It's very late.'

Although he's right, we *are* adults, and we're not going to turn into pumpkins. I'm being silly, I know, wanting him to stay awake so we can talk, so he can *be* with me instead of drifting away into a dreamworld of his own. However, his eyes have closed, his breathing resuming that slow, steady pattern, so I close my eyes and wait for sleep to come.

It does, eventually, and when I wake up, morning light is filtering in through the curtains. I flip over, expecting Antoine to still be sleeping there – but there are only rumpled sheets.

I lie still, listening for sounds in the apartment. There's the chink of crockery and a tap being turned on. Ah, he's in the kitchen. Perhaps he'll bring coffee for us to drink companionably. I remember now how nice it is to sit and drink coffee with someone in bed. David and I used to do that on weekend mornings.

I wait, scanning his bedroom for further clues as to what kind of man he is, but virtually nothing is on show: just a stripy dressing gown, hanging on a hook on the bedroom door, and a small blue vase on a chest of drawers.

I wait some more, deciding now that he must be making us breakfast too, and wonder what it might be. I'm pretty peckish. Perhaps he's nipped out to buy us some fresh croissants?

301

I slip out of bed, less confident about my nakedness in the morning light. It's 9.13 a.m., and I consider pulling on underwear – my navy blue scalloped lace ensemble, my second-best – as that would seem rather sexily French, wouldn't it, ambling through in lingerie while Antoine tends to domestic matters? Only, I don't have the nerve. I could borrow his dressing gown, but that might seem rather forward (ridiculous, considering what we got up to last night). Eventually, I decide to get dressed in my simple pale blue cotton shift dress – silly really as I still need to shower – and find him stretched out on the sofa. He is also fully dressed, in a white T-shirt and jeans, and is . . . *reading a newspaper.*

Seeing me, he smiles and folds it, placing it on his lap. 'Hey. Sleep well?'

I register the cup on the coffee table. One cup of coffee, not two.

'Yes, thanks.' I stand there, waiting for him to draw up his knees to make space for me beside him on the sofa, and wondering why he's chosen to lie here alone, reading, instead of coming back to bed with me.

I am being ridiculous. Of course he can read the paper if he wants to. After one night of passion I am in no position to start policing what he does in his own home. I clear my throat and perch my bottom next to his bare feet on the sofa, hoping there's enough space for it. Almost grudgingly, I feel, he draws his legs back to allow me a couple of inches more room.

'What would you like to do today?' he asks.

Be offered a coffee? Something to eat? I'm so hungry now, given that we didn't have dinner last night – too thrilled by each other to bother with food – and if that bread and cheese was still lying out now, I'd be stuffing it into my mouth. 'I'm happy to do some more exploring,' I say, trying to keep my voice light.

'Yes, we can do that.' He smiles brightly. I inspect my fingernails which I painted so carefully in La Beauté's Un Tendre Baiser: a tender kiss. Seems like none of those are forthcoming now. I look at him, trying to figure out what's going on. And I realise it's just like with Stu, when he announced he'll be moving into Bob's place: I am wondering what on earth I have done to make this happen.

Maybe I kicked off the covers during the night and he got the chance to have a proper look at my naked body and thought: *ew*. Or, despite rigorous teeth cleaning, my breath wasn't still pleasant after copious spiced lamb from our Turkish lunch. Or perhaps he's thinking, this is too much, too soon – and when we lay on the grass by the Serpentine and he asked me to come here, he didn't really mean it. Perhaps the wine had rushed to his head?

He picks up the newspaper and resumes his reading.

'Antoine?'

His gaze flicks up from the seemingly fascinating article. 'Yes?'

I squirm on the sofa and adjust the hem of my dress. 'Is everything all right?'

His eyebrows shoot up. 'Yes, of course?' He phrases it as a question. *Why do you ask?*

'Are you sure? Because it doesn't . . .' I feel myself reddening as I wonder how to put it. 'I'm just wondering if you feel okay about last night?'

He blinks at me and frowns. 'Yes, of course I do.' The newspaper is placed on the floor now, and his face settles into an expression of . . . what exactly? Not disgust or regret, so at least there's that. It's more a sort of resigned look. My heart seems to turn over as, for the first time

303

this morning, he turns to face me properly. 'Oh, it's nothing,' he adds off-handedly.

I peer at him, sensing a chill settling over me. 'Is there something you want to tell me?'

'No, no . . .' Brisk shake of the head.

My mind whirrs, spinning back to my conversation with Pearl: *One of those films where it all, inevitably, goes horribly wrong and there's actually a wife stashed away in Paris.* Christ, beautiful bra-less Nicole is still in the picture. 'Antoine . . . you're not still married, are you?'

'What?' he exclaims.

'. . . Or still, you know – together. With Nicole. You're not cheating on her with me, are you?'

He whirls round to face me. 'Of course I'm not! We've been apart for four years. I promise you, I would never do that. Why do you say it?' He looks appalled.

'Because you're acting a bit oddly.'

He sighs loudly and fiddles with a toe. 'Okay, I just, um . . . last night was very . . .' He breaks off. This is torture. It was very *what*, for crying out loud?

'You can say, you know, if something's bothering you. You can tell me anything and it won't freak me out.'

His face is impassive. 'Well . . .' He observes me over the rim of the cup. 'You were very . . . eager.'

'Eager? What does that mean?'

'You were very . . . keen.' *Keen?* I see his Adam's apple bob as he swallows.

I narrow my eyes at him. 'You mean . . . *too* keen?'

'Well, no, not exactly . . .'

'Would you rather I'd acted bored?'

'No, of course not!'

My heart is banging, and I take a breath, trying to bat down the humiliation that's welling inside me. 'Would you have preferred me to lie there, filing my nails, or doing some knitting?'

He lets out a little snort. 'Don't be silly, Lorrie, I just meant—'

'Or my Kindle? I could have reached for my Kindle while you were, you know – doing that thing. I did bring it, it's in my suitcase, although I'm not sure there's any battery left . . .' I know I'm being ridiculous, but I just can't stop.

'Lorrie, please, just leave it . . .'

'Leave it? How can I leave it when you're criticising me?'

'I don't mean it like that. Look, it's just a misunderstanding, okay?' He glances distractedly around the room, as if willing something to happen to curtail this conversation.

My mind races through the rest of our weekend together: today, and tonight, and the whole of Sunday until I fly home in the evening, none of which seems quite as appealing as it did yesterday.

'We should get ready,' he adds. 'My cleaner will be arriving soon . . .'

Sod your sodding cleaner! 'When you say keen and eager,' I remark, 'do you mean like a puppy? Because that's what it sounds like . . .'

'No,' he says, irritation growing in his voice now as he gathers himself up, towering above me now. 'I just mean you were shouting quite a lot.' Oh, Jesus God. I glance at the huge picture window and consider hurling myself through it. 'You were very enthusiastic,' he adds, 'and I wondered if people might hear, you know – the neighbours, the people below . . .' What did he expect? Three years, I've been celibate.

305

My mouth is bone dry and I feel quite sick. 'You mean,' I say carefully, 'you'd have preferred it if you weren't quite sure whether I was enjoying myself or not?'

'No! Please don't take this as a criticism . . .'

Miraculously, the tears that were threatening to spill over have dried completely. 'Right. So this is a sort of appraisal, is it? About my performance last night.'

'Don't be crazy . . .'

'It is! It's a performance review. You said you were devising new ways of monitoring progress and establishing goals, didn't you? Well I've had enough of those for one week. You might as well just come out with it and sum up my strengths and weaknesses while you're at it . . .' The simpering faces of Sonia, Dennis and Nigel loom over me, sniggering now.

'Lorrie, let's just stop this . . .'

'"Strengths: we'll come back to those in a minute. Weaknesses: bit overweight. Too enthusiastic in the sack."'

He frowns. 'In the sack? I don't quite—'

'In bed,' I explain tersely.

'Oh, I see. Well, yes, but I wouldn't say you're over-weight. Not really. You're not *slim*, of course; you're a larger woman . . .' Oh, good God. Just shoot me now.

'I'm a larger woman,' I repeat.

Antoine blinks at me. 'I'm just saying. You're very attractive, you know, but you'd be absolutely *beautiful* if . . .'

At this point my hearing seems to shut off as I glance around the room for my shoulder bag. Spotting it lying by the coffee table, I get up from the sofa and grab it.

'Lorrie?' Antoine says with a frown. 'What on earth's wrong?'

Instead of replying I stride into the hallway, aware of

306

his bare footsteps behind me and realising that my feet are bare too. I dart into his bedroom where I cram my feet into my flat pumps. He stands in the doorway, one hand clasped to his neck. 'What are you doing?'

'I'm going for a walk,' I mutter, already back out on the landing.

'Oh, don't rush out. Give me a few minutes and I'll come with you . . .'

'What, so you can go into more detail about how I'd be a decent-looking woman if I lost a stone or two?'

'I didn't mean that!' he protests as I push the front door open, making a mental note to burn my sexy undies as soon as I'm home and never sleep with anyone ever again.

Chapter Thirty-One

I keep glancing back, my breathing shallow and rapid, but there is no sight of a handsome and rather shell-shocked Frenchman emerging from the gate. I march down the hill, with not the faintest clue as to where I might be going, and find myself on the fringes of the old town, a warren of twisty, narrow streets filled with the smells of baking and coffee.

I find a cafe with just the right amount of customers inside – not too busy, but not deserted either, I don't want to sit there conspicuously alone – and order a coffee. The place is rather scruffy, its walls entirely covered with a dazzling collection of posters and flyers, the bar a mish-mash of bottles and crockery and artefacts.

The coffee is gratifyingly good. I must look a state, I reflect, un-showered, my hair unbrushed and not a scrap of make-up on – not that I care. I probably look about eighty-two. What would Sonia Richardson think of me now? What kind of image might I be projecting to younger customers? I fish my phone from my bag, wondering if Antoine has texted to apologise or ask if I'm all right.

There's just a message from Helena: *What's going on? Are you okay?*

I seem to have been put on gardening leave, I reply. *Don't worry, I'm okay. In France at mo. Will explain all xx.*

I scroll through my contacts and spot Stu's name there, and am seized by an urge to call him. My friend Stu, who would never say such disparaging things about my body or shoutiness – not that we would ever find ourselves in that kind of situation. But still.

I text Cam instead. *Hope all okay love, missing you x.*

Hi Mum all fine hope you having fun.

Yes thanks honey, Nice is amazing!

I pay the waiter – he gives my hair a brief, puzzled look – and step out into the warm, dusty morning, wondering what Stu is doing now, and craving the familiarity of a friend with whom I can just be myself. He has seen me being sick after eating bad prawns and terribly drunk at his fortieth birthday party. He has pulled a shard of glass out of the sole of my foot, and applied nit lotion to my hair. Never mind being spontaneous, or having an adventure. There is something to be said for the company of someone who knows you so well, the two of you are almost telepathic. There are none of those small, startling surprises that don't feel quite right – like Antoine's reaction to that woman with the cheap sparkly ring. Like seeing his kids twice in three months and thinking that's fine. Like reading a newspaper when he could have been back in bed with me, enjoying the morning because, really, what else would any sane person have done when we only have two days together?

I wander past small, cluttered shops smelling of incense and filled with leather goods and ethnic jewellery, wondering whether this scenario could be turned into an amusing anecdote at some point down the line – perhaps in seventy-five years when I might have recovered. Yet another bad date story to be howled over, like when Stu got his toe stuck between the glowing bars of an electric fire whilst having sex with a girl called Morna in a static caravan in Saltburn-by-the-sea.

The recollection cheers me a little and, somehow, I manage to while away a couple of hours with my wanderings. I buy a leather-bound notebook in which I decide to write a plan to sort out my life. Light-headed with hunger now, I find a tapas bar, chosen again not for its menu or ambience but the fact that it's not too busy, as I don't feel confident in grabbing the attention of harassed waiters, the way Antoine did. I order some kind of chicken in a paprika sauce, wondering what other diners think of me sitting alone, whether I seem like a woman of mystery or if traces of humiliation are still visible on my face. A boisterous group of young English men and women tumble into the cafe, all in high spirits, clutching each other and laughing. One of the men glances at me – am I imagining a hint of pity on his face? – and I take this as my cue to pay my bill and leave.

Now, as I amble along the promenade – I see the sparkly ring lady, swooping upon another unsuspecting tourist – it dawns on me that I must go back to Antoine's and try to salvage the rest of my stay. While his comments still sting, and I have no desire to sleep with him again – heaven forbid he should be faced with my 'largeness'! – we can at least hang out as friends. I'm in the South of France, after all, and I can still make the most of my trip.

I check my phone again – still no text from Antoine – and glance into the window of a department store. Behind the display of gazelle-limbed mannequins in chic taupe separates, it looks calm and inviting in there. A group of backpackers are approaching, all laughing loudly and taking up the entire pavement, and one of their rucksacks biffs my shoulder as they pass. No one apologises. No one even notices. I inhale slowly, push open the ornately carved wooden door and stride into the department store's beauty hall.

Soft jazz music is playing. I realise there is an actual pianist, an elderly woman with clearly dyed caramel-coloured hair, a string of glittery beads at her neck, wearing a pale pink twinset. What a lovely thing, having a real musician to make the floor feel even more inviting. I wander from counter to counter, my gaze skimming rows of lipsticks in enticingly weighty silver cases, and dazzling displays of fragrances. No wonder women love to treat themselves to beauty products when they're all so, well, *beautiful*. If you have the money, why not? Make-up never makes you feel fat, or too old, or in any way disappointed. I have always derived far more pleasure from a new eye shadow palette or nail polish than anything I've ever bought to wear.

The staff in here are all exuding an air of just quietly going about their business. Hopefully, no one will traffic stop me. Never mind the language barrier; I am not at all keen on an eagle-eyed beauty consultant surmising that I have spent much of the morning fighting back tears. And my hair – how could I have forgotten my hair? Hours of tumbling about on Antoine's bed, followed by a fitful night's sleep, and it still hasn't had a brush raked through it. I glimpse my reflection in a mirrored pillar and realise I look slightly mad.

311

And then I spot it, also reflected in the mirror: the familiar logo, blue lettering against white, back to front, naturally, but so familiar. Of course, why wouldn't La Beauté have a counter here? I make my way towards it. The young assistant – the only one manning the counter – makes eye contact as I approach and greets me.

'I'm sorry, I don't speak French,' I explain.

She smiles warmly. 'Oh, I see. Is there something you're looking for?' she asks in perfect English.

Hmmm. It seems silly to buy something here when I have a staff discount back home, but why shouldn't I treat myself? 'Just browsing, thanks,' I say. The girl nods and turns away to attend to another customer who's just arrived. I study the blusher testers – a pretty array of soft peaches and pinks – whilst tuning in to their exchange. Although I can only pick out the odd word the easy chatter between the women soothes me and that, coupled with the piano music and enticing scents, causes my anguish to fade even further. What does it matter that Antoine made a couple of clumsy remarks? It seems almost funny now – yet another chapter in my catalogue of dating disasters and one more reason, if it were needed, to opt for a quiet life of celibacy. I shouldn't be surprised really. Yes, I was infatuated thirty years ago – but how could I possibly have known the sort of man he'd grown into, just by lusting over a few Facebook photos? *You'd be really beautiful if . . .* Well, he prefers his women slim, that's obvious. He also seems partial to taking charge on a day out. While I did enjoy all the art yesterday, there's also something lovely about just wandering around, as I am today, and allowing the day to unfold naturally.

I test an unassuming pinky-beige lipstick on the back of my hand; it's one of the few shades I don't own already. The girl turns to me with an expectant smile. 'I'll have this, please.'

'I'll just get one for you.' She bobs down to open a drawer, selects the correct shade and rings my purchase through the till.

I was right, I decide as I step back outside, all those years ago in Goldings in Bradford. You get the feeling that nothing bad could ever happen in the beauty hall of a department store. Claudine and Mimi knew that; it's why they set up their little oases of calm in only the most beautiful, old-fashioned stores. Perhaps Sonia and her 'team' are right, in that things are changing, *have* to change, really – after all, what will happen when those stores are all gobbled up by huge companies until there aren't any left? Where will La Beauté fit in then?

I stand for a moment at the store's entrance, wondering how far Grasse is from here, the home town of our company's elderly founders. Could I get in touch, just to say hello to Claudine and Mimi and see how they are after the takeover? Will they even remember who I am? I picture the kind letter they sent, and their concerned faces when they took me for lunch after David had died. Of course they'll remember.

I pull out my phone from my bag, scroll through my contacts and find the number I have used only once, to express my thanks for the sisters' kind condolences. And now, on this busy pavement in the middle of Nice, I inhale the chocolatey aroma from a nearby crêpe stall as I call Claudine Renaud.

*

Antoine greets me with a sheepish expression plus the offer of coffee, a late lunch, a glass of wine and further explorations of the city. 'Maybe I was too pushy yesterday, deciding what we should do?' he suggests, rubbing at his chin. 'Is there anything you'd like to see today?'

His hair, I notice, is still a little ruffled. 'I'd just like to have a shower if that's okay.'

'Yes, yes, of course.' He narrows his eyes. 'I've been worried about you. You've been out for hours!'

Not worried enough to call or text me, though. 'I just fancied some time on my own,' I explain, 'and in fact . . . look, Antoine, I'm glad I came to see you. Yesterday was wonderful and, even after this morning, I'm still glad. But I just don't think it's right between us, do you?'

His face seems to droop a little. 'Oh, Lorrie, I'm sorry – it was a stupid comment and very thoughtless of me. The people in this block, you know . . .' He winces. 'They are terribly particular, many of them elderly. They complain a lot. Last time Nicolas and Elodie were here, someone complained about Elodie's violin. I told them, she must practise her scales and arpeggios every day, don't you understand? She's going to music college!'

A smile plays on my lips, but I manage to keep it down. 'That must have been difficult for you. Look, I do understand. I just felt a bit humiliated this morning. I probably overreacted . . .'

Antoine frowns. 'Actually, I'm still a bit confused, Lorrie. All I meant was—'

'Yes, I know what you meant. It wasn't really that part, though – about being shouty, I mean. It was the weight thing. That was harder to take.'

'The weight thing? I was just saying you'd be really beautiful if—'

'Okay,' I cut in, sensing my blood pressure beginning to rise again, 'I get it – you think I'd look better thin. Well,

314

you know what? This is me. I'm forty-six years old and I'm good at my job and I've raised two lovely kids . . .'

'Lorrie, I wasn't suggesting for a minute—'

'And I get enough of that from my mum,' I add. 'You know – "Have you tried this soup? It's hardly any calories at all. Just like hot water really!" And, "Have you thought of going back to that gym?"'

Antoine shakes his head in disbelief. 'Your mother sounds crazy.'

I laugh dryly. 'She is, I suppose – but anyway, I'm never going to become some slender little sylph of a thing. I've accepted that and, generally, I'm pretty happy with who I am.'

'Well, yes – you should be.' He nods approvingly and checks his watch. 'I like to see confidence in a woman. It's a very attractive quality. Now, shall we get ready to go out? I know a nice little bistro and if we hurry we could probably catch an exhibition before dinner . . .'

I touch his arm. 'Maybe we could have dinner another time, if you come to London again. I'd like us to be friends, Antoine. But the thing is, you and me . . . well, it's just not the same. I'm not upset anymore, but whatever we do, it won't feel like it did yesterday.'

'Yes, but—'

'So I made a call to someone I know,' I add. 'She lives in Grasse and used to own the company I work for with her sister. I was just curious to find out what they're doing now, and they've invited me to visit them.'

'You're going to Grasse?' he exclaims. 'When?'

'Well, as soon as I'm ready.'

'But that's mad, Lorrie. You're just storming off, trying to make a point—'

'No, I'm not. Look, it's only an hour away by train and

they were insistent about me visiting. I'd love to see them. I'll stay the night and go straight to the airport from there tomorrow afternoon.'

He looks down at the low table where this morning's coffee cup is still sitting, the newspaper beside it. 'Well . . . if you're sure,' he says sulkily. 'If that's what you really want.'

'Yes, it is,' I say gently. 'And you're right, it has been lovely seeing each other again. But we were just teenagers when we first fell in love and . . .' I pause. 'I don't think we can turn back the clock, can we?'

Antoine pauses. 'Maybe you're right.'

In fact, he is very decent about it, terribly gentlemanly, which makes me realise he is a good man and a real catch for someone – but not me.

I have a brisk but luxurious shower, and coffee is waiting for me when I emerge. Antoine compliments my rather demure choice of grey linen skirt and a flower-sprigged top, and insists on carrying my suitcase downstairs to the waiting taxi.

'I wish you'd let me take you to the station,' he says.

'It's fine, really.'

He sweeps back his hair with his hand and exhales as the driver loads my case into the boot. 'Well, have a lovely time in Grasse.'

'Thanks.' I smile.

'And, um . . . you're really welcome back here, if you'd like to visit again.'

I smile. 'Maybe one day I will, just as a friend? Would that be okay with you?'

A proper smile crosses his face at last. 'Of course, if that's how you'd like it to be.'

'Yes, I would,' I say, hugging him briefly before climbing into the taxi.

I glance back as the driver pulls away, and Antoine waves before turning back into his apartment block. I smile, my head filled with anticipation now as I pull out my mirrored compact and decide that my new lipstick – in a shade called 'Optimisme' – is just right.

Chapter Thirty-Two

'Of course we're happy,' Mimi exclaims, her silver bob swinging at her chin. 'It's been a very exciting time for us.'

'But La Beauté was your baby,' I remark, 'started right here in this garden. Wasn't it hard for you to let it go at all?'

'A little, but our baby is all grown up now,' Claudine says with a gravelly laugh. 'We were happy to send her off. We've spent forty years building the company and now, well . . .' The younger of the two – although both are well into their seventies – she wears her long, fine hair secured at the back of her head in an elegant plait. 'It was the right time,' she adds. 'Things are changing rapidly, Lorrie. We are a niche brand as you know, but perhaps we have taken things as far as we can . . .'

'La Beauté is ready for a new vision,' Mimi adds.

I nod and scan their barely cultivated garden. It's more of a wild-flower meadow, the flowers seemingly having sprung up at random, the haze of colour stretching to the river beyond. I feel honoured to be here; Claudine picked me up from Grasse station in her charmingly rustic Citröen 2CV, chatting all the way about my time here so far – reluctant to go into the Antoine scenario, I explained that I had stayed with an old friend – and presenting me with a great flourish as Mimi and their housekeeper, Anne, set out an early supper at the garden table.

We have tucked into delicious asparagus tarts, potato salads, and some kind of fine, buttery pastry draped with anchovies. There is wine, of course, and for dessert a simple platter of strawberries scattered with mint leaves and shards of dark chocolate. 'This is lovely,' I exclaim. 'It's all so simple.'

'That's how we like things,' Mimi explains. 'It's the whole ethos of the company, isn't it? Just the things you need – nothing more.'

'Oh, perhaps a few fun things,' Claudine chips in. 'That glitter for eyes . . .'

'Yes, for the young ones,' agrees Mimi, 'but for us, the whole point was that any woman, whatever her age, could find just what she wanted without having to make any confusing decisions, and know it would work.'

I nod, deciding that now is the time to tell the sisters about developments at head office since the takeover.

'Stool time?' Mimi exclaims, wrinkling her lips. 'What a ridiculous concept! You mean, customers aren't valued anymore?' She glances at Claudine in alarm.

'Well,' I say hesitantly, still unsure of how forthright I should be, 'it all comes down to cost-effectiveness – not that I agree with it. It's not the beauty business anymore, according to the new management. It's the *business beauty*.'

Claudine widens her eyes, her small gold hoop earrings catching the evening sun. 'The *business beauty*?'

'That's right,' I say.

'So are we all talking backwards now?'

I sip my wine. 'I know it sounds bizarre. It's as if they've stormed in and thrown everything the company stands for up in the air.' I glance at the sisters who are both looking quite upset. 'I'm sorry, perhaps I shouldn't have told you . . .'

'We'd have found out anyway,' Mimi says briskly.

'*Stool time*,' Claudine repeats, almost spitting out the phrase. 'It's the silliest thing I've ever heard. Don't they understand why women love to come to beauty counters? Are they idiots, these people, or what?'

I inhale, wondering how to respond when Mimi chips in. 'Oh, come on, Claudine. We talked about all of this. We made the decision because we were ready for a change – it was long overdue actually – and we have to accept that it's not ours anymore . . .' She turns to me, her expression firm. 'You have teenagers don't you, Lorrie?'

'Yes, I do.'

'It's like them flying the nest. You put in absolutely everything you can to help them to flourish and then, when they leave you . . .' She picks up a fragment of chocolate and pops it into her mouth. 'Then you just have to let them go and hope for the best.'

I smile, heartened by their stoical attitude, before telling them about my own predicament following the meeting at head office.

'Oh, I've never heard such rubbish!' Claudine gasps. 'Too old? A beautiful girl like you? How could anyone say such a thing!'

'I'd hardly class myself as a girl,' I say, laughing.

'But you're perfect, Lorrie. Your lovely face, your openness with people . . .'

'. . . So approachable,' Mimi adds. 'What are you going

to do? You can't accept this . . . this *stock cubes* thing.'
She shudders.

'Well, I'm not sure yet. They've given me a week off to think it over, but I can probably persuade them to let me have longer.' I shrug. 'It's a big decision. You know I'm a single parent, I have to think about Cam and Amy . . .'

'We understand,' Mimi says.

'I wish there was something we could do to help,' Claudine murmurs.

'You *are* helping by being so kind. I sort of . . . needed to come here today.'

We fall into a silence which is anything but awkward; I can tell they understand that something else has happened – something personal – and that I'd rather not share it right now.

The evening is turning cooler and Claudine, casually elegant in a leaf-print dress, gets up from her seat.

'I'm sorry about bringing bad news about the company,' I murmur.

Mimi shakes her head. 'When we decided to accept the offer, we also had to come to terms with the fact that things would change—'

'We didn't imagine it would be quite as dramatic, though, did we?' Claudine asks.

'Well, no.'

'But what makes things easier to accept is that we have exciting plans of our own . . .' She raises an eyebrow at her sister and they both beam at me.

'Would you like to see?' Mimi asks.

'Oh, yes, of course!'

'We're so glad you came here,' she adds, 'because we need some feedback. So far, well – it's just a dream we've had for a very long time and it's starting to come to fruition.

321

But it must appeal to all women – that's the whole point . . .'

Claudine touches my arm. 'And we need the opinion of a *young* woman like you.'

We make our way along the pebbled path and into the house, one of those classic French homes, square and solid with powder blue shutters and a thatched roof. I already know that the sisters inherited the former farmhouse from their parents. Neither woman has ever married, nor had children; from the very beginning, when they were blending plant extracts and concocting lotions to sell at markets, they have dedicated their lives to their brand.

'We should explain,' Claudine says as the three of us climb the steep wooden staircase, 'that we're starting something new. A *new* baby, at our age!'

'Really?' I hope I have managed to mask the note of surprise in my voice as Mimi leads us into a large, light-filled studio. The bare floorboards are painted white, the walls almost completely covered with huge pinboards adorned with sketches of women's faces, elegant and loosely drawn, reminiscent of the pictures in the La Beauté colouring books.

'What a beautiful room!' I exclaim. 'What are all these drawings for?'

Mimi perches on a stool at a drawing board on which two more sketches are attached. Again, they depict women's faces, one with a generous mouth and a tumble of dark curls, the other with a short, chic bob. 'It's us,' she says with a small laugh. 'At least, us when we were much, much younger. Hardly recognisable now!' Both of the sisters are still strikingly beautiful, the result of impeccable bone structure and, perhaps, a lifelong dedication to skincare. Claudine opens a drawer in a chest, lifts out a stack of sketches and, on her knees now, proceeds to spread them messily all over the floor. These drawings seem to depict some kind of shop. From the outside it looks like a chic boutique, its sign reading *Claudine & Mimi Beauté*. Baskets of flowers and rows of elegant bottles fill the window. The drawings of the interior show inviting sofas, squashy armchairs and dressing tables adorned with cut-glass bottles and make-up, a haven for any lover of beauty.

'Is it a beauty salon?' I ask.

'It's more than that,' Mimi says. 'It's an escape – somewhere for any woman to go when she needs a little time, perhaps to have a manicure, or simply to sit and have coffee with her friend and browse the make-up . . .'

'. . . She might have a facial,' Claudine adds, 'or perhaps she wants to talk about the kind of make-up colours she might wear for a wedding, a party, any special occasion . . .'

'So, you're launching a new range of products too?' I ask, aware of a palpable sense of excitement from the sisters.

Mimi nods. 'It's almost ready, the shops too – at least, we have the interior design just about right. To start with, there'll be one here in Grasse, another in Paris and one in London, of course – our most loyal customers live there.' She beams at me.

'Oh, that would be wonderful!'

'But we must make sure they look and feel absolutely right.' She jabs at one of the sketches. 'That's the most important thing, not to sell, sell, sell – women see through that, they feel panicked and pressurised and just want to run away.'

I laugh. 'Yes, I've seen that happen.'

'And that will never be the case at *Claudine & Mimi*

Beauté,' she adds, 'because the most important thing – the whole reason for doing it really – is to create a place for women to just *be*.'

We browse more drawings, and photographs of the prototype shop at various stages of development. There are mood boards showing scraps of pretty floral-printed fabric, and more sketches of elegant women having manicures, or their lips painted red. It's all thrillingly feminine and beautiful.

'We're launching a perfume too,' Mimi adds, 'to evoke the essences of the new brand. It'll be light and pretty, very delicate . . .'

'You're amazing,' I marvel, 'coming up with the whole vision. It all hangs together so beautifully, I can just imagine it now.'

Claudine smiles, her cheeks flushing pink. 'That's so kind of you to say, Lorrie.' Although the women seem eager for me to fire difficult questions about their venture, this seems different from when Stu and I sat around my kitchen table, discussing whether North Londoners might be persuaded to have porcini mushrooms delivered to their door. It just feels right, and I tell them so again, as Anne pops her head around the door to say goodnight.

We spend the rest of the evening watching a little TV, and by 11 p.m. both Claudine and Mimi are ready for bed. We say goodnight, with Claudine already having insisted on driving me to Nice airport tomorrow.

I sleep soundly in a powder pink room, the window ajar with soft floral scents drifting in, and in the morning we have hot chocolate and croissants at the sun-bleached garden table. The sisters take me into the centre of Grasse, where we stroll around the dappled squares filled with market stalls and cafe tables, before I am whisked to the airport, where we part with hugs and promises to stay in touch.

Mimi touches my arm before I head for the departure gate. 'I hope your visit to France hasn't been *all* bad . . .'

I shake my head, impressed by her perceptiveness. 'Oh no, it's been wonderful!'

She smiles. 'Remember that change can be a good thing, won't you? Babies grow up and life moves on, and that's fine – it's what keeps us young and engaged with life.' She looks at her sister and they both chuckle as if enjoying a private joke. 'We firmly believe,' she adds, 'that it's more effective than *anything* you can buy in a pot.'

Chapter Thirty-Three

Perhaps Stu feels that living with Bob is a new opportunity too. He's certainly jumped at the chance, so desperate was he to get away from us, apparently having taken just a small overnight bag earlier this afternoon. 'Just for a few days, he said,' Cam explains, hunched against the washing machine and looking rather bewildered. 'Why's he moving out again, Mum?'

I grimace. 'Says it'll be better for the business.' I shrug. 'Oh, I don't know, Cam. Sounds like a flimsy excuse to me. It'll be okay, though. It was only ever meant to be a temporary thing, him staying here, and it's his choice.'

'Maybe he'll change his mind?' He picks at a fingernail. 'I'll miss him. I like him being around—'

'I do too, darling . . .'

'Anyway, he said he'll be back in the week. He wants to sort out his stuff before he heads off to Venice for his sister's party . . .'

'Oh, right,' I say, trying to make light of the fact that he's clearly not planning to hang around. 'So, anyway, how have *you* been?'

'Yeah, great!'

'What've you been up to?'

'Just working and seeing people. This and that.' He smiles awkwardly. 'So, how was your trip?'

'Oh, fantastic,' I say, glossing over the Antoine part and focusing instead on my time spent with Claudine and Mimi.

'They're opening their own shops? You should do that, Mum!'

I can't help chuckling at that. 'The difference is, they've just been paid millions for their company.'

'Oh yeah, I s'pose there is that.' He chuckles. 'So, what *are* you going to do? Have you decided yet?'

Hauling my wheelie case up onto the table, I start to fish out clothes to be washed on a gentle setting: the red dress, linen skirt, floral top. 'No, not yet, but I saw a lawyer before I went to France.'

'Aw, that's great, Mum!'

'Well, it wasn't official. She's a friend of Pearl's and it was just a chat really. But, you know – she made me feel differently about the situation, and Claudine and Mimi did too, about the age thing. I mean, they're in their seventies. Can you imagine starting a new business at that age?'

'Yeah, uh, amazing . . .' His phone pings on the table and I see him twitching to check it, mentally wrestling between giving me the requisite attention and the clearly enticing communications of his friends. Ping! Ping! Another twitch. 'Well, I'm glad you had a good time, Mum.'

I smile, sensing his agitation. 'Thanks darling, and it's okay – it's good to be home actually. And now you can check your phone.'

Saying 'my lawyer' sounds strange coming from my mouth, but the more often I say it, the more it starts to feel as if I really have hired one properly, using the official channels instead of having a quick coffee with my friend's employer.

It's Monday afternoon, and Sonia was happy – no, *delighted* – to clear space in her diary for a meeting with me at Geddes and Cox Towers. Just the two of us this time, Nigel being unavailable and Dennis caught up in some kind of 'hideous nightmare' at the Tomo-Gro production plant. We are installed in the same bleak, windowless room, the documents outlining my 'choices' laid out on the table between us.

'So,' I start, 'my lawyer and I have been through my contract' – a small fib, as my contract was gobbled up long ago in the cupboard, along with the kids' drawings, school reports and ancient toy catalogues – 'and we discussed the fact that I am of course employed as a counter manager, specifically for La Beauté. There's nothing to stipulate that I can be moved to a different role, for a different brand, without my agreement.'

Sonia's mouth twitches. 'Yes, but you must understand that we're having to implement changes here in order to achieve market leadership as swiftly as possible.'

'That's fine,' I say, 'but *you* must understand that I am not prepared to move into the PR department, for Crumble Cubes, or anyone else for that matter, and if your reason for presenting me with the severance offer is due to my *age*, then—'

'We didn't say that exactly,' she says, turning a little pink.

My palms start to sweat. I inhale slowly, trying to conjure up the image of Romilly Connaught-Jones in her kitchen, scoffing at my boss's audacity at presenting me with such an offer in the first place. 'You did actually,' I say firmly. 'You said you had to consider how the brand was coming across to the younger demographic.'

She coughs. 'I think we should ask someone from HR to sit in on this.' She picks up the rather grubby-looking desk phone and stabs at a button with a burgundy nail. 'Jennifer? Get Nigel here, would you? Or Jim, Sarita, anyone?' She purses her lips and replaces the phone.

As Sonia seems unwilling to proceed until an HR person joins us, the wait is excruciating. 'I should ask your advice,' she says, attempting a more jovial tone, 'about make-up. This lipstick specifically . . .' *Ah yes, I've noticed your matching lips and nails approach; terribly dated, if I might say so, for a young person like yourself.*

'It looks great,' I remark. 'It's quite a statement. In a good way, I mean . . .'

'Really? I guess it's my trademark, but one doesn't want to get stuck in a rut, does one?' *Absolutely not, one doesn't want to stagnate . . .* 'Ah, Deborah!' she exclaims as the door opens. 'I didn't expect you. Thanks so much for joining us.' Immediately, the atmosphere changes as Sonia scrambles out of her chair. With her cropped greying hair and rangy build, the newcomer exudes the no-nonsense air of a gym teacher.

'I can spare a few minutes,' Deborah says briskly, taking the seat beside me.

'Thank you so, *so* much.' Sonia's cheeks flush even pinker as she sits back down and turns to me. 'Deborah Stonehouse is head of HR across the entire company. Deborah, this is Lorrie Foster, one of La Beauté's counter managers, we've been involved in discussions about her next move—'

'Yes, Nigel filled me in with the options you've put on the table.' Dressed in a sharp grey trouser suit, she gives Sonia a brief, brittle smile, which thaws slightly as she shakes my hand. 'So, how long have you worked for the company? I'm sorry, I haven't had time to look into this—'

'Ten years,' I reply.

'Right. And the issue here is?' She spears Sonia with a sharp look across the table.

'The issue is restructuring,' Sonia says quickly.

'Really?'

'Yes, and you'll be aware that we're shifting the brand younger—'

'Seems rather hasty in my opinion,' Deborah says tersely. 'I mean, we've owned La Beauté for less than two weeks. Surely, a major asset of the brand is the expertise that comes with it?'

I clear my throat, momentarily stunned by the fact that she seems to be on my side.

'Well, you know how it is,' Sonia murmurs. 'Move fast, seize the moment . . .'

'Yes, but in my experience fools rush in.' Deborah smirks. 'So, Lorrie, I gather you've been offered either an equivalent role in another division, or redundancy?'

'Well, not exactly equivalent.'

'And you say this is due to restructuring, Sonia?' Deborah's finely arched eyebrows shoot up.

'That's right.' She nods vigorously.

'Not exactly,' I say again. 'At our last meeting it was suggested that my age might be an issue which, as my lawyer pointed out, is clearly discriminatory—'

'Oh, we didn't mean—' Sonia blusters.

'. . . which,' I cut in, 'clearly goes against Geddes and Cox company policy, wouldn't you say?'

330

Deborah nods. 'Yes, of course it does. We are an inclusive company, it's very clearly stated in our recruitment policy.'

'Yes, I've read that,' I say.

'You've read it?' Sonia frowns.

'Of course I've read it. In fact, I have it right here.' I delve into the bag at my feet and pull out my laptop.

'Oh, no, it's fine,' Sonia says quickly. 'I think we're all familiar—'

'No, I'd just like to read it again, if that's okay.' I flip my laptop open, click onto the screenshot I've saved and begin to read: '"At Geddes and Cox we take pride in offering a stimulating and nurturing environment in which every employee is valued and respected, regardless of gender, race, religion, disability, sexual orientation or age."' I stop and look up. 'Or age,' I repeat, and Deborah nods. '"We are fervently opposed to discrimination in any shape or form,"' I continue, '"and firmly hold the belief that our inclusive approach benefits each and every valued employee."' I pause for effect, picturing Romilly Connaught-Jones smiling with approval. '"At Geddes and Cox, our people are our lifeblood and deserve the utmost respect."'

A hush falls over the room as I close my laptop. I clear my throat and try to wrestle my thoughts into order. 'So,' I conclude, 'as *my lawyer* pointed out, such an esteemed company, which is so proud of their non-discriminatory policy, would certainly not want to be seen to be forcing out someone purely due to—'

'No, of course not,' Deborah retorts, turning to give Sonia an exasperated look. Sonia purses her lips and shuffles in her seat.

'Because,' I add, the tension leaving my jaw now, 'La Beauté is for all ages. I mean, that is our slogan, isn't it?

"Because every woman is beautiful." Not, "Because every woman is beautiful as long as she is under thirty-five."'

'Ha, yes, I don't think that would be a very positive message,' Deborah says with a wry smile. 'So, look, here's the thing. I think we might be rushing in here.' She flicks Sonia another quick, vexed look, then turns back to me. 'Lorrie, let's take it that you will remain in your current role for the time being. Well, no – you'll just remain for as long as you wish. I assume there are no other issues?'

'Er, no . . .' Sonia fiddles with the gold band on her middle finger.

'Nothing else I should know about? No disciplinary matters, no performance-related concerns?'

'No, that's it,' she mumbles as Deborah gets up, shakes my hand again and makes for the door.

'Okay. Well, that's that, then.'

I, too, am out of my seat. 'Great. Thank you for your time—'

'You're very welcome,' she says, already striding out of the door, leaving Sonia and I looking at each other like two school enemies forced to be on the same netball team.

'Well, *that* was interesting.' She grimaces.

'Yes, it was. Thanks for seeing me, Sonia.' I slip my laptop into my bag and loop the strap over my shoulder. 'So, I'll be back at work as normal tomorrow, okay? I mean, I think I'd like to end my gardening leave now, if that's all right with you. I've never had terribly green fingers.'

'Of course,' she says, failing to acknowledge my joke. 'Just out of interest, did you really consult a lawyer over this?'

'Yes. I spoke to Romilly Connaught-Jones—'

Her eyes widen. '*The* Romilly Connaught-Jones? From

Connaught-Jones-Evans? Gosh. Friends in high places. I wouldn't have expected—'

'She's not a friend exactly.'

Sonia flushes again. Perhaps I should recommend our colour-corrective base? 'No, I mean excellent contacts,' she adds, quickly regaining her composure. 'I'm impressed, actually, about how you handled our meeting today. We are always looking for strong, forthright types to promote in this company. Perhaps, when things have settled down, we should have another chat about where you might like to go from here?'

'What d'you mean?' I ask, still not entirely trusting her.

'Oh, you know. Opportunities, training, the chance to further your career . . .' She pauses. 'I assume you don't want to spend the rest of your life selling make-up?'

'I'll think about it,' I reply, 'but if it's okay with you, right now I'd just like to get back to work.'

Chapter Thirty-Four

Back home, with Cam out with his friends, I unpack the rest of my case as my mind starts running through the events at Antoine's. *You're not a slim woman. I just mean you were shouting quite a lot.* Although his comments still rankle, I am so buoyed up by my meeting with Sonia and Deborah, I decide right now not to allow them to put me off meeting anyone ever again. Fuelled by a surge of rebellion, I open my laptop and Google 'over-40s dating sites'.

I'm just curious, that's all. It's struck me that datemy-lovelymum.com might seem sweet and endearing in its concept – 'I love my mum, and you will too!' is its catch-line – but might possibly attract the wrong sort. I suspect now that the three men I've met were all under the illusion that, as a single mother, I was so grateful to be out of the house, in male company, that I'd pretty much do it with anyone. How *dare* they?

And now, as I browse alternative sites, I discover that there are some amazingly specific ones out there: for horse lovers, bakers, Latin dancing enthusiast, even 'mature skateboarders', God forbid. Pausing at a rather bland-sounding site for the over-forty-fives – ha, just sneaked in there! – I discover that, even without signing up, I can access profiles within a ten-mile radius. I study the perfectly pleasant and approachable-looking faces of teachers, electricians, gardeners and IT types. No one seems obviously crazy. In fact, the profiles I study seem incredibly – perhaps suspiciously – normal. I fetch a pen and paper and start to draft out the beginnings of a profile for myself.

Hi, I'm Lorrie and I'm 46 years old. I live in East London and I am mother to two teenagers. I work for a beauty company . . .

The kids would say I'm not selling myself enough. Stu would tamper with it and put in some jokes. But he's not here and, feeling irked now – there's been no call, no text to explain what's going on – I sign up for the site's free trial, tweaking my profile and choosing a selection of pictures. And it's done. Rather than wait for a 'wink' – a note of interest from a potential match – I potter around, checking Cecily's Facebook (Amy refuses to friend me) and basking in the numerous pictures of my daughter and her best friend in the pool, on the beach and in various outdoor cafes in Portugal. With a surge of missing her, I fire off a text, to which she replies, *Having the best time Mum. Love you xxx.*

My mobile rings – could it be my daughter, missing me desperately? Ah. It's my own mother. 'Hi, Mum, how's things?'

'Well, you know . . .' I wait for her to ask about my trip. 'As good as they can be with the wedding around the corner,' she adds. 'Are you *sure* everything's going to work out okay?'

Without a crystal ball, no. I close my eyes momentarily

and conjure up Romilly Connaught-Jones's reassuring face, her firm voice, her aura of self-assuredness. *You can't let people trample all over you, Lorrie!* 'Yes, Mum. Everyone knows about the new venue, don't they?'

'Yes, of course. It's just, it is only four days away . . .'

'Mum, I know that.' I exhale fiercely.

'Anyway, how was France?'

Ah, she is interested after all! 'Great, thanks.'

'Could *he* be your partner at the wedding?'

I splutter with laughter. As if my man-less status is as embarrassing to her as if I turn up wearing a triangle bikini. 'I don't think that's very likely, I'm afraid.'

'Ah, didn't it go well? Anyway,' she charges on without even waiting for my response, 'I'm still not sure about that bleak little hall. Didn't you find it stark? I did. The bleach smell, the cracked washbasin, all those *old* people having sandwiches and cake—'

'Yes, but they won't be there, will they? And we'll decorate the place. Me and the kids, I mean. We'll get there first thing – I'll check with Walter to make sure we can get in – and we'll bring bunting. I'll make lots and lots of bunting' – *make* bunting? What am I saying? – 'in pastel colours for a sort of village fete theme, it'll look really pretty—'

'Village fete?' she repeats, interest piquing.

'Yes. Or perhaps more of a garden party, like the Queen has . . .'

'Oooh, I like the sound of that.'

'So we'll have bunting, gingham tablecloths, casual bunches of flowers . . .'

There's a beat's silence. 'Hmmm. Can I trust you to pull all that together?'

Well, why not? Apart from marrying Hamish I seem to be doing everything else for this wedding. 'Of course,

Mum – at least, everything apart from the flowers. Could you tell your florist you'd like wild flowers in jam jars? Would that work with the bunting, d'you think?'

'I suppose so,' she says guardedly.

'Great. Now, just try to relax. Honestly – there's absolutely nothing to worry about.'

While this seems to appease her, it strikes me that, as I am back at work tomorrow, I'd better make a start on the promised bunting. As I turn to close my laptop, a Facebook message appears: Antoine. This time, my heart doesn't leap at the sight of it; I merely smile as I read,

Hope you enjoyed your time in Grasse. I know we said we might see each other again. I'd really like to – as friends. You're such fun to be with and I enjoy your love of life very much. All those photos you took. I don't think I've ever seen anyone so enthusiastic about Nice! I should be in London close to Christmas – shall we meet for a coffee then?

That sounds lovely, I reply, deciding to leave it at that for now. Whether or not we'll actually meet up, who knows? But I like to think there's still the possibility of friendship after all these years.

Right now, though, I switch my attentions to the matter in hand. Burrowing in the airing cupboard, I find old sheets which, on closer inspection are rather depressingly – rather than charmingly – faded. So they won't do for bunting. Instead, I gather up a couple of old cotton dresses from my wardrobe, plus several rolls of strong ribbon, and unearth my sewing machine from the cupboard under the stairs, bought to run up the amazing Halloween costumes I never got around to making.

Having installed myself at the kitchen table, I make a paper template and cut out a neat triangle from the skirt of a daisy-print dress. I put my foot tentatively on the pedal, flinching as it whirrs. *Come on,* I tell myself. *You've just 'taken on' Geddes and Cox, so of course you can knock up a few lengths of bunting.* I cut and sew, cut and sew, then pause, wondering what else I can cut up, as a mere six triangles of bunting will hardly create the promised garden party effect.

David's shirts. There are dozens stashed in the attic in bin liners, waiting for . . . what exactly? A decision to be made; perhaps to be donated to charity. They'd be perfect for this, if I can bear to take the scissors to them. I haven't even looked at them for years.

I head upstairs to Cam's bedroom, from where the attic is accessible through a rather precarious hatch, and drag out the stepladder from the landing cupboard. I clamber up it, pushing the hatch to one side, always an awkward manoeuvre, and one which Stu has tended to take care of for me, bringing down the Christmas tree and boxes of decorations and putting them back when required. So why isn't he here, helping me now? Stu has a life of his own, I remind myself. His sole purpose isn't just to assist me with practical matters, and I *don't* need a man to access the attic for me.

I click on the light, spotting a heap of board games, including Buckaroo and Ker-Plunk which David and the kids would play for hours. I tear a small hole in one of the numerous bin liners and glimpse pale blue fabric with a fine pink stripe. Down it goes through the hatch, bouncing onto the floor of Cam's room. Then another, and another: three bags stuffed with faded cottons. Having replaced the hatch, I step carefully down the ladder, considering calling the one friend I need to talk to right now, to ask if it's okay to cut up these shirts and make bunting from them. Or will he think I've gone mad?

I drag the sacks downstairs and tear one fully open, hit immediately by the smell of David. Perhaps it's in my imagination. They have been bundled up in there for seven years, after all. The scent of a person must surely disappear in that time. I spread out a shirt I remember him wearing, casually slung on after a day's swimming in the sea in Cornwall, and place my paper template on it. I start to snip, then pause. I am cutting up David's shirts. It feels almost . . . *violent*. My vision mists and I try to carry on, but I'm making a mess here, cutting a jagged edge. My mobile rings and I answer it with relief. 'Hi, Stu?'

'Hi. So you're back then . . .'

'You know I was back yesterday,' I say curtly. 'But you weren't here.'

'No, um, I just thought it might be best—'

'What are you doing? Why are you at Bob's already?'

The pause stretches uncomfortably. 'I needed a bit of space, that's all.'

'Space? What for?'

I can hear his breathing. 'I'll be back this week, to sort out my stuff . . .'

'Fine,' I say tersely. 'So how's Bob's place coming along?'

'Uh, he's having this urge to paint everything a terrible grey colour.'

'Grey can be okay.' I pause. 'Must be nice, being somewhere uncluttered . . .'

'What d'you mean?'

'You know – without all the books, the magazines, the sports kit lying about . . .'

He laughs. 'Yeah, it's a veritable bachelor pad.'

339

'Since when have you started using words like veritable?'

Stu sniggers dryly. 'I use it all the time now. It's my new favourite word. So, anyway, how was Nice?'

'Not so great, actually.'

'Oh, that's a pity . . .'

'You don't mean that.' I sit there for a moment, sensing there's something he wants to say.

'Um, maybe I don't. So, what are you up to now?'

I scan the table, littered with bleached-out cottons in every conceivable pastel shade. 'I'm . . . cutting up David's old shirts.' Without warning, a tear rolls down my cheek.

'Christ, Lorrie. What are you doing that for?'

'To make bunting for Mum's wedding,' I say, batting away more tears from my cheeks. 'I needed fabric,' I add, 'and they're just shirts, right? I mean, no one'll wear them, it's not as if Cam wants them—'

'Lorrie, love, don't get upset . . .'

'But it's awful,' I exclaim, crying properly now. 'I keep remembering him wearing them. I can picture his face, Stu, I can't help it . . .'

'Hey,' he says gently. 'It's okay. Of course you're going to be upset. Can I come over?'

I grab a piece of kitchen towel and wipe my nose. 'Of course you can, if you want to.' *It's still your home after all,* I want to remind him as we finish the call.

In twenty minutes he's here, first hugging me tightly, then surveying the tumble of fabrics on the table, the snippets scattered all over the floor. 'Oh, Lorrie. This is some job you've landed yourself with.' He pulls off his leather jacket.

'Yes, I know. I must have lost my mind. I mean, it's only a wedding, right? I could have just gone out and *bought* bunting . . . so why didn't I just do that?'

'Because you're nuts,' he says fondly, taking the seat beside me and beginning to cut out more triangles from the shirts. We soon fall into a natural rhythm of cutting and stitching, lulled by the whirr of the sewing machine.

'I think my sister's lost her mind too,' he remarks.

I turn to look at him. 'Why? Is she okay?'

'Oh, it's nothing awful. It's just, the party's off. She doesn't want a big do for her fortieth after all.'

'Really? Why not?'

He shakes his head and smiles ruefully. 'She just got cold feet. Said she was only doing it because all her friends were pressurising her to . . .'

'I assume you're still going out to see her, though?'

'No, I'm not, because she won't even be there. She's taking off on her own. Booked a ticket on the Orient Express, it's running a special trip to Istanbul and she's going to spend her birthday there.'

'Wow – amazing!' I exclaim. 'But what about your flight?'

'I've transferred it over to Bob. He could do with a break.'

I look at him, knowing I should still be cross with him for concocting a flimsy reason as to why he's moving to Bob's. Yet now, with metres of bunting already made, I feel only gratitude that he's here. I pause, wondering if it's okay to ask, or whether the very idea will horrify him. 'So,' I say hesitantly, 'if you're free, maybe you could . . .' I cough awkwardly.

'I could what?'

'I was going to say you could come to Mum's wedding, but I guess that's the last thing you'd want, isn't it? I mean, she'll probably get tipsy, sexually molest you—'

He laughs and scratches at his bristly chin. 'Lorrie, I'd—'

341

'No, I'm *not* going to inflict that on you . . .' I go to lift a bunting triangle from the sewing machine, spiking my finger on the needle. 'Ouch!'

'Hey, be careful!'

I smile and look at him, and something faintly unsettling seems to happen. Perhaps I look at him a moment too long, because my heart seems to turn over. I've just missed him, that's all, and it feels so right, him being here with me now. I wish he'd stay here tonight – I just want him to be close by – but how can I ask him to without sounding needy?

Looking flustered, Stu turns away to select another shirt from the open bag. 'Any you want to keep?' he murmurs.

'No, I think we should use them all up . . .' I watch him, clearly unable to meet my gaze now as he pulls a selection of stripy cottons from the bag. What happened just then? I try to shrug off the feeling – I'm being ridiculous, even thinking there was some kind of spark there – and suck the bead of blood from my finger.

'Yes, I'll come to your mum's wedding,' he says quietly.

I stare at him. 'Really? Are you sure?'

He smiles wryly, and then turns his attentions to cutting out another perfect triangle. 'Honestly, there's nothing I'd like better,' he says, then mimics that painting, *The Scream*, with his hands at his cheeks and a look of sheer terror on his face.

*

It's Stu who fills my mind as I travel to work the next day. He stayed the night in his room here – without me even having to ask – and we had a companionable breakfast together as if everything was normal. However, he

342

made it clear he was heading back to Bob's today, and I made a decent job of hiding my disappointment. I'm just grateful to him for being there when I needed a friend last night.

I join the crowds surging from the tube station, grateful, too, for being able to get on with my job without any more Sonia Richardson meetings hanging over my head. It's a hot and humid Tuesday morning, and as I'm approaching the store, Nuala calls.

'Are you all right?' she exclaims. 'I heard what's been happening. Well, I found out eventually. Sonia was pretty cagey about things but I gather you went in there after seeing a hotshot lawyer and absolutely floored them?'

I laugh. 'Well, sort of – but how d'you know that? I can't imagine that's how Sonia put it . . .'

'No, I managed to get it out of the top woman in HR. Deborah someone. I'm very proud of you, Lorrie. I'm sorry I couldn't have stepped in and helped—'

'It wasn't your fault, Nuala.'

'No, well, I just hope they'll let us get on with our jobs now, and do what we do best.'

I thank her and step into the store, where I am greeted warmly by Helena who's desperate to know what's been going on. But now's not the time. There is work to be done. I am determined to prove to Sonia and the suits that it is possible to adhere to our relaxed and friendly approach, whilst still managing to achieve healthy sales.

Spotting a woman with a little girl in tow, I rev myself up to invite her over to our counter. However, there are no longer any colouring packs in the cupboard; heaven forbid we might be viewed as a creche. The little girl tugs hard on her mother's arm, and before I can even make an approach, they are gone. I make my way back to the counter and busy myself by checking stock levels and catching up on what's been happening in the store since I've been gone.

'Excuse me, could I ask your advice on something?'

I spin around. The customer, who's probably in her early forties, is wearing a rather shabby khaki jacket over a stripy T-shirt and jeans. 'Yes, of course. How can I help?'

She scans the counter. Her skin is in good condition, blemish-free and with few lines, but a little sallow. 'I just . . .' She shrugs. 'I've sort of given up on make-up but I thought, well, I have a job interview coming up. I just think it might . . .' She tails off. 'It might help, you know?'

'Great, so what sort of make-up d'you wear normally?'

She looks blank. 'I just said – I don't wear any.'

'Oh, of course. Sorry. Well . . .' I start to select a few products: a light base, a selection of browns for her greyish eyes, and an easy-to-wear natural shade for her lips. Oh, and blusher. Her rather washed-out complexion could do with a lift . . . 'Could you hop on the stool for a moment for me, please?'

She smiles wanly as she does so, and I start by applying a light moisturiser to her face, 'Just to soften your skin, plump it up a little . . . so, what sort of job are you going for?'

'Just an admin thing,' she says.

'And you want to feel well presented.'

She laughs quietly. 'Yeah, that's the idea.'

'Always nerve-racking, aren't they, interviews? Feeling under scrutiny like that?' My meeting with Sonia, Nigel and Dennis flits back into my mind.

The woman nods as I squeeze a little base onto a cosmetic sponge. 'It's my first one in years, actually,' she murmurs. 'I've been out of work for a while, doing a bit

344

of studying, trying to . . . you know. Retrain. Get myself together.' She tails off as I start to apply the base. Already, her skin looks brighter.

'Oh, yes, I do know that feeling. Well, you've come to the right place.' I move to the eyes now, applying a beige base to the lids, followed by a brownish shadow. 'Open your eyes, please.'

I check the shading, the dark, nutty brown against the soft grey of her eyes, and that's when it hits me: those eyes. I know them. I know this face. It's the face I pored over obsessively, even though I knew it wasn't helping – it only made things worse – until it haunted my dreams.

She frowns as I pause briefly, as if she has noticed a change in my demeanour. I click back to the present and clear my throat. However, I am no longer capable of making casual chit-chat as I stroke dark brown liner along her upper lids, followed by mascara, blusher and lipstick. I am on autopilot now, touching up the lips and blending the eyes: blend, blend, blend, as they taught us in training, for a soft and flattering effect. Perhaps I over-blend because, at some point, she shifts back on her stool, leaving me holding the brush in mid-air. And now she is speaking, or at least her freshly painted lips are moving. She tilts her face to the mirror, and at first I think she's saying, *I'm sorry, I'm so sorry for what I did.* She's not, of course. It's just in my head, mingling with the scents of the beauty hall which, for the first time ever, seem too powerful – suffocating, almost. No wonder children often complain: 'It smells in here!' Is it always like this?

'Lorrie?' I jolt at the sound of Helena's concerned voice. 'Your customer here . . .' She flashes a professional smile. 'She was just saying how much she loves her make-up . . .'

'Oh, I do,' the woman enthuses. 'I think I might treat myself . . .'

Normally I'd have lined up all the products in a tidy and tempting array, awaiting selection. However, now they are all scattered haphazardly on the counter, the used cosmetic sponge still lying there, and I could have been pinged down from the homewares department, so strange and bewildering everything feels. I am vaguely aware of the woman saying, 'Oh, God. I can't decide . . . d'you think the base, the lipstick or maybe the blusher? Or would the mascara be the most practical thing?'

I look at her blankly, incapable of helping her in any way. I don't want to help her. I just want her to disappear before my eyes like a spray of perfume.

Across the floor, the girls at the brow bar are bantering loudly, while Helena steps forward swiftly to help our customer decide what to choose for herself. Base, lips, eyes, cheeks: she's buying a lot, I realise. She smiles gratefully and turns to me.

'Thank you, you've made me feel a whole lot better about myself . . .' Then the face of Anneka Salworth, whose car skidded on that snowy road seven years ago, goes all fuzzy and I feel nauseous and unbearably hot, and then there is nothing.

Chapter Thirty-Five

It's Helena's face I see first, but it all seems wrong because we're not at the counter or even in the miserable yellow-walled sick room on the second floor. All I know is that I am lying down and her face is looming above me. 'You're okay, Lorrie. No need to worry. You just had a faint, that's all.'

'Low blood pressure,' comes the male voice, and I realise now that some kind of tight band is attached to my arm, and I am in an ambulance, although I don't know whether we are moving or stationary or where we might be.

'Are the kids all right?' I blurt out, trying to scramble up from the narrow bed.

'Just rest,' the man says. 'There's absolutely nothing to worry about.' I focus on his face. It's round and pink, shiny-cheeked, reassuring. There's a fuzz of white hair on his head. 'You were only out for a few minutes,' he adds, 'but we're taking you to hospital just to run some tests, to be certain . . .'

'But I'm supposed to be at work! Do the kids know what's happened? Can I phone them?'

'Lorrie, it's *fine*,' Helena insists. 'Andi had just arrived and, anyway, you shouldn't be thinking about that now. I'm sure the kids are fine too. Amy's in Portugal, remember?'

I nod, remembering now that it's Amy's birthday next week and I haven't bought her a present yet. I should have chosen her something in Nice. I should have explored the other floors of that department store, perhaps picked out some sportswear, a football top . . . Helena squeezes my hand and I close my eyes, registering that we are moving now.

We arrive at A&E where, despite my badgering – as I feel nothing more than a little dizzy now – Helena refuses to return to work. She remains at my side while a torch is shone into my eyes and my blood pressure taken again. We wait some more, parked on plastic chairs among people hobbling on crutches and with bleeding wounds, people who really do need the services of the NHS. Finally, clad now in a terribly unfetching backless hospital gown – which I'm sure Antoine would find as alarming as my shouting – I am told to lie on a bed in a curtained cubicle while sticky patches are pressed to my chest and my heart is monitored.

Hours later we emerge, with Helena holding my arm protectively even though the doctors found nothing wrong with me. 'I wonder what brought it on?' she asks as we stand at the kerbside, waiting for a taxi.

'Low blood pressure, they said.'

'Hmm. It was pretty hot in there today. But that's hardly unusual, is it? And it's never happened before—'

'Yes,' I cut in, 'but then, Anneka Salworth has never walked up to our counter before, either.'

Helena frowns at me. 'Anneka Salworth?'

I keep scanning the street for a cab. 'The woman whose car killed David.'

348

'Oh, my God!' she exclaims. 'You should have said! Why on earth didn't you tell me? You could have whispered, I'd have dealt with her or sent her away . . .'

I manage to smile, despite everything. 'Can you imagine how Sonia would react if she found out we'd sent a customer away?'

'Oh, come on, Lorrie. We could have done something. I don't know how you managed to carry on doing her make-up. I'd have . . .' She breaks off.

'What would you have done, though?'

She pulls a baffled face. '*Said* something.'

'No, you wouldn't. I mean, what would you have said? "Oh, you're the woman who killed the father of my children"?'

'Probably, yes,' she splutters.

I exhale. 'She'd have been horrified.'

'Well, maybe she *should* have been horrified . . .'

'Helena,' I say carefully, 'I know what you're saying and, of course, part of me wanted to tell her who I was, and how she ruined my life and our children's lives . . .' She nods and squeezes my hand. 'But what would have been the point? I mean, what would I have gained by that?'

'You might have felt a bit better,' she mutters, 'having the opportunity to tell her exactly what she did to you . . .'

'No, I wouldn't. Anyway, there's no way it would have come out rationally, like we're talking now. I'd have been in a state . . .'

'You *were* in a state,' she cuts in. 'You ended up flat on the floor! You were out cold, you could have cracked your head open or anything—'

'Yes, well, I didn't, and I'm okay now – and not just in the way the doctor said. I mean, I really *am* okay. I've moved on from it and it looks like Anneka Salworth's trying to do that too . . .'

Helena frowns in confusion. 'You mean, you want her to move on? You've forgiven her for what she did?'

I pause. 'In a way, yes, I have. She's been in prison. She was convicted of causing death by dangerous driving. She knows she killed David, and it wasn't deliberate . . .'

'But her doctor had said she shouldn't drive!' Helena catches herself. 'I'm sorry. It's none of my business . . .'

'No, it *is*,' I insist as a cab comes into view. 'You were there for me after he died. You helped me through it all – you were brilliant with Cam and Amy – and I hardly knew you then. But I'm okay, you know.' I hail the cab and smile at her. 'Honestly, I really am.' The cab pulls up beside us. 'You want to take this? I assume you're going back to work?'

'I will, but I'll be quicker by tube. You take it, go home and get some rest.'

'You know, I think I will do that,' I say, hugging and thanking her for being there yet again, and climb into the back of the taxi.

She waves as we pull away, and then strides towards the tube station, heading back to the store which has almost felt like home to me these past ten years – the kind of place where you sense that nothing bad could ever happen. But today it did.

As we crawl through the traffic I picture its frontage, so delightfully old-fashioned with its wooden revolving doors and brass plaques, one of the last left in London that hasn't been swallowed up by a huge company. It's all summer fashion in the window display at the moment: bright prints and sparkles and sequinned beach bags, which will soon make way for muted autumn shades, all the

browns and greys and burgundys, then Halloween –
seasonal celebrations are always embraced with gusto
– and then Christmas, January sales, Valentine's Day,
Mother's Day, Easter and summer again . . . On and on
it rolls, year after year. I have always loved being a part
of the place but after today – and my Anneka Salworth
encounter – it's Claudine and Mimi I'm thinking about,
determined to focus on their new venture instead of
clinging onto the past. And what did Sonia Richardson
say again? 'I assume you're not planning to sell make-up
for the rest of your life?'

Well, maybe I'm not, who knows? I settle back in the
seat of the cab, watching shoppers milling in and out of
the stores as the tiniest germ of an idea starts to form in
my mind.

*

Back home, having learned of today's events at the hospital,
Cam gamely knocks together our dinner: pasta with pesto,
not Stu's home-made version of course, just a jar from
the cupboard. However, it raises my spirits to watch him
doling out super-sized portions into cereal bowls, and I
bestow him with thanks.

We hang out together, watching TV, munching on crisps
and speculating on what Amy might be doing now, until
Mo shows up, and the two of them head out for the
evening. The house feels quiet without him, oddly still
and decidedly empty. Even the kitchen cupboards are
looking bare. Despite Stu often being out on deliveries,
he sort of filled the space here, even when he wasn't here.
I am missing seeing his biker boots lying in the hall, his
habit of storing bread in the fridge. And, okay, I am also

missing spotting a Post-it note stuck to the lid of the cake tin, saying EAT ME.

I decide to run a deep bubble bath and, while it's filling, I poke my head around his bedroom door – well, our spare room now, I suppose, even though most of his possessions are still here. I consider calling him, just to chat, to tell him about Anneka Salworth, but after my bunting emergency last night I decide it's best not to load more woes upon him. Perhaps that's why he's moving out: because he'd simply had enough of the ups and downs of my life.

I close the door and sink into my bath, determining that, as soon as Mum's wedding is over, I'll decide what to do about his room. Perhaps I should let it out to a student after all? Cam and Amy are so often out and about, doing their own thing, and I know I'll miss having young people about the place when they do fly the nest.

In bed now, I flip open my laptop and check for any activity on the dating site. I have several 'winks', all from seemingly decent-looking men, no obvious weirdos or anyone lacking in teeth. I flick through the profiles, gasping audibly as I spot a face I already know. It's Eric from the park. Handsome, red-haired Eric, with a wide, slightly crooked smile and crinkly eyes, as if he's been caught mid-laugh. Eric who owns an off-licence, for crying out loud – always handy in a crisis, as Pearl pointed out. So he's playing the dating game too. And he's winked at me! I study his profile and small selection of pictures. Even without having met him, I'd be interested; he's a nice-guy-with-a-dog, I decide. Kind, friendly, easy on the eye. Not the type to say *anything* about a woman's weight. I consider whether to wink back, fire off a friendly message or delay doing anything at all. Oh, what the hell . . .

Hi, Eric,
Fancy meeting you on here! What a lovely surprise. Would
you like to meet for a drink sometime? I am away at my
mother's wedding this Friday and Saturday morning, but
perhaps sometime after that?

I press send, then come off the site and check Cecily's
Facebook page. It's filled with pictures of the Kenton
family – and Amy – all gathered around their turquoise
pool at the Portuguese villa. With a twinge of missing her,
I send her another chatty text, deciding not to mention
the fact that Stu is moving out. Like Cam, she'll be disappointed. I scroll through Dad's recent pictures too, and
glance only briefly at Antoine's page – there's nothing new
on there – by which time Eric has replied:

Hi Lorrie, I couldn't believe it when I saw you here either.
How about Saturday evening? Shall we meet at the pub
in London Fields?

Sounds perfect, I reply.
So, another date to add to my diary. Surely there'll be
no nasty surprises with an amiable, dog-loving man?
Too charged up to sleep now, I sit upright in bed and
start to carefully compose the email I've been thinking
about ever since I left hospital today:

Dear Claudine and Mimi,
It was wonderful to see you. Thank you so much for your
hospitality. It was an honour to visit your home and garden
– the inspiration behind La Beauté. The good news is,
since I've been back, I've had a meeting with the new
management who have agreed that I can stay in position

as counter manager, and that nothing will change. But as you know, things have changed. It's just not the company we all loved anymore, and now I think it's time for me to consider moving on to something new. A fresh start, if you like – just like you're doing too.

I've been thinking about the sketches and photographs you showed me in your studio. I'm convinced you're right, and that this is something women would love – a sort of escape, where they can shake off their responsibilities and disappear from the real world for a short time. Somewhere to go with no pressure to buy. I know some people think beauty is trivial but I have never felt that. Doesn't every woman deserve to treat herself, and be looked after, once in a while?

So, when you are ready to look for premises for your first Claudine & Mimi beauty store in London, I'd like to put myself forward to head up things here in the UK. You know I am devoted to beauty. I manage my team well and have lots of experience of recruitment. My girls here are excellent.

Most importantly, perhaps, I understand what you are trying to do with the new venture, and I know I can interpret your vision and make the London store a wonderfully inviting place where any woman will simply love to be. I do hope you can keep me in mind.

With very best wishes,

Lorrie

Chapter Thirty-Six

Two days isn't nearly enough time to get ready for the wedding, according to Mum. 'What about underwear?' she laments down the phone. 'I can't get married in Primark knickers . . . can we go shopping again?'

'Sorry, but not this week, and don't tell me all your underwear is from Primark. That's simply not true. Bet Hamish has bought you some lovely fancy things.' Since my little adventure in Nice I'm finding it easier to brush off her demands.

'He might have,' she says reluctantly.

'Just choose something plain and simple so it doesn't spoil the line of your dress . . .'

'Plain and simple? I'm going to be a bride, not a nun!'

She can truss herself up in a rubber corset for all I care at this point, although I refrain from saying so. Instead, I explain that Stu can come after all.

'He's rearranged things just for me?'

'Not exactly, but—'

'Oh, isn't he a darling? I'm delighted, Lorrie. I was so worried about you sitting there all alone.'

Meanwhile, with Amy's sixteenth birthday just around the corner, I use my lunchbreak on Wednesday to acquire an entire new basketball kit, plus two concert tickets, a pair of Converse, underwear and multi-packs of sports socks. Tickets aside, it all seems rather functional, but it's what she likes. I'd never dream of buying her perfume; she takes after her dad on that score. 'I've never knowingly worn aftershave,' he quipped one Christmas as soon as his mother was out of earshot, having presented him with an enormous bottle of Gucci Homme.

On Thursday lunchtime, I make a beeline for my store's homewares department, where I buy gingham napkins and tablecloths, and then hurry onwards to the fashion floor – not my usual hunting ground, but time is of the essence now. The sales assistants rally together to present me with a selection of possible footwear options to wear with my dusky pink dress on the big day. 'Wow, you're cutting it a bit fine,' remarks one of the girls. I settle on gorgeous black suede sandals embellished with tiny pearlised beads.

Amy returns that evening, honey-golden and, I suspect, slightly relieved to be home. 'It was great,' she confides, 'but they're so competitive, Mum. We couldn't have a swim without it being turned into a race. The boys are unbelievable . . .'

'Well, they are all high achievers,' I remark with a smile.

'Yeah, I know. It's exhausting. I'm so glad we're just normal . . .'

'Well, the jury's out on that.'

She laughs, her sunny mood only slightly dented when I tell her that Stu is in the process of moving to Bob's. 'We will still see him, won't we?' she asks.

'Of course we will,' I assure her. 'I've been friends with him since I was your age, darling. He's not getting rid of us that easily.' She still looks disgruntled as I leave her to unpack while I try on my outfit for the wedding tomorrow, perking up only when I reappear downstairs in my dress and heels.

'You look gorgeous, Mum,' she exclaims as I parade up and down the living room in a jokey catwalk strut. Amy will wear a chic little sleeveless red dress with no embellishment whatsoever, plus her sole pair of heels; it's all put together with zero fuss, and when she appears downstairs in it, I'm quite choked at how lovely she looks. With Cam, I have to exercise rather more quality control, but we dig out a shirt for him, plus smart trousers and a proper pair of shoes.

Late on Thursday evening, I am overcome with panic about the next day. There is nothing specific to fret about; the bunting and table decorations are all packed up, and as long as Mum has dispatched proper instructions to the florist, everything should be okay. However, her agitation is infectious, and I can't settle until I have called Hamish to check that everything has come together at their end.

'Everything's fine,' he says. 'We've had a lovely evening – we've been out to dinner and she's had just enough wine to take the edge off things.'

'Smart move,' I say, smiling. 'So, we'll be at the hall first thing, decorating the place, and then I'll be at your place to do Mum's make-up . . .'

'I don't know what we'd have done without you . . .'

'Really,' I say, 'it's nothing, Hamish. I'd just like both of you to enjoy your day.'

On Friday morning we set off, Stu having shown up looking extremely dapper in a dark grey suit and crisp white shirt. 'It's Bob's,' he admits, and I resist the temptation to quip, 'So you're sharing clothes now?' Because

I am delighted he's coming with us, sitting beside me in my scrappy car, kids in the back, the boot stuffed with our overnight bags and boxes of neatly folded table linen and bunting.

As arranged, we first stop at Little Cambersham village hall, where Walter Fadgett lets us in to festoon the room with bunting. The stripes, the checks and bleached-out cottons look incredibly pretty when strung up about the place. Trying not to think of them as shirts at all, I busy myself with the help of the kids as we spread out the tablecloths. The florist arrives with numerous hand-tied bunches of flowers, plus the requested jam jars; the hall looks quite lovely when we've finished.

From here, we drive onwards to the pub where we are staying tonight after the wedding. The Laughing Duck is a delightful, low-slung whitewashed building, its hanging baskets a blaze of blue lobelia and pale pink geraniums. While the kids and I will be packed into the family room in the eaves, Stu is relegated to the 'staff room', no more than a bleak cubbyhole really, which was all that was available when I requested a last-minute addition.

'It's fine,' he asserts, when we confer on the landing. 'Anyway, you know what your mum's like. After a few wines she'll probably have me tucked up with her and Hamish.'

'Now there's an image I'll never be able to un-see,' I retort.

Bags deposited, we drive on to Hamish's family seat. It's the first time I've seen the place for real, and I'm taken aback by how neglected and faded it looks, not nearly as impressive as in those photos Mum's always wafting around. Window frames are peeling, the roof sags in several places, and precarious-looking scaffolding clings to one of the gable ends. Several dismal outhouses are dotted around the grounds. I suspect now that Hamish's parents were just being difficult in refusing to have a marquee, as from what I can see as we follow the curving driveway, the lawn is in a pretty awful condition. A sign reading 'closed until further notice' hangs on the tea room door.

We park alongside a row of vehicles – ranging from a dented silver Bentley to a scuffed red Mini – on a weed-smattered gravelled area and make our way to the huge studded front door, where I rap the large brass knocker. We wait, and Stu squeezes my arm reassuringly. The door is opened, finally, by a middle-aged woman in a stark black dress and orthopaedic-looking shoes, her sandy hair in a tight ponytail.

'Hi, I'm Lorrie,' I start.

'Ah, yes.' She glances at Stu. 'This is your husband?'

'Er, no, this is Stu, my friend, and Cameron and Amy . . .'

'Do come in,' she says briskly. 'Everyone's getting ready . . .' She ushers us through to the drawing room. 'I'm Christine, the housekeeper,' she adds. 'Can I get you all some tea or coffee?'

'Don't go to any trouble,' Stu says quickly. 'I'm sure everyone's very busy.' He turns to the kids. 'We're happy waiting here, aren't we, while your mum does Grandma's make-up?' Cam and Amy insist they're fine, and arrange themselves rather stiffly on brocade armchairs under the gaze of gloomy oil paintings and deer heads hazed with dust.

While I am expecting to meet Hamish's parents, it's the groom himself who greets us warmly in a cream linen suit, his hair oddly flattened, his cheeks flushed pink. 'Ah, Lorrie, I'm glad to see you. Marion's a little . . .'

'Nervous?' I suggest.

'Just a bit. She seems out of sorts. I do hope she isn't having a change of heart . . .'

359

'Oh, Hamish, of course she's not! What makes you say that?'

He shakes his head. 'Just her mood today. You know, I wish we'd done it my way, just a small ceremony without fuss . . .' He tails off, his hands shaking slightly, and I'm overcome by a wave of affection for him.

'You're doing this for Mum,' I suggest gently.

He nods. 'I'll do anything to make her happy, you know. Come on, I'll take you upstairs where she's waiting for you.'

I throw Stu and the kids a worried look as we head towards the hallway.

We climb the sweeping stairs in silence. Various voices float down as Hamish accompanies me to a bedroom entirely done out in pale peach, where Mum is perched on a dressing table stool in satin pyjamas with her hair freshly set.

'Good luck,' he whispers, then scuttles away as I embrace her. She sits rigidly, as if waiting for me to stop all my cuddly nonsense.

'Feeling okay, Mum?'

'Er, yes, I think so,' she says, sounding uncharacteristically timid. Her mouth is set in a straight line.

I pull up a chair and sit beside her. 'You look really worried. You know everything's going to be okay, don't you? It's all sorted—'

'It's not that.' She turns to the dressing table mirror and pulls a face. 'It's this.'

I frown. 'What d'you mean?'

'This old face,' she exclaims, leaning closer towards the glass. 'You know the thing about marrying a younger man? You just feel so *old*!'

For a moment, I'm stuck for words. I have never heard

360

her speak this way before. 'Oh, Mum, Hamish loves you,' I say, touching her shoulder. 'Your age doesn't matter to him, and anyway, you don't look anything like your real age. I doubt if he even considers it.'

Her eyes sparkle with sudden tears as I squeeze her hand. From the whiff on her breath, I assume alcohol has already been taken. Not too much, I hope. I know how tricky she can be after that third glass. 'I just wonder what the point is,' she adds crossly. 'Having my hair done, my make-up, trying to look nice . . .'

I start to unpack my make-up on the dressing table. 'Of course there's a point. It gives you, I don't know – a boost, a feeling of being all pulled together and ready for anything . . .'

'Is this the kind thing you say to your customers?'

'Yes, it is,' I say as I smooth moisturiser into her face, 'but I *do* mean it, you know – otherwise I wouldn't be able to do my job. Okay, shall we get started now? Go with those colours we talked about?'

She nods and I set to work, aware of gravelly voices drifting from faraway rooms. We don't talk as I stroke taupe eyeshadow onto her lids, then enhance her pale blue eyes with a soft brown liner. Cheeks, lips, brows groomed and defined: she looks wonderful.

'Well, what d'you think?'

She blinks at the mirror. 'It's not finished.'

'Mum, you don't want to look too made up. We said a fresh, natural look, didn't we? That's what we decided, when we practised—'

'Yes, fresh and natural, Lorrie, with *bronzer*.'

I wince. 'D'you really need bronzer? I honestly think blusher's enough. It's more modern, you know . . .' I catch her stony expression in the mirror.

361

'Bronzer please, if you *don't* mind. You think I want to get married looking like a corpse?'

'Mum, trust me. You won't look . . .'

'Come on, Lorrie. Just a little!' She stares into the mirror as, with a sinking heart, I take the lid off the pot of shimmery pearls that's sitting, ready and waiting, on the dressing table. *Whatever makes the customer happy*, I muse as I dip my biggest blusher brush into the pot.

Leaving Mum to get dressed in the *un*-Jacobean frock, Stu, Cam, Amy and I have coffee and cakes at a tea room in the village, before joining the guests all congregating outside the small and astoundingly pretty church. In fact, there aren't as many as I'd expected. While I recognise and greet several of Mum's friends, there are few relatives present from our side; over the years, various inexplicable squabbles have driven Mum to sever ties with most of them. I recognise Nancy, a cousin of hers, and there are introductions and polite small-talk. 'This is my friend Stu,' I say, feeling obliged to make it clear that he's not my husband.

Meanwhile, on Hamish's side guests range from excitable children, who are already charging around the church grounds, to elegant ladies in pastel-hued hats who could possibly be well into their nineties. Still no sign of his parents. I sense of a stab of sympathy for Mum, realising now how uncomfortable she must feel when they clearly object to her being part of the family.

'You must be Hamish's new stepdaughter,' remarks an older lady, her hair set in immaculate silvery curls.

I smile, feeling far too old to be anyone's stepdaughter but agreeing that they make a lovely couple, and isn't it wonderful that they're so happy together?

'It really is,' the woman says, extending her hand. 'I'm Nanny Bridget.'

362

'Oh, Hamish's nanny?' I shake her hand warmly.

'That's right, dear. A big grown-up man now, but he'll always be my little boy, scuffing his knees and stuffing his face with too many redcurrants in the garden.' She chuckles as the silver Bentley I spotted at Lovington Hall purrs to a halt at the end of the lane. 'I assume you've met Hamish's parents?' she whispers.

'No, I haven't actually.'

'Ah, well, they're not quite so delighted but they'll come round, don't you worry.' She glances at Cameron and Amy. 'You'll know how hard it is to let one's children go.'

'Oh yes, I do.'

'But he's, like, *fifty-eight*,' Amy sniggers as we all start to filter into the church, where low-key organ music creates a sense of calm.

As we take our places on pews, I realise my hands are sweating. Stu leans across Amy to whisper, 'Are you okay?'

'Just about,' I reply as the music grows louder, our cue to stand and turn as Mum and Hamish appear at the church door.

My heart seems to clench. They are gazing at each other, and now I realise that Mum's mutterings about his failings are just an act, when in fact she clearly adores him. Clasping her arm, Hamish is beaming at her as if she were the most beautiful woman he's ever laid eyes on. They start to walk up the aisle, Mum shimmering metallically but still radiant in her blue dress. She is all smiles now as she greets her public with a regal flutter of her hand.

The ceremony commences, and I spend the whole time fighting back tears. It really is beautiful, seeing a couple formalise things in such a gorgeous setting surrounded by the people they love. With a stab of regret, I find myself wishing – for the first time – that David and I had done it, not to prove anything or because we weren't fully committed, but just for the actual day, to have something special to remember. God, what's happening to me? I glance past Amy and Cam to where Stu is standing. He raises a brow and sends me a stoical smile, as if understanding exactly what's going on inside my head.

It's all over so quickly, in a torrent of confetti as Mum and Hamish leave the church.

The reception is everything Mum didn't want it to be, and it's *wonderful*. There's no stately home, no quarry reopened: just a hall in a pretty Hertfordshire village, decked out in bunting, with everyone sipping champagne and nibbling on canapés and bestowing Mum with the attention she craves. Even Hamish's relatives look impressed. I catch Nanny Bridget straightening his bow tie, and almost expect her to spit on a napkin and wipe his face with it.

At the buffet, Stu and I sit with Mum's friend Dolores, who has just about managed to forgive her for rejecting the Jacobean dress she made with such care. The mood is incredibly jolly, and I am showered with compliments on the bunting, and even the buffet, despite having had nothing to do with it. Yet Nanny Bridget insists on praising me as if I had lovingly fashioned every prawn and caviar canapé myself.

The band arrives in the early evening, a motley collection of middle-aged men in ill-fitting suits who, I believe, are friends of Hamish's from his bridge club. The music starts up – a mixture of big band show tunes and wonky cover versions of seventies hits – and Mum dances with Hamish, then with Walter Fadgett who has lingered on to check that all's going to plan, and then Stu, clutching him to her heaving bosom while Hamish merely gazes in adoration at his bride. Cam and Amy sip their champagne and watch, grinning, as though being treated to a live version of a wedding-themed reality TV show. Noticing Cam sneaking off outside, I wonder whether he's tippled a little too much champagne, and keep glancing at the door, itching to slip out and check on him. Hamish bowls up to our table, and introduces us all to his parents who, thankfully, seem to be doing a sterling job of masking their disapproval. In fact, they are quite charming, with Hamish's father declaring, 'This is the kind of thing I like. Being with regular people in simple surroundings like this. Salt of the earth . . .'

'He's enjoying mixing with the peasants,' Stu whispers with a grin.

I smile and make my excuses as I step outside to find my son. He is leaning against the rough stone wall, and I can tell immediately that he is a little drunk. He is also smoking a cigarette.

'I wish you wouldn't do that,' I remark.

'Yeah, well.' He shrugs and looks down at the moss-speckled gravel.

I study his face. He looks pale and worried, and I wonder now whether he came out here fearing he might be sick. 'Are you all right, darling? You don't look too well.'

'I'm fine, I've only had two glasses . . .' It's not true, not that I've been counting; it's my inbuilt teen-booze barometer and it's pretty accurate as a rule. 'Mum . . .'

Oh God, he *is* going to be sick. 'Hang on, let me get you some water or something, or a bucket—'

'I don't need a bucket!'

'But you look—'

'Mum, it's not that. I'm not drunk, okay?' He manages to raise a wonky smile. 'It's, it's Mo and me . . .'

'Mo and you?'

'Yeah, you know . . .'

'Oh, are you going to that festival?' I smile and wrap an arm around him. 'You want a loan, don't you? For tickets before they sell out?'

He is laughing now, shaking his head at my idiocy. 'Oh God, Mum. D'you really not know? Haven't you realised at all?'

A rather raggedy version of 'Livin La Vida Loca' filters out of the hall. 'Realised what?'

'That we're, y'know. *Together.*'

I peer at him and then I understand, and we're hugging, even though he's still clutching his cigarette, and I'm apologising for being such an idiot and not knowing, and he's saying it's fine, he knew I'd be okay. I want to stay out here for a while, just Cam and me, so I can ask about Mo, about whether he makes him happy. But Stu is at the door of the hall, beckoning us in. 'Come on, they're cutting the cake!'

I grab Cam's hand and squeeze it as we hurry back inside. As everyone else gathers around, Stu and I find ourselves loitering at the back of the hall, sipping our drinks, enjoying a few moments' respite from the music. I want to tell him about Cam, and I will, as long as Cam says it's okay. I want to tell Stu everything, I decide, glancing at him. Well, almost everything. Perhaps I'll miss out the bit about being ticked off for being too shouty in bed.

'So,' he ventures with a teasing smile, 'how *was* your boring fart in a suit?'

366

'That's a bit judgemental, isn't it?' I smirk. 'Pretty awful actually. I mean, not all of it. But I won't be visiting him again.'

'Oh, right.' In terms of masking his delight, Stu fails spectacularly.

'But some people do have to wear suits,' I add, skimming his wedding outfit with my gaze. 'They have corporate jobs that don't involve bombing around on a motorbike with bunches of coriander . . .' He chuckles, as I continue. 'You look great, by the way. Terribly dapper. You should wear one more often.'

He pulls a bashful face. 'You reckon?'

'Yes, you could even buy your own.'

'Okay, if you say so.' He glances at me, and something about his expression makes me look away.

'So how are things with Ginny Benson?' I venture.

He shrugs. 'There's no *thing* with Ginny Benson.'

'Not even deliveries?' I ask, raising a brow. 'No raw organic vinegar required at 2 a.m.?'

'No,' he says, laughing now. 'It was a bit of a sort-of-nothing-thing.'

'Oh, is *that* what you call it?'

He grins at me and my heart seems to quicken. He's standing so close, I sense him breathing. I'm just missing him, that's all. I'm missing his lovely lemon cake and his encyclopedic knowledge of the entire ranges stocked by virtually every North London supermarket and speciality store. I miss seeing my best friend every day; the man I love, really, when all's said and done. Because we really are best friends, and always have been. We leave personal correspondence lying about, we answer each other's phones, and his pants often whirr around in the washing machine with mine. He has seen me splayed on the sofa,

367

first with Cam and then Amy clamped to a veiny breast. He's wiped the tears and snot – copious snot, like a face full of glue – off my face at David's funeral. He helped me to box up his things and carry them up that shaky ladder to the attic, saying, 'So, okay, you know everything's still here but you don't have to see it all the time. I think it's better that way. We can deal with it at some point – together – when you feel ready.'

Further back – way, way back, to the eighties – he helped to pull me together after Antoine stopped writing and I was a heartbroken mess. There was that kiss, of course, our one little romantic slip-up in the thirty-odd years we've been friends.

I turn, realising he's saying something. 'Sorry? I was miles away there—'

He smiles. 'I just said you look pretty damn hot in that dress with your hair like that.'

'Jesus, Stu,' I exclaim, 'I'm too old to be hot. I'm well out of the hot demographic . . .'

'No, you're not,' he says, giving my arm a matey squeeze. 'You look bloody gorgeous actually. Am I allowed to say that?'

'Yes,' I say, kissing his cheek, 'but only because you're drunk.' Then, as the band launches into an enthusiastic rendition of 'Dancing Queen', I grab his hand and pull him across the room to the floor. 'Come on,' I say, 'let's dance before Mum gets her hands all over you again.'

Chapter Thirty-Seven

As Walter seems in no hurry to shovel us out, we overrun our allotted time slot and party well into the night until, finally, out we all tumble into waiting taxis.

'You won't forget about cleaning up tomorrow, will you?' is his parting shot before we are whisked back to the cosiness of The Laughing Duck.

On the landing I hug Stu, wishing for a moment that we could stay here like this for a few minutes more; I'm not sure if it's gratitude I feel or something more. 'I'm so glad you were there today,' I murmur, pulling away.

'Me too,' he says fondly. 'Seriously, a big bash in Venice wouldn't have been a patch on that.'

I laugh, and we part company, the kids already tucked up in their beds by the time I step into our room. In the bathroom I peel off my dress and pull on pyjamas. I fall asleep instantly, dreaming of speeding along a coastal road on the back of a motorbike.

Amy is the only one who isn't feeling fragile over breakfast. We lounge over a full English and the Saturday newspapers until my conscience pricks me and the four

369

of us take a taxi back to the village hall. Here, we literally roll up our sleeves and tear into washing up and sweeping, all of us working flat out.

As I drive us back to London, everyone dozes. I am grateful for this. If Stu started asking what I'm up to later today, I'd have to tell him about meeting Eric, and it doesn't feel like the right time. I glance at him snoozing, his dark eyelashes grazing his cheeks. *You look pretty damn hot in that dress with your hair like that.* Did he mean it? I'm not looking too hot today, I muse, with my bare, beleaguered face, ratty sweatshirt and jeans.

I sense a stab of regret as I drop Stu at Bob's. It still doesn't feel right, but then, it's where he's chosen to live, and anyway, I need to get home and sort myself out in time for this evening's date.

Back home, I change into a denim skirt and a reasonable dressy top, squirt my hair with a water spray and shoosh it up with my hands, then apply the lightest of make-up.

By the time I'm ready, I am already running five minutes late. I call out goodbye to the kids and speed-walk towards London Fields, past Eric's off-licence – there's a poster for a gin tasting evening in the window – and the cafe where I stumbled upon Ralph and the undead Belinda. I march across the fields, past groups of dog walkers all chatting, and a young mum with her little boy. The child is clinging to his mum, as Cam used to do with me, gripping my hand or jacket sleeve, eager for physical contact. Amy rarely did that. Instead, I'd be tearing after her across the park. Clinging tightly or running away – sometimes it seemed as if there was nothing in between.

I spot another woman with a child, her russet hair caught in an untidy ponytail, as she chases her son in a good-natured game. Her face is familiar, and I realise it's Jane, my customer; an NPC actually. The buggy is parked nearby. A handsome young blond man is absent-mindedly pushing it back and forth. Jane catches her son – Archie, that's what he's called. I'm pretty good with names, it's part of the job. I hear him laughing delightedly as I step into the pub.

'Hi, good to see you!' Eric is already here, wearing smart black jeans and a red checked shirt, and springs up from his seat to kiss my cheek.

'Good to see you too.' It feels a little awkward, the two of us here without Pearl and the dogs.

'Can I get you a drink?'

'Yes, a white wine please,' I say, taking a seat at the small table and reminding myself: *it's just a drink, that's all*. A nice simple date, no pretending to appreciate lobster pots or Brillo pads, no being cajoled to try on an outsized stinky jacket.

Eric returns to the table with a beer and a glass of wine, and as we fall into easy conversation my nervousness ebbs away.

I learn that Eric and his wife split up after she had a fling on a girls' holiday and blurted it all out in a fit of guilt. 'Things hadn't been right for a long time, though,' he explains. 'In fact, we almost broke up the second year we were together, and then Lily came along and, well . . .' He smiles and shrugs. 'She kept us occupied, as little children do, and we pottered along for years . . . I'm sorry, do you really want to hear this?'

'Yes, of course I do.'

'Well, I suppose it started to fall apart when Lily was gearing up for leaving home and it would just be the two of us.' He pauses. 'Amanda went on that holiday – said

371

she needed time away from me and just wanted to let her hair down with her mates.' He chuckles ruefully. 'Not a good sign, huh?'

'Probably not,' I agree.

'And that was that. Twenty years, we'd been together – and it was all over in a flash.' He sips his beer and shakes his head in wonderment. I suspect now that he's heartbroken, and is trying his darnedest to gloss over the fact. 'Mad, isn't it?'

'It is,' I agree. 'So, are you friends again now? I mean, is it okay between you?'

'Oh, yeah, it really is – I mean, we're always going to be parents together. I'm sorry, I've been going on about myself . . . what about you? How did things work out with your job?'

He is suitably impressed when I fill him in on my chat with Romilly Connaught-Jones and the subsequent meeting at Geddes and Cox Towers, listening with rapt interest and probing me with questions about what I might do next. I study his face, this handsome, red-haired man who hasn't done anything untoward. In fact, he seems interested in a terribly endearing and non-worrying way. Yet our conversation has remained at a certain level, and I am aware of holding back and giving little away. While he has told me about his marriage breakdown, I have no desire to tell him about the snowy night, and me asking for wine, and David obligingly setting out to buy me a bottle of chardonnay. I don't want to share anything about the accident, and the following terrible months, or becoming a widow at thirty-nine years old. There is only one man who truly knows how it was, and he was there, and has *always* been there for me. I miss him so badly, I realise with a pang. I know Stu says we'll still see each other, but what if it's too late, and I've already lost him forever?

I drain my glass as Eric finishes his drink. 'Would you like another?' he asks.

'Thanks but I'd better go,' I tell him. 'This has been really lovely but, you know, I was at my mother's wedding yesterday . . .'

'Yes, sure. I'm up early tomorrow anyway. I've really enjoyed it too.' There's a polite cheek-kiss as we leave together, and we part company without making definite plans to see each other again. 'See you in the park, hopefully,' he says before striding away.

I hurry home, having already been informed that both Cam and Amy have gone out for the evening – the stamina of young people! – and for once, I'm grateful to have the house to myself. Tonight, I have a serious job to get on with. First, I wrap Amy's presents for her birthday tomorrow. She is celebrating with friends next weekend – no input needed from me on that score, apart from hard cash – but still, I want to make the day special for her.

A cake, I decide. Of course I should make a cake. If Stu were here, he'd do it – funny how I've relied on him for little things without even realising. But how hard can it be? I find a recipe online and burrow about in a cupboard for the right sort of receptacles. 'Spring-form' tins are required, according to the recipe, which I take as an omen that my sponge will indeed be springy and feather-light. I assume they're the ones with a little lever for opening and closing, and unbeknown to me, we have them. We also have eggs, vanilla and both kinds of sugar (caster, icing) so I'm all set. Hell, what about flour? There's plain, but none of the required self-raising. I rummage through the entire cupboard just to make sure.

Of course, there's a shop five minutes away. This is London, after all. But still . . . it's drizzly out there now, and gone 10 p.m. and, actually, that's when our nearest corner shop closes. There's another a little further down the street, but I'm not sure they stock baking ingredients. I can't drive anywhere – I've had a large glass of wine – so really, there's only one option open to me.

I pick up my mobile and pause before selecting the number, willing him to answer my call.

'Lorrie? You okay?'

'Yes, I'm fine. It's just, um . . . look, I'm sorry, you're probably shattered after last night . . .'

'What's up?' Stu asks, sounding the very opposite of shattered. He's quite perky, in fact.

'Oh, I'm just trying to bake a cake for Amy's birthday tomorrow . . .'

Silence hovers between us. '*You're* baking a cake? Am I hearing this correctly or is there something wrong with my phone?'

'Yes,' I say, smiling, 'I really am – or at least, I'm trying to. But there's a small hiccup in my plan.'

'Really? What's that?' I can sense him smirking.

'I've just realised we don't have any self-raising flour . . .' I say *we*, as if he still lives here.

'Can't you just pop out and get some?' he asks.

'Yes, I could, but I wondered . . . what I mean is . . .' I lower myself onto a kitchen chair. 'What I mean is, Stu, the thing is, at the wedding, I realised . . . ' I break off and rub at my glowing face. 'I suppose what I'm *trying* to say is . . .'

'. . . You need Parsley Force,' he chips in.

'I really do. It's an emergency, actually. Would you mind—'

374

He chuckles and makes a big show of umming and arrring just to torture me. "Course I'll come over,' he says finally. 'Anything else you need while I'm at it?'

I laugh awkwardly. 'No. Just, er . . .' I pause, wanting to say so much, but not having the nerve. 'Just you,' I say lightly, hoping he'll understand.

'Okay. I'm leaving right now.'

I wait, my heart thumping, deciding there's no point in touching up my make-up or fixing my hair because he knows what I'm like. He knows me better than anyone. I pace the kitchen and wait, poised for the sound of his motorbike, every minute seeming to stretch forever.

Back up in my bedroom now, I check my emails, and my heart does a flip at the sight of a message from Claudine. *Sorry to be brief, Lorrie. We're getting ready for Mimi's birthday party. It's her 80th and quite a big occasion* – Eighty? I had her down for mid-seventies – *but we were very excited to receive your email and would like to meet you when we come to London, probably in November, to start to look at properties. Let's have afternoon tea. We always enjoyed that when we came to London . . .*

I break off at the sound of the front door opening. The email can wait, I decide, rushing downstairs to find Stu standing in the hallway, a huge grin on his face.

'I bring self-raising flour for the maiden!' he announces, holding the packet aloft.

'Thank you so much,' I say, hugging him. I pull away, not quite knowing what to do next.

'D'you know what?' he says, striding to the kitchen. 'At first, I wondered if you phoning for flour was just an excuse to get me over here . . .'

'As if I'd do that,' I say, laughing.

'Yeah, I know. That's what I thought. I reckoned, well, if you wanted me to come over, then . . .' He stops, his gaze meeting mine. My heart seems to stop as I study his face; his gorgeous greeny-blue eyes, framed by dark lashes, and that lovely sensuous mouth that I kissed once before, what feels like a million years ago . . . and now, all of a sudden, I so want to kiss again.

'Then I'd just have said so,' I murmur. Stu nods and smiles. 'Actually . . .' I clear my throat. 'I did want you here, and it *was* an excuse. I could have just gone out to the shops myself. I mean, this is London . . .'

'. . . Not the Shetlands,' he says with a grin. We laugh and look at each other. 'Well, it's okay,' he adds, 'because I wanted to come. I miss you, you know. It's crazy because I've only been at Bob's for a week but . . .' He shrugs. 'I'm not sure it was the best idea, moving out . . .'

'You don't have to,' I say quickly. 'You can just come back whenever you like. Now, if you want to . . .'

He takes my hand in his, sending shivers right through me. 'Are you sure? I don't want to mess you around—'

'Absolutely,' I say quickly, 'and you've never messed me around.'

His hand squeezes mine. 'I never will, I promise you that.' We fall silent then, as if neither of us can muster the words we need to say. Then he speaks, finally. 'Lorrie . . . you really must know by now.'

'Know what?' I whisper.

'That I'm completely in love with you.' I open my mouth to respond, but he continues: 'I mean, I've always loved you. You're the most important person in my life, you know that? But this past year, being here, being your housemate . . .' He breaks off. 'Well – it made me realise that I don't just love you as a friend. What I mean is . . .'

He stops as my lips touch his. It's the lightest of kisses, yet it sends my head spinning. He pulls back, and that's how we are for a moment or two, just looking as if seeing each other properly for the very first time. 'What I mean is,' he adds, 'I realised I'm madly in love with you, if that's okay . . .'

I move a strand of hair from his eyes and smile. 'Of course it is. It's more than okay. I love you too, and I hope you know that . . .'

'I think I do,' he says softly, and then his arms are around me, and we are kissing deeply for the first time since 1986. We are kissing and kissing, and I feel as if I could dissolve right here in my hallway, and then he takes both of my hands in his and says, 'Okay, my darling, now I'm going to show you how to bake a cake.'

If you enjoyed *The Woman Who Met Her Match*, we think you'll love *The Woman Who Upped and Left*. Turn over to read the first chapter . . .

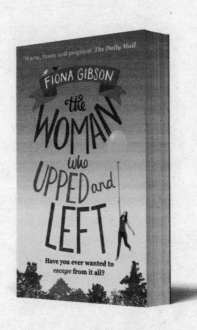

Out Now!

Chapter One
Fried Chicken

Pants. There's a lot of them about. Tomato-red boxers are strewn on the sofa, while another specimen – turquoise, emblazoned with cartoon palm trees and pineapples – has come to rest under the coffee table like a snoozing pet. A third pair – in a murky mustard hue – are parked in front of the TV as if waiting for their favourite programme to come on. I'm conducting an experiment to see how long they'll all remain there if I refuse to round them all up. Perhaps, if left for long enough, they'll fossilise and I can donate them to a museum.

Yet more are to be found upstairs, in the bathroom, slung close to – but crucially not *in* – the linen basket. The act of lifting the wicker lid, and dropping them into it, is clearly too arduous a task for a perfectly able-bodied boy of eighteen years old. It's *infuriating*. I've mentioned it so many times, Morgan must have stopped hearing me – like the way you eventually become unaware of a ticking clock. Either that, or he simply doesn't give a stuff. Not for the first time I figure that boys of this age and their mothers are just not designed to live together. But I *won't*

1

pick them up, not this time. We can live in filth – crucially, he'll also run out of clean pants and have to start re-wearing dirty ones, turned inside out – and see if I care . . .

Beside the scattering of worn boxers lies a tiny scrap of pale lemon lace, which on closer inspection appears to be a thong. This would be Jenna's. Morgan's girlfriend is also prone to leaving a scattering of personal effects in her wake.

I stare down at the thong, trying to figure how such a minuscule item can possibly function as pants. I have never worn one myself, being unable to conquer the fear that they could work their way actually *into* your bottom, and require an embarrassing medical procedure to dig them back out. I know they're meant to be sexy – my own sturdy knickers come in multipacks, like loo roll – but all I can think is: *chafing risk*. And what am I supposed to do with it?

Although Morgan has been seeing Jenna for nearly a year, I'm still unsure of the etiquette where her underwear is concerned. Should I pick it up delicately – with eyebrow tweezers, perhaps – and seal it in a clear plastic bag, like evidence from a crime scene? Tentatively, as if it might snap at my ankle, I nudge it into the corner of the bathroom with the toe of my shoe.

Stifled giggles filter through Morgan's closed bedroom door as I march past. He locks it these days, i.e. with a proper bolt, which he nailed on without prior permission, irreparably damaging the original Victorian door in the process. We've just had a Chinese takeaway and now they're . . . well, obviously they're not playing Scrabble. Having known each other since primary school, they've been inseparable since a barbecue at Jenna's last summer. Favouring our house to hang out in, they are forever draped all over each other in a languid heap, as if suffering from one of those olden-day illnesses: consumption or scarlet fever. They certainly look pretty flushed whenever I happen to walk into the room. '*Yes*, Mum?' my son is prone to saying, as if I have no right to move from room to room in my own home.

'Morgan, I'm off now, okay?' I call out from the landing. Silence.

'I'm meeting Stevie tonight. Remember me saying? I'm staying over, I'll be back around lunchtime tomorrow. Remember to lock the front door and shut all the windows and *try* not to leave 700 lights blazing . . .'

More giggles. How amusingly *petty* it must seem, wishing to protect our home from thieves and avoid a £2000 electricity bill . . .

'And can you start putting milk back in the fridge after you've used it? When I came back last week it had actually turned into cottage cheese . . .'

Muffled snorts.

'Morgan! Are you listening? It blobbed out into my cup!'

'*Ruh*,' comes the barely audible reply. With my teeth jammed together, I trot downstairs, pull on a black linen jacket over my red and black spotty dress, and pick up my overnight bag.

'Bye, Mum,' I call out, facetiously, adding, 'Have a lovely time, won't you?' This is the stage I have reached: the point at which you start talking to yourself in the voice of your own child. Where you say things like, 'Thanks for the takeaway, Mum, I really enjoyed it.'

The spectre of Jenna's lemon thong shimmers in my mind as I climb into my scrappy old Kia and drive away.

*

3

My shabby, scrappy *life*. It's not very 'Audrey', I reflect as I chug through our small, nondescript town en route to the motorway. Although I don't obsess about her – the real Audrey, I mean – I can't help having these thoughts occasionally.

You see, my name is Audrey too. It *was* Audrey Hepburn; let's get that out of the way. It'll come as no surprise that I am named after Mum's favourite actress, which might sound sweet and romantic until I also explain that she and Dad had had an almighty row on the day she was going to register my birth. She'd threatened to go ahead with the Audrey thing. 'Don't you *dare*,' he'd yelled (Mum filled me in on all of this as soon as I was old enough to understand). And she'd stormed off to the registrar's and done it, just to get back at him over some silly slight. 'What did Dad want to call me?' I asked once.

'Gail,' she replied with a shudder, although it sounded perfectly acceptable to me. To be fair, though, I don't imagine Doreen Hepburn anticipated the sniggery comments I'd endure throughout childhood and adolescence. You can imagine: 'Ooh, you're so alike! I thought I was in *Breakfast at Tiffany's* for a minute!' In fact our name is the only thing we have in common. I'd bet my life that the real Audrey never picked up a single pair of pants, not even her own exquisite little scanties, and certainly not someone else's unsavoury boxers. Nor did she drive a crappy old car that whiffs of gravy (why *is* this? To my knowledge there has never been any gravy in it). The real Audrey was arguably the most gorgeous creature to ever walk on this earth. Me, I'm five-foot-two (if I stretch myself up a bit) with a well-padded bottom, boobs that require serious under-wired support and over-zealously highlighted hair. I am a shoveller of peas, a disher-outer of sausages and mash. I am a 43-year-old dinner lady and my wedding ring didn't come from Tiffany's; it was on sale at Argos, £69.

While some women feel disgruntled about changing their name when they marry – or, quite reasonably, flatly refuse to do so – I was so eager to become Audrey Pepper that Vince, my ex, teased, 'It's the only reason you said yes.' I kept it, too, even when I reverted to a 'Miss' after our divorce, when our son turned seven. I never tell boyfriends my maiden name – not that there's been many. There was just the very occasional, casual date until I met Stevie nine months ago in a bustling pub in York.

I couldn't believe this charming, rakishly handsome younger man was interested. So intent was he on bestowing me with drinks and flattery, I suspected I'd been unwittingly lured into some kind of social experiment and that a reality TV crew was secretly filming the whole thing. I imagined people sitting at home watching and nudging each other: 'My God, she actually thinks he fancies her!' I even glanced around the pub for a bloke with one of those huge zoom lenses. In fact, Stevie turned out not to be an actor tasked with seeing how many middle-aged women he could chat up in one night. He runs a training company, specialising in 'mindful time management'. I don't fully understand it, and it still strikes me as odd, considering he seems to have virtually *no* time to spare for normal things like going out for drinks or dinner with me. Hence the venue for tonight's date being a two-hour drive from home.

Here's another un-Audrey thing: meeting your boyfriend at a motorway service station on the M6 on a drizzly Wednesday night. Charnock Richard services, to be precise. We are not merely meeting there before heading off to somewhere more glamorous. I mean, that's *it*. We are spending the night at a motorway hotel. We do this a lot, snatching the odd night together when he's 'on the road', as he puts it, which happens to be most of the time. However, I suspect it's not just for convenience, and that service station hotels are just his *thing*. His mission seems to be to make passionate love to me at every Welcome Break and Moto in the north of England.

It's just gone 7.30 when I pull into the car park. I turn off the engine and take a moment to assess the situation I've found myself in. I'm parked next to a mud-splattered grey estate with a middle-aged couple inside it; they're chomping on fried chicken and tossing the bones out of the side windows. I watch, amazed that anyone could possibly think it's okay to do this.

A lanky young man with low-slung jeans and a small, wiry-haired dog ambles towards my car. Spotting the scattering of bones, the dog starts straining on its lead and yapping like crazy. Dragging him away, his owner fixes me with a furious glare. 'You're disgusting,' he snaps.

Before I know what I'm doing I'm out of my car, shouting, 'They're not *my* bones, okay? Maybe you should check before accusing people!'

'You're *mental*,' the man retorts, hurrying away. The chicken-munching couple laugh as they pull away, and it strikes me, as I stand in the fine rain in my skimpy dress – my jacket's still on the back seat of my car – that I probably *do* look unhinged, and this is all a bit weird. This service station thing, I mean. This thing of Stevie expecting me to jump in my car to meet him with barely any notice.

Yet I do, nearly every time. I picture his teasing greeny-blue eyes – eyes that suggest he's always up for fun – and sense myself weakening. I imagine his hot, urgent kisses and am already mentally packing a bag. Never mind that I have another job, as a carer for elderly Mrs B, on top of pea-shovelling duties. At the prospect of a night with my boyfriend I quickly arrange for someone to cover my shift. Julie usually obliges. She's always keen for more hours.

So here I am, stepping through the flurry of pigeons pecking at the greasy chicken remains. Taking a deep breath, and inhaling a gust of exhaust from a carpet fitter's van, I make my way towards the hotel to meet the most beautiful man I've ever had the pleasure of sleeping with.

Midlife crisis?
WHAT midlife crisis?!

A warm, funny read for fans of Carole Matthews and Catherine Alliott.

The dreaded mums' race at school sports day – every mother's worst nightmare . . .

Laugh-out-loud funny, Fiona's writing deals
with those cringe-worthy moments in life
we all know so well . . .

A straying husband. A broken heart. And a crazy rescue dog in a town of posh pooches . . .

Laugh-out-loud funny, Fiona's writing deal's with those real-life embarrassing moments we all know so well . . .

What do you need a boyfriend for? You're a mum.

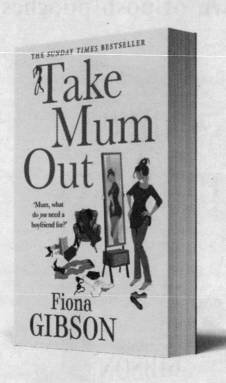

Sharply observed, laugh-out-loud funny, and *full* of dating disasters, this is the perfect read for fans of Carole Matthews and Catherine Alliott.